GOOD AS GONE

A NOVEL OF SUSPENSE

DAVID KAZZIE

OPUS CLUB

ISBN-13: 978-1-7350105-4-0

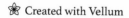 Created with Vellum

As Always, For My Kids

In Memory of My Father
David William Kazzie
(1932-2022)

ALSO BY DAVID KAZZIE

PROLOGUE

MAY 1973

Five of them entered the bank that morning, but they moved with the efficiency and precision of one. The pirate went in first, firing a single shot into the air but not saying a word. The shotgun blast showered the lobby with dust, plaster, and asbestos fibers. At first, some of the customers thought a car had backfired, but the bank employees recognized the sound for what it was. Glances were exchanged, and lips tightened with fear.

With a simple wave of the shotgun's barrel, the pirate shepherded the customers and tellers to the ground. They were compliant enough, lining up on the ground like freshly caught fish, their fingers laced around the backs of their heads.

The witch was the second one inside, a few seconds behind the pirate, and she made a beeline for Stephen Jewel, the young man who had recently ascended to the enviable post of bank manager. Jewel was thirty-five but looked seventeen and had to shave only twice a week. He had a pretty wife named Larissa and a new baby on the way, and he was very conscious of the fact that he had wet himself upon hearing the report of the pirate's shotgun. Now this lunatic wearing the green mask was headed right for him. Stephen would later tell police that the witch was a woman, but that he wasn't entirely certain. After changing his pants, of course.

The witch handed him a note. Scrawled on it were the words, *we want it all*. He handed it back, knowing full well what the robbers wanted.

"All what?" he asked with a quiver in his voice.

She pulled out a pistol and fired a shot at his feet, showering the cuffs of his wide-bottomed trousers with the dust of exploding marble.

"OK, OK," he said weakly, holding up his hands in surrender. "Follow me."

He glanced around the bank lobby, which resembled a still photograph. Nothing moved. The pirate had his gun trained on the hostages. A grizzly bear, a werewolf, and a vampire, who'd come in behind the witch, stood guard at the front door. The sixth robber was in the car, parked along the curb in the beaten-up sedan, waiting to whisk the sextet to a better place, a better life.

The witch followed Jewel around the velvet ropes to the corner of the bank, where the vault stood open, its armored door now as useful as an umbrella in a hurricane. A phone on a nearby desk began ringing, startling everyone. It jangled half a dozen times before the caller gave up. His hands shaking, Jewel used his key to open a second door inside the vault, leading to a smaller room and the robbers' ultimate target. The witch licked her lips when she saw the stacks of cash, delivered not twenty minutes ago via an armored car from the Federal Reserve down on Eighth Street. Two million dollars in neat ten-thousand-dollar bundles.

She reached inside her robes, whipped out four large burlap sacks, and handed them to Jewel. She tapped her watch with the muzzle of her pistol then retrained the gun on Jewel. He got the message and started filling a bag with the bricks of cash. When he finished with the first, the witch tied it off with a rubber band and slid it back out into the main vault. Jewel repeated the process with the next three bags until all the bundles were bagged up like groceries. She followed him out of the vault, and he took his place on the floor with the others. The pirate and the werewolf made their way toward the bags, and that was when everything went straight to hell.

A customer named Eleanor Hatfield began shrieking. She was a large woman with makeup that looked like it had been baked on, and she was terrified. Eleanor pushed herself to her feet and began running blindly, her arms covering her head. The desperate voices of the other hostages pleaded with her to lie back down, to take her place on the floor. It was too late.

The witch took one step forward and shot Eleanor in the neck. She tumbled to the floor in a heap, smearing blood across the fresh marble floor. The remaining hostages howled in terror, and another one, this one an off-duty police officer, saw the resulting chaos as his chance. In one graceful and life-ending move, he swept to his feet and drew a small pistol from the holster around his lower calf. He got off a single shot at the witch, but he missed badly. His bullet struck the vault door and rico-cheted into a wooden desk, lodging itself into the lumber.

The pirate returned fire, catching the officer full in the chest with a twin-barreled blast. The force of the impact blew the officer to the ground like a typhoon, and he lay perfectly still.

This time, the hostages didn't make a sound, rats that have learned not to pluck the cheese from an electrified platform. The pirate stepped over the body of the officer, silent and bleeding, and yanked one of the hostages to her feet. Her name was Denise Vaughan, and she was one of the bank tellers. The others were afraid to look, secretly thankful that they had not been selected.

With Vaughan in tow, the robbers each grabbed a sack and exited the bank less than ninety seconds after first entering and shattering the morning calm. Outside, they were greeted by a glorious morning, warm and fragrant, with that first hint of summer. The sky was a brilliant blue canopy over the clear air, the kind of day that just begged for a cooler of beer, some beach chairs, and a trip to the seashore.

The Olds was idling at the curb, its driver casually smoking a cigarette, as if he'd just dropped someone off to make a quick deposit. The group poured into the car, and the driver eased into traffic, heading east on Broad. They were nearly two blocks away before they heard the first sirens responding to the bank job. A block later, the car pulled into the parking lot of a no-tell motel, and the werewolf got out. The car sped away.

The robbers never said a word.

1

NOVEMBER 2002

The man hung up the phone and looked at it with a mixture of dread and relief. He rubbed his salt-and-pepper-stubbled chin, which hissed like sandpaper against the back of his hand. They'd talked about the possibility of such a phone call, even made contingency plans, but he hadn't actually believed it would happen. Especially now, after so much time had gone by. She had told him that they'd been too careful, covered their tracks too well. Nevertheless, the call had come. He stepped out onto the balcony, where his wife was sipping a glass of merlot and working on a crossword puzzle. He leaned over the railing, drumming his fingers against the metal. Not fifty yards away, the Pacific Ocean rolled lazily onto shore, calm and relaxed on this bright winter afternoon. The beach stretching out before them was empty; after all, they owned it.

After a minute, she finally rolled her eyes and asked: "What?"

He fiddled with his fingers and wet his lips as he

struggled with the words. She made him nervous, always had, and he wanted to be sure he got it right.

"That," he said, clearing his throat, "was a reporter."

"What did he want?"

"He wanted to talk about it."

The woman set down her puzzle book and took a long sip of wine. She waited for the warm buzz to spread through her, which would help calm her down. She didn't want to let on, but she was nervous too. Of course she would be. She didn't think they'd ever be completely free. All they could do was keep their heads down, stay out of the world's way, and hope everyone just forgot about them. The truth was, she was starting to think everyone had.

"Where was he calling from?" she asked, although she suspected she knew the answer.

"Richmond."

She stood up and went back inside. The chill of the cottage made her skin tighten with gooseflesh, and she threw a shawl around her shoulders. She went to the refrigerator and took out a bowl of fresh fruit. God, she loved it down here, she thought, as she sliced up a mango. The cottage, tucked behind a series of dunes, was small and neat and inconspicuous. She didn't want them to stand out. The neighbors were friendly but not too nosy, and that was the way she liked it. The thought of someone taking this life away made her cold, even after the chill of the air conditioning had passed. Her husband followed her inside and lit a pipe, mashing the tobacco leaves into the bowl.

"Not inside," she said, pointing at the pipe.

He looked at her with hangdog eyes, then pinched

out the snuff. He wasn't about to cross her, not with this new wrinkle.

There was one more bit of information he needed to disclose, but he was almost too nervous to tell her.

"There's one more thing."

He found it difficult to maintain eye contact with her.

"What is it?"

He rubbed the back of his neck nervously.

"He said his name was Charlie Dallas."

No visible reaction. Nothing. The woman's blood must have been ice.

"What did you tell him?"

"That I had to check my schedule and I would get back to him."

She nodded. "Good. That was smart. You have his number?"

"Yes."

"Call him back and set up an appointment. We'll fly back, and you can see him."

"You sure?"

"Yes," she said. She lifted his chin, which had dropped to his chest.

"It'll be just like the first time," she said warmly. "Remember how well you did?"

"It's been a long time," he said.

"I know. Think how much easier it'll be this time. This reporter--he's got nothing on us. You'll meet him, and that will be the end of it."

"You're sure?" he asked again.

"Relax," she said. "I've got a plan."

2
___

The sun dipped low over the island, lacing the sky with orange and red ribbons as the day began softening into twilight. It was just past seven, and the young couple observing the lightshow had dinner reservations in half an hour. Charlie Dallas stepped forward and wrapped his arms around his bride's narrow waist. He noticed the sun glinting from the new wedding band adorning his left ring finger, and he waggled it, still not used to wearing jewelry. It still felt strange. *You'll get used to it*, he thought to himself. After all, he'd only been married for thirty-six hours.

"Hungry?" Charlie asked his wife.

"I could eat," she said, winking up at him. She leaned back into his frame and kissed his neck. Her name was Susanna, and she was a schoolteacher back in Richmond, where the couple would make their new home. Her hair brushed his nose, and he took a deep breath. Raspberry jasmine-something or other. If there was a heaven, and

Charlie Dallas went to it, he hoped that it smelled like Susanna's hair.

He gave her a final squeeze and slid open the glass door behind them. Susanna stepped in first, then Charlie, into the cool dark suite that would be their home for the next five days. They had really wanted to go to Hawaii, but on their limited salaries, Sanibel had been a decent enough compromise. It was a tiny finger-shaped island just off the southwest coast of Florida, famous for its secluded beaches. Beaches with sand so white that it absorbed no heat and made walking barefoot on it no more painful than walking on wall-to-wall carpet.

They were even able to drive here, which had saved them nearly two thousand bucks in airfare to Maui. Two thousand bucks they didn't have. Well, at least two grand that they could spend down here. It had been a hell of a long drive, complete with one night spent in a motel in Gainesville that looked like it rented rooms by the half hour. They'd only spent a few hours in that room, just enough to catch a few z's before the final four-hour push south to Sanibel. But they'd made it. Finally, they'd made it to their honeymoon.

They were staying in a privately-owned condo suite, which was a fancy way of saying that the furniture had that cheesy floral-print upholstery. It was nice enough, though, with no television or phone to disturb newly-weds. The view was what they were paying for, a stunning view of the Gulf of Mexico, where the sun kissed the water before dropping below the horizon.

"I'm going to take a quick shower," Susanna said. "I've got sand *everywhere*." After settling into their room, and a quick lunch of shrimp and lobster salad, they made a beeline for the water. Susanna loved playing in the water. She liked waiting for the waves to reach their crest, then ducking underneath them as if sneaking behind a curtain.

"Need help?" He was only partially kidding. Susanna was not a tall woman, but she still made men stop and look wherever she went. Born of Irish bloodlines, her skin was creamy white, and her eyes burned a fiery green. Curly tendrils of strawberry blond hair cascaded from her head, and rarely a month went by without a stylist offering to buy locks of her hair.

She scrunched up her face in mock disgust.

"Haven't we done it enough yet?" she asked playfully. Well, maybe they hadn't gone straight to the beach after checking in.

Charlie cocked his head, as if in deep thought.

"Nope."

"If you're nice to me for the rest of the night, who knows what might happen?"

"I'll keep that in mind."

"You do that."

With that, she disappeared into the bathroom. A few seconds later, Charlie heard the steady hiss of the shower, and he briefly debated joining her. Then his stomach rumbled, as if to state unequivocally that its needs were just as important as any other he might be considering satiating, and he decided he didn't want to risk their dinner reservation. That, plus the fact that her patience only stretched but so thin.

As the shower stall filled with steam, Charlie slipped his cellular phone from a side pocket of their suitcase and dialed his messages. Susanna would kill him if she knew he was even thinking about work, let alone actually doing any; he needed to make it fast. He followed the digitized instructions in his ear and pulled up two messages that he'd gotten since his last day in the office. The first call came in just as Charlie and Susanna were exchanging their vows on Saturday, but the caller had not left a message. No caller ID information was available. The second message was time-stamped at 11:21 that morning.

"Hey, it's Mick. I got a lead on that bank robbery. Call me back."

As the flow of water shut off, he quickly pressed the End button on his cell phone and dropped it back into the side pocket. He'd have to follow up on the message later. He picked up a magazine and settled in on the couch, his bare feet propped up on the coffee table. It was an old Delta Airlines in-flight magazine. Charlie worked the simpleton crossword puzzle at the back. He wondered why the airlines made them so easy. Probably didn't want to piss off the paying customers.

Susanna stepped out of the shower, looking demure in the towel wrapped around her torso. She crossed the room and delicately crouched at his feet.

"Hey there, handsome," she said.

He winked at her.

She glanced down at his feet, which made him slightly self-conscious. They were large and bony, and he always worried that they smelled. He wasn't thrilled with the rest of his body either. He was tall and lanky and felt like he'd been put together poorly, like a cheap toy. Susanna rubbed his heel gently, which felt great and made Charlie forget about his issue with his feet. Then she stopped suddenly.

"Charlie?"

"Yes?"

"What's this?"

"What's what?"

"This tattoo on your foot," she said, turning the sole of his foot toward the dust-laden beam of sunlight filtering into the room. A small starburst had been tattooed on the bottom of Charlie's right foot, in the dark recess just underneath the toes.

"Haven't I told you before?"

"Uh, I think I would remember any tattoo story you were telling."

"Well, we did have a whirlwind romance."

"So. How long have you had it?"

"Since the day I was born."

"What?"

"I'm serious."

"How the hell did you get it?" Susanna asked, sitting on the floor with her knees drawn up to her chest.

"Well, on the night that I was born," Charlie said with the verve of a camp counselor around a roaring fire, "a huge storm hit Waynesboro. Like an inch of rain an hour for eight hours straight. All the power got knocked out. Then the generator failed, and the hospital was in total darkness. They had about a dozen kids born that night, and all the records were destroyed when a fire broke out in the nursery."

"Why didn't they just use wrist tags with the babies' names?"

"Apparently, it was total chaos all over town and in the hospital. Emergency surgery by flashlight, that kind of thing. The nursery had been destroyed. All the healthy babies spent the night being passed around by the nurses, who held us while we did whatever newborns do in their first twelve hours. A guy came in – a tattoo artist – and he had a broken ankle. He heard them talking about not being able to keep the babies straight, and he offered to tattoo them in exchange for a free ride. The doctors were terrified that the babies would end up getting switched, so they went for it. He had his kit with him, and the staff cleaned his needles. Remember, they weren't as careful about things back then."

"How did I ever not notice it before?"

"You spend a lot of time studying my feet?"

"No, I guess not."

"Seriously, the tattoo guy did it in a way that it would be very difficult to see. Plus, it's so small because our feet were little newborn feet."

"Why that design?"

"Something my mom picked," he said. "Some of the other kids got ID numbers, but she asked the guy to put something a little less..."

"Less prison?" Susanna jumped in.

"Exactly."

"And the parents went for it? Getting their brand-new babies tattooed up?"

"My parents said that after the docs told them they couldn't guarantee keeping the kids straight during the storm, they went along with it pretty easily."

"Did you ever think about getting it removed?"

"No," Charlie said. "It's part of me. It's probably why I never mentioned it to you. It's just as much a part of me as my ears are. And I didn't sit down one day and tell you about my ears, did I?"

A smirk crossed her face. "You didn't have to tell me about your ears," she said, pulling on his lobes. "Those are the first things I saw when I met you."

TEN MINUTES LATER, they were ready to go. Charlie wore a pair of khaki pants and a Hawaiian print shirt that his buddy, Dave Guinness, had bought for him when he'd been on his own honeymoon in Maui--the lucky bastard. The shirt sported a classic beach theme, dotted with old roadsters and surfboards. He looked presentable enough, but next to Susanna, he knew he looked like a lech. At best. She was stunning in a sleeveless dress that accentuated her toned, creamy-white arms.

"You look amazing," Charlie said, wrapping his arms around her.

"Thank you."

"Seriously. A vision."

"You're a lucky man."

"I know."

"Keep it up, Dallas. You're off to a good start."

She kissed his nose, and they left the room. They still had fifteen minutes to spare, so they took the long way around to the restaurant. They walked hand in hand, and Charlie couldn't remember the last time he'd felt so relaxed.

THE RESORT WAS CALLED 'Tween Waters, situated on the tiny sandbar that connected Sanibel to Captiva Island. A couple of thousand yards to the east, soft waves lapped against the mainland. The blue-green waters of the Gulf of Mexico stretched westward hundreds of miles, giving the small island the best sunset on this side of the Pacific Ocean.

A five-star restaurant called Kimo's highlighted the main level. Just because it sported that rare five-star classification, however, didn't mean Kimo's had forgotten its beach roots. The theme was nautical, its walls paneled with dark balsa wood. Original artwork commissioned by local artists lined the walls. The dining room was situated on the north end of the resort, open-air style. To their left, a tuxedo-clad bartender served up drinks to a group of young women carousing at the bar. They laughed, smoked, and sipped brightly colored drinks from glasses the size of fish bowls.

Charlie approached the maitre'd.

"Reservation for Dallas?" he said. "Seven-thirty."

The man traced his finger down a list of names in his reservation book.

"Ah," he said. "Mr. Dallas. We'll be with you shortly. If you'd like to have a seat at the bar."

Charlie's face tightened into a scowl. The clock above the bar read exactly seven-thirty. *Guess these guys don't understand the concept of reservations*, he thought. He stepped back and took a seat with Susanna on a bench in the foyer.

"What was that about?" she asked.

He shrugged.

"Said our table wasn't ready yet."

"Oh," Susanna said. "They must be on island time."

"I guess." Charlie took a deep breath and exhaled it slowly. *Jesus*, he thought. They were probably going to drop two hundred bucks on dinner. The least they could do was have the table ready on time.

Susanna leaned back and took her own deep breath, but she was clearly in a better mood. A breeze blowing through the open-air deck rustled her hair, and she took Charlie's hand in her own.

"Relax, big guy."

Just as he decided to let it go, another couple approached the maitre'd. The guy was about Charlie's age, maybe a bit younger, and was the kind of guy that looked like he could use a good ass-kicking. He wore aviator sunglasses and fired a pretend gun at the maitre'd as he stepped up to the podium. On his hip was a waif of a woman, arms and legs like pixie sticks, with a deep tan and hip-looking sunglasses. Charlie thought about sending an extra cheeseburger to their table. She could use it.

"Name's Graham," the man said in a steep Alabama drawl, loud enough to annoy the crap out of Charlie. "I believe we had an arrangement." He extended his hand to the maitre'd, and Charlie noticed a fifty-dollar bill clipped between two of the man's fingers.

"Mr. and Mrs. Graham," the host said, "so good to see you." He took Graham's hand and swallowed up the fifty into his sweaty, meaty paw. The bill disappeared into his pocket as he extracted a pair of menus from under the podium.

"Right this way," he said, leading them deeper into

the restaurant. "We have some lovely specials this evening. . ." His voice trailed off.

Son of a bitch! Charlie thought, tugging his hand away from Susanna's.

"What now?" she asked.

"That jackass just slipped the guy a fifty," Charlie said through clenched teeth. "He sold our reservation."

"Are you sure?" Susanna asked.

"Yes, I'm sure!"

"Watch the tone, mister," she snapped. "You don't have to take it out on me."

"But he's giving our table away," Charlie said. "Doesn't that piss you off?"

"We'll get a table," she said. "You in a big rush to get somewhere? Look, if it bothers you that much, then say something when he comes back."

"I think I just might."

Charlie turned the problem over in his head, his eyes glued to the corridor down which the Grahams had disappeared. Damn right he was going to say something. Give that asshole a piece of his mind. He'd really let the guy have it but stay cool at the same time because he didn't want to cause a scene. Classy like.

The maitre'd returned to his post and immediately began scanning his reservation book with great interest. *Look at him*, Charlie thought. So smug, studying that book like it contained a message from an alien civilization. *He just doesn't want to look at us.*

Ten minutes passed, then twenty. The maitre'd never made eye contact. Charlie couldn't quite figure out what to say. *Screw it*, he thought. *I'm getting up. Now.* A minute passed. *Now I'm definitely getting up.*

"Well, are you gonna do something?" Susanna asked. Charlie noticed a hint of acid in her tone, and he snapped his head toward her.

"I guess not," he said, his voice cloaked with disgust. "What's the point?"

"Mmm."

Charlie looked at her again. *Are you gonna do something?* Her question echoed in his head as if she'd shouted it from the edge of the Grand Canyon. She'd appeared to have forgotten about the incident. Her eyes were closed. She had one leg crossed over the other, rocking her foot back and forth to the beat of some unheard tune.

"Mr. and Mrs. Dallas?"

Charlie looked up into the oily grill of the scumbag maitre'd. This was his chance.

"Katie will escort you to your table," he said; he quickly retreated to his station.

Susanna patted him on the knee. "Let's go, sweetie. It's over."

A young woman with sun-bleached brown hair and bronze skin led Charlie and Susanna up a flight of stairs to an outdoor patio, where they would have a view of the Gulf. Susanna ordered a glass of Australian Shiraz, Charlie a martini. The hostess laid a leather-ensconced menu in front of each of them. Charlie glanced around the patio; there were a dozen other tables out here. Most were occupied by couples, the rest by larger groups. Everyone seemed to be enjoying themselves immensely.

The Grahams were two tables away, their annoying fingers interlaced at the center of the table. Charlie wanted to shoot him.

"Martini, huh?" Susanna asked with a slight scowl on her face when the hostess had vanished from the table.

"I need it to settle down after that bullshit."

"Charlie..."

"Sorry. Seriously, it's a special occasion."

"You mean like my birthday?"

"Hey, that was an accident," he said, referring to an incident a few weeks earlier that ended with Charlie's head in a toilet.

She winked. "It's your honeymoon, too. Have your martini. Better just have one, though."

Charlie held back his tasteless retort as their waiter arrived. He looked like a professional, mid-forties with silvery, spiked hair and a deep tan. His name was Mark. He announced the specials of the day. Charlie ordered risotto with jumbo sea scallops; Susanna went with blackened tuna drizzled with a sauce bearing an unpronounceable name. They also ordered a spinach and artichoke dip to share.

Charlie leaned back in his seat and sipped his drink. The wind freshened, and a cool breeze rippled across the dining room. Twilight was falling like a curtain, and candlelight flickered on each table.

"Comfy?" Susanna asked.

"Very."

"Nice to see you relaxed for once."

"I know."

Susanna tucked a stray lock of hair behind an ear. "I wish you weren't so stressed all the time."

"I'm working on it."

"Well, we'll see what your new wife can do." She narrowed her eyes. "Wow. Wife. Strange word. It makes me feel old."

"Yeah, two days ago, you were my fiancée. That sounds a lot more hip than husband and wife. If someone calls you Mrs. Dallas, I'm going to think my mom is here."

"You really know how to romance a girl, don't you?"

"You know what I mean."

Mark returned with the appetizer.

"Is there anything else I can get you?" he asked as he set the steaming bowl and a tray of warm bread on the dark cherry table.

"Thank you, we're fine," Susanna said.

He disappeared.

"He's good, isn't he?" she asked, tearing off a hunk from the freshly baked bread. "Barely notice he's there."

"I guess," Charlie said. "He seems to have his eye on you."

"Why, Mr. Dallas, you should be flattered. It speaks volumes about you."

"Wouldn't it be charming if I beat the crap out of him?"

"Again with the romance," she said, spooning a bit of the dip onto her bread. "You should teach a class."

Charlie smiled and took another sip of his drink. It was strong, and his head started to swim. *Definitely better make it just one*, he thought.

"So what did you think of our little wedding?" Susanna asked.

"What wedding? I barely remember being there."

"I know. Can you believe it? Everyone told me that

would happen, but you just never understand until you go through it."

"It almost makes me wonder why we went to all the trouble."

"Don't be a jerk."

"I'm just kidding." *Well, maybe only partially*, he thought. Thousands of dollars for everyone else to have a good time. He looked out over the water, where he saw the running lights of the sailboats, yachts, and fishing trawlers dotting the surface of the Gulf. He looked back at Susanna, her dark eyes wide and bright in the candle-light, and he decided that she'd been worth it. If he'd had to pay twice as much money and make idle chitchat with a thousand guests he barely knew, she was worth it. He vowed never to disparage their wedding again. At least not in front of her.

Their meals arrived a few minutes later, one dish perched in each of Mark the wonder-waiter's arms. He set them softly on the table and pulled a pepper mill from out of nowhere. *Okay, so maybe he is good*, Charlie thought, as he nodded his assent to freshly cracked black pepper.

The food was magnificent. Charlie's scallops tasted fresh and clean, and the risotto virtually melted in his mouth. Susanna raved about her tuna. She had a second glass of wine, and her cheeks began to flush with the alcohol. Charlie switched to ice water after killing off the martini, but he was still pleasantly buzzed.

When the plates had been cleared, Mark brought out the dessert tray. He rotated it like a DJ working an old turntable, pointing to cheesecakes, chocolate tortes, tiramisu. Susanna chose the tiramisu, and Charlie went with the torte.

"I think I have to pee," Susanna said, giggling, while they waited for their desserts.

"You're drunk," Charlie pointed at her.

"Am not."

"Susanna Dallas--" he began.

"Well, so are you!"

Charlie laughed out loud. He stood up and helped her out of her chair.

"My, my, aren't we the gentleman?"

"Hey, I told you I was a romantic."

She kissed him, a quick brush of the lips. "Be right back. Why don't you get those desserts to go?" She winked at him before making her way to the restroom.

Charlie flagged down Mark.

"Can we get those desserts to go?" he asked.

"Absolutely, Mr. Dallas. I'll notify the kitchen."

Charlie gazed out over the water again. The remainder of the week stretched out before them like an unopened gift. He wanted to go snorkeling. Susanna had mentioned parasailing. He took a deep breath and exhaled it slowly, thrilled that these were the important decisions he'd have to make this week. Hundreds of miles away from the newsroom. From his laptop. From his cell phone. OK, so he had the cell phone with him. But it was off. Didn't that count for something?

Mark returned with the check, and Charlie placed their Visa card in the leather billfold.

"I'll be right back with your receipt and your desserts," Mark said. "Thanks for coming in tonight."

"Thanks."

Charlie decided there was no reason to bear the man any ill will. The man made his living by turning on the charm. He wondered if he would be able to pull it off. He leaned back in his seat and looked out over the water.

Night had scrubbed away the last remnants of daylight, as if an invisible hand had erased a blackboard. The stars weren't out yet, and it was a moonless night. A gentle breeze blew in from the west; toward the horizon, heat lightning flashed like a distant camera. Charlie felt an upward tick in the humidity, and he wondered if it might storm.

A few minutes later, Mark returned with their packages, wrapped expertly in small gift boxes. It was a nice touch, and considering they'd just dropped two hundred bucks on dinner--before tip--it was the least they could do. Still, he was planning to enjoy the hell out of himself this week, and when the credit card bill came home to roost, well, they would just deal with that then.

Charlie glanced at his watch and looked out across the dining room. No sign of Susanna yet. He smiled. The conventional wisdom stated that women took longer in the bathroom. Not in the Dallas household, despite her apparent dilly-dallying tonight. Susanna could go from deep sleep to out the door, including showering, shaving her legs, spritzing, and whatever the hell else his wife did to smell so good, in under fifteen minutes. Good thing, too, because she hated to get up in the morning more than anything, and so all she left for herself was fifteen minutes to get ready before she had to leave for St. Mary's, the private Catholic school where she taught fourth grade. Mornings in their home were nothing less than organized chaos. She had somehow reduced it to an art form.

Charlie looked at his watch again, this time with a shallow fissure forming in his brow. She normally didn't take this long, no matter what nature was calling for. Maybe her dinner hadn't agreed with her. Wouldn't that be something? Seventy-dollar entree and she gets food poisoning. He checked around her seat, wondering if she'd taken her small handbag with her. She had. Maybe she was touching up her makeup. Charlie didn't think so. She barely wore any to begin with.

He swept his gaze around the dining room again, this time focusing on anyone loitering in the aisle. The flickering candelabra lining the outer perimeter was romantic, without a doubt, but it didn't offer much help in the way of lighting. Elvis could've been at the next table, and he wouldn't have been able to tell.

A hostess swept by the table, and Charlie reached out and grabbed her elbow.

"Excuse me," he said.

"Yes?"

"I'm sorry to trouble you, but my wife went to the bathroom about fifteen minutes ago, and she hasn't come back yet. I'm worried she might be sick. Would you mind--"

"Certainly, Mr. Dallas."

"Thank you."

Wow. He was impressed. The hostess remembered his name. He was going to come back here. *Listen to you. You're not coming back here. This is a once-in-a-lifetime-maybe-once-in-a-decade meal, and you plan on coming back here. Right.* He took a sip of his water and crunched a piece of ice between his teeth. He did it quickly; Susanna always got on him about chewing ice. She had told him that some uncle or something of hers ruined his teeth by crunching ice. She never believed Charlie when he said that was the kind of thing grownups told little kids when they wanted them to stop doing something.

Out of the corner of his eye, he saw the hostess returning to his table. He noticed she was fumbling with her fingers.

"I'm sorry, Mr. Dallas," she started, "the women's restroom is empty."

"What?"

"It's empty. There's no one in there."

"What do you mean, it's empty?"

"I'm sorry, sir, but the bathroom was empty."

"Did you check the stalls?"

"All we have are stalls."

He laughed out loud, aware that she had not meant to make a joke.

"What about the other bathroom?" he asked, growing confused.

"That's the only restroom in the restaurant."

"So where is she?"

The hostess, who was nineteen years old and working here during her summer break from Florida State University, was at a loss.

"Are you sure she went to the ladies' room? Perhaps she went to the bar," the hostess said. "I'll check there."

"Thank you."

Charlie signed the credit card receipt and left the restaurant copy in the leather billfold. He stuffed the other in his wallet and got up from the table. He did a quick loop around the patio, even pausing at each table just to make sure Susanna hadn't buddied up with some other diners. He wouldn't put it totally past her. She had a disarming way about her, one that might even lead complete strangers to ask her to sit down with them for a drink.

He took a deep breath and told himself to relax. She had just wandered off somewhere. That was all. Probably buying a t-shirt and grabbing some matchbooks at the bar. He calmed himself down a bit then headed downstairs to the main level. He took the steps two at a time.

As he descended the last step, he saw the hostess and Mark hunched over the oak bar, deep in discussion with the bartender. Susanna was not at the bar.

"Mr. Dallas!" Mark bellowed happily.

Uh-oh. This can't be good.

Charlie ran a hand through his blond hair and stepped up to the bar. Mark clapped a hand on his shoulder.

"She's had enough of you, huh?" His ensuing laugh was forced. The hostess and bartender joined in.

"I'm sure she just stepped outside to grab some air," the bartender said with a look that said, *Buddy, I'm glad I'm not in your shoes.*

"We were sitting outside." Charlie noticed his voice had taken on a mechanical tone.

"Where are you staying?" the hostess jumped in.

"Fifth floor."

"Well, I'm sure she just went on ahead of you," Mark said. "You're a newlywed, right? Of course you are, look how shiny that wedding band is. Look, the wives, they do crazy things on honeymoon. It's all part of the excitement."

Charlie nodded, twisting his wedding band around his finger.

"Careful with that thing," the hostess said. She was blond and sweet, and she smiled her toothiest smile. "How would it look if you lost it right before you get back to your room and find her there?"

"Thanks for your help."

Charlie shoved his hands in his pockets and ambled toward the door.

3

The night had grown stickier since Charlie and Susanna had left the room. The long, thick leaves of the palm trees dotting the walkways swayed in the warm breeze, silhouetted by the soft lights glowing from inside the hotel lobby. Except for the glow of the hotel lights, however, the night was pitch black. Sanibel had little in the way of nightlife, and the island was far enough away from the mainland to avoid the harsh glare of south Florida's electrical grid.

Sweat beaded on Charlie's body, and he felt cold inside. He became conscious of his breathing, and he was thankful that it was an involuntary response. Otherwise, he didn't think he could remind himself to inhale right now. Back in the room. She must be back in the room, he thought as he crossed the courtyard to the main lobby of the hotel.

He passed the concierge desk; a young man was starting to break it down for the night.

"Good evening," he said with a thick African accent.

"Hey, did a woman just come through here?" Charlie asked.

"No, sir. I see nobody."

Charlie punched the button for the elevator; the panel of lights flashed at seven before beginning its slow descent to the first floor. *Screw this.* He walked quickly to the end of the hall, where he pressed the fast-release bar of the door leading to the stairwell. Taking the steps two at a time, he felt panic setting in like the chill of a cold winter day.

By the time he reached the fifth-floor landing, his undershirt was soaked through, and he felt rivulets of sweat coursing down his body. The door onto the floor banged into the wall with a loud thud, and Charlie sprinted down the hallway to their room. Naturally, their room was the last one on the end. He fumbled in his pockets for the keycard and slipped it into the door slot.

"Susanna!" he called out. He didn't care if anyone heard him. "You in there?"

The green light on the door panel lit up, and Charlie threw the handle down. He charged into the room like a drunk. The lights were on. Relief cascaded over him like a summer shower. He distinctly remembered turning them off when they left for dinner.

He took a deep breath and exhaled it slowly. All worked up for nothing. She had already come back to the room. Probably ready to enjoy her dessert. *Shit!* He had left them sitting on the bar. Oh well. He'd just have to make it up to her. He threw the deadbolt and began unbuttoning his shirt.

"Susanna, I'm back," he called out. He stepped through the small corridor and into the room proper.

Empty. He stepped back and ducked his head into the restroom. The light was off; he flipped it on to be sure, just in case she was hiding or playing some crazy newlywed game she'd read about in one of those bridal magazines the size of a small moon. Empty.

Patio. She must be on the patio. He willed himself to walk to the patio despite his urge to sprint the distance. He slid the glass door open, and his heart skipped a beat. Or twenty. The patio was deserted as well. The roar of the ocean, just fifty yards away, filled the summer night. He leaned over the patio railing and peered down to the pool area. A figure was skulking around down there.

"Susanna!" he called out. "Is that you?"

The figure stopped and called back.

"I sound like someone named Susanna?" a deep voice rasped back.

"Sorry."

He stepped back into the room and slid the glass door closed behind him. For the first time since they'd been there, he locked it as well. He looked around the empty room, which seemed dead without Susanna. It was as if the life had been sucked out of it.

He sat down in a rocking chair in the corner of the room. Leaning forward, he set his elbows on his knees and tented his index fingers to his lips. Nausea swept through him. Before, it had been a generalized sense of panic. Now, it was a growing certainty that something was wrong. Dark images flashed across his mind as if they were illuminated by strobe lights. He imagined her falling prey to a psychotic serial killer, her violated body dumped in a river. Wasn't Ted Bundy from around here?

The images continued marching through until he was close to madness.

Then he saw it.

A folded piece of paper was propped up on the night-stand. His name was printed on it in black lettering. CHARLIE DALLAS. It most certainly had not been there before they had left the room for dinner.

"This can't be good," he said, jumping at the sound of his own voice.

He stood up and crossed the room. He knelt down and examined the missive. It appeared to be a four-by-six-inch index card, folded lengthwise. He picked it up by a corner, careful not to disturb any latent fingerprints that he hoped were on it, and flipped it over. The three short sentences printed on the card felt like three hot bullets to Charlie's chest. He dropped the card, and it fluttered to the floor, where it landed face up. He looked back down at it and read it again.

IF YOU TRY TO FIND HER, SHE DIES.

IF YOU CALL THE POLICE, SHE DIES.

WE ARE WATCHING.

4

Charlie pushed himself to his feet, but the sudden rush of blood to his head staggered him. Stumbling across the room, he collapsed in a heap on the couch. His heart was beating quickly and erratically. It felt like he was being tickled from the inside of his chest. His mouth went dry, and he felt like he might pass out. He gave his head a violent shake, like a small child refusing his vegetables. A good, hard shake back to reality.

"Stay calm," he said. "Stay calm."

He took several cleansing breaths, and his heart slowly decelerated, like a racecar sliding in for a pit stop. His years as a reporter had instilled him with the ability to observe the world around him with a sense of detachment. His unconscious mind was attempting to do the same thing here as a defense mechanism. It was working, but only barely.

"Susanna," he whispered.

He clapped his hand to his mouth, as he felt panic rearing up inside him.

Think, dammit, think!

He began pacing the room while running through his options. His first two instincts were pretty much addressed in the note. So those were out for now. He started replaying their honeymoon in his head. They'd arrived in Sanibel about thirty hours earlier. It had been mid-morning, about ten or ten-thirty. He closed his eyes and tried to recall it in his mind's eye. The lobby had been empty except for the desk clerk. Attractive middle-aged woman. Perfect hair. Mandy or Amanda. He remembered giving the lobby the once-over, but he couldn't remember if he saw anyone there, let alone anyone suspicious. It wasn't like he was scoping for kidnappers on the first day of his honeymoon.

He checked the room for additional messages. On the shelves, on the end tables, in the bathroom. Nothing. He picked up the ransom note again. Ransom? Is that what this was? If so, they, whoever *they* were, were going to be sorely disappointed. He and Susanna were pretty much broke. What the hell did they want him to do? Was he supposed to wait in the room?

A second later, he got his answer. The dead silence in which he'd been living for the previous ten minutes shattered when the phone started jangling. He lunged for it and grabbed it in the middle of the first ring.

"Yeah?" He hoped his voice didn't sound as shaky as he thought it did.

"Mr. Dallas." The voice sounded mechanical, and Charlie realized the caller was using voice alteration equipment. So that shit really existed. Was there a catalog that today's modern kidnappers used to outfit themselves?

"Yes," Charlie said.

"Be back home by noon tomorrow."

"Noon?"

"Remember the instructions in the note. They still apply."

"I can't make it by noon. It's already--"

Charlie checked his watch. 10:45 p.m.

"Ten forty--" he started to plead.

The line clicked dead.

Jesus. It was real. The note had been otherworldly, almost surreal, but the phone call had driven it home. Charlie ran his hand through his hair, then massaged his temples with the tips of his fingers. He checked his watch again. 10:48. *Move, Dallas, time to move!* He bolted from the edge of the bed like he'd been launched from the deck of an aircraft carrier. Like a man possessed, he grabbed their suitcase and emptied the contents of the bureau drawers into it.

As he gathered their few belongings, he did some math in his head. Noon was barely thirteen hours away. If he drove, he was going to have to average better than seventy miles an hour to make it. Impossible. And yet he had no choice. As he zipped the bag shut, he picked up the phone and dialed the front desk, clipping the receiver between his shoulder and ear.

"Room 1109," he said. "I'm sorry, but we have to check out early. Death in the family. I'm leaving the key in the room."

"I'm very sorry to hear that."

He was already hanging up the phone. He tossed his

card key on the bed, and he pawed through the detritus on the nightstand, looking for the second key to the room. He remembered leaving it there earlier that afternoon.

They can bill me.

Wait. Maybe there was another way back to Richmond. He dug out the yellow pages, stacked under the Gideons Bible, and flipped to the listings under Aviation. He wondered if he could charter a flight to Richmond. He dialed a few of the numbers, hoping for a miracle at this hour, but all he got were answering machines. He found one charter pilot's home number and punched the number into the keypad of his cell phone.

"Hello?" the voice said against a backdrop of thumping music.

"Is this Michael De Golia?"

"Yeah, who the hell is this?"

"I need a pilot," Charlie said, already losing hope. The man was slurring his words. "Tonight."

"Sorry, bud, I've had a little bit to drink. Call me tomorrow afternoon. You know, twelve hours, bottle to throttle."

"Dammit!" Charlie bellowed, throwing his phone back into his satchel. He couldn't afford to waste any more time looking for a pilot. He was going to have to drive home.

Charlie darted out the door, dragging the new suitcase he and Susanna had received as a wedding gift behind him. He wondered why he'd even bothered with the suitcase, and it dawned on him how hard it was to kill habit. When you check out of your hotel, you pack your bags, wife kidnapped or wife yelling at you all the way back to the car. Simple as that.

Charlie and Susanna's Ford Escape was parked near the exit, and Charlie dumped the case in the cargo area. He jumped in and fired up the engine, which roared to life. The fuel gauge needle swung over to F, flooding Charlie with relief. *Thank God*. He had decided to stop for gas on the mainland, just before crossing the bridge to Sanibel. He didn't even want to think about how many problems he had ahead of him, but a least he had a full tank.

Taking only enough care to make sure he didn't drop the transmission into the parking lot, he dropped the car into reverse; the thick, knobby SUV tires squealed as he shifted into drive, but the car didn't miss a beat. It leaped forward out of the parking lot and onto the main road, and Charlie and Susanna's honeymoon came to an abrupt end.

HE PICKED his way back through the darkness to the mainland and then onto Interstate 75, which hugged Florida's Gulf coast before twisting through the heart of the state and plunging deep into Georgia. The highway was black and deserted at this hour. This portion of Florida was punctuated by resort towns and nothing but large stretches of undeveloped wilderness connecting them. In the distance, heat lightning flashed. Hurtling through the darkness, Charlie could only see as far as the sweep of his headlights. It occurred to him that the illu-minated road ahead of him was all he could see of his future. What had been so happy, so certain just a few hours ago had been thrown out like yesterday's garbage.

As he raced north through the darkness, he turned on the radio to break up the painful silence engulfing him. Finding nothing but static on the FM band, he flipped to AM, which carried farther at night. He found he had his choice of idiot sports talk show hosts in the East or desperate, lonely men and women seeking advice on love in the Midwest. He picked up one station from Boston, lamenting the current state of the Red Sox, and lingered on that one for a bit. Susanna was a die-hard Sox fan.

Thoughts of his wife drew a smile across Charlie's face, like a child finishing a crayon drawing of a loved one. He touched his wedding band, still amazed at how quickly it had all happened, stunned as to how quickly it had all been ripped away from him.

Almost two years earlier, Charlie had decided to check out a support group for people who'd lost both parents. Granted, he wasn't Oliver Twist, running the streets in ratty clothes, but not having any family hadn't been easy. At first, it hadn't been so bad. His father had died when he was a kid. He was a freshman at N.C. State when he lost his mother, and so he'd sponged holidays off his roommates' families or his girlfriend Renee's family.

As he got older though, his friends began starting their own families, and there wasn't room at the table for Charlie anymore. He and Renee stayed together for a year after college, but that had finally fizzled out too. By then, he was settling into his new job as a reporter, willing to work holidays, which definitely made him a fan favorite with his coworkers with families.

As he got older, however, approaching the dreaded three-oh, he began to hate the holidays, finally admitting to himself that he wanted to wake up on Christmas morning in a house full of people. Wanting to need a few stiff drinks to put up with the family.

So he talked to a counselor, who turned him onto a group that met once a month at different restaurants around town. Booze and food always seemed to take the edge off; the meetings helped a little, especially around the holidays, when he could at least be certain that he wasn't the only one dreading the six weeks between Thanksgiving and New Year's. He'd made a few friends, even hosted the dozen lost and lonely souls in the group for the previous Thanksgiving. He cooked a sixteen-pound turkey, everyone brought a covered dish, they all got hammered and had a grand old time.

At the first meeting after the new year, the group welcomed a new member. Her name was Susanna, and she immediately drew the attention of the group's eight men. She wore jeans and an Arizona State sweatshirt, and her strawberry blond hair was pulled back in a pony-tail. Her dad had been killed in action in the first Gulf War, and her mother had died in a car crash the previous summer. Like all the other group members, she was an only child. She had recently moved to Richmond and taken a position as a fourth-grade teacher with a local private school.

At the end of the meeting, she asked Charlie to join her for a drink at a nearby bar, and he did. He liked her immediately. The drink turned into dinner and an all-night talk. Charlie did most of the talking, but she seemed happy to just listen. That was followed by another date the very next night, and by the weekend, the platonic phase of their relationship had ended. The intensity of his feelings frightened him a little; it was something he'd never experienced before. Before he could stop himself, he was picturing what their children might look like. He told himself everything was moving much too quickly. In response, he tried to imagine his life without Susanna. Dark and cold. Lifeless. Dead. And that was how he knew he wanted to spend the rest of his life with her.

He sat her down three months after they met and asked her point-blank if she thought their relationship was moving too quickly. They laid out their hopes, their fears, their dreams. He told her he wanted kids. Like any poor struggling reporter worth his weight, he wanted to become a successful novelist. Neither of them flinched. They split a bottle of wine, had dizzying sex, and they decided to get married. Charlie kept waiting for that little voice inside to sit up and shout, scream, plead with him, give him a little of the old, "Hey, what's the rush, muchacho?" It never said a word. Either that, or it went out for coffee. By the time it got back, it was too late.

Two months ago, he happily relinquished his shithole apartment and moved into Susanna's house. He remembered running the broom one last time through his empty apartment, then locking the door behind him. He never looked back.

They got married at Maymont, a small park and nature center near Richmond's downtown. A friend of Charlie's performed the ceremony after getting ordained via the Internet. Two of Charlie's buddies stood in as groomsmen. Susanna, who told Charlie she'd moved around a lot growing up and didn't have a lot of close friends, asked two teachers to serve as her bridesmaids. A local jeweler handmade their rings, and the happy couple bought the thirty guests dinner at Cabo's, a tasty local bistro owned by a friend of Charlie's. The owner liked Charlie a lot, but he liked good publicity even more, so he had cut a deal with Charlie for the reception. Everybody wins. Charlie wore his best suit, which was also his only suit; Susanna wore an off-the-rack wedding dress that she found for less than a hundred bucks.

And just like that, Charlie Dallas was a married man.

By 4:00 A.M., Charlie knew he needed a break. He'd been hunched over the wheel for five hours without a break, the speedometer tickling ninety much of the way. He was in decent shape to make his noon deadline, but his body's reserves were fading quickly. He needed some coffee and some food. Gas, too. He was on I-95 now, having cut east along I-10 at Lake City and swinging around Jacksonville. Each state was melding into the next, and it occurred to him that he wasn't even sure which state he was in.

The glowing marquee of a 24-hour gas station an hour north of the Florida/Georgia border beckoned him. He took the exit ramp and followed the small blue signs to his destination, where he found a deserted mini-mart and a thick middle-aged woman manning the counter sleepily. Charlie filled a twenty-ounce cup of coffee and grabbed a few candy bars from the inviting rack by the register. He set them on the counter and waited for the woman to ring up his purchases. As she did so, he glanced out the glass front door. He noticed a man loitering by the pumps, and more disturbingly, by his car.

Charlie fished a ten-dollar bill from his wallet and dropped it on the counter.

"Keep the change," he said, grabbing his coffee and shoving the candy bars into the pockets of his khakis. He stepped outside into the still-sticky night. The man lit a cigarette and stepped away from Charlie's car. Charlie went around the back and started to get in.

"How about a ride, man?"

The stranger was young, about twenty years old. His hair was cut high and tight, and he wore a wife-beater T-shirt, pulled out over his jean shorts. Beady blue eyes stared hard at Charlie; the kid made him very nervous.

"Sorry," Charlie said, pulling the door behind him, his hands fumbling with his keys. He was desperate to start the car and get the hell out of there. As he turned the key over, he heard a heavy tapping on his window. Too late. He swung his head to the left and found himself looking into the maw of a semi-automatic pistol.

"Shit," he muttered.

"Out of the car," he heard the punk's muffled voice say.

Charlie looked down at the shifter and decided he would never get into gear before the guy had a chance to get a shot off. He glanced back at the mini-mart; the clerk was deep into a magazine. Maybe this kind of thing was part of the late-night mini-mart experience in this state. Reaching slowly for the door handle, he formulated his plan as he cracked the door open. He gave it a sudden shove, and the door knocked the pistol from the stunned kid's hand. It clattered to the ground and went off. A bullet pierced the thin skin of Charlie's back door, continued through the cabin, and shattered the rear cargo window. Charlie closed the door and opened it again, this time putting all his weight into it; he didn't want to give the kid a chance to get up and get a shot off as he drove away.

The edge of the doorframe caught the kid square in the chest, eliciting a hissing noise as he collapsed to the ground. It was his first move since pulling the gun, apparently shocked that Charlie had put up a fight. Charlie started to get back in, then stopped. He reached down, grabbed the gun, and tossed it on the seat next to him. It might come in handy later; that thought came twinned with another--how surreal the day had become that a gun might come in handy later.

He pulled out of the gas station, checking to see the clerk's reaction in the rearview mirror. She had come to the door, where she could see the boy writhing around on the ground. After scanning the scene for a moment, her hands on her plump hips, she turned around and went back to her magazine.

Charlie sped back to the interstate and screamed north toward Richmond.

5

S hortly after ten, Charlie crossed the North Carolina/Virginia border. He was less than eighty miles from home. He stopped for food and gas again, this time without incident, and was back on the interstate in minutes. He rolled north through the hills of Emporia, the industrial feel of Petersburg, and closed in on Richmond. The downtown skyline shimmered in the warm, clear morning, and a sense of relief flooded Charlie.

Charlie and Susanna were living in a small house in the Fan district, just west of downtown Richmond. The Fan was the city's historical district, so named because on a map, it appeared that the neighborhood's dozen or so main streets fanned out from a central location near Virginia Commonwealth University. Homes in the area ran the gamut, from the million-dollar colonial homes along Monument Avenue, a tree-lined thoroughfare dotted with monuments to Civil War heroes, to rundown brownstones occupied by young single professionals, to crack houses just a few blocks further south.

Susanna had bought the home two years ago, before Charlie met her, shortly after having moved to Richmond. She had taken advantage of a low-interest, no-down-payment program offered to schoolteachers to encourage them to live in the city, which desperately needed good teachers. It was a brilliant move. Susanna paid $130,000 for the house; last year, it had been appraised at $275,000. The Fan had become the "in" place to own real estate, and Susanna got in at just the right time. Her luck continued when a major movie studio chose to film one of its summer blockbusters in Richmond. In exchange for the use of Susanna's home for six weeks, they offered to put her up in the Jefferson Hotel, the only five-star hotel in Richmond, and Susanna kept the $50,000 worth of renovations that the studio did on the house when they were done. There was little debate about where they would live after the wedding.

At this time of day, curbside parking was plentiful, and Charlie found a spot just in front of their home on Hanover Avenue. The house was sandwiched between a four-unit apartment building and the Georgian-style home of a city councilman. He killed the ignition and checked the dashboard clock. Eleven thirty-seven. He had made inhuman time. His eyelids were stuck together, and his head was throbbing. After grabbing the handgun, he got out, stretched, and headed up the cobblestone walkway to his front door. The mailbox mounted on the exterior wall was overflowing with mail--he realized he'd forgotten to put a hold on their mail like Susanna had asked him to before they left Richmond.

Two days ago, was it? It seemed like a month ago. Charlie tried to get his bearings on what day it was. *The wedding was on Saturday. Drove to Sanibel Sunday. OK, today was Tuesday.*

He grabbed the mail and went inside. He checked the phone to make sure there was a dial tone; then he went to the living room to wait for whatever was next.

~

THE PHONE RANG PRECISELY at noon. Again, Charlie grabbed it on the first ring.

"Yes?"

"Listen carefully. I'm only going to say this once. Be at the boat landing on Belle Isle at six o'clock sharp. Just east of the footbridge. Come alone. If we see anyone else, she dies."

"Can I talk to her please?" Charlie said quickly, hoping to get it out before the caller hung up.

"Six o'clock." The line clicked dead.

"Dammit!"

Charlie reared back and hurled the phone against the wall, where it blew apart in a symphony of wires, batteries, and shattered microchips. He ran his hand along his face, which hissed with two-day-old stubble. He replayed the call in his mind.

The boat landing at Belle Isle. A fairly obscure location. The kidnapper had to be local. He had suspected that since the kidnapper had ordered him back to Richmond. Now he was even more certain. He didn't think anyone but a local would pick such a meeting location. Unless, of course, the kidnapper got it from Susanna.

Which brought him back to square one, where he didn't know shit.

He needed help. The kidnappers had said only that he couldn't call the police. This situation was way beyond his powers of comprehension, and he didn't think he could keep his shit together until six o'clock, let alone jump through another one of these hoops. He pulled the note from his pocket and read it again. It didn't say he couldn't call anyone. Just that he couldn't call the police.

He pulled out his cell phone, scrolled through its internal directory to the name he was looking for, and pressed the Talk button. No answer. It kicked into voice mail.

"Devo, it's Charlie. I need your help."

He slid the phone back into his pocket.

HIS CELL PHONE rang at two o'clock. He checked the caller ID, fully expecting to see Devo's number flash on the screen. Another number, however, popped up.

"Yeah?" he said, nervously taking the call.

"This Dallas?" a man's hushed voice said.

"Yes," he said. A chill ran down his spine, like someone had traced an ice cube against his skin.

"Meet me at the Stonewall Jackson statue on Monument. Twenty minutes."

"Who the hell is this?"

"Do you want to find your wife?" the caller asked angrily, his voice booming.

"Yes. Yes, of course."

"Then just do what I say," the man said. "I have the proof you're going to need to find her."

"Why should I believe you?"

"Because I'm the only chance you've got."

The line clicked dead.

Jesus. Charlie didn't know what to do. He checked his watch. Four hours until he was supposed to get to Belle Isle. Certainly, he had time to make it and see what this joker had to say. Maybe he was telling the truth. What motive would he have to lie? And really, did he have any other choice?

He went out to the shed and dragged out his mountain bike from under a dusty plastic tarp. It was an older one, a Raleigh, but it was still in good shape. He climbed on and started pedaling, first west, then north to Monument Avenue, a wide, tree-lined thoroughfare unlike any other in America. Starting at the corner of Monument and Roseneath, at the western tip of the Fan district, majestic thirty-foot statues of Civil War figures dotted nearly every block running east toward downtown. J.E.B. Stuart. Robert E. Lee. And then in a strange juxtaposition in a city full of them, Richmond sports hero, Arthur Ashe, the first African American Wimbledon champion.

Nestled in the middle of a grassy roundabout, the Stuart statue stood watch over the corner of Monument and Stuart Avenues. The campus of Virginia Commonwealth University stretched east toward downtown. Large Victorian-style houses peppered the neighborhoods in the other directions of the compass.

The sun was high and unfettered by any cloud cover when Charlie pedaled up to the statue. With no shade, Charlie baked while he waited astride the bike, panting like an overworked dog. He was ready to hightail it out of there if needed, but he couldn't take the chance of passing up any information this guy might have about Susanna.

Right on schedule, Charlie noticed a man watching him from across the street in the shadows of the church on the corner. The man checked for oncoming traffic, then jogged across the street. Charlie reached inside his bag and wrapped his fingers around the handgun.

"Mr. Dallas," the man said when they were face to face. He wore wraparound sunglasses, which hid his eyes and much of his face. He was short, about five-six, and was built like a powerlifter. He wore khaki pants and a plain blue T-shirt.

"That's me," he said.

The man chuckled softly. "You look just like your old man."

"What?" The statement was like an uppercut to Charlie's chin. "You knew my father? Who the hell are you?"

"It doesn't matter who I am," the man said. "What matters is what I can give you."

"Why should I trust you?"

"Because this is how I'm going to make myself right with God."

Charlie's eyebrows rocked upwards in surprise. The man reached inside his pocket and brought out a small envelope. *Enough with this cloak and dagger shit*, Charlie thought, his eyes locked on the envelope. *Just give me the goddamn envelope!*

Charlie reached out and touched it with his fingers just as a loud squeal filled the intersection. Both men's heads turned toward the sound, coming from the north.

A small, red car was accelerating through the intersection, with apparently no interest in slowing down as it approached the roundabout.

"Shit," the man said, turning to flee, tucking the envelope back into his pocket.

Charlie hopped back on his saddle and started pedaling west. *Dammit*, he thought. He hadn't gotten the envelope from his mystery guest. When he was safely clear of the little car's trajectory, he stopped and watched the scene unfolding before him. Traffic was light at this hour, and there were few pedestrians out in the heat of the day. Something bad was about to happen, and Charlie couldn't do anything to stop it. As he pedaled west, he threw desperate glances over his shoulder.

The car ran up over the curb and the grassy expanse, zeroing in on the man like a heat-seeking missile. He was running, but predictably, he wasn't moving nearly fast enough to escape the oncoming car. With one hand, he reached back and planted his palm on the hood of the car as it plowed into his side like a blitzing linebacker. He flipped up and over the hood, smashing the windshield and flopping over the roof like a rag doll. When the man's body had rolled to a stop, the driver got out, crouched over his victim, and plucked the envelope from his pocket. He looked around, presumably for Charlie, then got back in his car and sped away.

6

The afternoon ticked by slowly, like the wait on the hard bench outside the principal's office. After getting back from the disastrous rendezvous at the statue, Charlie roamed the house aimlessly, hoping the phone would ring on the one hand and dreading it on the other. He desperately wanted to hear Susanna's voice, if only for confirmation that she was alive. Several times, he picked up the phone and started to dial 911, but the echo of the mechanical voice banged around his skull, and he abandoned the idea. He thought about the man's comment that Charlie looked just like his father. The man must have confused him with someone else. Charlie didn't look anything like his father, who was short and stubby. Where Charlie was built like a ladder, his dad, Edwin, more resembled a fire hydrant.

He drifted into their bedroom and sat on the edge of the bed he shared with Susanna. The room was small, and an air-conditioning unit rambled noisily in the window. The room was set at the rear of the house, giving them a view of their garden, in which Susanna usually took great pride. Charlie stepped over to the window, widened the slats of the blinds with his fingers, and peered down into the garden, which, in all honesty, had seen better days. With the wedding plans consuming her the last few months, Susanna had let the garden go a little. Some weeds had sprouted up where normally, black-eyed Susans and gladiolas stood guard. She had mentioned getting the garden in order when they got back from Sanibel. Tears welled up in Charlie's eyes, and he brushed them away with the back of his hand. He slumped facedown across the bed.

The bed was new, a sleigh-cut style made of sturdy pine; it was the first item they'd bought when they moved in together. The purchase put them in the poorhouse for a short time, but it was one thing they agreed on--never skimp on bedding. A Tommy Hilfiger comforter blanketed the surface, and they slumbered underneath 600-thread count sheets that made you feel like you'd slipped into a warm bath. Charlie stroked the comforter gently. He lifted Susanna's pillow to his face and inhaled the scent of her shampoo, still redolent in the fabric, as if her ghost. . . *Stop it,* he told himself. *Don't think like that.*

On the nightstand, a framed five-by-seven photograph of their engagement picture stared back at him silently. She had been wearing a black spaghetti-strapped tank top; he was in a blue button-down oxford. There had been no need to fake their smiles for the camera. Charlie had never once doubted his decision to propose to Susanna. Cold feet happened to other people. And now, it had all been taken away from him.

Stop thinking like that, he told himself again. *It won't bring her back.*

AT FIVE-FIFTEEN, Charlie loaded a backpack with some granola bars, a bottle of water, and an envelope of cash that they kept for emergencies. He decided this constituted an emergency. He checked the gun and made sure the safety was on. He held the weapon in his hand, tracing a finger along the cool steel barrel. He'd never owned a gun before and firmly believed that it was way too easy to get a gun in this country. Still, the heft of it gave him a certain sense of security, even if his entire gun experience consisted of a trip to a shooting range during a college rush event. He hoped he could get a shot off. If it came to that. *Please be alive, Susanna. Please be alive.*

He rolled the bike back out to the sidewalk and headed east along Hanover toward downtown. Under any other circumstance, it would have been a lovely afternoon for a bike ride. Would've been a lovely afternoon for a lot of things. Charlie pushed those thoughts from his head and concentrated on pedaling. Crank, crank, crank. He passed joggers pushing baby strollers, young couples walking hand in hand, little kids riding bikes. An ordinary Tuesday afternoon in early summer.

A few miles away, the boat landing at Belle Isle was only accessible by foot or bicycle. It was a hundred-acre island in the middle of the river and home to numerous walking and biking trails. On a sunny afternoon, hundreds of people walked dogs and jogged around the flat gravel trail circumventing the island. In the middle of the island, dense singletrack and rocky downhills were popular with mountain bikers. It was quite a sight--a serene river park nestled among the skyscrapers that dotted Richmond's skyline.

A thought hit him as he wove his way through westbound traffic. Maybe Susanna would be there. The thought died as quickly as a summer storm. No way. They had gone to a lot of trouble to pull this off. They wouldn't take such a chance. Not for the first time, he wondered if he would ever see her alive again.

He turned south at Laurel and doglegged east again at Cary Street, which ran through the heart of downtown, somewhat parallel to the James River. The James was the spiritual center of the city, which itself had sprung from the river's loins in the 1700s. The river twisted past the southern edge of downtown and served as the centerpiece of the James River park system, Charlie's ultimate destination.

At Fifth Street, Charlie turned south again, then doubled back up Tredegar toward the pedestrian footbridge connecting the mainland to the island. Charlie pedaled slowly across the bridge, mindful of the other bikers, joggers, and walkers using the bridge as well. He descended from the bridge onto the island slowly, then turned his bike east toward the boat landing the kidnappers had specified. He pedaled through knee-high grasses as they swayed in the late afternoon breeze. The grasses covered one of the island's darker secrets. During the Civil War, Union troops had used this site as a prisoner camp, and hundreds of Confederate soldiers died here of cholera, malaria and just general misery. The place gave Charlie the creeps, and he felt gooseflesh pop up on his arms.

Charlie leaned his bike against a tree and stepped down to the boat landing. A group of people was busy at the shoreline, dropping four kayaks into the water. The kayakers were all dressed in blue shirts, members of an extreme fitness class run by an ex-Navy SEAL. Charlie checked his watch; it was a few minutes before six. His heart was pounding.

CHARLIE WATCHED the group as they checked their gear and settled into their seats on the kayaks. They were laughing, joking, generally having a hell of a good time. Charlie dropped his chin and shook his head.

"Mr. Dallas?"

The voice startled him, and he jumped. He turned and saw a man in a dark suit and aviator sunglasses approaching him. He looked to be about forty, give or take, although it was hard to tell because the man's face was smooth and unlined. He was about Charlie's height but much more well-built. There was something about him that Charlie couldn't quite put his finger on.

The man seemed calm, relaxed. As he drew nearer, he reached into the inside pocket of his jacket, and Charlie froze. *Shit, he's going for a gun.* Before Charlie had a chance to react, the man was already displaying what he had extracted from his pocket. It appeared to be some sort of identification. Charlie took one step forward and looked at the brass shield pinned to one half of the bifold, symbolizing the man's employment with the Federal Bureau of Investigation.

"I'm Agent Mike Vitelli."

"I'm sorry?" Charlie blurted.

"With the FBI?" he said quizzically. "You said you had some information for me?"

Charlie blinked hard and tried to process the scene. Something wasn't right here, but he wasn't sure what. He glanced around, looking for something, anything that would shed light on his growing sense of unease.

"Mr. Dallas," he said, "it's illegal to file a false report with the FBI." But the man's voice bore no ill will. "Now, what is it you want to tell me? It's OK."

Charlie's eyes darted from side to side, and he knew he was making the FBI agent nervous. As his gaze swept past Vitelli, he saw the man brush his hand against his side, where he almost certainly kept his sidearm. Vitelli took a step backward.

A rustle in the thick brush along the shore caught Charlie's attention. It appeared to catch Agent Vitelli's attention as well, because the gun came out, partially draped by the lapel of his jacket.

"What the hell--"

The sound was subtle, no louder than a whisper. Had Charlie not been standing downwind, he would never even have heard it. He looked back at Vitelli, whose hand was suddenly clutching his chest. Vitelli looked Charlie directly in the eye, a look of bewilderment on his face, shock that his life was now ending. A dark stain bloomed on his charcoal suit, and he crumpled to his knees before toppling face-first into the dirt. Behind him, Charlie heard a woman scream.

"He's got a gun!"

Charlie turned and saw some of the fitness class members dropping to the ground; others went headfirst into the river, anxious to avoid it, whatever *it* was. Charlie's eyes darted back to the brush, but he couldn't see anything. A thought took root in his mind, a growing certainty that he was in a whole world of trouble.

Shit. Got to get out of here.

Charlie hustled back to his bike, swung a leg over, and pedaled his way back to the footbridge. Behind him, he could hear a cacophony of yells and screams. Echoes of *There he goes!* and *He just shot that guy!* swirled up to him as he made his way onto the bridge. Riding with a little more abandon than on his inbound trip, he glanced back to the shore, where Mike Vitelli's body now lay. A group of the kayakers had surrounded him, and someone appeared to be checking his vitals. Charlie churned his legs harder and flew north across the bridge.

As he descended the bridge to the mainland, he looked across the river to the far shore, some five hundred meters away. The crowd seemed tiny from this distance, but he could sense the hive of activity surrounding the fallen agent. He prayed the man would live, but he knew he couldn't go back. He would most certainly be fingered as the shooter. Pedaling north toward Cary Street, he looked back over his shoulder one last time. Witnesses were pointing toward the footbridge, like the desperate young men in the photo capturing the moment after Martin Luther King's assassination.

7

A few miles to the west, John Hood was taking his own last look, this one at an apartment in which he'd spent a lot of time over the past few months. The apartment belonged to Bonnie, an assistant U.S. attorney in the Richmond office. She was young and lovely and driven and brilliant, and John hoped this wouldn't hurt her too badly. He knew that at twenty-eight, she was probably looking for more than a good time. He was thirty-six, and he knew he should probably be doing the same. But he would not be doing it with this one. She just wasn't the one.

He picked up his duffel bag and glided down the stairs of the small Fan apartment building. It wasn't much of a place, and she always talked about moving somewhere a little nicer, but her work as a federal prosecutor left little time for personal needs. Still, it had felt more like home than anything in a long time. A long, long time. He crossed the street to his car, a beat-up Ford Bronco, and tossed his bag in the rear cargo area. A check of his watch told him it was almost seven. Bonnie wouldn't be home for hours. She was working late tonight, a big RICO trial that started Monday. As one of the FBI agents leading the investigation, John was supposed to testify late next week. This would not go over well.

He turned the key in the ignition and was greeted with a sound that more resembled a wounded animal than a car engine. Finally, the motor caught, and Hood headed west on Floyd Avenue. As he prepared to turn south on Robinson, his cell phone rang. He checked the caller ID on the digital display; it was a city detective he'd become friendly with over the years.

"Special Agent Hood."

"Hey, John, it's Daniels," a familiar voice said in a grave tone. "I'm down on Belle Isle. I think you better get down here."

"What is it?"

"We got a body here. Looks like it's one of your guys."

Hood's ears perked up, and he immediately began mapping his route downtown.

"Got an ID?"

"We got a bunch of witnesses, checked him for ID," Daniels said. "Mike Vitelli. Couple of them tried to revive him, but it was too late. Picture on the ID matches the body."

"Jesus. I'll be there in ten minutes."

John rubbed his bare scalp as he turned east on Cary Street, following a very similar route to the one Charlie had taken about an hour before. He reached under his seat and removed the portable emergency light. At the next traffic signal, he popped the bubble light onto the roof of his car, then raced downtown to the crime scene.

THREE CITY POLICE cruisers were parked near the access to the footbridge, their drivers already down at the crime scene. Behind them, an ambulance idled, and two paramedics smoked cigarettes and chatted while waiting for the signal to recover the body. It was still warm; John's FBI t-shirt clung damply to his chest.

John jogged across the bridge and down to the boat landing, where yellow tape had been strung around a grove of trees. A number of people were already at work, but he was the first person from the Richmond field office on the scene. As the Assistant Special Agent in Charge, John bore primary responsibility for responding to incidents involving other agents. The Office of Professional Responsibility would wade in soon as well.

"Agent Hood," a voice called out. John recognized Ben Daniels's voice behind him.

He turned and shook the man's hand. Daniels was black, with skin like dark chocolate. He was small, looking tiny next to John's six-foot-four frame. Most importantly to John, though, the man was a fantastic detective. On the whole, the city's detectives cleared less than a quarter of its homicides, but Daniels always seemed to deliver.

"I'm sorry, man," Daniels said.

"It happens," John said.

"One of your own though," Daniels said. "Never easy."

"So what do we have?" John said, anxious to get off the subject.

"This group over there," Daniels said, pointing to a gaggle of onlookers about twenty yards away. "They were pushing their kayaks into the water when Vitelli approached another man. Young guy, early-to-mid thirties. Khaki hiking shorts, some say blue t-shirt, some say green. Curly blond hair. Took off on a bike. We've got patrol scouring the area for bikers, but you know how that'll go."

"Can we get a sketch artist?"

"One on the way," Daniels said. "You can get a copy of his schedule for the day, right?"

"Yeah," said Hood, referring to the written schedule that was prepared every morning for every agent for this very reason. "Yeah, we'll get on that now."

"Weapon?"

"Still looking, but nothing yet."

"I want to talk to each of these witnesses," John said, pointing to the crowd. "Separate them now, before they talk too much and they all get the same picture in their head."

Daniels motioned for a uniformed officer and relayed Hood's instructions to the young officer. Daniels had no problem falling in line with Hood's assertion of jurisdiction. He did not play politics because there was no need to. There were enough murders in this city that fell under his jurisdiction, murders that no one else was eager to claim.

"Want to take a look?" Daniels said, jabbing a thumb over his shoulder.

"Not particularly."

Daniels gave a half grunt, half chuckle, and the pair crossed the field to Vitelli's final resting place. John Hood knelt down and pulled back a corner of the yellow sheet of plastic covering Vitelli's body. A strange thought zoomed across Hood's brain as he came face to face with his now-deceased co-worker. *How come they referred to it as Vitelli's body? An hour ago, this was Vitelli. Was it just an object that belonged to Vitelli now? Belonged to his estate?*

"He took two in the chest," Daniels said, crouching down next to John and startling him out of his morbid daydream. "Lost a lot of blood, probably tore through some major arteries. The paramedics said he was dead before he hit the ground."

Hood studied the scene carefully. Vitelli's sidearm was a few yards away, covered with a light sheen of dust. He wondered if Vitelli had gotten a shot off. As John leaned forward to examine the wound, the sleeve of his t-shirt rode up his bicep. Beneath was a giant scar, starting at the crook of John's elbow, running the length of his bicep before disappearing underneath the thin fabric of the blue T-shirt.

"Where'd you pull that?" Daniels asked, motioning toward the scar.

John tugged the edge of his sleeve down, and the ruined flesh disappeared back under the shirt.

"It was a long time ago."

Daniels dropped the subject.

Behind them, the area had become a hive of activity. Members of the FBI's evidence response team were working the scene now, and all three network affiliates had reporters just outside the yellow-taped perimeter taping reports for the late local news. John peeked in on various technicians attending to their duties, one trying to take impressions of footprints, another searching for trace evidence--difficult in an outdoor setting, but not impossible. Still another was photographing and measuring the scene. Made up of five FBI technicians, an Evidence Response Team was responsible for collecting evidence, cataloging it, photographing the scene, and just generally seeing what they could see.

Crime scene investigations always made John very nervous. Scenes were compromised the instant the offense ended. Bodies shifted, shell casings rolled across floors, breezes blew hair and fibers away. Throw people into the mix, even people trying to solve the crime, and the integrity of the scene deteriorated faster than the body itself. Even the people that had tried to revive Vitelli had accomplished nothing more than bringing third-party trace evidence to the scene and possibly destroying the markers that the perpetrator had left behind. Still, there was nothing he could do. He just had to hold his breath and hope there was enough left over.

He pitched in with the ERT, filling out forms for each item of evidence that they bagged. A latex-gloved technician emptied each of Vitelli's pockets into small plastic baggies. As John helped out, he scanned the scene, trying to imagine the last few moments before the shots rang out. Based on the location of the entry wounds, Hood could guess that the shooter had been standing in front of him, but he couldn't determine much else.

And that fact was a little strange itself. Broad daylight, witnesses everywhere, and someone had gotten the drop on Vitelli, apparently while having a chat with him. He wondered if they should be looking for a scorned lover.

Maybe this was an affair gone bad. He tried to remember if Vitelli was married, but he just couldn't recall. He never really got too involved with the guys' personal lives. In John's opinion, that's why they were called personal. Of course, now that Vitelli was dead, the curtain would be drawn back from his personal life.

The inventory of Vitelli's personal items continued. Hood didn't have the foggiest idea if they had found a single item of value, but that wasn't his job right now. If they didn't stick it in a plastic bag, seal it, and record it, then the mad scientists in the FBI labs couldn't decipher it. They were the ones that made the big finds these days.

HER NAME WAS MAYA BEVINS, and she was an auditor with a large accounting firm in Richmond. She was an attractive girl, with shoulder-length brown hair and milk chocolate eyes, but a little on the heavy side, and that was why she had signed up for the fitness class with the former Navy SEAL. Another summer was underway, and she was too embarrassed to go to the beach, even with a one-piece, so this year she had decided to do something about it. *Look where that got you*, she thought sadly, dabbing her eyes. She had seen that poor man shot to death right in front of her.

It was a little after ten in the evening, and Maya was in the Richmond Police Department's new headquarters on Grace Street. They had set her up in Interview Room Four, where she was nursing a soda and a package of peanut butter crackers. She'd already given a twenty-minute statement to somebody from the FBI, and now it looked like they wanted her to do it again. When they let her go home, she was going to hit Taco Bell and pretty much go to town on the combo meal menu. She figured she deserved it.

The door opened, and a woman stepped in, carrying a sketch pad. She was tall and thin, a model's build. Her skin was pale. Behind her, a large man followed her through the door. Maya remembered him from the crime scene. He was massive, and she felt nervous around him.

"My name is John Hood," the man said. "I'm with the FBI. This woman is a sketch artist for the police department. I want you to describe the guy you saw down on Belle Isle to her."

"Hi, what's your name?" the artist asked. "I'm Donna."

"Maya." She felt the tears starting again. "I've never seen anyone die before."

Jesus, Hood thought. *Keep your mouth shut,* he told himself, *Just keep it shut.*

"It's OK, Maya," Donna said, flipping open her pad to a fresh page. "You just start describing what you remember about his face and leave the rest to me."

"OK," she said. "OK. He had blond hair. Curly, big curls, almost wavy."

"What did his face look like? Was it round, long--"

"It was round-shaped. His face was pretty full, like he hadn't lost his baby fat. But he wasn't fat."

"Sure, I think I get it." Donna was scribbling furiously on her pad. John stepped up behind her and peeked over her shoulder. Already, a face was taking shape. The woman was remarkable. They went on like this for another thirty minutes or so, Donna sketching, then erasing, then redrawing. The pair had found a groove, and

Donna seemed to grasp what the girl was describing to her. John kept quiet in a corner of the room, hoping that they would be done soon.

"Does this look like him?" Donna asked, turning her pad toward Maya.

Maya held the pad in front of her and eyed it carefully.

"My God," she said softly. "That's incredible."

John had heard enough. He grabbed the pad from the girl's hands.

"Hey!" the girl yelled.

John tore the sketch from the pad and dropped the pad back to the table, then tucked the sketch under his arm and exited the room.

"What's with that guy?" Maya asked.

"He's tense," Donna said.

"No kidding."

JERRY BLAINE FIXED himself a bourbon and water and settled into his tattered recliner in the living room. His wife, Bonita, was already in bed, and thank God. She'd been whining about a migraine all night, driving him up the wall. But now she was asleep, and he could enjoy the late SportsCenter. He flipped the channel to ESPN, and his face sank upon seeing that a WNBA game was still on. Four minutes left in the game. *Christ*, he thought. Women's pro ball. He decided to switch it to the news until the game was over. He reached for the remote and punched in the channel number.

"--released a sketch of the suspect. Again, this man is

wanted in connection with the brazen killing of an FBI agent in downtown Richmond earlier this evening. Police consider the man armed and dangerous."

The sketch flashed up on the screen, and Jerry nearly choked on his mixed drink. He sat up in his recliner, kicking down the chair's built-in footrest. After setting the drink on the end table, he reached for the phone and pushed in the three familiar digits.

"911. What is your emergency?" said a pleasant female voice.

"I saw the sketch of that guy who killed the FBI agent," Jerry said, shimmying his considerable girth to the edge of the recliner. "I know who he is."

"Please hold while I transfer you."

The line clicked once. Jerry studied the sketch one more time before it disappeared from the screen. The newscaster moved on to the next story, something about a flight attendant strike. No question, it was that Charlie boy. He remembered his name because Jerry was a huge Cowboys fan, and Charlie Dallas was not a name you forgot if you were a Cowboys fan. Jerry knew him because the kid stopped by Jerry's newsstand almost every morning for coffee. He liked the boy, thought he was friendly enough. He was a Cowboys fan too, but hey, who else could you root for if your last name was Dallas? Still, if he killed that cop, Jerry had no problem turning him in.

"Detective Daniels," a voice said when the line clicked back on.

"I seen the sketch of that boy who killed the FBI fella."

"You know him?" Daniels asked.

"Yeah, I know him. Comes by my newsstand every morning."

"You know his name?"

"Charlie Dallas," Jerry said. He could hear the detective rustling some papers.

"And your name?"

"Jerry Blaine."

"Where's your newsstand?"

"Down Cary Street and First. You know it?"

"Sure, sure I know it."

"We're gonna want to talk to you again," Daniels said. "Can you give me a number where I can reach you?"

CHARLIE JOGGED up the steps to his house and quickly let himself in. He knew he was taking a huge risk coming here, but he needed to collect a few supplies before going on the run. Easier to do it now before they figured out who he was. Especially now, on the backside of twilight, he could move on foot in relative anonymity, having dumped the bike a few blocks east.

Leaving the lights off, he took the steps up to their bedroom two at a time, where he grabbed a few changes of clothes and threw them and some toiletries into his pack. As he turned to exit the bedroom, he saw a picture of Susanna that he'd taken during a weekend trip to Hilton Head a few months ago. She was sitting on a rocking chair on the balcony of their room, toasting the camera with a frozen margarita. He grabbed the framed photo and tossed that into his bag too.

Once he got downstairs, he set his sights for the front

door. *Almost there*, he thought. As he reached for the knob, he heard it. Rustling noise outside. He leaned to his right and peeked out the bay window that overlooked the front walk. Two men approached the door; he scanned the street and counted three more cars that didn't belong. Unmarked police cruisers.

Charlie tiptoed down the hall. He needed another way out, and he needed it now. The back door was out, as more officers were undoubtedly converging on that as well. They'd be covering the windows too. He figured he had about three seconds before they kicked down the door.

"CHARLES DALLAS!" a voice bellowed through a megaphone. "The building is surrounded! We have a warrant for your arrest! Come out with your hands up!"

Charlie's insides liquefied. He shut his eyes tight and waited for the sense of nausea to pass. He needed to keep his composure. Susanna was still out there somewhere. He opened the front hall closet and ducked inside, pulling the door shut behind him. At the back of the closet, a gaggle of winter coats and ski jackets concealed a smaller doorway, which he unlatched and quietly pulled open. He reached inside the dim corridor with a blind hand, searching for the dropoff that signaled he'd found the steps.

As he began crawling down the steps, he heard his front door explode behind him. At the same time, his back door blew in, and his house filled with police officers, as if a hurricane had hit and flooded his home. He accelerated his pace down the steps, knowing they'd find his escape route soon enough.

"Living room, clear!" someone shouted.

"Downstairs clear!"

A stampede of footsteps up the stairs followed. A few seconds later: "Upstairs all clear!"

Charlie reached the bottom of the steps and lowered himself to a crouching stance. He was in their crawlspace, which was pitch black. Luckily, he'd been down here more times than he cared to count to bail out standing water after a big rain, so he knew it pretty well. A grate leading to the alley was about thirty feet away, in the northeast corner of the house; the grate was partially covered with ivy and brush and would be difficult, if not impossible to see. At least he hoped it was. If not, they would arrest him, try him, and convict him of murder, and who knew if he'd ever even find Susanna? Hell, they'd probably saddle him with her murder, too.

He scrambled along the damp floor in the infinite dark. Cobwebs he couldn't see strung themselves to his face and neck, and he felt at least a couple of rodents scurrying around his ankles. Above him, it sounded like an army had been dispatched to hunt him down. For all he knew, they had.

He reached the wall, where he began feeling for the grate with his hands. The brick wall of the crawlspace was cool to the touch, but he couldn't find the metal grate. Panic began to swell inside him like a balloon. He couldn't even see his hands in front of him, let alone the grate.

"In here! In here!" a voice yelled from above. *Shit!* They'd found the access door to the crawlspace. "Send someone around the side!"

"Dallas, we know you're down there!"

An officer shined his flashlight down the staircase,

giving Charlie an unlikely ally. With the beam of the flashlight bouncing around, acting as his savior, he finally found the grate, his fingers touching the distinct metal. He fiddled with the latch, swinging it down, and gently lifted the grate from the wall. He set it on the floor next to him and squeezed up through the access panel. It was a tight fit, but he could just wriggle his body through. Using his forearms, he pulled himself out onto the gravel path and took a quick look up and down the alley. Footsteps echoed across the brick pathway in the backyard. Only a few more seconds before they pinned him in. He scurried across the alley to the wooden privacy fence that bordered the neighbor's yard. Grabbing the pointed tips of the fence, he pulled himself up and over and dropped down into the yard next door. Thankfully, their neighbor was not a dog person. At least not a Rottweiler person. She did have a huge calico cat that spent most of its time in the kitchen window.

A light was burning on the porch about fifty feet away, and Charlie could see his neighbor silhouetted on the front steps. Her name was Asia, and she was an artist-in-residence at Virginia Commonwealth University. She and Susanna had become friends shortly after Susanna bought the place. They often walked down to the hippie coffeehouse on the corner on weekend mornings when Charlie was working, as he often was.

"Who's there?"

Charlie hustled across the yard. "It's Charlie," he whispered as forcefully as he could.

"What's going on?" Asia asked softly. She was standing on the steps with her arms folded across her chest. She was thin, and her clothes hung loosely on her frame. She wore a pair of faded jeans, stained with various paints and oils. Her fingers constantly were caked with the raw materials of her work.

"They're looking for me."

"The police?"

"Listen to me, Asia," Charlie said. "Whatever you hear about me, it isn't true."

"Why aren't you on your honeymoon?" she asked, her voice soft and soothing. Even with this chaos surrounding her, she managed to keep a calm aura about her.

"It's a long story," Charlie said, peeking over his shoulder toward the fence line. They were still scouring the alley. It was only a matter of time before they turned their sights on the yards lining the alley. "I'm in a lot of trouble, but I didn't do anything. Please believe me."

Asia stepped down from the porch and touched her hand to the side of Charlie's face.

"I believe you." She looked over Charlie's shoulder toward the gate. Flashlight beams danced around the darkness; an officer knocked on the wooden gate.

"Police! We are coming in!"

Asia nodded her head toward her back door.

"Hide in there," she said. "I'll get rid of them."

Charlie slipped into the small kitchen and dropped to the floor. Using his elbow, he propped the screen door open and waited to see what Asia could do.

ASIA RUSHED to the gate and swung it open. It creaked on its rusty hinges, revealing three Richmond police officers.

Behind them, the darkness of the evening was broken by the oscillating blue lights of the half-dozen police cruisers surrounding the house. One officer stepped forward.

"Ma'am, we're looking for a neighbor of yours," the lead officer said. He was heavyset and graying. "We think he–"

"Yes, yes!" she said as excitedly as she could. "I was sitting on my porch and a guy jumps in my yard from over there." She pointed toward the spot where Charlie had appeared. He ran-

"You said-" She nearly slipped and said Charlie's name. "-my neighbor?"

"Yes, ma'am," the officer said. "Charles Dallas."

"Wow," she said. "Well, he ran clear across my yard and jumped over the back fence. There's another small alley down that way, cuts up to Stuart."

The officer tipped his head over to his shoulder-strapped radio and barked out sharp commands; his two cohorts came through the gate and sprinted across the yard. They were young and fit, and they disappeared over the north fence of Asia's yard.

"Suspect is headed north between Strawberry and Shields," said the officer, eyeing Asia carefully. He seemed to be deciding whether to believe her or not. Finally, he thanked her and headed back out to the street.

FROM HIS NARROW VANTAGE POINT, Charlie watched the two officers scale the fence. *She did it*, he thought. *She did it!* As if to confirm this, the spiraling blue lights began receding from Charlie's block. The brusque shouts and calls softened in intensity as the dragnet shifted north.

Charlie slithered backward on his chest, deeper into the house and away from the windows. In the hallway, he pushed himself up to a seated position against the wall and pulled his knees up to his chest. He rocked back and forth, barely conscious of the passage of time. About fifteen minutes later, Asia slipped inside the house silently, closing the screen door behind her.

"Charlie," she whispered.

"In here," Charlie said.

"What the hell is going on? Where's Susanna?"

His chin dropped to his chest and shook his head. Then he rose to his feet and took Asia's hands in his own. He looked into her light green eyes, which stared back at him, puzzled. He couldn't believe the risk she'd taken for him. If he ever found Susanna, she would owe her life to this tall, thin, pale woman that drew landscapes for a living.

"Thank you," he said. "I promise, someday, I'll tell you everything."

He slipped down the hallway, one that was similar to the one that bisected the first floor of his own home, and stepped out into the warm summer night. He glanced up the street toward his house. His car was being winched onto a flatbed tow truck, headed for the police impound lot. A pair of officers stood guard near his front door, on the off chance that Charlie decided to come home.

He turned east on Hanover and disappeared into the darkness.

8

"I'm sorry, Agent Hood," said the officer. Rivers of perspiration were coursing down his face, darkening his undershirt. Partially because of his unsuccessful foot chase of Charlie Dallas, but mostly because it looked like this fed was about to completely go postal. "We think he may have had some help from a neighbor. We're looking into it."

The officer was standing, shuffling his weight from one foot to another, in the spartan environs of John's private office. John worked at an old oak desk that had been there for years. In its top was carved the ghostly residue of hundreds of reports and evaluations, layered upon one another like a fossil bed. A spare leather executive chair sat neatly behind the desk, but it also wore its age poorly. Tiny tears and scratches pocked the skin of the chair, giving it moonscape. When John had ascended to the position of Assistant Special Agent in Charge, he had refused the opportunity to furnish his office and told Personnel to use the money to buy better guns for his agents. He hadn't even let them repaint the office. On the wall across from his desk was his sole concession to decorating. The certificate he'd received upon graduating from the FBI Academy in Quantico hung in a simple black frame, and that didn't help much. It merely accentuated the industrial feel of the room.

John pushed his chair away from the desk, feeling the anger seep inside him like condensation in a damp basement. His teeth were grinding away at each other like angry dance partners, fueling the tension headache that had been slowly building since Daniels had first called him.

"You're looking into it?"

"Yes, sir," the officer said, his voice softening with each word.

"I don't believe this," John said, the tone of his voice moving in the opposite direction. "I just don't believe this!"

The rage broke loose as if a dam had burst. John put a boot to his chair, which flipped up against the wall, leaving a black streak against the fading paint. A small banker's lamp on his desk became the next victim. Hood grabbed it by the post and hurled it at the wall, where it exploded into a million pieces, showering the room with bits of green glass.

The officer decided that he'd seen enough and retreated from the room. Hood didn't notice he was gone. He turned his boot on the side of the desk and continued pounding on it. The thin siding vibrated at first, then splintered inward under the fierce pressure of John's size twelve foot. He was completely out of control now, barely conscious of what he was doing. He ripped the top drawer out of the desk and threw it like a Frisbee across the room. It crashed against his FBI certificate, sending office supplies flying, and everything plunged to the ground. It was like someone had split open a very strange pinata.

"Shit!"

He turned toward his desk, his back toward the door.

At that moment, his door burst open, and a pair of agents working white-collar crime rushed in; the first one went for John's legs, which buckled underneath him. The second one came in hard into John's back and drove him face-first to the ground.

"John! Calm down!"

John slumped to the ground; his chest heaved up and down as he struggled to catch his breath, and his heart beat wildly. Hot tears stung his cheeks, but he wasn't even aware he was crying.

"Relax, just relax," said the second agent, a fifteen-year vet named Eugene Hicks. Hicks was the senior agent in the white-collar crime unit. The other agent remained silent while they helped John into a chair. His name was Jerome Hudson, a rookie agent from Chicago.

Hicks knelt by John's chair and looked into his eyes. The guy looked very bad. His skin was pale and clammy, and his eyes darted wildly around the room, as if they couldn't focus on anything.

"I'm alright," John said, pushing himself to his feet. "See, I'm fine."

He took one step forward and slumped to the ground, unconscious.

"Shit, call 911!"

Six hours later, John walked out of the emergency room at the Medical College of Virginia Hospital. His EKG and EEG had come back clean, and the treating physician had given him a clean bill of health. Physically, at least. The incident itself had been written off to extreme stress, and the ER had plenty of work to do. This was Richmond after all, the murder capital of the East. In his pocket, John carried short-term prescriptions for Xanax and Zoloft, and the doctor had suggested that he be evaluated by a psychiatrist.

In the pickup/dropoff circle, John saw a car he recognized. A blue Dodge Stratus with government plates. He ignored it and continued toward the main road. He would just take a bus home. It wasn't that far. The horn beeped and lights flashed.

"Dammit," he said to himself.

He stopped, turned back, and climbed into the front seat of the Stratus. Robert Bagwell sat behind the wheel, staring straight ahead. When John had strapped himself in, Bagwell pulled away from the curb and into traffic.

"I spoke with your doctor," Bagwell said.

"So much for patient privacy," John said, looking out the window at the deserted downtown area. Bagwell crossed over Broad Street and zoomed up the on-ramp to the interstate.

"You know better than that," Bagwell said. "I'm the SAC. It's my duty to know what's going on with my agents."

"Yeah, yeah," John said. He glanced over at Bagwell, still looking fresh and crisp in his expensive Joseph

Abboud suit and solid red tie that was still tied in a perfect knot.

"For once, just cut the shit out," Bagwell said, his voice elevating just a hair. "As of right now, you're on probation." Bagwell checked his rearview mirror and merged to the center lane of northbound I-95. A few minutes later, Bagwell turned south on the Powhite Parkway and headed away from the city.

"For what?"

"This has been building, John," Bagwell said. "You're out of control. I'm not working with a lot of options. I'm supposed to take your badge and piece. You're on probation as of right now."

"I have a right to a hearing."

"Yes, you do," Bagwell said. "But if you'd let me finish, I'd explain to you why you're better off on probation."

"Oh, please enlighten me."

"First, if you appeal, I'll suspend you--"

"But--"

"Shut up and listen," Bagwell said, pounding the dusty dashboard with his fist. "If you do this my way, you'll be on probation, but you can return to active duty immediately. Your doctor said that you'd be fine with the meds. If you appeal, you'll be on administrative leave, and you will have to turn in your creds and weapon pending the outcome of the appeal. Do it my way, and you keep the badge, the gun, everything. There's just one condition."

"What's that?"

"You have to go into therapy."

"You must be kidding me."

"I'm not."

"The hell with that."

Bagwell had had enough. He closed his eyes and rubbed them, the fatigue of the day setting in.

"You want to head the investigation on Vitelli or not?"

John massaged the crown of his hairless dome in an attempt to stave off the headache that was building. He hoped the dose of psychotropic medicine they'd given him in the hospital was still working. Punching a hole through Bagwell's windshield probably wouldn't help his case much. His fists clenched, his muscles drew taut, like a beach resort awaiting a hurricane's landfall. Finally, the rage crested and subsided quietly, waves on a calm summer night. He rolled down his window and took a deep breath, inhaling the warm breeze into his lungs. The air smelled of rain.

A few minutes later, Bagwell slowed and turned down John's street. John hadn't even realized that he was almost home. His street was lined with century-old oak trees and small Cape Cods built after World War II. He'd bought the house after his latest promotion. He kept it spartanly furnished, but it provided a temporary respite from the stress of his job. On warm nights, when he was off duty, he liked to pull a lawn chair and cooler full of beer into the small square backyard and look at the stars. Sometimes, he'd throw back one too many and sleep under the black sky, waking up with a thin sheen of dew on him.

Bagwell turned the wheel, and the car dipped and bobbed up into John's gravel driveway. John stared out the windshield toward his house. A huge spiderweb, backlit by the soft glow of the porch light, guarded the sidewalk up to the front door. John made a mental note not to walk into it.

"OK," he said. "I'll do it."

THE DINER SITTING ALONE in the corner booth of the Waffle House wondered how much longer he'd have to wait. He sipped his coffee, already his third cup. He wasn't too worried about the effects of caffeine. He didn't think he'd be sleeping much for a while. Not until all this was resolved. He hoped resolution came sooner rather than later because this wasn't good for a man his age. But the waiting was driving him nutty.

The waitress approached his table again, armed with another fresh pot of coffee. He decided to order some breakfast. That would make him just another patron here during the graveyard shift rather than someone who looked like he was for nefarious purpose. This lonely, bored waitress might take notice, and he couldn't afford that right now.

"Think I'll start without the wife," he said loudly and happily. "Man can't wait forever, right?"

"I guess not, sugar." She was thick and oily-looking, probably a lot younger than she looked.

"I'll have me three eggs, hash browns, bacon--burnt to a crisp--a side of flapjacks."

She grabbed the pencil behind her ear and scratched out his selections on the green order book that she had tucked in her dirty apron.

"Be ready in a few minutes."

A steady thrum drew his attention, and he turned his head toward the window. It was raining, sheets washing across the plate glass. Thunder rumbled deeply in the distance. He drew his focus back in and caught his reflection in the plate-glass window. He couldn't believe he was the old man in the mirror image. Well, maybe not one-foot-in-the-grave old, but fifty-nine was a hell of a long way from twenty-five. His hair remained thick and mostly brown, but grey had made significant advances over the past half-decade. Soon, it would overrun his head, like the American beachhead at Normandy.

His name was Patrick Jessup. At least, that's what it was now. It had been his name for more than thirty years, more than half his life. Back then, starting a new life with a new identity had been a relatively easy process. Amazing what you could do with a fake birth certificate back then, and getting one of those had been a piece of cake. Especially when you had the right kind of money.

A car pulled in from Broad Street and parked in an open spot near the door. The driver jumped out and hightailed it to the front door. Upon entering the restaurant, the newcomer lifted her hands to her head and ran her fingers through the sopping wet hair.

She scanned the dining room until she spotted Patrick. She slid into the opposite booth and removed her jacket.

"You're late," he said, the cup of coffee inches from his lips.

"Sue me," she said, wrapping her arms around herself tightly. "I got drenched. That enough punishment for you?"

They sat in silence, awaiting the inevitable visit from the waitress. Again, Patrick wondered why they met in public places like this, but again reminded himself that hiding in plain view was usually the best approach. That was what she had said. People remembered things that seemed out of the ordinary, things that didn't fit in the paradigm of normalcy. That was what they feared. Her name was Lindsey, but that too was an old alias, one so familiar it didn't seem like an alias anymore. She ordered a cup of coffee and some toast, and they were once again alone.

"So he got away?" he asked.

"For now."

"Dumb luck, eh?"

She took a deep breath and exhaled.

"Well, who would have thought he would have been the reporter?" she asked rhetorically. From her wrist, she removed a small rubber band, then tied her long red hair into a ponytail. Even damp, it still looked good. It reminded the man of when she got out of the shower, often a good memory. "We always suspected someone might dig back into it. What are the odds it would have been him?"

"I still think we should've--" He paused, looked around, then slowly drew his index finger across his throat.

"We talked about this, remember?" she said impatiently, like a teacher scolding a bad student. "If we had done that, we might have made a martyr out of him. Someone might have followed his work. This way would've disgraced him, and everything he's ever done is ruined."

"So you actually saw it?" he asked.

"Yes, that was the plan," she said. "I wanted to see it myself. Only way to be sure. I even gave a statement to the police."

"You what?"

"Relax," she said. "I gave them a fake name."

She paused and tapped a finger to her lips.

"Now--" she began.

"Now what?" the man said, his voice rising.

"Shh."

He felt his blood pressure rising. He hated it when he couldn't follow her thinking. He knew she was smarter than him, but that didn't mean he had to like it.

"Never mind," she said.

"Never mind what?"

"They'll find him. They always do."

"You don't sound too sure."

"Relax, baby. This is all going to be over in a few weeks. Then we can disappear. No one will ever bother us again. This is the last loose thread."

"You've been sayin' that for years."

"This time, I promise."

She kept his gaze for a long time, and the anger and worry began to bleed away. The waitress returned with their orders and set the plates on the table. The smell of the blackened bacon tickled his nose, and he forgot about their problems. He drowned the sizzling pancakes with half a bottle of maple syrup, drizzling the sticky liquid on the vinyl tabletop.

Lindsey took a long look at what he had ordered, but she bit her tongue. Typically, she'd have torn him a new one for eating like this, but it had been a rough day. She sat quietly and watched him enjoy his breakfast.

9

C harlie gave up on sleep at around dawn. He blinked a few times to clear his eyes, then sat up with a start, his reality flooding back. He stood up and switched on the lamp that was mounted to the wall above the nightstand. Harsh yellow light spilled across the room, and Charlie decided that the room looked a hell of a lot better in the dark.

He was staying in a cheap motel just east of downtown, having checked in just after midnight. A loud party had been underway in the adjoining room. His room reeked of fast food grease and cigarette smoke. Eschewing the very questionable-looking bed, he had slept instead on the floor. After seeing the bedspread again in full light, he was glad he'd racked on the floor. He didn't even want to think about the sheets underneath. After a quick and cold shower, he packed his few belongings and exited the room. There was no need to worry about checking out--this was a cash upfront kind of place. The motel clerk had eyed Charlie very carefully when he walked in the door. Few white people ventured this far east at night. Like in many places that had fought for the Confederacy, the ghosts of the old South lived on in Richmond.

The night sky had given way to a soft blue, but the stars were still out on this moonless dawn. The parking lot was relatively quiet, now emptied of the half-dozen crack dealers patrolling the motel when Charlie first checked in. No birds were chirping, as if they knew to avoid this area.

Charlie's phone began ringing, breaking the early-morning quiet. Ducking behind an all-night convenience store next door to the motel, Charlie reached in his pocket and pressed TALK. The caller ID screen flashed: JORGE CORREA. The man worked strange hours.

"Devo--" Charlie started.

"Dallas," Correa said in slightly accented English. "What the hell is going on? I thought you were on your honeymoon, and now I see your picture--" As Devo rambled on, an image began to form in Charlie's head. The image was of his cell phone as a tracking device and a phalanx of police cruisers and SWAT vans closing in on him from every compass point. Suddenly, he wanted it out of his hands very badly.

"Devo, just shut up and listen. I need you to get me a prepaid cell phone. Load it up with minutes. Meet me at--" He paused and wondered how close they were. Maybe Devo's phones were tapped.

Devo seemed to catch his drift. *That was loyalty in a friend*, Charlie thought. No unnecessary questions. Charlie was in trouble, and Devo would do whatever it took to help his friend out.

"I get you," he said. "You remember that big yard you had growing up?"

Charlie smiled. The Yard was a notorious dive bar on the north side of town. It was a rough establishment, but it was popular with people who wanted anonymity. Popular with the city's criminal element. Motorcycle gangs. Drug dealers.

"Yes," he said. "When?"

"Eleven," Devo said. "Wear a baseball cap. Don't shave."

"Why not?"

Devo laughed loudly.

"You hair up like Sasquatch," he said. "You'll be harder to recognize."

Charlie's hand drifted to his cheek, where he felt a thin beard already growing. He realized he hadn't shaved since the afternoon of the wedding. Devo was right; he was one hairy bastard.

"Got any idea what I should do till then?"

"Don't get arrested."

The line went dead. Charlie debated whether he should call his cellular carrier's customer service center and cancel his account, but he worried that might create another trail for the police to follow. He dropped the phone to the ground and crushed it underneath his shoe. The small device splintered easily under the pressure and was soon nothing more than a mixture of broken plastic and shattered computer circuitry.

Charlie slung his bag over his shoulder and took a mental inventory of his supplies. The bag contained a couple of changes of clothes and some personal effects, some leftover toiletries designed for a quick trip out of town. He still had about two hundred in cash. And he still had the gun.

Thoughts of his missing wife popped up in his brain, and he struggled to maintain his composure. He closed his eyes and tried to imagine what she was doing at this very moment. Asleep? Terrified? Dead? He prayed to God that she was still alive. *Wasn't that why God was there?* Charlie wondered. *To answer prayers like this? To watch over us? To protect us? Well, who was protecting Susanna?*

As he headed west toward downtown, his mind drifted back to his years as a child, when his parents made him go to church. The other kids with whom he had grown up often put up a fuss, but Charlie didn't mind it. He liked the quiet, the peacefulness, the idea that someone or something great and powerful was looking over them. Even after his parents died, he rarely missed a week. He missed it occasionally, when he was covering a story or working on deadline, but not too often. He didn't really listen to the sermon that often; it was more of a place to come and feel safe. When his relationship with Susanna turned serious, she started joining him. It made her feel safe, too. He didn't feel very safe anymore.

A police cruiser passed by him, slowing as it did so, but it continued west on Broad Street without incident. Around him, the world was starting to wake up. The sun had just peeked over the horizon behind him, and the air was thickening like a good gravy on Thanksgiving morning. It was going to be a very hot day. A traffic helicopter buzzed overhead, scanning the freeways for the first delays of the morning. Trucks rumbled down the street on their way to their deliveries. Charlie had never felt so alone.

JOHN HOOD WAITED until the first hint of dawn licked the windows, then carefully extricated himself from the bed in which he found himself. It was not his own. He padded across the room gently, or as gently as his six-four frame would allow, and collected his jeans and boots. His shirt, if he remembered correctly, was still in a heap by the front door, where the sole occupant of this apartment had dropped it after ripping it over his head about four hours earlier.

After Bagwell had dropped his ultimatum, John went to a hole-in-the-wall place called Alydar's, just around the corner from where he lived. It was a crumbling concrete structure with plastic chairs and long tables, run by an Egyptian immigrant. He served a limited menu of finger foods from his homeland and kept the locals inebriated when they needed it most.

John sat at the bar and drank scotch for two hours, making small talk with Farid, the owner. Just as he was getting good and sloshed, he made the acquaintance of a woman named Mary, who was probably a lot younger than she looked. Maybe it was Maria. Something like that. Could've been Ashley for all John knew. She matched him drink for drink, and then they had retreated to her apartment a few blocks away. The sex had been, well, sex. A mindless distraction. It beat staring at the ceiling all night. And she had been willing to go all night.

He sat in a chair next to the bed and pulled on his boots. He glanced at the nightstand, where the empty box of condoms served as a testament to the enthusiasm that now seemed pointless. The girl stirred under the sheets and pulled herself to a sitting position. She was wearing a t-shirt and nothing else.

"Where are you going?" she asked sleepily. The room was dark, and John could just make out her features. She was thin and pale and had a thick mane of curly black hair.

"I gotta go to work." He held his breath for the imminent explosion. The work excuse never seemed to pan out, even when it was true. You take a guy home at two in the morning, especially from that dump, you really shouldn't expect...

"Try and keep it down," she said, rolling over and pulling the covers up to her chin. "My kid's asleep in the next room."

A few seconds later, John could hear the steady, even breathing of slumber.

Perfect, he thought. *Just perfect.*

On his way to the front door, he picked up his shirt and pulled it over his head. He stopped and looked back at the other bedroom door, the one he had missed upon their two-thirty arrival. He thought about the kid behind that door, a child he hoped was a very deep sleeper.

BAGWELL CALLED JOHN AROUND SEVEN, informing him that his appointment with Dr. Elsa King had been set up for eight-thirty. Bagwell included the customary warning of the consequences of not taking the therapy seriously. John wrote down the address and got off the phone as quickly as he could.

With a steaming cup of coffee in hand, John headed across the James River. His route took him south along the Powhite Parkway then turned slightly east on the Chippenham Parkway. From there, he turned west on Midlothian Turnpike, a crowded, bustling thoroughfare, jammed on both sides with strip malls, car dealerships, and fast-food joints. The southside of Richmond had a reputation for being the redneck cousin of the metro area, an embarrassment to the soccer moms of the western suburbs and to gentrified blue bloods on the north side. The reputation was somewhat deserved, having a much higher ratio of little Calvin stickers urinating on the logos of NASCAR foes slapped to rear windshields than most areas in the country.

The shrink's office was in an office park a few miles inside the county line, and John eased the Bronco into a very tight spot out front. A few maintenance workers tooled around the grounds of the office park, watering the well-manicured plants, cutting the grass, and justifying the high cost of health care in so many different ways.

The lobby of Dr. King's office was spartanly furnished. Two neutral-colored cookie-cutter couches, a coffee table, and little else. A magazine rack was bolted to the interior wall, but it was empty. The room smelled of something familiar, but John couldn't quite place it. At the far end of the room, a sign was mounted to a closed door. The sign read: PLEASE PRESS THE BUTTON NEXT TO THE DOOR FIVE MINUTES BEFORE YOUR SCHEDULED APPOINT-MENT. THANK YOU.

A small box was mounted on the wall next to the door and, as promised, sported a black button. John pressed the button once and took a seat on one of the couches. He struggled to find a comfortable position, but it was impossible. His ass kept sliding down the smooth industrial-strength fabric of the couch. Fortunately, he did not have to wait long.

At eight-thirty, the interior door opened, and a short, stout woman emerged. She was dressed in a cream-colored pants suit, and she wore little makeup. She was not a bad looking woman, Hood thought. Hood put her age at around sixty.

"Special Agent Hood?" she said with a soft, lilting voice bearing a hint of a southern accent that had been deadened over the years. Without waiting for a response, she turned and retreated into her chambers. John stood up and followed her into the office.

His eyebrows rocked upwards slightly. The contrast between Dr. King's office and the waiting room was stark indeed. The walls were painted a champagne color, the couches leather. A dozen framed certificates and diplomas lined the walls like trophy heads. The room smelled of rich coffee; water bubbled through a filter into an unseen coffeepot. Dr. King took a seat in a beige wing-back chair and waited silently while John gave her office the once over.

When he turned back to face her, she was sitting comfortably in the chair, one leg draped over the other, her elbow propped on the armrest of the chair. She wore a pair of reading glasses, and she looked like someone about to start working on a crossword puzzle. She had no notepad.

"Please, have a seat," she said, gesturing toward the center of the room. She folded her hands in her lap.

John took a seat on the couch closest to the doctor.

"Harvard, huh?" John said, nodding back toward the large parchment hanging on the ego wall, certifying Ms. Elsa King's transformation to Dr. Elsa King.

"I was a geek," she said. "I wasn't sure my looks would last, so I wanted something to fall back on." Then she laughed, rocking her head back with pure unadulterated glee that John was having a hard time comprehending.

"So how does this work?" John asked.

"Well, I've got some electric paddles under the desk. I'll hook them up, and we can go to town."

John blinked and started to open his mouth, but nothing came out.

"Why don't you tell me why you're here?" she said, her playfulness now a memory.

"They made me."

"They did, huh?" The smile returned.

They were quiet for a few minutes, making John feel uncomfortable.

"How long have you shaved your head?" she asked, breaking another interminable dead spell.

"Since I was fifteen."

"Ever tried growing it back?"

"No."

"You shave it every day?"

"Just about."

"Why did you start shaving it?"

"Just seemed like a good idea. No muss, no fuss."

She nodded as though they had made a major psychological breakthrough.

"I know you've been required to meet with me," she said. "So let me tell you a little bit about myself. When the session is over, you can decide whether you want the therapy to continue."

John nodded.

"I'm fifty-seven years old. I was married for twenty-one years, but I've been divorced for ten. I've been in practice for eleven. You do the math. I've concentrated my practice on people in high-stress jobs. I treat a lot of police officers, doctors, firemen, that kind of thing. Any questions?"

John shook his head.

"Chatty, aren't you? You law enforcement types, you're so strong and silent. And you, you're as big as this room. So, why don't you start? Call me Elsa, by the way. I never got used to being called Doctor."

John didn't feel like going through introductions with a new therapist in a week or in a month, so he decided to stick this one out. It wasn't a very conscious decision; he just didn't feel like getting up just yet. He leaned forward and propped his elbows on his knees.

"I had an incident," John said, feeling a stab of heat up his back. He waited for a response from Elsa. He got none.

"I'm working a murder case. Something got screwed up, and I overreacted."

"Overreacted?"

"Overreacted. That's all."

Elsa King tapped an index finger against her lips.

"How would you define 'overreacted'?"

"I'm sure you've got my file," John said. "Why don't you read about it?"

"I do have your file," she said, jabbing a thumb over her shoulder, toward the small, pine desk in the corner of the room. "A courier brought it over last night. I didn't read it yet."

"Why not?"

"I like to meet my patients first. Before I get an impression in my head. The minute you open a file, especially one as detailed as an FBI file, it imprints a picture. One that's always flawed."

"Flawed how?"

"You begin developing biases the instant you hear someone's name for the first time. You immediately form a picture in your head when you hear the name Kate or Larry or Mac or Genevieve. I pictured you as a thin, suit-wearing G-man, a little gray around the temples. Obviously, I was wrong."

She got up and went to her desk, where the small coffeemaker had been percolating. She poured a cup and returned to the seat. John noticed she took her coffee black, no sugar.

"You ever seen yours?" she asked when she'd sat back down.

"My file?"

"Yes," she said, blowing the steam from her mug. She took a sip-*"ow, shit,"* she muttered--then balanced the cup on the armrest.

"No," he said, popping his head up. He'd been concentrating on an ant marching across the cream-colored carpet. It appeared to have a crumb locked in its pincers. John wondered where the ant was headed. How many ants that crumb would feed. Now there was an ant getting some shit done.

"How come? You guys usually sneak a look at your file. Can't stand not knowing what's in there."

"I guess I'm not that curious." John stood up and started pacing the room. He wondered where the ant was, hoping not to crush it under his boot.

"You know that's a load of crap," Elsa said, her eyes tracking John like radar.

"None of my business what's in that file."

"Only your entire professional life."

"I know what I've done," John said. "Why the hell would I need to look at a file?"

"Some people are curious."

"Well, you know what they say about curiosity."

Her eyebrows bobbed upwards, and she crossed her right leg over her left.

"Why don't you tell me what happened?"

John checked his watch. It was nine-fifteen. He was exhausted. He crossed his arms over his body and took a deep breath. Slipping the fingers of his left hand under the right cuff of his t-shirt, he gently rubbed the scarred flesh underneath. He wondered how much of *that* was in his file.

"Are you going to read it?" he asked, stuffing his hands back in his pocket.

"Maybe," she said. "If I think there might be something that could help with our sessions. Not right now though."

"So when do we do this again?" he asked.

She got up again and got her desk calendar. She flipped a few pages back and forth, then said, "I can see you day after tomorrow. How about Thursday at eight?"

"I'll see you then."

When he was back in the parking lot, he pulled the two bottles of anti-depressants from his pocket and unscrewed the tamper-resistant lids on each. He started to dump them out on the asphalt, but then had a vision of some strung-out teenager skateboarding by, finding them and OD'ing on them. He carefully fed the pills back into the orange-toned bottles and returned them to his pocket.

He climbed back in his truck and cradled his head in his hands for a long time. A very long time.

10

The Yard was wedged into a run-down section just north of the I-64/I-95 interchange. It sat in between a medical supply store and a tattoo parlor. The food was better than one might expect, and if you spent enough time and money there, the wait staff tended to pay closer attention to you. A smallish place, the dozen booths lining one wall were usually full by ten o'clock. On the other side sat a huge oak bar and a small kitchen.

As he stepped inside, he wondered if it was a mistake to come here, even given the clientele. Someone might be willing to turn him over to curry favor with law enforcement for some future offense. But the place was jammed. Each booth was overflowing with revelers, and the rest of the place was standing room only. Charlie pulled his baseball cap low over his eyes, and he rubbed his steadily growing beard. He picked his way through the crowd, stretching his neck to catch a glimpse toward the back.

Sure enough, Devo was already there, nursing a gin

and tonic. It was the only thing the man drank. It was the only thing he drank because he was an alcoholic who believed that gin and tonic was the only thing that kept him from drinking everything else. A bourbon sat waiting for Charlie. Devo's sense of timing was uncanny. The ice hadn't even started to melt.

"Thought you could use a drink," Devo said. He pulled out a cellular phone from his pocket and tossed it across the table. "Loaded up with minutes."

"Thanks," Charlie said, catching the phone and sliding it into his pocket. Then: "What the hell were we thinking meeting here?"

"Take a look around," Devo said. "No one cares."

"Why didn't we just meet at your place?"

"I wanted to see if anyone suspicious followed you in."

Charlie looked over his shoulder. Devo was right. People kept to themselves.

"Now then," Devo said, lighting a cigarette and propping his elbows on the table. "What the hell is going on?"

"I didn't kill him."

Devo nodded.

"A lot of people seem to think you did. What were you doing with him, anyway?"

Charlie plucked a cigarette from Devo's pack and lit it. He took a long drag, closing his eyes as the nicotine fired up his synapses. It made him feel alive and alert. He thought back to the warning in the kidnapper's note. It didn't say anything about talking to a friend. It just said he couldn't call the police. He took another puff and set the smoke in the slot of a plastic ashtray.

"Susanna's been kidnapped."

Devo took this news without emotion or reaction. Charlie continued.

"The kidnappers set that meeting with the agent up. I didn't know who he was. I didn't know what was going to happen. They just told me to be there at six."

"They? How do you know there's more than one?"

"I don't," he said. "Try and stay with me."

"Sorry, big guy. And then?"

"That's it. No more contact from them. No ransom. Nothing. I don't have any idea where Susanna is. Or even if she's--"

"Don't say it," Devo said, jabbing a stubby index finger across the table. "Don't even think it."

Charlie picked up his drink with a shaky hand and demolished half of it in one gulp.

Devo stroked his beard for a while, as if deep in thought.

"They told you not to call the police, right?"

Charlie nodded.

"But no ransom?"

"Nothing."

They sat in silence for a while. The alcohol soothed Charlie's nerves, and for the first time since Sanibel, the tightness in his stomach loosened.

"It sounds like you're being set up," Devo finally said.

Charlie took another drink, a sip this time. This possibility hadn't occurred to him. Not too surprising, considering he hadn't slowed down long enough to even take a breath in forty-eight hours. He thought back to his brief meeting with the FBI agent. The man had said that Charlie had tried to contact him.

"I never thought of that."

"That's why you need me," he said.

Charlie smiled. Devo was a true friend. A raving lunatic, but a true friend. He never doubted, never questioned. His loyalty was pure and true. The pair had been friends for a long time, through some rough times. Devo's past was sketchy, at best, but Charlie trusted him with his life.

They'd first met on a story that Charlie was working, when local utility workers had threatened to strike after a long, tense labor negotiation had collapsed at the eleventh hour. A source came forward and gave Charlie proof that a captain in the Guarino crime family had told the union leaders to reject the contract offer from Mid-Atlantic Power & Light. Charlie confirmed the story via other sources, and the paper ran it, causing the mob influence to recede like a doomed hairline. The workers voted to accept the contract, and the strike ended less than twenty-four hours after it started. Devo had been the source.

After the story ran, Charlie began receiving threatening phone calls at home. One evening, on his way home from a night of drinking, he was cornered by a pair of goons who seemed interested in only one thing: rearranging his teeth. Before they got a chance to work him over, however, Devo appeared out of nowhere and went to town on the thugs, Robert DeNiro-in-Cape Fear style. Devo hung around for a couple of weeks after that, close enough to keep an eye on Charlie, but far enough to let him live his life. Or so he thought. Charlie called him out on it, and the two had been friends ever since. Occasionally, he drifted out of Charlie's life, sometimes for months at a time, but he never seemed to be too far away.

Charlie had never really figured out what Devo did for a living. He never really knew why he was called Devo. There were whispers that he was an arms dealer. Rumors that he had been a hitman for the Sacramoni crime family.

"Why would someone want to set me up?" he asked. "You hearing anything on the street?"

"Don't flatter yourself," Devo said. "You're poor, and you don't really have anything to offer. Seriously, the first thing that comes to mind is you're a reporter. You stumble across any government conspiracies lately?"

"Jesus, I'm a metro reporter," Charlie said, lighting another cigarette and leaning back in his seat. "I've got about fifty different leads I'm chasing at any given time, and maybe five of those will pan out for an actual story. If I'm lucky. And of those, none warrant, *oh*, kidnapping my wife and framing me for murder. Believe me, it's not like *All the President's Men*."

"Here's what we're going to do," Devo said. "Keep growing your beard, dye your hair, that kind of thing. Try to find you a place to stay. And then we're going to figure this out. Stick with me. I know the right kind of people. We'll find her before the cops catch you. You hungry?"

Devo's question made Charlie's stomach rumble.

"I haven't eaten in two days," he admitted.

He felt guilty for feeling hungry. Susanna was probably not getting ready to order the dinner of her choice. But he needed to eat. Devo raised his arm and motioned for a waitress; Charlie's body tensed like a rope pulled taut.

"Relax," Devo said as the waitress approached their table. "I'm banging this one."

She was short, and her arms were tattooed from elbow to wrist. Her name was Anna, and she seemed quite smitten with Devo. They ordered burgers and cheese fries and more gin-and-tonics. Charlie could not remember the food ever tasting so good. He ate two burgers, his digestive system be damned, and the gin slowly relaxed his cable-tight muscles. He felt his eyes drooping.

"I need some freaking sleep," Charlie said. "I can't even see straight."

"Let's get out of here," Devo said. He dropped a fifty on the table. Devo sauntered casually out of the bar, stopping twice to shake hands with folks he knew. Charlie pulled the brim of his cap as low as he could, holding his breath on his way out the front door.

An hour later, Charlie was in bed, but the sleep that seemed so close back at the bar had deserted him. Devo had set him up in the guest room of his spacious apartment in downtown Richmond. Located on Tobacco Row, where Philip Morris had once churned out cigarettes by the billions, the building was a refurbished warehouse, gutted and painstakingly renovated. Painstakingly owned, too, as each apartment sold for about $750,000. On clear days, sunlight filtered down through large skylights in the cathedral-style ceilings, and the walls were exposed brick.

Charlie climbed out of bed and opened the blinds, giving him a fantastic view of the city lights below. The hardwood flooring felt cool and refreshing under his tired feet. In the distance, the James River was a twisty black vein through the heart of the downtown. As the lights twinkled below him, Charlie thought about Devo's suggestion that he was being set up. For the life of him, he couldn't have imagined such a scenario. Sure, like all reporters, he dreamed about the One, the story that would bring down a presidency or expose an international conspiracy. He just hadn't found it yet. Or had he?

He went through the Rolodex of his active stories in his mind. A feature on safety procedures in the city's water systems. Another story on a police brutality trial currently underway out in Henrico County. A story about the thirtieth anniversary of the most famous bank robbery in the city's history. A piece on a city council-woman accused of taking bribes in exchange for her vote to fill another council seat, vacated when the incumbent was arrested and charged for soliciting sex from a sixteen-year-old boy.

These were ordinary stories, albeit important ones, in any newspaper in any city in the country, no, the world. You read them every day. He leaned closer to the window and pressed his forehead to the glass pane. *Come on, Dallas, you need some sleep.* Another night staring at the darkness, and his mind would be as useful as a baby food jar of strained carrots. And he needed his wits about him. Again, the lunacy of the situation rocked his brain like an earthquake. *Susanna, gone. Police officer, no, FBI agent*, he corrected himself, *dead. Charlie, wanted fugitive.*

He climbed back into bed, his head spinning and feeling heavy. He was asleep before he was even able to pull the covers back over himself. He slept deep and hard, waking only once to a rumble of thunder as an overnight storm soaked the city.

∼

HE WAS AWAKE BEFORE SEVEN, the rich aroma of good coffee tickling his nose. It made him think of those cheesy TV commercials where people woke up, noses crinkled, in bright, sunny bedrooms with apparently no job to get up for. *I'll bet the coffee tastes good*, Charlie thought. He grabbed a quick shower, threw on his clothes, which were starting to develop some serious personality--he really needed to do some laundry--and headed downstairs. Devo was on the couch in his bathrobe, one hand wrapped around a mug, the other holding a bowl of Froot Loops, a cigarette dangling from his lips. Charlie often wondered how the man ever convinced anyone to have sex with him, although it seemed to happen quite often.

"Dude, you're famous!" he said, pointing at the television. Devo was watching the Today Show, and the perfectly coiffed newscaster was delivering the day's top stories. In the box over the newswoman's shoulder, Charlie saw his photograph, the picture from his ID badge at work.

". . . Virginia, federal and local law enforcement officers are conducting a huge manhunt this morning for Charles Dallas, a newspaper reporter who is the prime suspect in a brazen shooting two days ago that left a decorated FBI agent dead. Officials say they are baffled by the killing."

"Oh, Jesus," Charlie said, dropping against the couch.

"I take that as a sign that we need to get started," Devo said, setting his coffee and cereal on the glass coffee table as the newscast moved on to the next story.

Charlie nodded his head vigorously.

"First, you probably shouldn't stay here anymore. I'm

pretty far off the grid, but you never know. They might show up here with a warrant."

"Yeah, thanks for letting me crash here. You didn't have to do that."

"Don't mention it. Now follow me," he said, standing up, burning out his cigarette in the leftover milk.

Charlie trailed behind him to the bathroom. Devo was on his knees, rooting through the cabinet under the sink, tossing one personal hygiene product after another over his shoulders and onto the floor. A set of clippers sat on the edge of the sink.

"Where the hell is it?" he muttered. "No, no, no--here it is," he said, holding up a strange-looking bottle. "Grab that towel and wrap it around your shoulders."

Charlie did. Devo grabbed the bottle from both ends and twisted each half in opposite directions. An internal seal cracked, and the liquids from each half mixed together. He twisted the cap off.

"I'm not even going to ask why you have that here."

"Probably best that you didn't. Stand still," Devo said, grabbing the clipper and turning it on; it buzzed like a low-flying plane. Devo was merciless, wasting no time in reducing Charlie's locks to a thin layer of fuzz covering his head. Then Devo began applying the dye to Charlie's once-curly blond locks, pressing the applicator to the roots of Charlie's hair and working his way out to the ends.

"Shampoo it in," Devo said.

After pulling on a pair of latex gloves, Charlie began rubbing the dye into his scalp, a very strange sensation. The only thing he ever put on his head besides shampoo was his Red Sox baseball cap. After a minute or two, his gloves were as black as a mechanic's hands at the end of a busy day.

"Now what?"

"Wait five minutes, then run your head under the faucet for about thirty seconds. That's it."

"How long's this stuff last?"

"Beats me," he said. "Long enough for you to find Susanna." He paused, and a smirk lit up his face. "Or get caught."

"Hilarious."

"Just trying to keep the mood light. What else can I do?" Devo clapped Charlie on the shoulder. "I'll wait for you out front."

Charlie sat on the edge of the tub, waiting for the dye to take hold. When the five minutes had passed, he ran his head under the faucet, and streaks of black dye stained the ceramic tub. Charlie got the eerie sensation that he was washing blood from his hands, trying to hide the signs of some terrible crime.

He went back out to the living room, where Devo had set up a stack of legal pads and a box of pens. A laptop was roaring to life, and Devo was connecting a small printer to the back of the computer.

"Hey there, handsome," Devo said, looking up from his work.

"I look like a freak," Charlie said, glancing at his reflection in a small mirror that Devo had mounted by the front door. *Not a bad plan*, Charlie found himself thinking as he looked at the virtual stranger looking back at him.

"There's only one way we're going to find her," Devo said. "We got no police to help us, and to be honest, we're probably better off. We're going to have to do some good old-fashioned detective work. Lucky for you, my last brother-in-law was a P.I. He taught me a few things, showed me a few tricks."

"You're a piece of work, you know that?" Charlie said.

"Get your thinking cap on, slick," Devo said. "We need to figure out a plan for you."

"OK."

Devo's cell phone began chirping.

"Yeah?"

Devo stepped into the kitchen, leaving Charlie alone in the living room. Charlie knocked down the volume on the television a few ticks, anxious to hear Devo's conversation. He still wasn't totally comfortable letting Devo run the show. But what choice did he have? Life on the lam wasn't exactly his specialty. He primed his ears as Devo became increasingly animated.

"I told you, it was gonna be next week," Devo barked.

Silence.

"No, we're not changing it."

Charlie couldn't be sure, but he almost detected an undercurrent of fear in Devo's voice. Not good.

"We had a deal," Devo said, his voice mellowing and softening with each word. Finally, it devolved into whispers, and Charlie couldn't hear anything else. A few minutes later, a loud boom echoed through the flat; Charlie's stomach nearly exited his body through his mouth. Devo had punched a wall.

He stepped out of the kitchen, a smile back on his face.

"Everything OK?" Charlie asked.

"Sure," Devo said. "You've got bigger fish to fry. I've got an errand for us to run."

"What kind of errand?"

"You'll see. It's going to help us both. And then you'll be on your own, buddy."

JOHN HOOD CRACKED open his third Mountain Dew of the morning. People always looked at him strangely for drinking the stuff, but he didn't care for coffee, and he certainly didn't care for having to clean up a coffeemaker every morning. He took a sip of the ice-cold soda and began reviewing the murder book on Vitelli, still in its infant stages.

On top was a photocopy of Vitelli's desk calendar from the day he was shot. In the square for June 17, he'd penciled in: *Mtg. 6:00. Belle Isle boat ramp. CI.* Law enforcement officers frequently depended on confidential informants to feed them information about what was happening on the street. Most of the informants were criminals themselves, willing to rat out their own mothers in exchange for a better deal with the prosecutor. As part of the narcotics trafficking unit, Vitelli had a wide network of informants to whom he spoke often. John wondered if a rat had sold Vitelli out to someone big time, someone that Vitelli was getting close to. They'd have to check each of his active cases, of course, a task that could take weeks or months.

Much of the office was in shock. John could tell when he'd gotten to work this morning. He didn't understand it.

This was still a dangerous job, and agents sometimes got themselves killed. After all, that's why they carried guns.

He wondered how Dallas fit into all this. Based on what little information they had on him so far, he didn't seem the type to do the dirty work himself, even if he was involved with drug trafficking. And so what if he looked like some preppie white kid? He could still be in the biz. John scratched a few notes out on a legal pad and was holding the pen to his lips when a knock at his door interrupted him. Agent Jerome Hudson was holding a thin manila folder up in the air.

"We got some stuff on Dallas," Hudson said, handing the folder across the desk to Hood. "Get this. He's a reporter for the Richmond Gazette. I sent three agents down to the newspaper offices."

Hood nodded, almost imperceptibly. He was already flipping through the file, which contained some biographical information about Dallas. Date of birth, social security number, that kind of thing. John did some quick math--Dallas was thirty-three years old, born in Waynesboro, Virginia. The last known address matched the one where the failed raid had taken place the night of the shooting. The name on the copy of the deed was Susanna O'Donnell. Landlord? Wife? There wasn't enough information in the file to answer that one right now.

John pointed at the young agent before him.

"Get his boss down here, right now," John said. "I don't feel like waiting for more information."

≈

DANNY FREYHOGEL WAS an assistant city editor at the Richmond Gazette and Charlie's immediate supervisor. He was thin, his teeth were yellowed from years of double-barreled abuse, coffee and cigarettes. He looked to be in his late forties, but truth be told, John thought he could have been in his thirties had life not beaten the man down so badly. His hair was thick and short and spiked upwards, and he wore a pair of dirty khakis and a blue button-down oxford. His clothes were rumpled and draped across his frame like it were a wire hanger.

"Have a seat," John said.

Freyhogel did so, sitting on the edge of one of his visitor's chairs. His eyes darted back and forth across the room.

"I just don't get this, don't get it at all," Freyhogel said quietly and rapidly. "I was just talking to him Friday before he left for vacation."

"Vacation?" Hood asked, leaning back in his chair.

"Yeah, sure, he got married Saturday and was going on his honeymoon."

Hood frowned.

"We're talking about Charles Dallas, right?"

"Yeah, sure, Charlie, blond hair, you know."

"Do you know where he went?"

"No, I really don't," Freyhogel said, his eyes either unable or unwilling to focus on anything specific.

"What do you know about his wife?"

"Sure, Susanna, lovely girl. I think she's a teacher, but I'm not sure."

John scratched the top of his head. The guy gets married, supposedly goes on his honeymoon, then comes back and bumps off an FBI agent? John tried to fit that piece of information into the puzzle of Mike Vitelli's murder. Assuming that Dallas was a big-time trafficker, John supposed it was possible Dallas got word of a federal agent getting ready to make a move against him, and said, *Sorry, honey, I've got to get home and whack this FBI agent so I can continue to provide you with the lifestyle to which you've been accustomed.*

"How long's he been with the paper?"

Freyhogel looked up at the ceiling and did some quick math.

"I think about five years."

"I'm going to need copies of all his work."

Freyhogel winced like he'd eaten something bitter.

"Oh, geez, that's gotta be a thousand stories," he said.

"Well, you'd better get cracking, Mr. Freyhogel."

"Do I have to?"

"Would you prefer a dozen FBI agents personally delivering a federal subpoena to your desk?"

Freyhogel looked like he might cry.

"Fine, I'll do it. OK?"

John gripped the edge of his desk. The guy had the social graces of a seven-year-old boy. He wanted to bash the man's head in. *Dammit, why hadn't that doctor given him any relaxation techniques?*

"Now get out of here," John said, pointing to the door. "I want those stories by six o'clock tonight."

"Did Charlie really kill that guy?"

"I don't know," Hood said. "I wasn't there."

Freyhogel got up and retreated from John's office like a beaten puppy. John leaned back in his chair. He was exhausted, and it wasn't even noon yet.

Carrollton Oaks was the best-known neighborhood in the city of Richmond. Not because anyone famous lived there, or because it sported beautiful Victorian houses, or even because it had a decent high school football team. Carrolton Oaks was famous because it was the most dangerous place for a hundred miles in any direction. Rarely a night went by without a drive-by shooting or execution-style killing. Even rarer was any sort of police presence, the area written off by the city fathers. A figurative siege was underway here on the city's eastern border.

It had a refugee camp feel about it, with long rows of crumbling concrete-block apartment buildings, drug dealers that swarmed like flies on carrion, and shootouts that resembled the streets of Beirut during Lebanon's civil war. Everyone knew the place was in desperate shape, but no one knew what to do about it.

The children of the 1980s crack dealers were coming of age now, and many had grown up even deadlier and more violent than their now-deceased parents. Teenage dealers and prostitutes roamed the streets at all hours; the sound of automatic weapons fire crackled each night. The law-abiding citizens of the neighborhood, those with no other place to go, ran home from the bus stops, locked their doors, and drew their curtains tight, like the British during the German air raids of World War II.

On this hot, sunny Thursday morning, Devo and Charlie took the bus to 31st Street and disembarked, conscious of the eyes that locked on them the second they stepped down to the weed-choked strip of grass fronting an abandoned storefront. Brightly colored sale flyers advertising rib roast for $1.99 a pound still hung in the dusty window. Across the street, Charlie looked at the wrought-iron gates leading inside the Oaks, heavy and majestic as if they were guarding a billionaire's compound. A close inspection of the bars revealed a thousand pockmarks of long-ago fired bullets. Behind them, the bus accelerated away from the curb like a jackrabbit on speed.

"Stay close," Devo said under his breath. "They cut me a little slack here, but not much."

Charlie felt hot with terror. Young men looked at him with lost, desperate eyes. A basketball game on a cracked court in the center of the complex came to a halt, and everyone watched the two strangers who were encroaching on their turf.

They crossed the street, and Devo led Charlie up a rickety open-air staircase, treading cautiously to the end of the corridor to Apartment 331. Devo performed a series of knocks at the door and stepped back. He pitched his half-smoked cigarette over the railing.

Rustling on the other side of the door gave way to muffled shouts. The door cracked open, and Charlie caught a glimpse of a young woman in the narrow void that had opened up.

"The hell do you want?" she asked.

"I need to see Smoky," Devo said, his voice strong and unwavering. "Now."

"Brianna!" a raspy voice exploded from inside. "Open the damn door!"

The door slammed shut, the bolt in the chain door guard sliding in its groove, before popping open again. The girl wrenched Devo and Charlie inside quickly, and the door closed as quickly as it opened. The apartment was dark, darker still in contrast to the brightness of the day. The pungent odor of marijuana and old fast-food grease permeated the room.

Rough hands shoved Devo and Charlie against the wall and patted them both down for weapons. The searcher found Charlie's automatic under his shirt. He felt the steel barrel pressed against the nape of his neck.

"You even know how to use this?" his searcher asked. Then, he turned his head and barked, "They clean."

"Devo, Devo, Devo," the raspy voice said. "You must be a damn fool, bringing that boy here."

"I need your help, Smoky," Devo said, turning away from the wall. "He needs a new life."

Charlie followed Devo's cue and turned toward the room. His eyes had started to adjust. Fast-food wrappers and empty bottles of beer cluttered the coffee table. Besides him and Devo, three other people were in the living room. The girl, the fellow who had searched him, and Smoky himself, were seated on a couch. Smoky, true to his name, was smoking a cigarette.

He was a bear of a man. He was wearing knee-length basketball shorts and an Atlanta Falcons football jersey. His hair was braided into cornrows. Smoky eyed Charlie up and down, and Charlie got the distinct impression that the man did not miss much, despite, or perhaps because of, his surroundings.

He pulled his considerable girth off the couch and engulfed Devo in a warm embrace.

"Been a long time, my man," he said, clapping his paw of a hand on the side of Devo's face. There was a warmth in his voice and touch that took Charlie by surprise. When the reunion was complete, Smoky turned his attention toward Charlie.

"Seen you on the news," the man said, poking a thick finger in the center of Charlie's chest. "You killed a cop, that might bring the cops down here."

"No one knows we're here," Devo said.

Smoky placed a finger of his other hand against Devo's lips.

"Gonna cost you," Smoky said. "Hazard pay and whatnot. Five large."

Devo guffawed, and Charlie nearly wet his pants. The last thing they should be doing was disrespecting this man in his home.

"Three," Devo replied nonchalantly, as if they were negotiating the price of a used car.

Smoky smiled, revealing two rows of blinding white teeth. Then he started to laugh, a big, belly-shaking laugh.

"Four," Smoky said. "And then I don't want to see that mug of yours 'til I'm old and grey. You got that?"

Devo glanced over at Charlie.

"Deal."

Devo reached in the outer pocket of his cargo pants and pulled out a thick wad of cash, nearly two inches thick. He counted out forty hundred-dollar bills and pressed them into Smoky's hand. Smoky took the money, looked over at Brianna, and nodded his head toward the back of the apartment.

"This way," she said, as if she were a waitress leading them to their table.

What awaited them at the end of the hallway could not have surprised Charlie more. The room was outfitted like the White House Situation Room. Seventeen-inch flat-panel monitors occupied three tables, state-of-the-art Hewlett-Packard computers powering away underneath them. A collection of oddly-sized printers, flatbed scanners and digital cameras cluttered the room.

Charlie whistled softly.

"You like it," Smoky said, laughing.

"Yeah, I do. But don't you worry about--"

Smoky held up his hand, palm out. "Nobody steals from Smoky," he said without a trace of ego or machismo, the cool confidence of a man who'd spent his life surviving and thriving. Then he pulled up his jersey, revealing a cannon of a handgun tucked in his waistband.

"Nobody."

As he lowered his shirt down, Charlie caught a glimpse of a twisted scar running across the length of Smoky's body and around his hip.

Smoky took a seat at one of the computers and

tapped a few keys, bringing the screen to life. A couple of clicks of the mouse activated an icon on the Windows-based operating system, changing the pointer into its spinning hourglass. Meanwhile, Devo had settled on the couch with Brianna, and the two seemed to be enjoying themselves immensely. Smoky tossed a few glances their way. Charlie hoped that Devo wasn't moving in on Smoky's girlfriend. She was beautiful with dark eyes and angled features. Her legs went on for hours. Charlie looked away, a pang of guilt shooting through his gut.

"I'm gonna give you a driver's license and birth certificate with a new name, new social, new DOB. I'll even give you some sweet pimpin' glasses for the picture."

Charlie nodded.

"Gimme your social," Smoky said, "see what kind of blocks have already been thrown up."

"Blocks?"

"You're a fugitive, man. Social's like a GPS tracking device. I'm sure it's flagged. You try to use it anywhere-- they'll be on you in a heartbeat. Also, I wanna get some dirt on yours, so I can give you a completely fresh one, different year and state of issue than your own."

"331-73-0913," Charlie said.

Smoky tapped the number into a new window on the screen. Window after window of information that most Americans probably thought was secure popped up on the monitor.

"What are you doing now?"

"This is spy software," Smoky said. "I can look around all I want in here. Long as I keep quiet, I can look at everything."

"How do you--"

"I got me a guy," Smoky said softly, "and that's all you need to know."

He studied the screen for a moment. "Hmm. Give me that number again."

Charlie repeated the number with which he'd become intimately familiar during his life. Social security numbers had always given him the creeps. The idea that every man, woman, and child in this country had an identifying number was bizarre. Who said Big Brother wasn't watching?

"You sure about that number?" Smoky asked. He pulled a cigar out of a desk drawer and lit it. The room filled with pungent smoke.

"I'm sure."

"Well, then, according to this, you died in 1969."

"What the hell you talking about?"

"This number was assigned to Charles Xavier Dallas, born June 12, 1969, died December 11, 1969."

"I don't get it."

"This been your number all your life?"

"Of course it has."

"Is June 12, 1969, your birthday?"

"Yes."

"You ever received paperwork from the Social Security Administration?"

"Sure," he said, not feeling too sure at all. "I guess."

Smoky rubbed his chin, deep in thought.

"Must be a mistake," he said finally. "Don't matter much anyway. Let's move on."

"Doesn't matter much?" Charlie barked. "It matters to me that my ID is all messed up."

"Keep your eyes on the prize, little man. Eyes on the prize. We got a lot of work to do."

He began tapping away at the keyboard, mumbling to himself in a tone that belied no emotion. Charlie watched him work through the Social Security Master Death Index, a roll call of anyone who had been issued a social security number and then had the misfortune of dying.

"The best numbers to use are from people who had no surviving relatives," Smoky said. "That's where this software comes in handy. This guy here," he paused, pointing at a name in a sea of others. "Robert Winston McWilliams. Died 1955."

"How do you know he's got no relatives?"

Smoky pointed at the screen, clicking on the name. "Look here," he said, as the window for Robert McWilliams popped open. The window included a brief biographical sketch. An entry marked Beneficiary was marked *None*.

"See, his death benefits went to the government because there wasn't any next of kin," Smoky said. "Congratulations. You're now Robert McWilliams."

"Won't it raise a red flag that I'm using a dead guy's social?"

Smoky leaned back in his chair and puffed on the cigar. It smelled rich and good, and Charlie wished he was with Susanna, smoking his own stogie, sipping Jefferson's Reserve, while she drank a frozen margarita.

"It looks like you've been doing just that yourself," Smoky said.

That was true.

Smoky got up and fed some light-green card stock into one of the printers. He clicked a few icons on the screen, and the small printer whirred to life. The computer delivered the information to the printer, which in turn inked the paper as it was instructed to do. Smoky tore off a section, looked over it, then handed it to Charlie.

Charlie examined his new social security card.

"Incredible," he whispered. It was not merely a terrific forgery, it was an authentic social security card. Charlie wondered how many pies Smoky had his fingers in.

"Next step, driver's license. Stand over there," he said, pointing toward the corner of the room, in the crosshairs of a digital camera mounted on a tripod. Charlie stood against the wall while Smoky snapped a half dozen head shots to go on the phony license. Smoky returned to his workstation and downloaded the digital photographs to the desktop. He opened a new program, titled, appropriately enough, *Driver*.

"So which picture do you like?" Smoky asked, pointing toward the two rows of photographs on the screen.

"Whatever," Charlie said.

"Hey Devo," he called back over his shoulder. "Your boy can get a bit moody."

"Tell me about it," Devo said, looking up from his liaison with Brianna.

"Sorry," Charlie said.

"Just thought I'd lighten the mood," Smoky said.

Smoky highlighted the first picture and double-clicked the mouse. From a drop-down menu of U.S. states, he selected Maryland and waited while the program worked its magic. An authentic-looking license template appeared on the screen, absent the photograph and biographical information. The software made Charlie extremely nervous. This was the kind of thing that terrorists used. Smoky tapped in the necessary biographical data, including an unfamiliar street address.

"What's that?" Charlie asked.

"You ever watch the X-Files?"

"No," Charlie said.

"Too bad. Best show on TV back in the day."

"I don't get it."

"It was Mulder's address on the show."

"Nice touch," Charlie said, rolling his eyes and trying to imagine this man settling in one night a week to catch his favorite television show.

Smoky got up again and turned on an oblong-shaped machine propped up on a wall-mounted shelf. It was a license printer, and it created the supposedly forgery-proof, heat-sealed picture identification that each state issued. A beam of laser light glowed inside the machine, and then it spit out Charlie's new driver's license into the plastic drop tray.

Charlie fished it out; it was still warm to the touch. Like his new social security card, the license was perfect. With it and his new social security card, he could do just about anything. At least for a while. He pulled out his wallet and tucked his new identification into the appropriate slots.

"Alright, time for you to go," Smoky said. "Don't ever come back here."

Charlie nodded. "Thanks, man." He stuck out his hand.

Smoky shook it.

~

DEVO BID BRIANNA A FOND FAREWELL, and he followed Charlie down the hallway. Smoky ushered them quickly to the door, and they were quickly alone on the landing. As soon as the door shut behind him with a distinct click, Charlie felt his body buzzing. He scanned the neighborhood below him, slow and quiet on this hot, humid morning. The courtyard, which had been crawling with life when they got here, was empty. As if everyone had snuck out of the bar and stuck Charlie and Devo with the tab. Devo didn't seem to notice; he lit a cigarette and started down the stairs. Charlie reached out and placed his hand on Devo's shoulder.

"Wait," he whispered. "Something's up."

"Listen to the kid," Devo said, continuing down the stairs without breaking stride. "Relax. I'm cool here."

Charlie refocused his attention on the courtyard. A slight movement near--or was it in?--the pool caught his eye. Technically, the pool was out of service, but on very hot days, they would fill part of it with a hose. Then the adults would come in and smack the kids around for turning the area into a mosquito breeding ground.

But now it looked like someone was down in the pool, up against the near wall, just out of his line of sight. Charlie started down the steps after Devo, anxious to get out of here. Probably just a couple of kids messing around, but he didn't want to take that chance. He reached in his pack and felt the reassuring steel of the handgun.

Devo got to the bottom of the stairs and turned right, back toward the street. He looked like a man without a care in the world, his shirttail flapping in the soft breeze that had kicked up. They were in an open square, walking toward a narrow corridor that led back to the bus stop. Behind the dirty windows of the closest apartment, a young woman held a cute baby against her breast. His eyes were still locked on the woman when she drew back from the window and yanked the curtain shut.

The distinct sound of metal scraping against concrete drew Charlie's attention back to the pool, and now Devo had become interested as well. He focused on the empty basin like a lion zeroing on its prey.

"Get down," Devo whispered.

"Devo!" a voice called out. It was loud, high-pitched, reedy. The shrillness of it made Charlie's blood run cold. "Time to pay the bill!"

Charlie pulled his weapon, not a hundred percent sure what he was going to do with it, and dropped to the ground as the air filled with the staccato burst of semi-automatic weapons fire. The shooter was inside the pool, propping his assault rifle on the edge of the deck, less than thirty yards from where they were standing. Flames licked the long black barrel as the shooter emptied a clip at them.

Charlie checked their surroundings. A few trees about fifty feet away could provide meager cover. Otherwise, they were completely exposed. A perfect killing zone. Devo was flat on his stomach, elbows propped up, a nine millimeter in each hand, firing as fast as he could.

Jesus, Charlie thought. *Jesus Christ, they were dead.* The situation had finally registered in Charlie's mind as the terror inside him started to crack and survival instincts began seeping in like cold under a door.

Shaky hands flipped the safety off--how Charlie remembered to do that, he'd never know--and he squeezed the trigger of the Taurus .22-caliber semi-automatic. The gun shimmied in his hand, shots flying wildly, but the new threat seemed to catch the shooter off guard. The raking of bullets paused, and Charlie decided to make a run for the alley between a row of apartments and the perimeter fence, using the trees for cover.

He jumped to his feet and bolted, firing blindly behind him, as the shooter regained his composure and recalibrated his sights. Tears filled Charlie's eyes as he neared the relative cover of the concrete building. He ducked behind the thin, dying trees, bullets tearing through the soft wood and melting what little foliage had managed to grow here. He had to make it. Had to. Otherwise, he'd never see Susanna again. He pumped his legs harder, and they began to burn, all the while waiting for a slug to rip through his side. Twenty yards became ten, and then he dove for the cover of the building. His ears rang with the sound of bullets chipping at concrete, dust filling the air and his nostrils.

Safe for the moment, he bent over and drew oxygen into his lungs, then looked up, expecting to see Devo a step behind him. What he saw instead burned itself onto his conscience for the rest of his life.

Devo was down on the ground, holding one leg gingerly, returning fire with his free hand. Blood was flowing freely from the wound, pooling underneath Devo's body.

"Dallas!" he called out over the din of the gunfire. "Get the hell out of here!"

The shooter, sensing the kill, gave up on Charlie and focused his fire back on Devo.

Charlie held his hands to his head, barely noticing the mild burn the still-warm barrel of his gun left on his forehead.

"No!" Charlie fired at the pool, trying to draw the flying lead away from Devo long enough for him to crawl for cover. It didn't do any good.

A final burst from the automatic weapon caught Devo in the side of the head, spraying the courtyard with bone, blood, and brain matter. His body rocked backward, twitched once, and was still. The scene galvanized Charlie, and he sprinted down the alley toward the street. Behind him, the courtyard was silent and smoky, a burnt acid smell hanging in the air like a ghostly replay of what had just happened.

12

Charlie spent the next twenty-four hours wandering the streets of Richmond. When he got tired around sunrise, or more accurately, became aware of the exhaustion racking his body, he stopped at Byrd Park, just on the north bank of the James River, and took refuge on a park bench. With his dirty clothes and even shaggier beard, he passed for a vagrant, and because it wasn't illegal to spend the day in the park, nobody harassed him. He spent most of that time huddled on his bench like a refugee, his knees drawn up to his chin, his arms wrapped around his legs. The previous day passed by in the blink of an eye, which was fortunate, because every time Charlie did close his eyes, he saw Devo's brain erupting from his shattered skull.

He knew that he needed to get moving, but the enormity of the situation was becoming more than he could bear. With Devo at his side, he felt like he had a chip in whatever game he was being forced to play. He was confident that with whatever connections the man had, they'd find her in no time. Charlie had even suspected that Devo could front whatever ransom the kidnappers might want.

And now he was alone. Susanna was just as vanished now as she had been two days ago. *Was that how long it had been?* He tried to imagine what they would've been doing today, had things gone according to plan. She had mentioned giving parasailing a shot. He could just see it now. The boat accelerating, the parasail whipping her up into the jet stream, and Susanna cussing him out for letting her go through with it. They both loved to snorkel, and the clear blue waters around Sanibel provided numerous opportunities.

Tears ran silently down his cheeks. He wept silently for Devo, for himself, but most of all, he wept for the woman he'd promised his life to just a few days earlier. He removed his wedding ring and held it up to his face, where the platinum band glinted in the morning sun. He read the inscription on the inside: *Let Eternity Begin.*

Well, *Eternity* had been stopped in its tracks. Pulled over by a demented patrolman and taken downtown. And Charlie didn't know how to spring Eternity free. He had no help. He had no idea what he was doing. And yet, he had no choice. As he looked at the ring that he had once joked would be nothing more than a shackle, he thought about what their vows had said about the ring. An unbroken circle representing the permanent bond between him and Susanna. The other vows he'd repeated without thinking scrolled through his mind. *For better or for worse.* Well, this was definitely in the 'worse' category. *Until death us do part.* He chuckled to himself, aware of how silly it all had sounded on Saturday but amazed by how much the words meant to him now. *Until death us do part, all right, but not so soon. No way it would be so soon*, he promised himself.

He was going to get off his ass, and he was going to find Susanna. He would not stop until he found her or until he was dead, whichever came first. He knew that the police would be turning over every stone to find him. He was a cop killer, after all. No matter. He would not let them catch him. It was time to start cashing in every favor, calling in every source, calling every informant he'd ever had. Charlie's hand had been dealt, and he was pushing his chips to the center of the table.

It was time to call.

JOHN HOOD PARKED his car in the visitor lot on Tredegar Street, just under the train trestle bordering the river. With him was Jerome Hudson. It was late afternoon, and the day had broken cool and cloudy. Rain seemed likely. John locked the door, and the pair made their way across the pedestrian bridge toward the murder scene. Now that the area around the boat landing had been inventoried, the on-lookers a memory, John wanted to examine the scene just as it had looked immediately before Vitelli and Dallas's fateful meeting.

The threat of rain had left the island relatively deserted, which John preferred. He stood where the ERT had estimated that Vitelli had been standing when the bullets hit his chest. To his left, a line of young saplings bordered the river. A thicket of brush and river grasses was on his right, swaying in the gentle breeze. The ground beneath him was an uneven mixture of ruddy clay and gravel.

The ERT had found very little useful forensic evidence at the crime scene. One of the technicians had been able to take a footprint cast leading away from the scene, casts that had matched the size of shoe seized from Charlie Dallas's apartment. Nothing to get excited about, though. Charlie wore a ten, the same size worn by roughly fifteen million men in this country.

"How far away was the shooter?" Hood asked.

"Preliminary estimate was about eight to twelve feet," Hudson said. "Might change after more ballistics."

John counted off eight feet, then twelve, which brought him to the very edge of the water lapping softly against the bank. Water kissed gently at his shoes, wetting the soles.

"Strange."

"What?"

"Most of the witnesses said that the shooter was further up on the bank." He pointed back toward the gap between the trees and bushes. "Right about there."

"Well, like I said, they're running more ballistics tests. Plus, witnesses have terrible depth perception."

"True."

Still, something began to gnaw at John, like a puppy chewing at a blanket after its owners had gone to work for the day. No fewer than a dozen witnesses had placed the shooter further up the bank, the ballistics report notwithstanding.

John continued to study the scene, trying to coax out its secrets. The place was trying to tell him something, he just didn't know what. Something that would shed light on what had led Charles Dallas, cub reporter, to cut his honeymoon short and gun down a federal agent. Something that might shed light on where he was. What his next play would be. How this fit into the big picture. There had to be a big picture. The odds that Dallas had just killed Vitelli for kicks were about as good as the odds that the Red Sox would win the World Series in Hood's lifetime. As painful as that was to admit.

"Did the Sox win last night?" he asked.

The Sox were two games up on the Yankees, but it was only late June. Plenty of time to design and execute a late-season collapse.

"Don't know," Hudson said. "Not much of a baseball fan."

"The hell good are you then?"

John scanned the area again, but the whispers were gone. If the scene was trying to tell him something, it was not going to give up any more today. The sky had started to clear, and John could see the pedestrian traffic on the bridge thickening.

"Let's get out of here," Hood said.

"You want to grab a bite?" Hudson asked.

"No."

"You sure? My treat."

"I gotta go," Hood said.

HALF AN HOUR LATER, John was back in the waiting area of Dr. Elsa King's office. An aquarium in the corner of the room caught his eye, and he got up to check it out. *Was*

this here last time? he wondered. Couldn't have been. He would have noticed it.

Brightly colored fish darted around the tank as John approached. He counted about a dozen fish, some striped, some solids. A few of them ducked behind a twisted, mangled rock in the corner when they realized that John wasn't there to feed them. Others bobbed at the surface of the bubbling water. Just in case John was the new guy in charge of feeding them.

They'd had a tank when he was growing up, back in the little apartment in Hoboken. His dad was an aquarium nut back before people thought they were cool. The Hoods never had much money, so his dad would scrape together a few dollars a month, save up his cash until he could buy a new fish or a new piece of equipment up at the Fish Hut on the north side of town. John's mother tolerated it because it kept him on the sunny side of alcoholism, just barely, which was more than could be said about many of the men in the neighborhood.

John used to spend summer evenings plopped on the couch, its cover frayed and threadbare, watching Yankee games with his dad. His old man drank Pabst Blue Ribbon, usually a six-pack a night after coming home smelling like blood and raw meat. Behind the couch, his mother would feed the fish when his dad forgot, as he often did after a few beers. She had no love for the fish, but John did, and she did it for him.

Thinking back, John couldn't recall the last time he'd even seen an aquarium. *And too bad*, he thought now. So simple. Swim around this artificial world, never a care in the world. He should be so lucky. No wonder his father had liked fish so much.

"They're lovely, aren't they?"

He jumped, not hearing the door to Dr. King's office open behind him. Instinctively, his hand went to his side, where he holstered his weapon.

"I'm sorry," Dr. King said. "I didn't mean to startle you."

"I like your tank," he said, hoping that she hadn't noticed that he'd passed through more than one of the stages on the way to firing his weapon. Shooting his therapist probably would've reflected poorly on him. Even shooting her accidentally.

"They bring me a lot of peace," she said. "I've got two more at home. A fifty-five and a one-twenty-nine."

"What does that mean?" John asked. The jargon had long been buried, locked in a place with a sign that read CHILDHOOD, a sign that was draped with heavy chains.

"Gallons."

"How big is this one?"

"Thirty," she said.

John whistled.

Elsa motioned to her door with an open hand. "Why don't we get started?"

John stepped inside her office, which was getting dimmer as the afternoon sun faded. The sky outside had softened to that indigo fog that immediately preceded darkness. The intermittent yellow flash of fireflies illuminated the courtyard outside the building. He appreciated that Elsa had agreed to see him so late in the day, but she seemed to take it as a matter of course. As she followed him inside, she spun a dimmer on the wall, and the room brightened instantly.

"There, that's better, isn't it?" she said to herself. Then

she took a seat in her chair and folded her hands in her lap.

"Why don't you tell me what's been going on since we last met," King said.

"Work," John said. "Nothing but work."

"You know, you can talk to me about your work," she began. "Our conversations are privileged."

"I don't know," John said. "Goddamned defense attorneys. . ."

"Trust me, Agent Hood, I've come across my fair share of defense attorneys. My ex-husband's one."

A smile passed across John's face.

"I'm investigating the murder of a fellow agent," he said.

Elsa's face sank. John wondered how long she'd practiced that face, considering that death in his business was not unheard of. Especially by the time it had gotten to her. People didn't come see her when nothing was wrong. And the FBI sure as hell wasn't going to pay for it unless something was wrong.

"I'm sorry to hear that," she said.

"It's a dangerous job," John said.

"Still. So, how's the case coming along?"

"We know who did it," John said, "but he's on the run."

"I'm sure that's frustrating," Elsa said.

John shrugged his shoulders and leaned back against the couch. "Part of the job."

"Is there a lot of that in your position?"

"Can be. I'm the ASAC, so a lot of the responsibility for the day-to-day operations falls to me."

"Was this agent a friend of yours?"

"Not really. I mean, I thought he was a good agent."

Elsa nodded.

"So what happened?"

"Not sure," John said. "Shot in broad daylight."

"Oh, yes," Elsa said. "I read about this in the news-paper this morning. But why would this reporter kill your agent?"

"Probably drugs."

"What do you mean?" she asked, leaning forward, her arms crossed across the top of her legs.

"The reporter was probably dealing, Mike got a little too close, and he got popped."

"You think it's that simple?"

"It usually is."

"Is that so?"

"I find it to be."

Elsa leaned back in her chair and made a sound.

"What?" John asked.

"Nothing. We'll go back to your work another time."

John got up and moved toward the window. From his vantage point, he could see the tail end of rush hour on Midlothian Turnpike, mixing in with the post-work errand rush. Folks rushing around checking mindless tasks off their to-do lists, speeding home to eat dinner out of a box and watch the latest craze in reality television programming before heading off to bed and starting all over the next day. He felt tired again, and his head hurt. He massaged his temples, noticing the stubble was thicker than usual. He realized he hadn't shaved his head in a couple of days.

"Where did you grow up?"

"Aaah, the childhood," John said. "I was wondering when we'd get to all this. It's such a cliche."

"True," Elsa said. "But how does a cliche become a cliche?"

John glanced back over his shoulder toward the doctor, who had a tiny smirk on her face.

"I grew up in Hoboken."

"Is it as bad as they make it out to be? The way some people talk, you'd think it was a partially deformed, homicidal stepson of New York City."

"Just your basic industrial town," John said, feeling a spike of heat shoot up his lower back. "No better. No worse."

"What did your parents do?"

The heat spread throughout him, making him warm. Sweat beaded on his skin like condensation on a cold can of soda. He didn't like where this was going, but he felt powerless to stop her.

"My dad was a butcher. My mother was a nurse in the school system."

"Are they still alive?" she asked.

"No," he said. His lips tightened, reducing them to a thin red line, and he wrung his hands together slowly. Then he cracked his knuckles, all ten of them, one at a time. She closed her eyes and chewed on her lower lip, waiting for the series of tiny explosions to cease.

"I'm sorry about your folks," Elsa said.

"It was a long time ago."

Elsa sat back in her chair and looked at the man carefully. The death of his parents was still a sore spot, but he didn't want her to know she had exposed a nerve here. He lowered his head and said nothing more.

"Why don't you tell me about growing up in Hoboken?" she asked.

"What do you want to know?"

"What's your happiest memory?"

"Playing street football."

They eyed each other for a few moments.

"Care to elaborate?" she asked.

"We played it. My friends and I. Used to bet on the games. Losers bought sodas and candy bars. Supposed to, at least. Usually the game ended in a fight, and some kid would get a black eye or lose a tooth, and then everyone would take off and run home. That was usually how the games ended."

"Did you go to high school in Hoboken?"

"Yes."

"Then?"

"College at Rutgers, law school at Princeton."

"You did well in your studies."

"I got lucky."

"Why did you join the FBI?" she asked.

"You know, I gotta be honest," John said, rubbing a palm over his shiny dome.

"Please," Elsa said, her eyes narrowing, curious where this was going.

"That's the dumbest question I've ever heard. No offense."

"None taken. Why do you say that?"

"I mean, why else would I join the FBI?" he asked sternly. "To catch bad guys. To throw them in jail. To stop them from committing crimes. And it's not just you, but I get that question a lot. Why else would someone become a cop? If you want to stop crime, you have to catch the bad guys."

"That's true," Elsa said, twirling her reading glasses now. "But what about other reasons to join the Bureau? Fulfilling civic duty? The adventure of it? The intellectual challenge?"

"Whatever," John said. "If they're not there because they want to catch criminals and terrorists, then I've got no use for them."

"Are those reasons any less noble than wanting to catch criminals?" Elsa countered. "As long as they do their job well, that is?"

"If you think like that," John said, "then it becomes a job. Something you do for a living. But it doesn't work like that. This is not something you quote-unquote *do*. This is who you are."

Elsa glanced at the clock on the wall.

"Our time's up."

13

Charlie stole a quick shower from the homeless shelter downtown, a concrete monstrosity at the corner of Adams and Second. The folks who ran the shelter were happy to let him use the facilities, especially when he told them he didn't need any food or a place to sleep. During the summer months, the workers secretly hoped that more people stayed outside. It cut down on the smell, which naturally was worse during the warm months. They certainly didn't recognize him as the fugitive of the century, overworked and underpaid in their quest to look after the city's several thousand homeless. Either that or they didn't care.

A check of his watch told him it was just past four in the morning. He headed south for one block, then turned east onto Franklin. Less than a mile away, the city's high-rises tickled the early dawn, their lights twinkling on the skyline. The night was clear and warm, but the humidity was low. *Good thing*, Charlie thought. The shower, as basic as it was, was going to have to last him for a while.

His destination loomed ahead, the lights bathing it in the early morning darkness. Life was beginning to rustle, but it would be a good hour before things really got rolling. Still, he didn't have much time, and he was going to have to work fast.

The offices of the newspaper occupied a low-rise compound of glass and concrete, quiet and deserted at this hour. The deadest a newspaper ever got was during the couple hours after the day's edition had been put to bed. On a typical night, that usually happened around 2:30 or 3:00. The editors beamed the last sections of the paper in a digitized format to the printing facility located twenty miles east of town, which then ran 100,000 copies for delivery onto front lawns and porches by six a.m. The process never ceased to amaze Charlie.

He loped up the steps to the front doors, through which he could see the security officer at the desk. The guard, a young black man, was sipping coffee and eyeing the various monitors at the security desk. His name was Roger or Richard. Started with an R, that much Charlie could remember. Didn't really know much else about him, as their communication was pretty much limited to a nod of the head and a "good night." *Too bad*, Charlie thought. He could use a man on the inside for something like this. In the movies, guys in trouble always had someone helping them on the inside. With his luck, Charlie figured, the guy would have a SWAT team here before Charlie could say hello.

Charlie took a quick look around the quiet block. A homeless man napped on a bus stop bench about fifty yards away. The eastbound traffic signal shone bright green, but there was no traffic headed this way just yet.

Charlie counted less than half a dozen parked cars lining the curb in front of the building. Most would be gone before sunrise, but he was willing to bet at least one car's owner would return to find a bright green parking citation clipped to the hood by the windshield wiper. Charlie wondered what traffic cops would do without wiper blades. Probably just jam the ticket in the tailpipe.

He refocused his attention on the guard. Beyond the security desk was the bank of elevators and stairwell that led up to the newsroom. That was where Charlie needed to go. Getting out would be simpler. Charlie knew some back hallways and corridors that led to the loading dock in the back of the building, and that was far less secure. At least from the inside.

OK. Problem number one. He needed to get inside the building, but the glass doors were electronically locked, and he was certain that his newspaper ID badge, which deactivated the lock in the access panel just outside the glass door, had been turned off. And he couldn't take the risk of trying. Problem number two. He had to get past the guard. Granted, this wasn't going to be like trying to break into the Pentagon, but the guard probably wasn't just going to open up and let him in with a slap on the back and a "Welcome back, Charlie. I heard you were framed!"

Charlie was going to have to get the guy to open the door himself. *Think, goddammit, think!* He saw an empty beer bottle in the bushes flanking the front door, and an idea hit him. He grabbed the bottle, inched his way across the front portico and hid behind a column. A huge potted tree provided additional coverage. He cleared his throat.

And then he screamed. As loud as he could, in as high-pitched a tone as he could. Nothing brought the cavalry running like a woman in distress. He felt his throat burning as he forced the pitch higher. He peeked around the column toward the security desk. Bingo. He'd gotten the guard's attention. The man stood up, stretched, and tried to peer outside from his seat.

Time to reel him in. Charlie cleared his throat again, and then let loose a second bloodcurdler, this one lasting a good ten seconds. Charlie prayed he'd only hook the guard and not some well-meaning Richmond city police officer out on patrol down here. The guard gave his monitors a quick scan, came around from behind the desk, and made his way toward the glass doors.

Shit, Charlie thought, getting his first good look at the man. The man was huge; Charlie must have never seen him out from behind the desk. He was at least six-five, two-fifty, and ripped. His biceps were taut against the thin fabric of his sleeves. Not someone he wanted to tangle with. The man's long strides ate up the thirty feet between the desk and the door in a few seconds. Charlie pressed his body against the pillar, wishing he could make himself invisible. Then he saw it.

"Shit," he whispered. He realized that when the guard opened the door, it was going to swing open toward him. He would have to slide around the edge of the door before slipping inside. If he'd just set up on the other side, the door would have opened away from him, and he could be inside within a second. Now it would take two or three seconds, an eternity, and that was assuming the guard turned his attention away from the door. He gauged the distance to the opposite pillar but quickly realized that he'd never make it without the guard seeing him.

He edged his way around the curved pillar, bringing him within ten feet of the door. The guard popped his head out and primed his ears. Charlie was positive that the man could hear his heart thudding away in his chest. Any more of this, and the man might end up with Charlie's heart all over his clothes.

"Who's there?" the guard called out.

Charlie held his breath and lobbed the glass bottle toward the street. It exploded with an echoing tinkle, the sound of silverware hitting a plate. The guard's head turned in the direction of the noise, and he burst through the door and down the steps.

"Who's there?" he repeated, bounding down toward the street.

Still holding his breath, Charlie skulked around the edge of the door, which was now slowly closing, and slipped inside the building. He sprinted across the lobby, bright white with fluorescent lighting. His sneakers made rubbery echoes on the tile flooring. He dismissed the idea of using the elevators. That could be monitored from here.

He burst through the stairwell door and checked the steps above him. Silence. He dropped to a crouching position and kept the door open a crack. About a minute later, the guard returned. He was walking casually, yawning. A hand rubbed a sleepy eye. He dug through a backpack that was stashed under the desk, pulling out a magazine.

Charlie allowed himself a tiny smile. It had worked. He carefully guided the door closed again, which sounded like a gun cocking as it clicked shut. He counted to ten, and hearing nothing, made his way upstairs.

HE BOUNDED up the stairs two at a time to the second floor, where the newsroom made its home. It had a warehouse feel to it, nearly four thousand square feet of cubicles and desks, computers and phones. The overhead lights were dark, but emergency lighting and still-illuminated lamps in several of the cubicles gave Charlie some light to work with. He held his breath and listened for any sounds of life, a stray reporter or copy editor burning the way-past-midnight oil. Nothing. He checked his watch. Four-twenty. Even the cleaning people wouldn't come in until about five, and he planned to be long gone by then.

He tiptoed his way down the maze-like corridors to his cubicle, which was about fifty feet away from the door through which Charlie had entered the newsroom. His cubicle was neater than usual, having fulfilled a promise to himself to clear as much crap out as he could before the wedding. It was a standard cubicle, about six-by-six feet square. Framed pictures of him and Susanna littered one corner. A small boombox occupied another corner. An old desktop computer sat in the middle of the desk, wallpapered with nearly a dozen sticky notes. Some bore phone numbers with no names, others bore the initials of Charlie's confidential informants, and still others bore addresses that Charlie had visited while pursuing a story. He peeled each of the notes from the monitor and pasted them to the inside of his portable desk calendar, still open to the previous week. Across the individual boxes for each day of the week, he'd written in big block letters: SANIBEL!

He slipped the planner into his backpack, then turned his attention to the computer, which was in sleep mode. He shuffled the mouse around, bringing the computer to life, and began scrolling through his files. He scanned the file names, each triggering one memory or another in Charlie's head, but nothing jumped out at him as terribly controversial.

No time for that now, he thought. Just drag and drop. He grabbed an empty floppy disk and jammed it into the disk drive. Staring at the list of names, he decided to focus on investigative pieces that he'd worked on in the last three years. He was willing to bet that his articles covering the school board and city council meetings did not motivate anyone to kidnap his wife. Using those parameters, he hoped to narrow the index of possible links to Susanna's disappearance considerably. When he was done, he popped the disk out, placed it in a protective sleeve, and slipped it into his pocket. He repeated the process two more times. He flung open the drawer, which rattled loudly on its track, and began digging out thick files, wrapped in frayed folders and bound together with rubber bands. Those went in his backpack.

Under the desk, his laptop computer was still tucked away in its carrying case. Charlie grabbed it, slung the carrying strap over his shoulder, and scanned his desk area one more time. A pair of his reporter's notebooks caught his eye, and those went in the laptop case too.

Time to go. He peeked over the cubicle wall and gave the newsroom a once-over. Still dead. The back door

Charlie had planned on using was on the northwest side of the newsroom, about ten yards from his cubicle. The last five feet would be completely exposed, and he'd just have to move quickly. He checked his watch again. 4:28. Less than ten minutes. Each minute that passed increased the odds that the guard he'd already hood-winked once tonight would look at his newsroom monitor at the very moment the camera swept over Charlie.

Just as he cleared the last cubicle, the back door opened. Oh no. He'd forgotten that this stairwell fed back down to the room with the vending machines. A young woman stepped into the newsroom. Charlie's insides turned to water, and his head darted around as he looked for a place to hide. Nothing. He froze. The girl gasped.

"Who's that?" she asked, unable to identify the silhouette.

Charlie recognized the voice as that of Sara Deveron, another metro reporter. She was about thirty, with a thick build and short blond hair. They'd been friends since joining the paper within a few months of each other. Susanna had become good friends with her as well.

"Sara, it's me, Charlie."

"Holy shit," she said, clutching her hand to her chest. "You scared the crap out of me! What the hell are you doing here?" She took a deep breath and exhaled it slowly, regaining her wits about her.

"It's a long story."

"I bet," she said.

"Listen," Charlie said. "I gotta get out of here. I didn't kill that agent."

"Alright," she said. "I believe you. I wasn't buying that shit on the news. You need anything?"

Charlie gnawed his lower lip and shook his head slowly.

"I've got to hide out for a while. Try and get some work done."

"You got my cell number?"

She took a scrap of paper from the closest desk and scratched out her mobile number.

"You need anything, you call me," Sara said. "If I can't talk right then, I'll start talking about my sick aunt or something."

Charlie nodded while he tucked the paper into his pocket. Sarah stepped forward and squeezed his shoulder.

"You gonna be OK?"

Charlie patted his briefcase. "I hope so."

He ducked around her and through the back door. Except for the red glow of the Exit signs mounted on each landing, the stairwell was dark, forcing Charlie to descend cautiously. He wanted to sprint down the steps, but he really couldn't afford to turn an ankle at this particular juncture.

When he got to the first level, he pushed through the door into a chilly corridor that led to the newspaper's primary mail sorting facility. He noticed a few workers sipping coffee and smoking cigarettes at the ramp down to the loading dock. It was still very dark, and Charlie was fairly certain that they wouldn't be able to identify him. He strolled down the ramp past them.

"Good morning," he said.

"Late night, eh, guy?" one of them said, raising his coffee toward Charlie in greeting.

"Always," Charlie said, laughing a real laugh. It felt good.

He headed back east on Franklin Street, breathing a sigh of relief, and almost feeling normal. It felt good to not have to duck for cover around other people, if only for a moment. He paused at the door of the Third Street Diner, a city institution that did most of its business between the hours of midnight and six a.m. Charlie had eaten more than his share of meals here, and he was especially fond of the grilled doughnut with a scoop of vanilla ice cream on top. Looking through the diner's plate-glass windows, he could see the place was fairly empty. A few hard-core regulars worked through eggs and bacon and a couple of tired-looking, uniformed police officers chatted with Carol, the night-shift waitress.

It was too risky to chance it.

He caught his reflection in the glass. The dye in his hair was holding fast, and his beard was filling in nicely. Add in the horn-rimmed glasses, and he barely recognized himself. OK. The disguise was working. He had the raw materials he needed to try and track down Susanna. Now he just needed to sit down and work. Figure things out.

14

A knock at John Hood's door jarred him out of his trance. He'd been elbow deep in Vitelli's active files, trying to find a link to Charlie Dallas, but nothing was lighting up the radar. The files had taken up all of the free space on John's desk and most of the floor. He looked up and saw Agent Williams standing at the threshold of the office, behind a cart carrying a TV/VCR unit.

"We've got something here," Williams said, holding up a videocassette.

Hood motioned him in, and Williams inserted the cassette into the VCR. He pressed Play and stepped away from the screen.

"This is a security tape from the newspaper where Charlie Dallas works," Williams said, as the picture snapped into view onscreen. "Early this morning. Guard on duty saw it about half an hour after it was taken. He reported it to his supervisor, and the paper called us."

In the black-and-white video, Charlie could be seen entering the camera's view and scampering across the lobby toward the bank of elevators, then disappearing into the stairwell. The time-stamp across the bottom of the screen read 04:21:37. The screen cut to black before blinking to a new scene, this one of another part of the newspaper. Charlie at a cubicle--his, presumably--collecting files, computer discs, a laptop case--then disappearing as the camera swept across another portion of the newsroom. John checked the time stamp again. 04:29:11.

"He sure has a hard-on for his desk," John said.

Williams nodded.

"No one saw him?"

"Some mail guys said they saw someone leaving the loading dock around a quarter to five, but they didn't know who he was. Just assumed it was one of the reporters. Had to be him though."

"Any idea how he got in? I'm guessing his ID badge had been deactivated."

"The guard reported hearing a woman screaming around 4:20, and he went outside to check it. Didn't see anything."

"Why would he go back to the newspaper?" Williams asked.

"Not sure," Hood said. "Maybe he left some personal items there. Knew he was never coming back to the office. Thought it would be his last chance to get those sentimental items."

"Seems like a pretty big risk to take," Williams said.

"Then he must have really wanted whatever it was he

took," said Hood. Then: "Why was there anything still at his desk? How come it hadn't been inventoried yet?"

Williams reared back like a puppy facing a disappointed owner.

"It was set for today. A couple of guys are over there now."

Hood shook his head in disgust. Again, his people letting him down. He thought about what he and Dr. King had talked about. This was why people made mistakes. They treated it like a job, as if being an FBI agent was no different than bagging groceries at the local supermarket.

"I want an inventory of what they send to the labs," Hood said.

Williams exited the room, leaving John with the tape. He rewound it and watched the tape again, concentrating on the seven-and-one-half minutes that Dallas was rifling through his desk like a Watergate burglar. Details that John had missed the first time began to sink in upon a second viewing. Dallas had been intent on taking as many files with him as possible. Agent Williams' words echoed in his head as he watched Charlie copy his computer files to a floppy disk. *Why would he go back to the newspaper?*

BREAKFAST WAS a stale bagel and a cup of bad coffee from a small breakfast cart near downtown. A heavily tattooed girl working the truck had been reading a book about Nietzsche. *God is dead*, Charlie remembered from his English Lit class.

He sat and took his meal in an alleyway near the Capitol building. The streets were quiet; it was still a couple of hours before the lunch rush. Across the street sat the law firm of Willett & Hall; eighteen months earlier, a bizarre scandal involving a lottery jackpot had been birthed in the august recesses of that building.

He pondered his next move while he sipped his coffee. First, he needed a place to work. The main branch of the city's public library was just a few blocks over, but he might be recognized there. Librarians were a nosy bunch, especially considering the kind of clientele a public library could draw. Homeless people looking for a break from the hot summer sun and pedophiles hunting for potential targets. What Charlie needed was a decent hotel where he'd be safe and where he'd be left alone. With his disguise and his new identification papers, he felt ready to give it a shot.

He threw his trash in a dumpster. The day was heating up quickly; the sticky warmth wrapped itself around him like a shroud. There was a payphone on the corner, and, as luck would have it, the phone book had not been stolen yet. He called a cab and waited on a nearby bus stop bench.

The taxi arrived within ten minutes, and Charlie climbed in the back seat, which reeked of dried sweat and old bourbon.

"Comfort Inn Midtown," he said, not making eye contact with the driver.

The driver reset his meter and merged back into traffic. The city was bright and alive on this sunny morning, but it felt cold and different to Charlie. Like he was a stranger in a new city. As a reporter, he felt plugged in, he knew the secrets, he knew what was behind the pretty face the Chamber of Commerce tried to put on. But now, he didn't know it at all.

The taxi struck a pothole, jarring Charlie from his daydream. Ahead of them, the tall, gray motel loomed in the bright sun. The driver slowed the car and stopped at the curb.

"Eight-fifty," the driver said.

Charlie threw a ten over the seat and told the driver to keep the change. With his backpack and computer case secure, he got out of the cab and went inside the motel. It was a drab structure, with all the architectural imagination of a shoebox. The lobby was dim and small. In one corner, a short, stout cleaning woman was dismantling the coffee dispenser.

A pretty young woman greeted him as he approached the counter. She looked fresh out of hotel management school, probably in the lower half of her class, considering her assignment. Charlie rubbed his beard. Her nametag identified her as Barbara. Underneath her name, the phrase *One Year of Service* was stenciled on the badge.

"I'd like a room, please," he said. "King-size if you have it."

"Certainly, sir," the woman said. "I'll just need your credit card."

Here we go, Charlie thought.

"Actually, I was going to pay cash," he said.

Barbara, who had been focused on her computer screen hunting for the best darn king-sized room available, did a double-take. Imagine! Cash in this day and age!

"Alrighty, then!" she squeaked. "I'll just need a photo ID."

Charlie worked to keep his hands steady while he fished his wallet from his pocket. He handed her his new driver's license, and she entered his false information into her computer.

"OK, Mr. McWilliams," she said, looking up from her screen. "How many nights will you be with us?"

"Three," he said.

"Terrific," she said.

If I'm not in jail in three days, that'll be terrific.

Charlie paid upfront for the room. It cost him ninety-six dollars, nearly half of the cash he had on him. But it had worked. Devo had saved his ass. As had Smoky. Time to cash in on the freedom that had been paid for in blood.

THE ROOM WAS CLEAN, spacious, and unlike his previous room, didn't look like it had been the scene of a recent murder. When the door clicked shut behind him, he threw the deadbolt and dropped his belongings in the small corridor. The air-conditioning unit was cranking steadily, cooling his overheated and fatigued body.

He took a long, hot shower, washing away the grime that had built up over the past few days. As he toweled himself off, he felt his eyelids drooping, the stress and wear of the past few days eating at him like battery acid. Instead of treating himself to a nap, however, he took advantage of the in-room coffeemaker. While the coffee machine bubbled and hissed, Charlie put on his last set of fresh clothes, slowly feeling a little more human. He drank one cup before doing anything else, taking in the top stories on CNN and wondering whether he was a top story.

The coffee fired Charlie's synapses like a car's spark plugs, making him more alert than he'd been in hours. He propped himself up on the bed and set out his files, computer disks, and laptop in front of him. He would work backward, starting with the most recent features that he'd been chasing.

First, he isolated his notes from a bribery case involving city councilman Brian Powers. A source had told Charlie that Powers had sold his vote on a proposal to increase police presence in the Carrollton Oaks because of a little cocaine habit that Powers had developed. The source claimed Powers' secret was quietly bankrupting the man and his family and that he was willing to sell his vote in exchange for a week's worth of groceries. Charlie was still working to verify the story, make sure that it really was a story, as opposed to what Charlie expected--that Powers had smoked a little dope sometime in the last decade, and rumor had snowballed into a full-blown crack addiction with Powers selling his vote in exchange for an eight-ball.

Charlie opened the manila folder he'd dedicated to this case and reviewed his notes, a transcript of the tape-recorded interview that he'd had with the councilman himself. Charlie had spoken privately with Powers, given him a chance to respond to the allegations while trying to verify them. Naturally, Powers had vehemently denied the charges, but Charlie was inclined to believe him. It wasn't that Powers had just denied the charges. He actually looked hurt by them, the broken look in his eyes that said he wasn't used to the high-powered microscope under which all public figures operated, that it was incomprehensible to him that someone might be out to ruin him when he was just trying to do his part to help out his wounded city. This wasn't the one, Charlie decided.

He next turned his attention toward a sturdier piece, one about the safety of the city's utility workers. Three city workers had died and eight had been injured in four separate incidents during the past twelve months. In one of the incidents, two men who had been on the job for less than two weeks were electrocuted when their earth mover had touched some power lines. Witnesses at the last two scenes spoke off the record with Charlie, telling him that the city had been cutting back on training and equipment in these "uncertain economic times." Charlie planned to run the story a week or two after the honeymoon. Again, though, it just didn't seem reasonable that a cabal of local government officials had conspired to keep the story out of the papers. After all, nothing in Charlie's notes suggested that the officials had any personal financial interest in the case. Although a solid story, it was more a piece on misguided fiscal policy rather than on any misappropriation of funds.

A rumble in his stomach broke his concentration, and a check of his watch showed that he'd been at it for nearly five hours. He stood up, stretched, sighing as blood delivered oxygen to cramped muscles. He stepped outside to the room's east-facing balcony, the shadows now receding as the sun ascended to its daily peak. His stomach growled again. *Lunch would be nice*, he thought. Help him buckle down for the rest of the day.

He ordered a cheeseburger and fries from room service, which he ate while continuing to review his notes. When he was finished, he brushed the crumbs from the front of his shirt and stepped back onto the balcony for a quick smoke. As he pulled on the filter, a bolt of panic surged through him like he was an over-loaded electrical outlet. *What if he couldn't find anything in his notes? What if he'd sent himself on a wild-goose chase? What if Susanna was just gone? No explanation. No reason. Just gone. It couldn't be*, he told himself. *Couldn't be.* That was just the nicotine talking.

By NINE O'CLOCK, Charlie was down to his last at-bat. He peeked outside as he picked up the last folder, a thick one with a rubber band holding it together. The evening, which had been clear and bright with starshine, had darkened considerably. Already, fat rain drops were smacking against the window, cutting channels through the layers of dirt and grime that had built up on the windows. Hopefully, the power would stay on.

He snapped the rubber band from the folder and, in an unexpected burst of playfulness, he shot it across the room at the can of soda that he'd downed during his dinner. The band struck the empty can with a satisfying twang. He flipped the folder open and set it on the comforter, pushing his laptop out of the way to make room for the beefy file. He'd been working on this story for the better part of a year; the file was stuffed with old newspaper clippings, copies of crime scene photos, and transcripts of witness interviews with the investigating officers. He unfolded the clipping on top and read the headline. The article was dated May 16, 1973.

DARING BANK ROBBERY LEAVES TWO DEAD

By Mark Bradshaw

Staff Writer

(May 15) Five robbers wearing Halloween-style masks entered the downtown branch of the First National Bank early Friday morning and stole $2 million in cash, killing an off-duty police officer and another customer in the process. The robbers also took one hostage, which helped facilitate their escape. The hostage, a female bank employee, remains missing and is feared dead.

"We are pursuing several leads at this time," Detective Howard Collinsworth said. "We encourage anyone that has any information about these crimes to come forward."

The dramatic scene unfolded just minutes after the bank opened for business. Witnesses told police that the quintet of robbers entered silently, already wearing the masks, and did not speak during the robbery. When the police officer, who was cashing his paycheck, attempted to intervene, one robber shot him twice in the chest. The other victim, a 42-year-old mother of three, was shot while attempting to flee the bank during the robbery.

"I think she got scared and just became hysterical," said Lana Staples, another bank teller. "She just snapped and ran."

A source speaking on the condition of anonymity told the Richmond Gazette that police are investigating the robbery as an inside job. The source said that the robbers were familiar with a large amount of cash that was being distributed to other branch offices that afternoon. The source added that Federal Reserve officials had delivered the cash less than an hour before the robbery. Bank officials had no comment about this scenario.

"They seemed very organized," said another customer, who asked not to be identified. "They moved like they had a plan, and I don't think they said two words to each other, not even when they started shooting people."

Police are looking for a dark-colored, late 1960s Oldsmobile Cutlass Supreme, the robbers' suspected getaway vehicle.

Charlie placed the clipping face down on the night-stand next to him and moved on to the next article.

STILL NO LEADS IN FNB ROBBERY/MURDER
By Mark Bradshaw
Staff Writer

(May 18) – Sources close to the investigation tell the Gazette that local and federal law enforcement officials remain "baffled" by Friday's daring and violent robbery that left two people dead. Nearly a hundred FBI agents and city detectives have shaken down known criminal elements in Richmond and throughout Virginia, but without any apparent success.

"They really have no idea who did it," the source said. "The size of the take and the precision with which the job was done made them think it was a Mafia job, but so far, they've found no evidence linking it to any organized crime outfit for a hundred miles."

The article continued, but Charlie had read it so many times that he had virtually committed it to memory. He flipped through a few more clippings, all familiar ground to Charlie. He came across one dated June 11, 1973; he was familiar with this one too, but it always depressed him when he saw it.

BANK HOSTAGE FOUND DEAD
By Mark Bradshaw
Staff Writer

(June 11) – Police confirmed today that a body discovered floating in the James River a week ago was that of Denise Vaughan, the bank teller taken hostage by five bank robbers during their daring daylight assault on the First National Bank nearly a month ago.

"The coroner has determined that Ms. Vaughan died of a gunshot wound to the head," Detective Howard Collinsworth said.

Police continue to hunt the robbers, who made off with about $2 million in cash, but even Richmond Police Chief Andrew Buck admitted that the investigation had "stalled."

Outside, the rain had intensified and was now battering the city. Frequent lightning forked down from the heavens, splitting the sky like a cracked mirror. Low rumbles of thunder made Charlie's insides quiver, interrupted by explosive claps that made him jump. The lamps flickered a few times, but the power held.

Charlie's head was throbbing, but he forced himself to continue digging through the file. He read more clippings highlighting even more police futility on the case. Six months later, the police still had nothing. Thousands of man-hours had been expended on tracking lead after lead, but the trail had gone cold. The robbers had simply disappeared.

Charlie got up, stretched, and stepped over to the window, wondering if this was the break he'd been looking for. The rain came down in sheets now, forming a virtual wall in front of him. He went over the bank robbery in his mind. This had to be it. This was the only one that would warrant taking revenge on a reporter. But that would mean Charlie had actually come close to discovering the identities of the bank robbers. If the kidnappers had, as Devo--*may he rest in peace*--surmised, tried to set Charlie up for the murder of the FBI agent, that would mean he had scared them badly enough to poke their heads up and create a rather elaborate frame-up.

Charlie believed the robbers had split the take and disappeared from the radar. Probably assumed new identities, started families, scattered around the world. That meant the answer was in those files. A phone call. A recent interview. A background check. Something he had done had tipped off the robbers in a way that Charlie didn't notice.

As Charlie continued paging through the files, something began to gnaw at him. That feeling you get when you've left for work and think that the stove is still on. Not just your average paranoia but getting home that afternoon and discovering that the stove was indeed on. The tumblers in his mind were spinning, trying to click into place, rehashing already-traveled ground.

He picked up the news clippings again, starting with the first one. The accompanying picture, the headline, the caption, the byline, the date of the story. Then it hit him. Denise Vaughan's picture. He flipped through the clips to it and pulled the one with her photograph free. How had he never noticed it before? It was an employee ID photograph, provided to the newspaper by the bank. Despite the photo's age, Denise Vaughan still looked radiant and young. She was wearing a light-colored sweater and a blouse with a plunging neckline. A simple necklace ringed her slender neck, and that was what had attracted Charlie's attention. He squinted his eyes and drew the picture to his face. There was no mistake. The pendant resting against Denise's skin was a starburst. Identical to the image tattooed on Charlie's foot.

15

Vitelli's investigative file, also morbidly known as the murder book, continued to grow, now measuring about three inches thick. The latest addition to the file was a copy of Charlie Dallas's marriage certificate and a photograph of his new bride, Susanna Dallas, maiden name O'Donnell. They'd been able to determine that much from the freshly-minted marriage certificate, which had been filed that morning by the officiant, the minister who'd performed the Dallas marriage. The Bureau's Identification division was trying to determine whether a file existed on Susanna, and a couple of street agents were looking for the next of kin. Problem was, it looked like Charlie was the only next of kin, which was too bad, considering that John was willing to bet that Charlie knew exactly where she was.

John flipped through the file again, needing a break from the hundreds of press clippings that constituted Charlie's body of work with the Richmond Gazette. That avenue had proved a dead end so far. Nothing John had seen so far had linked Charlie to Mike Vitelli, or to anyone in the FBI for that matter. His private notes would have been nice to look at, John thought, but he'd been smart enough to snake those during the nighttime raid on his cubicle. Instead, he read through the initial police report and the preliminary autopsy report, but that served merely as background noise. Death had been nearly instantaneous, brought about by massive internal hemorrhaging thanks to the explosive-tipped round that had torn through his chest. And where did this reporter get an explosive-tipped round anyway? Did people sell them on eBay?

At the end of the file, John found Susanna Dallas's smiling face. Her wedding photo. Hair pulled back and tucked into a neat bun, not a single strand out of place. A string of pearls ringed her slender neck. Her disappearance was just another piece in the puzzle, the problem being that John didn't know where it fit or what the puzzle was supposed to look like. He batted a theory around his head, just to see how it felt. Charlie Dallas was running drugs or smuggling aliens or something else on the side. Vitelli caught wind of it, and Dallas was in deep enough to have enough motive to bump off a federal agent. His wife threatens to rat him out--or maybe she's the one that *did* rat him out to Vitelli--and he gets rid of her, too. The theory didn't thrill him, but at least it had legs.

His cellular phone rang.

"This is Hood."

"Hi John, this is Nadia," a soft voice with a lilting southern accent said. Nadia Dufour was a forensic technician for the Bureau. She'd been doing the ballistics work on the Vitelli scene.

"What's up?" John asked.

"I'm fine, John, how are you? The kids are great. Bob got a promotion at work."

Pleasantries were very important to Nadia, and she knew that they were not important to John. She loved to torture him. She had no children and was divorced.

"Please, Nadia, not today."

"You're such a pain in the butt," she said.

"I try."

"Well, you want to come take a look at what I found? Or do you just want the bad news up front?"

"You know how much I love bad news," John said.

"Ballistics came back," she started. "And the preliminary report suggests that the shot came from about twelve feet away. That's based on the compression of the bullet. Plus, I talked to the medical examiner--Dr. Reed--you know her?"

"I've heard of her," John said, his mood darkening.

"She's of the opinion that the bullet entered Agent Vitelli's body at about a thirty-degree angle. Not face to face."

Agent Jerome Hudson poked his head in the door; John waved him into his office.

"OK, thanks." He snapped the flip phone closed and slipped it into his pocket.

Jerome folded a stick of gum into his mouth and waited for his superior's instructions.

John took a deep breath and let it out slowly.

"Let's go."

AN HOUR LATER, Hood and Hudson were back at the boat landing. The police tape was still up, but it was more for show than anything. The crime scene had long been compromised by weather, squirrels, and well-meaning crime scene technicians, so Hood was hoping for more of a lucky break than anything. A light rain was falling.

John knelt by a grove of saplings lining the bank, about three feet deep, thick with summer foliage. According to the ballistics report, which he had read in the car, the shot had come from this direction. Each one of the witnesses had told the investigators that Dallas had been between two and four feet from Vitelli.

Snapping on a pair of latex gloves, John pushed his way into the dense tangle of leaves and branches. He turned around and found himself with a prime vantage point of the meeting between Dallas and Vitelli. He scanned the shooter's nest and saw an exit point through the brush running east along the river, away from the boat landing. A person could slip around the island down along the water line without being seen.

"Can you see anything in there?" Hudson called out.

"Yup," Hood said. He removed his weapon and aimed it through a gap in the leaves. "I could put a hole in your head from here. Can't you see me?"

"No," Hudson said, staring blankly at the bushes. "And I'm looking for you. No one would've seen a shooter in the bushes that day."

"So I guess Dallas had an accomplice."

"Could be," Hudson said.

"You don't agree? Please, Agent Hudson, regale me with all your expertise."

"Well, it seems like an awfully big chance to take, setting up a hit out here. Broad daylight. Popular with the locals."

"Maybe it was the only way they could flush Vitelli out," Hood said.

Hudson paced down to the banks of the river, rushing hard today, scrubbing away the stagnancy and detritus of a river that had been low all summer, which rinsed away like dirty bath water.

"Still taking a big chance," Hudson said.

"Sure, so he didn't count on a truckload of witnesses standing right there," Hood said, pointing at the river-bank. "It worked, didn't it? Vitelli's dead."

"Yeah. I guess."

"Did the ERTs sweep this spot?"

"I'm not sure. We'll have to check the report."

"Better have," John barked, his temper spiking like a dangerous fever.

Hudson glanced away, focusing his sights on a kayaker working the boiling rapids in the center of the river.

"Fuckin' A," John muttered. If there was a second perp, and John was willing to bet there was, he now had a several-day head start. "Get an ERT back down here right now. I want them to check every square inch from here to the other side of the island, where the bridge crosses the river."

Hudson stepped away and called for the ERT on his mobile phone. John's head began to throb. Situation normal. All effed up. It had been four days since the murder; virtually every useful piece of forensic evidence would have been destroyed by now.

"I'm gonna follow the bank around the island and see if I can find anything," he told Hudson, who waved him off as he began jabbering to someone on the line.

A FEW YARDS EAST, the growth thickened to the point that he had to drop to the ground. He pulled himself along the damp riverbank, wincing as dirt and gravel worked their way under his clothes. It reminded him of the beach. He hated the beach. Finally, he was clear of the brush, and he hopped down a gradual slope to a gravel path that circumvented the island. A perfect-looking young couple wearing matching sweatsuits jogged by. John watched them for a moment, wondering if he'd be doing them a favor if he put a bullet in each of their heads. When they disappeared around the south curve of the island, he returned his sights to the fringe of the path, cataloging everything he saw, dropping each item into a mental sorting facility. Crushed aluminum cans. Broken beer bottles. Granola bar wrappers. A used condom wrapper. He began to write off another item as trash, then stopped suddenly.

A small piece of paper caught his eye. He bent down for a closer look, careful not to get his hopes up, careful to keep his judgment clear. It was a piece of stationery that looked like it had been torn off a pad. A familiar logo--a smiley-faced sun rising over a freshly made bed--was stamped at the top. The Sleep Rite Inn, a hotel near downtown. John had been ready to dismiss it as garbage when something clicked in his head. A corner appeared to be burned away, the jagged yellow edge a stark contrast to the charred paper.

John remembered a lesson from his recent firearms evidence certification class. If a person handled a piece of paper shortly after firing a gun, the chemicals in gunpowder residue were often still active enough to char the paper. John removed a plastic evidence bag from his pocket--he always carried a couple extra with him for situations like this--then pinched the corner of the paper with two still-gloved fingers. He dropped the paper into the bag, sealed it shut, then turned it face up. Something had been written on it, but the ink had faded beyond comprehension.

A second perp may have stayed at this hotel, possibly the night before the murder. Maybe the night after, although John doubted that the shooter would have stayed in town after knocking off a federal agent. *Calm down*, he told himself. Assuming the killer did drop the paper, there was no guarantee that he had actually stayed there. Even if he had, he certainly wouldn't have used his real name. But it was something. Something that would lead to John Doe. And to Charlie Dallas.

THE SLEEP RITE INN, occupying a refurbished warehouse at the corner of Cary and 14th Streets, had long been a thorn in the side of the Richmond Police Department and of Sleep Rite corporate. It was a hive of drug trafficking and prostitution under nose but just out of sight, like the creepy crawlies you found after pulling up a rock from damp soil. John Hood tapped the bell twice, hoping to draw someone's attention to the unmanned front desk. He peered over the counter at the desk, which was cluttered with empty fast-food drink cups and ashtrays overloaded with cigarette butts.

"Jesus," Hood said as they waited for the clerk to amble her way to the desk. "This is a dead end. We're wasting our time."

"Take it easy," Hudson said. "Maybe we'll catch a break."

The clerk finally made her way behind the counter, where she found both Hudson's and Hood's badges thudding heavily against the chipped Formica countertop. She was heavy-set, and her hair was stringy and oily, like a dirty mophead.

"Need a list of your guests the last two nights," Hood said.

She narrowed her eyes and cocked her head, as if she were trying to size the two men up.

"Got a warrant?"

"Let me get one," Hood said. He withdrew his phone from his pocket and began dialing.

"I'm gonna get one of these local guys to run over to the magistrate," he said to Jerome while scrolling through his preprogrammed phone numbers. "Yeah, it'll be no problem. Probably have a handful of cops down here, running around, digging through all this shit to find these records. Sure."

He held up a finger.

"Just another five, ten minutes."

"Forgive my partner," Jerome said. "He forgot to eat breakfast this morning."

"Alright," she said, reaching out and smacking John's hand. "Forget the warrant, mister man. Think you so smart. I got your guest list."

She disappeared through a small door behind the desk, where Hood and Hudson could hear her rooting through creaky file cabinets. A roach skittering across the floor caught Hood's eye, shortly before it died under Hudson's heavy boot.

"The hell you do that for?" Hood snapped.

"Cause they're nasty," Hudson said.

"Perfect organisms," Hood said. "You know that? Be here after we're done screwing the planet over."

"Not this one."

Hood shook his head and glanced out into the parking lot, where a drug deal appeared to be in progress by a rusty pickup truck. A skinny guy with pasty skin looked around furtively while he handed a dark-skinned Latino man a fist-sized clump of aluminum foil. And Hudson was killing roaches. Hood wondered what harm would come if he stepped outside and emptied his Glock into the two junkies by the pickup. One less avenue for drugs, one less user robbing some poor schmuck walking back to his parking garage after a day trapped in his cubicle.

"Here's your list," the woman barked. Two crumpled pages, stained, stapled together. Handwritten. Luckily, the motel was small, around a dozen rooms, and they hadn't had a full house on either of the nights that they were curious about.

With list in hand, the pair turned to leave; Hood stopped and turned back toward the counter.

"You see anyone didn't fit the last couple of days?" he asked her.

"What?" Hood noticed she seemed taken aback by the question, as if she'd been hoping he wouldn't ask it.

"Someone new hanging around?"

"No."

"You sure?"

"Yes."

Hood nodded his head and followed Hudson back outside, sending the drug dealer running for the safety of a narrow alleyway adjacent to the motel, much like the roach that Hudson had squashed inside.

"You buy that?" Hudson asked.

"No. She saw him."

TWENTY MINUTES LATER, a dozen police cruisers had surrounded the Sleep Rite Inn, and an ERT was scouring each room for evidence. Obviously, none of the guests were still around, and none would ever return to the inn, as its usefulness as a den of bad behavior had been compromised. Within a year, a group of investors would buy the property, raze the building, and install a new Irish pub that would become very popular among the locals.

It took the rest of that day, but by dinner time, Hood and his agents had accounted for eleven of the twelve guests that had registered at the Sleep Rite Inn on the nights before and after Vitelli's murder. Not that it had proven terribly difficult. Six of the ten were known dealers that conducted business from the motel and rented rooms by the week. One was a pimp whose girls used three of the rooms to peddle their wares, a modern-day wild West brothel. The tenth belonged to a small-time arms dealer wanted on various federal firearms charges. Hood didn't contact his liaison at the Bureau of Alcohol, Tobacco and Firearms, as courtesy generally dictated. Vitelli's murder investigation took priority over ATF's small-time hood. Besides, John didn't like the guy anyway.

Twenty-four patrol officers working in two-man teams fanned out into the city to hunt down the eleven regis-tered guests of the Sleep Rite, but Hood was more concerned with mystery guest No. 12. That was the one, he was sure of it. Grabbing Nadia, they climbed the wooden stairs to Room No. 9, wherein Ulysses Grant had been registered. A couple of technicians were already in the room working.

"Lovely," Nadia said.

"We can't all come from the suburbs," John said. The woman was getting on his last nerve. He was getting punchy. Time to pay Dr. Elsa King another visit before he shot someone. He had an appointment the next afternoon.

The room was squalid. A light-blue mattress, bruised and torn, sat precariously on a rickety metal frame in the corner. Dark stains on the wall looked suspiciously like dried blood. Nadia went to work hunting for trace evidence, while John worked on a big-picture view of the room. Fortunately, it looked like the room had been last cleaned during the Reagan administration, which hope-fully meant that anything that Mr. Ulysses Grant had left behind would still be there.

A bureau pushed up against the corner, flush with the warped front door of the room, caught Hood's eye. About six feet high, wooden, it had that cracked, weather-beaten look about it, sanded to the bone. What had piqued Hood's curiosity was that the dresser was slightly off center, as if someone had bumped into it. John quickly scanned the room, which was awash in the overcast gloom of the day outside. It gave the room a sick-dead feeling. Definitely not your bed-and-breakfast, Belgian waffle, French roast vibe.

He returned his attention to the dresser, keeping its silent, off-kilter vigil over the room. A fly buzzed lazily around John, and he made an equally lazy swat at it with his hand. He dropped to one knee and peeked behind the dresser, expecting to find a thick layer of dust and grime. He did. Behind the front right leg of the bureau, John found a small necklace, its chain coiled around the leg like a snake. The charm was thin metal and resembled a small bowtie. With the poor light, he couldn't discern anything else about it. The one thing that did stand out was that it was not covered in a thin sheen of dust, which meant that it hadn't been here very long. He pinched the chain between two gloved fingers and dropped the necklace into a plastic baggie. He stood up and moved to the window, where he held up the item to the natural light filtering in through the dusty panes. The silver chain glinted in the sun, and John could see that the clasp was broken.

"You find something?" asked Nadia.

"I'm sure it's nothing you wouldn't have found."

"Check 'one silver chain with charm' into evidence," John said. "I'll follow up on this."

16

Charlie spent much of the night on the covered balcony, watching a series of thunderstorms pulse across the area. Perched on his lap was a six-pack of shitty light beer, which he'd purchased from the all-night gas station/mini-mart across the street. A carton of cigarettes was lying on the ground. Charlie had asked the clerk for a single pack before changing his mind. *Why screw around*, he had thought, *just go whole hog, and buy the entire goddamn thing.*

As he sipped his beer and smoked, the grainy black-and-white photograph of Denise Vaughan dominated his thoughts like a hurricane lurking just offshore. Maybe he was just imagining the similarity between his tattoo and the charm on her necklace. His mind was trying to make connections, blaze new trails, and this could simply be a function of trying to grasp onto something concrete when there was just nothing there. But the question continued to eat at him. *Who was she?*

One after another, the beers disappeared, and Charlie

lined up the empties on the railing in front of him. The lights glowing from nearby businesses glinted from the raindrops collecting on the cool bottles, creating a tiny prism of colors. Charlie watched the rainbow before him, transfixed, but fully alert. Normally, this much beer would have sent him to dreamland long ago, but the nicotine coursing through his veins primed him like jet fuel. But he was no closer to understanding what, if any, connection there was between his tattoo and the photograph. He wanted to write it off as coincidence, but it stuck with him like a hard-to-reach splinter in his brain. Then a thought occurred to him. He certainly did not know the story behind the origin of Vaughan's necklace, but maybe he could check the story behind the origin of his tattoo. He dropped his smoke into his half-full bottle of beer, which hissed loudly as the cold liquid extinguished the cigarette.

Taking a seat at his laptop, he fired up the portable computer and signed onto the Internet through the hotel's Internet portal. He ran a Google search for historical weather information. After several failed attempts, he finally found a promising website called Weather History, which provided daily weather recaps for each of the past forty years. A strange feeling began to gnaw at him. Thoughts of another storm, the one that had been raging as he entered the world, raced through his mind. It occurred to him that he had never looked up any news clippings about the storm, never seen any information about it, never heard anything about it, apart from what his parents had told him.

He typed in the ZIP code for Waynesboro, Virginia, and waited as the current conditions popped up in a browser window. Eighty-two degrees with seventy percent humidity. This kind of weather blanketed the valley like a shroud. A few clicks of the mouse later, he was scouring the record books. As he did so, his head began to swim, finally succumbing to the effects of the alcohol. He willed his eyes open as he clicked on the year of his birth, the month, and finally the date. He paused for a moment, then changed his entry to the day after he was born. He'd been born around ten in the evening, just as the storm was reaching its peak fury. A shaky finger clicked OK, and the hard drive began to hum. Charlie leaned back against the headboard and closed his eyes. He was asleep instantly. The tiny hourglass on the screen spun silently, then disappeared as a new page of information popped to life. Charlie slept on.

THERE HAD BEEN many hangovers in Charlie Dallas's life, nights spent on bathroom floors, in backyards, even one in the county drunk tank when he was a senior in college. This one announced its Hall-of-Fame credentials the instant that Charlie realized he was awake. The combination of beer, cigarettes, stress, and exhaustion had collided like malicious weather fronts to create a super-storm of misery and pain. His head felt like it was trapped in a vise, and his lungs burned with the residue of a dozen cigarettes.

He was still sitting up, his head having lolled back against the couch cushions, so the first thing he saw was the stucco-style ceiling. Slowly, he rolled his head forward, feeling a twinge in his neck as he did so. *Great,* he thought, the very act of thinking making his head pulse with pain. A pinched nerve would really make the morning complete.

In front of him, the computer screen was dark, having switched into sleep mode during the night. He tried to recall what he'd been doing when he passed out, exhaling when it finally came back to him. Leaning forward, he pressed the Enter key and realized that his stomach was about to quit on him. He lunged from the couch, his desire to make it to the toilet stronger than the pain urging him to sit down and yarf all over the floor.

When he was done, he swirled some old toothpaste in his mouth and spit it out, which went a long way to making him feel somewhat human again. Outside, the sun was licking the rooftops of the surrounding buildings, telling Charlie that it was just after dawn. He tottered back into the living room like an old man after a hip replacement and spilled onto the couch, anxious to see if any useful information was still on the screen. An icon in the corner of his desktop informed him that he was still online. He scanned the page for information. His date of birth was striped across the top of the page, the weather capsule underneath.

June 12, 1969 Weather Summary

A high-pressure system remains in place over the Mid-Atlantic. Mostly sunny skies, some high, thin clouds in the evening. Fourteenth straight day with no precipitation in the Waynesboro area. High 91. Low 65.

Mystified, Charlie checked the reports for the two days preceding and following the day he was born. No mention of any storm. No mention of any rain. The implications of what he was learning chased away the hangover like a guard dog scaring off an intruder. The very essence of his being, the story of his birth, had been a lie. There were only two logical inferences he could derive from his latest discovery. Either he hadn't been born in Waynesboro, or the story surrounding the origin of his tattoo was a lie. Possibly both.

A second thought began bouncing around his head, joining the first like a new lottery ping-pong ball. Amid the horror of Devo's death at Carrolton Oaks, it had been lost in the shuffle. Something that Smoky had said. He closed his eyes and tried to remember. Something about his social security number. The Death Index indicated that Charlie Dallas had died in 1969. All of a sudden, it didn't seem like a clerical mistake, as Smoky had suspected. All of a sudden, Charlie began to wonder who he really was.

Charlie spent his professional life on the fringes of society, looking for people and places and things that had fallen through the cracks and drifted away from center. When he found a loose thread out there, he would grab it and pull, following it to its sometimes logical, sometimes interesting, often boring conclusion. But sometimes, the thread ran through the very fabric of a life or a career, and yanking on it would dissolve whatever it had been holding together, like a baseball without its rawhide cover. He felt like he'd found the thread running through his own life, one he hadn't even known was there.

His thread stretched back through three decades, back to the very night of his birth. He needed to go out there, where the thread was exposed, and work his way back to the center. That would mean digging into his own past, which he had assumed was well-settled territory.

He'd known some tragedy, sure, but no more than most families.

Charlie realized he wasn't breathing. How had he never checked this out before? *Because there was no reason to, you dumbass.* You didn't do a background check on your parents. You were born when they said you were born. If they said there was a pisser of a storm the night you were born, well, there was a pisser of a storm the night you were born.

When you were little, you could count on everything you heard, because your parents were the only ones who told you anything. Then you got a little older, and the stuff they told you got diluted with the crap you learned from your friends. Like it or not, you learned about sex from Playboys that your buddy stole from his dad's stash in the back of the closet, you learned smoking hurts when you try it for the first time, you learned that three beers make you sleepy, four make you happy, and six give you a bad headache.

By the time you hit your teenage years, what little you still hear from your parents is drowned out by an ever-widening assault on your senses, from friends, television, movies, music. But deep down you still know you can trust them. That's why even in your worst moments, they're still going to be there for you. Because they were there from the beginning. If you couldn't count on that, what could you count on? Like the U.S. dollar. If the rest of the world couldn't count on good old American green-backs, where would this planet be?

Right about here, Charlie told himself. *Where I'm sitting right now.*

His childhood had been fairly normal. School,

friends, homework, sports, and later, girls. And the beach. Their beach cottage had been the center of his universe, the crucible in which his happiest memories had been forged. Entire summers had been spent there, carbon copy days spent in the sun with sand jammed in every possible bodily crevice. Evenings, there were cook-outs and ice cream and mini-golf. He knew he was sugar-coating the past a bit, forgetting about the hard work involved with maintaining a beach house. It didn't matter. The good memories were still there.

When his father died, the trips became a little less frequent. Every weekend during the summer became every other weekend, and they rarely went down while school was in session. And when they did go, it was never the same. Even with a house full of people, it still seemed empty. The house certainly made him a hit with his friends, and they often caravanned to the little hamlet of Holden Beach, N.C., where the house was located.

Then his mother had died, and the life was sucked right out of the house, as if a giant vacuum cleaner had been set on top of it. He sold the house in which he'd grown up, but he couldn't bear to part with the weather-beaten cottage. So in a nice compromise, he loaded all their belongings in Waynesboro and moved everything to the cottage. He hadn't been back since.

It was time to go back.

~

"How's your case coming along?" asked Dr. Elsa King.

John Hood shrugged his shoulders and leaned back in his chair. Some of the tension he'd felt back at the motel had dissipated like a puff of frosty breath, but he still felt the urge to beat the crap out of someone. It was late afternoon, and bright sunshine filled Elsa's office, making it uncomfortably warm. John heard the drone of a substandard air compressor struggling to keep up with the heat.

"I don't get it," Hood said. "I'm surrounded by idiots at work. This is a simple case, and some of my people can't seem to find their asses despite having their heads shoved up 'em."

"Interesting image," she said, chuckling a little. "Sorry, potty humor gets me every time."

"Glad I can amuse you," John said.

She cleared her throat, then leaned forward in her chair. "John, can I share something with you? Something I've noticed about you?"

He spread his arms, inviting her comment. "Please. That's why I'm here, isn't it?"

She clasped her hands into a fist and tapped her lips.

"I'm finding that you tend to see the world in black and white. That's a simplistic way of putting it, but it's fairly accurate. When things don't fall into a neat little category..."

"Go on," he said, as she paused, apparently struggling with her next statement.

"Well, it seems to drive you batshit."

John was silent.

"Let me ask you another question?"

"Shoot."

"Are you a good agent?"

The question startled him. The answer that shot from his lips surprised him even more.

"I- I-I don't know."

"You don't know?" she said rhetorically. "You've had a distinguished career. You've been decorated several times, promoted through the chain of command."

"The bad guys aren't that smart," he said. "They make it easy on me."

"Do you feel that you might be underestimating your opponent? And yourself?"

"That's not what I meant," John said. "These guys that I'm chasing, these bad guys, I never underestimate their ability to kill me. I never underestimate their ability to get lucky."

"Don't you think that you deserve some of the credit in your career? Your ability to analyze, make inferences, make deductive leaps?"

"The evidence usually does the work for you. We just have to find it, and the bad guys usually don't do a very good job hiding it."

"What about the ones that have gotten away?"

"Sometimes they get away. The chips don't always fall into place for us. An informant changes his story. Cover gets blown. It happens."

"Has a suspect ever just outsmarted you?"

"Rarely happens," John said. "With our resources, it just doesn't happen too much."

"But it does happen?"

"Once," John said, cutting his eyes away from Dr. King's piercing stare.

"What happened?"

The memory of John's biggest professional failure began rolling through his mind, an unwanted matinee flickering on a cranial movie screen. He had only been on the job a few months, just twenty-five years old. He was with the narcotics trafficking unit then, working undercover on a joint task force with DEA. After months of work, he and his partner, a DEA agent named Richard Zetlan, had infiltrated a drug ring run by a gang of white supremacists in southern Virginia; they gained the trust of the group's leader, a ruthless skinhead and neo-Nazi named Del Thomson. The group funneled much of the region's cocaine supply and then hid its profits in a maze of dummy corporations and fake identities.

Two days before the planned raid on the group's compound, John got a call on his portable phone ordering him to Thomson's residence. When he arrived, he found Zetlan, dead, strung up from the porch rafters, shot twice in the head and once in the genitals. The words *WE KNEW* had been scrawled on his chest in blood. The rest of the cartel had disappeared into thin air. The DEA accused the FBI of blowing Zetlan's cover, the FBI counter-accused the DEA of moving too early, and everyone wanted to drop everything on Hood.

A disciplinary proceeding ensued, but the FBI's Office of Professional Responsibility ultimately determined that Hood was not to blame for the operation's failure, and his record stayed clean. A few of Thomson's goons went down, but Thomson himself and his closest advisers were never captured. Simply thinking about the incident made John's heart rate accelerate like a Formula One racecar. Immediately after the Thomson mess went down, he'd spent ten minutes with an FBI shrink, part of the official debriefing process in the real-agents-don't-need-help, good old days of the Bureau. Until this moment, he had never spoken of it since.

"That's a terrible thing," Elsa said when he finished relaying the story. "But how did Thomson outsmart you? Wasn't that a case of cover getting blown?"

"The op was doomed from the start," John said, feeling like he was in confessional. "They lured us in, knew we were cops from the beginning. They knew that we were watching them, so they figured the best way to keep an eye on us was to bring us in close. You know the old saying."

"Keep your friends close. Keep your enemies closer," she said softly.

"Yeah."

"So you see," she said, treading carefully. She was getting into dangerous territory, the therapeutic equivalent of traipsing through gator-infested swampland. "Sometimes we have shades of gray mixed in. Think about the Thomson case."

Their session ended, and Hood stepped out into the main corridor. The office door clicked behind him, reminding him of the sound his weapon made as he chambered a round. The hallway was silent, as it was long past five o'clock. Pressing the forefingers of each hand to his eyes, John felt his inner strength fail him, and sobs racked his body. The image of Robert Zeltan's final indignity roared back to life, and John Hood cried like he hadn't cried in a long time.

17

"He's still on the loose," Lindsey Jessup said, signing off her computer. She'd been checking the Associated Press website, which provided brief updates of all stories great and small. She'd found one little tidbit on the Mid-Atlantic wire--*FBI Hunts Suspected Cop Killer*. It had been posted less than fifteen minutes ago. Lindsey pushed herself up, wincing as her hip throbbed with pain. *Great. Something else to worry about.* Fifty-five years old, and her body was starting to fail her. If they got out of this, she was going to start an exercise program. Seriously this time.

"Are you listening to me?" she asked her husband.

Patrick was on a sofa, leafing through an old issue of Sports Illustrated. He dog-eared his page and tucked the magazine between the seat cushions.

"Sorry," he said absently.

"Sometimes, I swear to God."

"I said I was sorry," Patrick said, his voice rising. "Jesus."

He edged his way forward on the couch, propped his elbows on his knees.

"What do you want to do?"

"I think we should send our friend to get rid of him."

"I thought you said--"

"I know what I said," she barked, making Patrick jump. "It's been a week. I thought he'd be in jail by now. Or dead."

"You don't want to give the cops a little more time?"

"No," she said. "The longer he's out there, the greater the chance that he starts to piece things together."

"What do you mean?" Patrick asked, a tone of alarm punctuating his voice. "He wasn't supposed to figure anything out."

"It's possible that he's going to trace this back to us," she said as Patrick's eyes widened. "But it doesn't matter. He was already getting close, even if he hadn't figured it out yet. He wasn't going to just go away just because we did nothing."

"Oh," Patrick said, taking a deep breath and exhaling it slowly. He got up and ambled across the room to the window. Lindsey watched her husband's profile at the window, and briefly, she wondered if she should get rid of him, too. She'd put up with him for nearly forty years, and her patience had long since worn out. She couldn't afford to leave him. He was too dependent on her, and if she left him, she knew it wouldn't be long before he wandered into another woman's arms or into a police station and blurted out a full confession.

Besides, the years had been pretty good otherwise. More money than they knew what to do with, money that had grown steadily in various investments and had been laundered so many times it smelled like freshly bleached hotel bedsheets. *Amazing how easy it was to make money when you had money*, she thought. And it wasn't like life with Patrick was all bad. He was a decent man, good to her, would die for her if it came to that. You didn't just throw that kind of loyalty away.

Now, they had to take one more tiny step. Granted, it was a step they should have taken to begin with, but too late for that now. Had her strategy worked as she'd planned, it would have been perfect, and they'd have been in the clear. Forever. No matter. Getting rid of Charlie Dallas would slam the door shut on the past, a door that had been left cracked open for far too long.

"You ever think about how this all started?" he asked suddenly.

"Sometimes," she said softly. She gazed out the window of their suite, which looked east over the downtown skyline, shimmering in the early dusk. The suite was thickly carpeted. To her left sat a silver tea service on a cherrywood sideboard. When she was growing up, she never imagined she would ever stay in a place like this. Granted, she was staying under an assumed name with one of her multiple sets of identification papers. *But still.*

They hadn't been back in years, but the city didn't look much different. It still looked dirty, still felt divided, still seemed old. Lindsey had hated it here. Surrounded by so much wealth, Lindsey had grown up in abject poverty. Her mother worked as a housekeeper for a rich family living on River Road, the kind of people that showed up here on the Mayflower, and her father worked in a rock quarry before a stroke ended his life in 1958. Her mother often worked at her employer's home during dinner parties and cocktail hours and regaled her only daughter with tales of the rich and famous.

She met Patrick in high school, and they had gotten married a week after graduation. College was never an option. Neither of them had been academically inclined. No football scholarship for Patrick either. A wide receiver, he'd hauled in a grand total of seven catches during his unremarkable high school career. Lindsey worked two jobs to help out at home, and so when the hell was she supposed to study?

Continuing the cycle of hopelessness that encircles so many low-income families, they both entered the work-force, neither job paying particularly well. Patrick worked crazy hours, never knowing from week to week when he was going to be home. He didn't like the work much, but he became fairly good at it, and he was promoted through the ranks quickly. Promotion, however, meant a hell of a lot more responsibility, not more money. Lindsey found a job as a secretary, which was still the best gig many women could hope for back then.

Then Patrick's draft number had come up, and he shipped out to Vietnam in the spring of 1970. Instead of seeing it in black and white with Walter Cronkite's gravelly voiceover, he was going to see it live and in person. He was twenty-six, an old man for a draftee, and the other boys shipping out with him called him Gramps. He didn't mind going to Vietnam. All other things being equal, he would've rather been home in his light blue recliner listening to Washington Redskins games on the radio, but he was OK with serving his country. No big deal. He was there for two years and saw things that he hoped no other generation of boys would ever have to see.

He came back and went back to his old job. He was well-respected and well-liked, and he didn't mind the work. But there was never enough money. Every month was a race between days and cash. Sometimes cash lasted longer than the month. More often than not, though, it was the other way around. And, brother, did he hear about it from Lindsey. Then she'd gotten pregnant, and forget about Kent State and the march on Washington-- things were tough on *his* home front, that was for damn sure. Then this idea, this ridiculous idea somehow sparked to life. It seemed to take a life of its own, refusing to die. Before he knew it, they were scouting out loca- tions, arming themselves with stolen guns, mapping out escape routes. Lindsey had been a very convincing woman. Had been then. Still was now. The truth was, he didn't hate the idea. If he hadn't really wanted to do it, he could've talked her out of it. That's what he told himself.

"Sometimes I wonder how things would have turned out if we hadn't--"

Lindsey held up a palm, like a menopausal cop directing traffic.

"Don't you ever wonder?" Patrick asked.

Jesus, she thought. *What was with him today?*

"Yes, of course I wonder," she said.

"It wasn't a bad job," he said, digging in the inside pocket of his barn jacket. He removed a pipe, used his thumb to stamp down the tobacco, then lit it with a plastic lighter. The warm, rich smoke curled from the bowl and filled the room like a fog. Lindsey loved the smell. It had been one of the things that first attracted her to Patrick. He'd been smoking pipes since he was fifteen years old. He'd never been one for cigarettes.

"I know," she said. "But did you really want to go through life like that? Struggling from month to month, wondering whether we'd make our rent payment on time?"

"Part of life," he said, taking a long, crackling pull from the pipe stem. He sat back down on the couch and smoked in silence.

"Not for me!" she exploded. "I didn't want to live that way! I hardly ever slept! I cried every night. Did you know that?"

Patrick cupped the underside of the pipe bowl, but he said nothing.

"Yeah," she continued, drawing closer to him, "and on the nights you were actually home, wow, what a lucky girl I was. Remember, you'd throw back your twelve-pack for the night and pass out in that piece of shit recliner. Or on the nights I was privileged enough to have you stumble back to bed and grace me with your presence before farting and blacking out."

"I didn't know that," Patrick said.

"How could you?" she snapped before going on. "Then we did the bank," she said. Tears welled up in her eyes, giving them a glassy, shiny look. "And then every-thing changed." A laugh tried to escape from her throat, but her spastic sobs captured it like a spider's web.

"Those first few days after we did it," she continued, "I felt so happy. Relieved. Like we had a future. I wasn't going to let anyone get in the way of that. Anyone. I wasn't scared of getting caught. I knew we wouldn't get caught.

"I wish things had turned out differently," she said, her voice softening again. "But I don't regret what happened, if that's what you're asking." They had made their choice. They had to live with it.

"What about you?" she asked, wiping her cheeks with the back of her hand. They were warm and red.

"What about me?" he asked, studying the tobacco grinds like they were mystical tea leaves.

She crossed the room and sat next to him on the couch. She took his hand, rough and coarse, into her own.

"You know I'm right behind you," he said, never lifting his gaze from the pipe bowl. "All the way."

She patted his knee. "That's what I thought," she said.

"Now what do we do?" he asked.

"We call Ulysses back," she said. "We end this."

ULYSSES WAS NOT his real name, but that had been his nickname since April 1968, when he entered the Army as a bloodthirsty private with a burning desire to kill North Vietnamese soldiers. During the bus ride to Fort Benning, Georgia to begin basic training, a recruit named Hollis Thornton began razzing a fellow grunt about the James Joyce novel that he was reading. That literarily inclined recruit did not take it well, breaking Thornton's nose with a single punch, a punch that no other passenger on the bus reported seeing. The reason was that most of the other guys didn't like the kid who'd been reading *Ulysses*, but they liked Thornton even less, and amazingly, not one passenger on the bus had seen Ulysses, as he came to be known, pop the annoying Thornton. The drill sergeant was not impressed, and they all did five miles in the Georgia sun when they got to Benning before they even went to Requisitions. Every one of the sixty-four new soldiers vomited up their induction breakfast inside of three miles.

Within ten days, Ulysses had distinguished himself as the best marksman at Benning. Some people play piano. Others are virtuosos with a paintbrush. Ulysses turned killing into an art form. He was snatched up from his infantry unit and trained as a sniper, where he displayed deadly accuracy from distances ranging up to 1,500 yards. Almost a mile.

In July 1968, Ulysses's squadron shipped out to Vietnam, arriving in Saigon in a hot, steamy downpour, which didn't let up for four days. By then, Ulysses was in country, transformed by terror into a cold killing machine. He loved killing. He thrived on it, never feeling more alive, from the top of an outhouse or perched on a thick tree branch, a single round, the cold bore shot, piercing the skull of some NVA officer, sending the army unit under his command into disarray.

For three years, Ulysses roamed the countryside like the boogeyman, turning down more than one chance to go home because nothing was waiting for him there. He became the deadliest American sniper in the war, amassing ninety-nine confirmed kills during that time. And then, one day, he had missed. Scheduled as his hundredth kill, it was supposed to be an easy shot, through some trees in clear weather. No wind. The target had been a middle-level diplomat, visiting the troops in Hanoi. Ulysses was on the roof of an abandoned farmhouse about four hundred yards south of the podium. Everything had gone according to plan. He peered through the 10X telescope sight of his U.S. M40A1 sniper rifle, the target's head appearing as big as a watermelon. After proceeding through his mental checklist, Ulysses took the shot and was breaking down his weapon before he realized that something had gone wrong.

What exactly had gone wrong was a matter that still kept Ulysses up at night. Maybe the target had sneezed, rocking his head forward just as the bullet screamed through the unexpectedly empty kill zone. Or maybe he'd bent over to scratch an itch on his leg. Ulysses escaped easily, but the incident had shaken him to his very core. Thoughts of the failed hit followed him like a shadow on a late summer afternoon.

It haunted him until October 29, 1972.

JUST SOUTH OF the Georgia-Florida border, Ulysses's Ford Bronco raced deep into the Sunshine State, its speedometer tickling ninety, the driver nipping a bottle of Southern Comfort. A radar detector mounted on the dashboard squawked, announcing the presence of a nearby Florida Highway Patrol radar gun, and Ulysses reluctantly eased the pressure on the accelerator. He spun the cap back on the bottle and tucked it between the seats.

Dammit, he thought, as the huge truck decelerated to the speed limit. He'd been really enjoying himself. His cell phone chirped, causing him to forget his mild annoyance. He checked the caller ID.

Christ. Now what?

"Yeah?" he barked loudly, over the din of the Bronco's engine.

"We need you for another job," Lindsey Jessup said.

"Lemme call you back," he said, ending the call. If there was one thing Ulysses hated, it was people blabbing away on their cell phones while driving. *Oh, I'm stuck at a red light. Oh, I just passed Adams Street. Oh, Food Town's got rump roast on sale.* Just once, he wished he could point his Glock at one of these chit-chatty drivers and hear them say, "Oh, I'm about to get my head blown off."

But he restrained himself. Never a good idea to kill someone unless he was getting paid for it. Too much of a risk and an inefficient use of resources. He shook his head. Amazing how strong the residue from his Special Forces days was. He'd been discharged more than thirty years ago, but the lessons stuck with him like a birthmark. If this cell phone idiocy kept up, however, maybe he'd take out a few, just enough for the media to catch wind of the fact that the only real piece of evidence they'd been able to pin down was that each of the victims had been on a cell phone when they'd bought it. That'd teach them.

He pulled off the interstate at the next rest stop, about twenty miles down the road. After using the facilities, he strolled down into the woods where he could get some privacy.

"What's the job?" he asked when she picked up the line.

"Dallas."

His eyebrows rocked upwards.

"Seriously?"

"Yeah," she said, sighing loudly. "It's time to tie up all the loose ends."

"He knows who we are, doesn't he?" asked Ulysses nervously. He was chewing on a ragged fingernail.

"It's possible," Lindsey said.

"Do you know where he is?"

"No."

Ulysses was almost pleased to hear this. If she didn't know where Dallas was, that would give Ulysses some additional leverage on the fee. Killing people was risky business, and he expected to be compensated for it.

"It's going to cost you," he said.

"Like hell," she said. "We're all in this together."

"Wrong again, babe," he said. "I personally could not give a shit about Charlie Dallas. I want a hundred thousand."

"Why don't you kiss my ass?"

"Good luck finding someone to do the job," he said. "Have a nice life." He made no move to hang up the line; he knew she wouldn't call his bluff.

"Fine," she said. "Fine."

Wow.

Dallas must have gotten close. Ulysses should have demanded more.

18

Hudson tapped on Hood's door and stepped inside his office. John, who was reviewing field reports from the various units in the office, motioned him in with a wave of his hand. It was late evening, the skies outside a light shade of purple. A rumble rolled through Hood's stomach, reminding him that he hadn't eaten since an energy bar he'd thrown down at breakfast.

"I've got some news on the wife," Hudson said, taking a seat across from Hood. He crossed one leg over the other and opened a manila folder in his lap. Hood had placed Hudson in charge of investigating Susanna Dallas's disappearance. Twelve agents were now working on the Vitelli investigation, and keeping a handle on the flow of information was getting complicated. Especially since none of the information seemed to be fitting together. A bunch of puzzle pieces that may or may not fit into the same puzzle. Always reassuring.

Hood looked up from the file he was reviewing--an investigation into an international microchip price-fixing scheme. It was mind-numbingly boring, and he was dying to hear about something else. One of the downfalls of a management position. As much as he wanted to devote his full attention to tracking down Vitelli's killer, the presence of the word *bureau* in the full name of his employer pretty much guaranteed he was going to have to always deal with bullshit red tape. Some days, he wished he was still just a field agent, and he often thought about putting in a request to return to street-level duty. Maybe a transfer to a new office. As an ASAC, he could probably have his pick of field offices. San Diego sounded nice. He'd heard the Padres had been rained out once in the last twenty-five years. Eighty degrees every day, the place crawling with beautiful women. Maybe he'd look into it after this Vitelli mess was wrapped up.

"Here's what we've got so far," Hudson said, studying the folder. "We already knew that they checked into a resort on Sanibel on Sunday. Dallas checks out Monday night, leaves one of the keys in the room, and takes off. His car was in front of his house back in Richmond, so it seems reasonable to conclude that he was the one who drove it back. Also, I finally caught up with the manager of the restaurant at the resort. He says they came in for dinner around seven-thirty or eight Monday night. Then after dinner, he remembers Dallas wandering around looking for his wife. He even asked a waitress to check the bathroom for her. None of the employees remembered seeing her leave. They said he seemed pretty frantic."

"Did he file a MP?" Hood asked, twirling a pen with his finger. It was a bad habit. Sometimes he spun it around until his wrist ached.

"We're checking on that still, but it doesn't seem like he did."

"Vitelli was killed Tuesday evening," Hood said, thinking out loud. "The wife disappeared Monday night. We know that Dallas was back in Richmond less than twenty-four hours after dinner with his new wife. We're assuming that Dallas drove his car back to Richmond. But what if he didn't? Have we checked flights out of the closest airport? Fort Myers, right?"

"We checked the passenger manifests for all commercial flights out of Tampa, Miami, and Fort Myers," Hudson said. "Nothing on that front. We're also working on the charter companies, but that's going to take a few days. Plus, the only prints in the car were his and his wife's. We haven't found any trace evidence of any third parties either."

John Hood closed his eyes and focused on his last session with Elsa King. *Shades of gray*, he told himself. Charlie Dallas had been there when Vitelli died. No doubt about that. A second person was there, in the bushes. Probably the actual shooter. They'd been assuming--*OK, I had been assuming*, John thought--that they were working together. But what if they weren't? That would mean what? That Charlie had been set up? Had been the intended target? The more John thought about it, the more possibilities flooded his mind like storm surge. Maybe Dallas was planning to report his wife's disappearance as discreetly as possible. If she had been kidnapped, then perhaps Dallas had received a message from her captors. Another thought lit up his mind like a Roman candle. If Dallas had been meeting the kidnappers, wouldn't he have tried to arrange a meeting where he had last seen her--in Florida?

Like all law enforcement officers investigating a disappearance, John also had been wondering if Susanna Dallas had orchestrated her own disappearance and tried to knock off her husband. He made a note to check Dallas's net worth, the life insurance policies--the crappy policy he got through his newspaper--anything that would provide a financial incentive for Susanna Dallas to try and kill her new hubby.

"How much do we know about her, anyway?" asked Hood, motioning for Hudson to hand him the file.

"Schoolteacher, from the area," Hudson said. "Went to Elon College, got a master's in teaching at VCU. Works at one of the private schools in town."

"I want to find her," Hood said, tapping an index finger against his lip while leafing through the file. "Soon." He wanted to know how Susanna Dallas fit into all this. Whether she was kidnapped, whether she set it up, whether she was still down in the plush honeymoon suite, wondering if Charlie was ever coming back with that bucket of ice.

"I'll have to stop sitting on the couch with my thumb up my ass then," Hudson said.

"Quite a mouth you've got on you," Hood said, leaning back in his chair, lacing his hands behind his neck.

"We're working on this," Hudson said. "You gotta have a little faith in us."

John patted the top of his head, stroking the soft fuzz

that had sprouted from his scalp. Three days since he'd shaved, and he was feeling ratty. He sighed heavily, then tossed the file on his desk. This case was draining him like a tick feeding from a dog's back.

19

Charlie caught a ride south on I-95 with a long-haul trucker for Hanlin Systems, headed for Columbia, South Carolina. The driver, a middle-aged black guy named Lenny, was carrying a load of computer parts from a warehouse in Paramus, New Jersey to a regional distribution center for the southern states. He'd been on the road for nearly a week, and he was happy to have the company. The huge rig ate up the miles like a giant worm burrowing its way south, while Lenny chatted nonstop about baseball, politics, his kids, and his favorite strip clubs along the I-95 corridor.

Shortly after dark, he eased the semi into a truck stop in Benson, N.C., near the I-40/I-95 interchange, a gaudy hive in the otherwise sleepy center of tobacco country, where truckers and locals ate and drank and commiserated about their tough lot in life. Two dozen trucks sat in the overnight parking lot, purring softly as the electrical systems powered the air conditioning, portable TVs, and refrigerators that helped make the rigs a little more like home. The parking lights dotting each of the trailers like Christmas lights glowed ominously, giving each of them the feel of a sleeping beast.

Charlie used the bathroom and bought a bottle of soda from the vending machine while Lenny worked a plate of steak and eggs, sunny side up, at the front counter. Charlie studied the huge map of North Carolina pinned to the wall in the lobby area of the restaurant, trying to estimate how much further he had before he reached the cabin, as well as the tricky matter of how he was going to get there. He traced a finger from his current location, east along I-40 into Wilmington, then south along Route 17, where he found the tiny hamlet of Holden Beach. He wondered how the place had held up; he hadn't been there in five years. He wasn't sure if anyone had. He paid the taxes on the property and the electric bill, but that was about it.

"Hey, buddy," Lenny said, stepping up behind Charlie and tearing his attention away from the map. A dollop of yolk stained the stubble above his upper lip. "I'm gonna sack out here in a minute, but I got you a ride east toward Wilmington. Pretty lady there on the end." He pointed toward the crowded main counter.

"That's great," Charlie said, extending his hand. "I appreciate it." Lenny shook it; his hand felt rough and callused in Charlie's.

"Don't mention it."

Lenny pulled a cigarette from the pocket of his flannel shirt, placed it between his lips, and stepped out into the muggy night. Charlie looked over at the woman sitting in the last seat on the right edge of the counter. Long brown hair. Dirty blue jeans and denim jacket. She was reading a tattered paperback book, the front cover folded over the back. Charlie always thought people who did that got their money's worth for the book. Don't just crack the spine, dammit, get it all rough and mussed up. He watched her read for a moment; when she reached some natural break in the story, she dog-eared the page and tucked the book under her arm. She spun her seat around and hopped down onto the floor. She barely acknowledged Charlie as she pushed her way out the door. Charlie briefly wondered what kind of a woman would have no objection to inviting a strange man into what was effectively her home on the back country roads of North Carolina.

"Let's go, cowboy," she said with a rough voice. She was about five-eight, just a couple inches shorter than Charlie, with leathery, tan skin. Her hair was black, not brown as Charlie had guessed, and straighter than a table edge. Though small, her green eyes burned with such intensity as to draw attention away from the rest of her face. She was a little on the heavy side, Charlie noticed, which he was certain was attributable to the lack of exercise or decent meals that were commonplace in a trucker's life. If she'd had it as easy as most people he knew, she'd have been a knockout. Like her buddy Lenny, she lit a cigarette the minute she stepped outside.

Charlie stepped in behind her and trailed her to her truck, a behemoth vehicle with a trailer marked with the Wal-Mart logo. Charlie climbed into the cab, having mastered the art with Lenny's help, and plopped down into the leather seats. He glanced around casually, not wanting to get busted for looking around too much. A single mattress and comforter appeared to provide the woman's sleeping arrangements. Several stacks of books littered the area. In the corner, he saw a small TV/VCR combo unit.

"Name's Donna," she said, throwing her paperback into the living area just behind the front seats. Charlie wasn't sure, but it looked like she'd been plowing through Ayn Rand's *The Fountainhead*. He immediately felt guilty. He didn't know what he'd been expecting her to be reading, but it certainly wasn't that. She peeled off her jacket and dropped it to the floor. Charlie gasped softly when he saw the chrome-plated handgun strapped to her torso via a leather body holster. That pretty much took care of Charlie's concerns about her safety. She caught him staring.

"A girl can't be too careful, right?" she said.

Charlie laughed nervously. "I guess."

"Lenny says you're headed for Wilmington?" she said, bringing the rig to life. She popped the clutch and guided the truck toward the on-ramp feeding onto the interstate.

Charlie nodded. He was immediately afraid of this woman. She seemed too smart to not know who he was. He had visions of her driving him straight to the local sheriff's office and collecting whatever bounty had been placed on his head. She merged onto the interstate and joined the light traffic headed east.

"Don't mind me smokin', do ya?" she asked over the din of the engine.

Charlie shook his head.

"Good! Cause I wasn't gonna put it out!" She laughed heartily but stopped when she saw Charlie wasn't laughing.

"Come on, man!" she huffed. "We got a hundred miles

to go, we might as well enjoy it. How about a smoke?"

Charlie took it eagerly. He'd smoked long ago, but he'd given it up before he met Susanna. Still, sometimes there was nothing like a good drag to take the edge off. And did he ever need it taken off today.

NINETY MINUTES LATER, Donna guided her rig against a loading dock just on the outskirts of Wilmington. An industrial section of the oceanside city, this was where the dirty work got done. The warehouse belonged to the Aircraft Engines division of General Electric, a sprawling ten-acre compound that shimmered in the light of the full moon.

"End of the line," she said.

"Thanks," Charlie said, extending his hand.

She grabbed it and pulled him close, brushing her lips against his cheek.

"You're a sweet kid," Donna said. "You're in trouble, aren't you?"

Charlie dropped his chin to his chest.

"This about a woman?"

"Kind of."

"You hang in there," she said.

Charlie hopped down from the cab and jogged across the gravel lot, the tiny pebbles crunching under his feet. Behind him, Donna greeted a pair of GE workers approaching the truck. He continued around the edge of the main building and headed toward the employee parking lot. It gave him an idea. He'd planned on hitching a ride the rest of the way, but that was getting risky. The more people he saw, the greater the chance someone might recognize him, even on these back country roads. Maybe some of these guys left their keys in the car overnight. Who would steal a car out here?

He crouched near some bushes ringing the lot and waited until the shift change ended. He checked his watch. Just after midnight. Another few minutes, and the night shift would be underway. He gave it twenty minutes, accounting for the few stragglers that showed up until nearly twelve-thirty.

Finally, the lot was quiet. Only a few cars were out at this hour, zipping past the parking lot every minute or so. The full moon made it a little brighter than Charlie would have liked, but it would have to do. He approached the first car, a dirty Ford F-150 with oversized tires and adult-oriented mud flaps. Too obvious. He passed on it. Second car was a dark Honda Accord. Charlie lifted the handle gently. Locked. He met the same result with the next dozen cars, but he finally got a nibble on the thirteenth. A white Mazda sedan. He held his breath and felt around the ignition.

Bingo!

The keys rattled against the plastic casing. He crawled in and pulled the door closed behind him. The cabin reeked of stale cigarette smoke. A cardboard pine tree dangled from the rearview mirror, giving the car a nice menthol aroma. Charlie buckled his seat belt and turned the key; the engine roared to life, sending Charlie's pulse through the roof. Guilt washed over him like a rogue wave. *Relax*, he told himself. *You're just borrowing it. The police will find it in the next day or two. You'll even leave it in a nice, well-lit gas station.*

He eased the car out onto the highway and picked his way through the deserted outskirts of Wilmington until he got to Route 17 South. The four-lane divided highway stretched interminably into the darkness, broken up by billboards and mobile home dealerships. Half an hour later, he turned east onto Holden Beach Boulevard and cruised the eight winding miles, passing tiny ranch houses situated on desperate plots of land where families sold corn and tomatoes and cucumbers from roadside stands.

Finally, the gas station marquee marking the town limits of the little hamlet appeared in the distance. At this hour, the sign burned like a beacon, sending shivers of relief through Charlie's body. After slipping the car into an empty slot in front of the station's mini-mart, Charlie took a deep breath and let it out slowly. He stepped out of the car into the warm night and inhaled the humid, salty air. Three miles to go. He draped the laptop case over his shoulder and continued his trek.

He walked quickly. Past the jungle-themed mini-golf course, the all-you-can-eat seafood place where the seafood tasted like it had been trucked in from the Midwest, the cheesy, oversized beach supply store. The causeway to the island rose before him like a concrete mountain, and as he ascended the steep climb, he could see the line of demarcation between where the lights of civilization ended and the eternal blackness of the ocean began. The roar of the ocean seemed magnified at night, a restless beast sleeping fitfully. At the bottom of the bridge, the commercialism faded away, leaving a quiet peaceful island.

Charlie covered the three miles in forty-five minutes;

by the time he turned off Ocean Boulevard onto Dolphin Avenue, he was slick with sweat, and his shoulders ached from carrying the heavy bag. The house was at the end of the street, toward the sound. An A-frame house with a wrap-around deck, this had been Charlie's home away from home growing up. His paternal grandfather had built it by hand, wooden plank by wooden plank. He had poured the concrete and raised the support posts that kept the house from flooding when the Atlantic threw one of its summertime temper tantrums and hurled tropical systems toward the coast.

Charlie knelt by the lamppost by the driveway and flipped up a slat of wood fitted into a slot in the ground, home to the house's main water supply. He turned it on, then climbed the step to the front door. Reaching over the doorframe, he retrieved the key and unlocked the door.

Old, stagnant air and mustiness tickled Charlie's nose as he stepped inside. He reached against the wall, feeling for the light switch, and flipped it up, washing the living room in a sick yellow glow. He dropped his bag on the couch, wooden and ancient with its thick, rough cushions. Plastic sheeting gave the furniture a cold, inhospitable feel, and Charlie felt a chill sweep his body, even though it was oppressively warm in the shut-up house. The living room was the centerpiece of the house, about thirty-by-twenty square. A small kitchen piggy-backed the room, and two small bedrooms branched off either side. Old nautical maps decorated the walls.

The place was just like he remembered it. It was as if it had been flash-frozen more than a decade ago. Issues of *Newsweek* and *Sports Illustrated* with cover dates from the late 1980s and early 1990s were stacked on top of the cherrywood coffee table. A Stephen King novel sat open, face down, on a rocking chair in the corner, as if its reader had only meant to put it down for a few moments.

Charlie went to work making the place a little more livable, opening the windows, turning on fans. For the most part, everything worked. A few lamps blew their bulbs, unable to handle the shock of being rushed into service. The water ran rusty brown for a few seconds before turning clear. He couldn't find any bed linens, then decided that was just as well. He'd sleep out on the sofa.

Every time his eyes drifted across the room, a different spot triggered a memory from years gone by. In the kitchen, he could see giant stockpots roiling with boiling water and live crabs. The couch he was leaning up against was the site of his first kiss, shared with ... *Emily*, he thought her name was. *How could you forget that, Dallas?* The big floor console TV, where he and his dad had watched Atlanta Braves games while here on vacation. It was as if someone had started a mental slide show, forcing Charlie to sit through it.

After his mom died, the family's assets had passed into a trust, with Charlie as the sole beneficiary. He never even knew who the trustee was. When he was twenty-one, he received a copy of the deed and the keys to the Waynesboro property and the beach house. Both had been long since paid off, but he never felt right coming here. He made a few more trips after his parents died, occasionally bringing down college friends after final exams. He'd been on his own ever since. Strange, the way things worked out. The truth was, if his parents hadn't died, he never would have met Susanna.

His head swam with fatigue, and he gave it a quick shake. He needed to start digging through the mound of material on the table in front of him. He grabbed a notepad and stretched out on the couch. His eyelids drooped once, then twice, then shut again. A thunderstorm ravaged the area overnight, but Charlie never even budged.

SUNLIGHT FILTERING through dusty blinds woke Charlie up shortly after seven the next morning. He rubbed the crust from his eyes and pushed himself to a sitting position. A thin sheen of sweat covered his body. He hadn't checked to see if the air-conditioning unit wedged into the front window still worked. He ran his fingers through his hair, still surprised to feel the soft fuzz rather than the curly loops. His head ached--he needed some coffee. Luckily, coffee was the one thing he might be able to find here. He padded across the room, his muscles stiff and his back sore, to the refrigerator.

The freezer was an arctic wasteland, thick with ice. But fate was smiling on Charlie this morning. A small can of instant coffee was stuck in the door-mounted shelf, and Charlie nearly ripped off the door in his attempt to extract the can before popping it free. He put some water to boil on the avocado-green electric range. While the water swirled and steamed up, Charlie ran his body under the low-pressure outdoor shower. The water was ice-cold, but it felt good in the soupy humidity that had already blanketed the island this morning.

CHARLIE WAS fourteen when his dad died. Edwin Dallas sold brake pads for a large national outfit and was on the road about two hundred days a year. He was about fifty pounds north of a healthy weight, and he had a pack-a-day habit to boot. He wasn't a philanderer, and two stiff drinks usually put him right to sleep, so he didn't have much else to do to pass the time besides smoke and eat. On his final business trip, he was waiting for his double cheeseburger at a Wendy's in Toledo when, as luck would have it, a massive coronary hit, killing him well before he hit the freshly mopped floor.

Charlie remembered going to the airport and waiting in the cargo area where the box carrying Edwin Dallas's body would be unloaded from the United Airlines flight from Toledo to Richmond. A strange thought had occurred to Charlie while they loaded the wooden crate, laden with dry ice to preserve Edwin's considerable remains, into the medical examiner's van. What would the passengers on the flight have thought had they known they'd been flying with a dead man below deck? Was that bad luck? Or was it good luck? Considering the dead guy had already died once, weren't the odds pretty good that the plane wouldn't crash?

Edwin was buried two days later in the Oak Glen Cemetery in Waynesboro. A small headstone inscribed *Husband, Father, Friend* marked his grave. The last one always made Charlie wonder. He didn't remember his father having any friends, let alone enough to warrant the inscription on the headstone. When the creepy coffin machine lowered his father's casket into the ground, Charlie did not cry. He knew that he would miss his father, miss the way he yelled at the TV during Dallas Cowboys games, the smoky smell of his clothes after he burned the leaves each fall. The way you missed anything that had been part of your whole existence. It wasn't sadness, though. He remembered feeling very guilty because he hadn't felt sad.

And so it had been Charlie and his mother, living in the house on Wrigley Avenue for the next three years until he finished his tour of duty at Stuarts Draft High School. When Charlie left for N.C. State, Emma Dallas was devastated. Since Edwin had died, Charlie had become her whole life, and now he was gone. One night, two months after Charlie left home, Emma Dallas died in her sleep. An autopsy determined that she had died of an aneurysm in the chest--a broken heart, the medical examiner had joked to his assistant. Had Charlie heard this bit of gallows humor, he probably would have agreed. Charlie sold the house and financed the rest of his education with the proceeds. The beach house, however, he couldn't bear to sell. Instead, it had become a storage facility for the Dallas family legacy.

A builder by trade, Charlie's great-grandfather, Robert Dallas, first laid eyes on Holden Beach Island in 1956, when he was driving south along Route 17 toward a hotel project in still-fledgling Myrtle Beach. A wrong turn had sent him east toward the ocean, where he found the little hamlet, still undiscovered and pristine. On the strength of a handshake, he bought a plot of land from the Holden family and promised to return. He came back the following summer with a shitload of lumber and nails, and he set to work building his dream home one two-by-four at a time. It took him three years, working every weekend and every holiday. He hammered and nailed twelve hours a day and installed the plumbing and wiring himself.

A week after Charlie's mother was in the ground, alongside Edwin, Charlie and his college roommate loaded a station wagon with anything worth keeping and gave the rest to Goodwill. The Goodwill people were quite impressed. Furniture, old jewelry, clothes. Charlie kept boxes of memorabilia, things he felt too guilty to get rid of, photographs, papers, those things that were supposed to be stored in safes hidden in the closet.

That was what had driven Charlie down here. He hadn't set foot in this room since the day he and his roommate had unloaded the boxes in here, stacking them floor to ceiling. The room was musty and felt a little damp, probably not the best conditions for long-term storage, now that he stopped to think about it. Standing on his tiptoes, he nudged the highest box from its perch, then grabbed it by its corners. The cardboard bottom, long since decayed in the punishing, salty atmosphere, collapsed and showered the floor with pictures, old holiday cards, even some of Charlie's elementary school papers.

Sitting Indian style, he began digging through the scattered remnants of his life. Pictures of birthday parties, his own and those of childhood friends whose names he could no longer remember. He came across snapshots from a mini-golf course, that birthday party by which all other birthdays would be measured and fall short of matching. Just one of those days he remembered climbing into bed, pink with sunburn, thinking he'd just lived the finest day of his life. He then went through the holiday cards, one by one, all the while telling himself he didn't have time to be taking this stroll down memory lane, yet unable to stop himself. LOVE YOU MOM scrawled in crayon. ROZES ARE RED, VYLETS ARE BLUE, MOMS ARE SWEET, ESPESHALLY YOU!

He missed his mother. It was funny. All he remembered of her was a love for him he could feel even when she wasn't around, as if she worried he might forget her if he drifted too far out of her orbit. She had been thin and pale and probably enjoyed a few too many cocktails when she got home every night from her job as a paralegal for Wilson & Lewis, Waynesboro's biggest law firm. Charlie used to think it couldn't have been much of a law firm because it didn't advertise on television.

He didn't remember his mother being especially fun, or funny, or even much of a talker, except when he screwed up and she tore him a new one. Basically, she had been his mother and that was it. She wasn't his friend; being his friend wasn't her job. Not for the first time, he wondered what she would have thought of Susanna. Probably would have thought he was getting married too fast. "What's the rush, Chuckie?" she would ask. She didn't call him Chuckie too often, only when she was worried he was getting a little too smart for his own good and decided to show him he really didn't know his head from his ass.

Charlie put his memories aside and continued digging through the boxes.

20

Ulysses lay awake, his hands folded behind his head, until he got tired of waiting to fall asleep. He needed little sleep to function. As an eighteen-year-old sniper in Vietnam, he'd learned to get by with a few winks here and there. He never really trusted his fellow soldiers to stay awake on their shifts, and more often than not, that paranoia had been justified. When he found them asleep, usually standing up, he liked to wake them up by cocking his weapon and jamming the barrel into their half-open, drool-stained mouths. Every now and again, he knocked out a few teeth, and the soldier would wake up, blood dripping from his lips. No one ever complained because that would mean explaining how they'd let someone jam a gun in their mouths while they were on the night watch.

He got out of bed and padded across the room to the sliding glass door dividing the room from the balcony. With a flick of his thumb, he unlocked the door and stepped out into the humid night. It was still warm, in the eighties, but Ulysses was in a pair of shorts, and the air felt good against his bare skin.

There was a pack of cigarettes and a lighter perched on the railing; Ulysses lit one, took a drag, and leaned over the railing. The sky was black, no moon out tonight to cut the uncompromising darkness. In the distance, the light of a water tower shimmered like a star.

He glanced back at the digital clock glowing atop the nightstand. It was nearly four in the morning, but Ulysses wasn't tired. Charlie Dallas weighed heavily on his mind. As did Lindsey Jessup. The woman really had him by the short and curlies. She'd owned him for years. If he hadn't been so careless with the money!

It had been such a beautiful day. After the job, they had driven out to the pre-selected location, an empty field where they'd stashed three stolen cars with home-made plates. Lindsey--naturally--had been in charge of splitting the take. Nearly half a million in cash for each of them. The heft of the small duffel bag, stuffed to the gills with a hundred $10,000 bricks, felt good against his back, and he had never felt so free.

Per Lindsey's directive that they all permanently expatriate themselves, Ulysses had driven straight to Atlanta. There, he caught a flight to London, carrying the bag of money on the plane with him. That memory made him smile. Back then, you could've walked onto a jumbo jet with a nuclear device strapped to your back. As long as you didn't look like you were planning to use it.

He made his way to Ireland and spent a year there, little of it sober. He also developed an affinity for gambling in illegal betting parlors, wagering on virtually every soccer game played in the western hemisphere. By the time he staggered to the airport in Dublin, he'd blown through a quarter-million dollars and had little to show for it besides a tremor-inducing addiction to booze. He still had the money in the same weathered duffel bag, the load noticeably lighter.

From Ireland, he flew to Rio de Janeiro, where he spent more than a decade. His addiction evolved into a lifestyle, and he was drinking twenty-four hours a day. Tequila became his drink of choice, buying thousand-dollar bottles that tasted like nectar. After a six-month stay in the Hilton, he bought a little flat in the teeming barrio and hid the cash in the floorboards. The money was never far from his mind, and he checked it every day, sometimes twice, afraid to be away from it for too long. When he was able to tear himself away from the cash, he sat on his balcony overlooking the downtown area and watched life race by. He rarely left his home, and the money continued to dwindle. He knew he should invest the money, but he was too afraid to move it. They'd ask questions. They'd trace it to the robbery. They'd drag him off to some Brazilian prison, where he'd have to drink sewage to stay alive.

One afternoon in 1988, Ulysses was nursing a hang-over with a little tequila in the watering hole across the street when he overheard two men discussing the need to eliminate a business competitor. They weren't talking about simply putting the man out of business, and the killing machine buried inside Ulysses came to life. One of the men was Mexican, and the second man spoke with a loud Texas twang. Bored out of his mind, Ulysses approached the men and offered his services for $10,000. Their first instinct was to run, but Ulysses convinced the men that he was not a cop and that he knew what he was doing. He ordered a round of drinks, and the men shared their story with Ulysses.

The target was a Brazilian cattle rancher named Eduardo Hayek, in Rio for Carnival, and Ulysses's clients, who owned a rival farm, wanted to corner the market. Hayek was a well-known and well-respected business-man. His ranches were huge, and he sold so many head of cattle that he kept prices depressed. Not that it kept him from becoming filthy rich himself--he just stopped anyone else from getting rich, too.

After trailing the man for a week, Ulysses had Hayek's routines down. Every afternoon at two, he ate a bowl of frijoles and drank two beers at a little place just south of Rio. When he was done, he went outside toward his armored Ford Expedition to make the dusty twenty-mile drive back to his ranch. Nestled in a rocky hillside, Ulysses waited until Hayek stepped outside into the bright sunshine and then put a round into the man's head.

Ulysses felt alive again. His clients were pleased, and, plugged into a number of other illegal business ventures, they put Ulysses on retainer for more work. Over the next three years, Ulysses assassinated a Brazilian Supreme Court justice, a DEA agent, a cartel leader, and two Rio police officers. He worked cheap, and that made his employers happy. He worked too cheap, though, and the money trickled away like sand through an hourglass.

By the early 1990s, homesickness had settled into Ulysses's heart like a damp chill. Despite Lindsey's warning that they could never go back, he was certain that enough time had gone by. They were safe. And the money was nearly gone. He didn't know what else to do, where else to go. The contract work had dried up when his employers were indicted, arrested, and executed for murder and narcotics trafficking. He'd never bothered to learn Spanish, and he was tired of eating beans. Unlike what most Americans thought about their neighbor to the south, it wasn't all cheesy quesadillas and nachos down there. Beans, beans, beans.

In 1995, he bought a used Nissan Sentra and drove across the border at Del Rio, Texas. Tears of joy streamed down his cheeks as he passed unmolested through the customs checkpoint. The U.S. Customs agent didn't give him a second look. Anxious to get out of the heat and humidity he'd been living with since the Reagan administration began, he traced a route north and arrived in Boone, North Carolina a week later. On the way, he ate hugely of everything American. Chili, fried chicken, barbecue. A ton of barbecue.

He bought a little cabin, paying in cash and earning a pair of raised eyebrows from the seller, who nonetheless took the money without objection. He had his own money problems, and he didn't care where Ulysses came up with the money. After outfitting the cabin, Ulysses was down to his last $20,000. He took a job at the local grocery store and ran the place for the old man who owned it. Luckily, the owner didn't ask a lot of questions about his new employee. During the summer, Ulysses spent the evenings on his porch or puttering around his house. When the snow started falling, he liked to build a fire and read. Occasionally, he played chess with Eddie Gillen, who lived about a quarter-mile down the road.

And so he had lived, happy for the first time in years,

until Lindsey Jessup had called. He was tempted to tell her to kiss his ass, but he knew he couldn't. The police would be happy to fire up a cold double murder case. And he didn't fancy a trip to the electric chair.

WHEN THE SUN finally peeked over the Blue Ridge Mountains the next morning, Ulysses was still awake, now as busy as a dog with a new bone. He filled a duffel bag with a week's worth of clothes and loaded up his Barrett M82A2 sniper rifle, two SIG-Sauer P-229s, and several boxes of ammunition into a small footlocker. He also packed his laptop computer, which was loaded with software popularized by private investigators, having picked up a little PI work in Rio. After making a few sandwiches for the road, he was ready to roll by seven.

The little cabin grew smaller in his rearview mirror as he kicked down the dusty gravel road. He'd been so happy to see it when he got home a few days ago, and now he was filled with the opposite emotion, the negative pole of the magnet. He wondered if he would ever see it again.

Ulysses sped north on I-95, arriving in Richmond around noon. He checked into a hotel in the west end and unpacked his belongings with military efficiency. When he was settled in, he set up a workstation and got down to business. Although it had been nearly a decade since his last hit, the framework for each was the same. Eliminating the target with as little risk as possible. Typically, that meant trailing the target for days or even weeks, learning their routines, their habits, when and where their guard was down. It was difficult, tedious, and absolutely necessary.

Charlie Dallas was a fugitive, however, and that required a different mentality. Because there was an additional variable in the equation--the cops. Plus, there was no routine or habit to learn. A target on the run was far more dangerous than a corporate exec who'd been marked for death by his main competitor. In a case like that, you just followed him home from a golf club a few times until you had the routine down.

After taking his various databases for a spin, he'd found Charles and Susanna Dallas's address, news clippings about their engagement and subsequent wedding. He also found obituaries for both of Charlie's parents, several years apart. He collected a few more scraps of information, enough to start a trail to track down his target.

Ulysses closed his eyes and placed himself in Charlie Dallas's shoes. Dallas was a fugitive, on the run. More importantly, Ulysses knew that Dallas was innocent. Dallas would try to clear his name before the cops caught him. And sooner or later, they would. Ulysses was careful never to underestimate law enforcement, if not for their intelligence, then for the sheer volume of resources they could throw at a case. Ulysses suspected that Dallas knew this as well. So Dallas would have to hide somewhere, probably not too far from Richmond, somewhere he could feel comfortable and try to piece together the mess in which he'd found himself.

An hour later, Ulysses had a half-inch-thick stack of documents in his hand, detailing Dallas's education and financial history. He also had a computer-generated

DMV photograph. Ah, the beauty of the social security number. Using a dummy corporation he'd set up for these kinds of investigations, under the guise of checking Dallas's credit for a job application, Ulysses pulled his reports from the major bureaus. Dallas owed about $9,000 in student loans, carried little credit card debt, and contributed heavily to his employer's 401(k) plan. There was a car payment on a 2001 Ford Escape, plus the house that he owned jointly with his wife.

Ulysses wondered if it was a blessing or a curse that Charlie was the one chasing this story. For one thing, it gave him the creeps, as if some vengeful spirit from the past had tapped them on the shoulder and wanted to collect an overdue bill. On the other hand, maybe it didn't matter who was working on the story. Whether it had been Charlie or some other Bob Woodward wannabe, the response would have been the same. Try to discredit the reporter. Ulysses supposed he agreed with Lindsey's logic--killing a reporter in America was a very tricky business. The engine of conspiracy was always humming in this country, and a reporter's death merely fed more coal into the fire. But the setup had failed for now. And the longer Dallas stayed out there, the bigger the chance that he might start connecting the dots. That was why he had to find him now, wherever he was. Like a hotel.

A shady place like the one in which the Jessups had set him up. A disgusting place, but useful, because no one asked any questions or paid too much attention. Ulysses could see Dallas bunking in a place like that. But, even assuming he'd disguised his identity, he couldn't spend too much time in a public place. Especially if a reward had been posted. He wouldn't be safe anywhere.

Ulysses decided to start at the Department of Vital Records, taking a cab to its office, which was tucked in a strip mall in the city's western suburbs. The interior was stark white, like a hospital, but without the hustle and bustle of the business of birth and death. This was the record of birth and death. The hum of computer hard drives and laser printers interrupted only by the muted ring of advanced telephone systems. He approached a thin man at the reception desk, who was leafing through an old copy of Newsweek. His skin was as white as the walls and seemed even pastier against his blue shirt. Short-sleeved.

"I need a copy of a birth certificate, please," Ulysses said as neutrally as he could. He'd soon know what tack he'd have to take.

The man never looked up from his magazine.

"Fill out this form in triplicate," the receptionist said mechanically. "If the birth occurred within the last fifty years, you'll need to provide evidence of kinship to the person."

Ulysses sighed. A civil service drone who would go out of his way to be as unhelpful as possible. Fortunately, he had some experience with this. He flashed his long-expired PI badge, which conveniently resembled a law-enforcement badge.

"I'm with the Bureau of Alcohol, Tobacco & Firearms," he said firmly, tucking the badge back in his pocket. "My authorization number is--"

The man held up a hand as if to say: "I don't want to go through this."

He'd never even glanced at Ulysses's badge.

"Just fill out this form," he said, flipping through another file and withdrawing a tablet of forms. Anything to get Ulysses out of there so he could get back to his magazine. A good article about the latest boy band craze. *Government workers were so predictable*, Ulysses thought. When confronted with the possibility of actual work, they usually folded like a cheap picnic table. Sometimes, it took a little cash to grease the skids, which Ulysses had been prepared to do. But, more often than not, it just required throwing out some official-sounding names.

THE RECEPTIONIST PRODUCED Charles Dallas's birth certificate, but he wouldn't let Ulysses take it from the front desk. The document had faded, the words *Certificate of Live Birth* smudged. Ulysses copied the information by hand, using the nub of a pencil he found on the desk when his own cheap pen ran dry. Place of birth, Waynesboro, Virginia. Date of birth, June 12, 1969. Father, Edwin Dallas. Mother, Emma Dallas. *Who the hell were these people?* he wondered.

With that information in hand, Ulysses rented a car from a nearby Alamo and headed west on I-64, arriving in Waynesboro about three hours later. The weather was clear and he made good time. He picked his way downtown and made his way to the town hall, which housed, among other things, the county assessor's office. The assessor maintained a register of all properties in the city and more importantly, where the tax bill was sent for each of the parcels. The downtown area was quaint, with a real-life Main Street peppered on both sides by short, stout buildings with brick facades. The dogwoods were alive and green, lining a shady median strip in the center of the main drag. It was lunchtime, and men in suits sauntered casually into one of two small cafés with signs that said *All You Can Eat Pie $4.50!*

Inside the large foyer of City Hall, Ulysses paused and enjoyed the cool crispness of the air-conditioning. He checked the directory and found the listing for the county assessor's office. Second floor. He marched upstairs, going against the lunchbound flow of traffic. The office was nearly empty when he reached it. A lonely-looking clerk date-stamping a stack of files about a mile-and-a-half high. Using a public access computer that was set up by the information desk, Ulysses typed in Charlie's full name, as well as his wife's, and waited while the machine spit out the info. Nothing. Then he ran his parents' names through the index. Emma Dallas's name appeared in the Grantee index, establishing that she'd taken title to a piece of property in Waynesboro in June 1984. Two-sixteen Wrigley Avenue.

He followed the trail of the property through the index and found that it had transferred by will in October 1987. That date corresponded to the date of Dallas's mother's obituary. The grantee was Cowboy Limited, and it held the property in a trust for an unnamed beneficiary. Ulysses raised an eyebrow and did some quick math. Charlie was seventeen in October 1987, technically still a minor. Ulysses was willing to bet that Charlie was the unnamed beneficiary. He checked the name of the trustee, which was the party legally responsible for administering the trust. Cowboy Limited. Ulysses smiled, the thrill of discovery rushing through him. *Charlie Dallas. Cowboy Limited*. Clever. He checked the index one more step back, learning that Emma Dallas had taken title to the property by right of survivorship when her husband had died three years prior.

After making a few notes, Ulysses thanked the desk clerk and stepped outside into the hot sun. The warmth felt good and fresh against his skin, which, truth be told, had grown uncomfortably clammy in the frigid confines of the county office. He stopped in at the café with the fantastic pie offer and ate a club sandwich; he passed on the pie. When he was done, he pushed his plate to the center of his table; munching on a few stray potato chips, he pulled out his cell phone and retrieved the number for the State Corporation Commission from Information.

"I need some general information on a corporation," he said when he finally got through to a human being.

"Name?" barked a tired-sounding voice.

"Cowboy Limited," he said.

A pause, while the sound of tapping keys filled his earpiece.

"Cowboy Limited, incorporated in 1987," the operator said rapidly, shooting information out machine-gun style. "Says here that the corporation is in default."

"What's that mean?" Ulysses asked, taking notes furiously.

"Could mean a lot of things. Let's see here," she said. "He hasn't paid the annual fees since 1998."

"Who're the officers and directors?"

"Only one listed. Charles X. Dallas. President."

Ulysses's eyebrows were up now, and he was scribbling like a madman.

"No one else?"

"No. Only one person required to incorporate. It's an S corporation."

That meant it was a small corporation, closely held. Nearly all corporations carried such a designation because most were small, family-held operations that didn't trade publicly.

"Where can I find a list of the corporation's holdings and assets?"

"In its most recent annual report," the SCC operator said. "I can fax you a copy."

"Terrific," Ulysses said.

"Your fax number?"

He recited it for her.

"Okay, I got it."

Then he realized he'd given her his home fax number.

"Actually, that's not the right number," he said.

He read her the hotel's fax number and ended the call.

He was in such a good mood that he ordered a slice of pie to go. Apple crumb. His favorite. He left a large tip-- but not too large--and made his way back to his car. The meter had expired, but he hadn't gotten a ticket. *Must be my lucky day*, he thought. As he drove east toward Richmond, he fought the urge to mash the accelerator to the floor. He was confident that he had a jump start on finding Charlie Dallas, and the odds were good that when the feds caught up with Dallas, he'd be too dead to tell them anything useful.

Ulysses began pondering his own future. As much as he hated to do it, he decided to make his way back to

South America and hang out for a few months, let the heat die down a little. Maybe wait out the winter there. He'd run from the heat and humidity nearly a decade ago, but as he grew older, he hated the cold more than ever. The prospect of bypassing it entirely again excited him. *Yeah*, he told himself. Mexico. On the Pacific. A snatch of dialogue from his favorite movie, *The Shawshank Redemption*, grabbed him. At one point in the film, Andy Dufresne had told his friend, Red, about a little town on the Pacific Ocean, Zhiuataneuo, where he wanted to live out his days. Ulysses thought it sounded awfully good.

THREE MINUTES LATER, the SCC operator faxed the document to Ulysses's home fax number.

21

By the time Charlie's stomach began firing warning shots of hunger around noon, the room was a mess. He'd excavated a dozen boxes of photographs, bank statements, copies of utility bills, and the other random detritus of a life lived in the twentieth century. Piles of useless paperwork surrounded him like a World War II bunker, and his head ached from digging through his past.

He'd tried to maintain some order in his search, trying to keep anything that related to his own life in a single pile. Old report cards, certificates of achievement, his college acceptance letter, certificates of stock for a long-defunct company that his father had purchased for him when he was a boy. He stacked photographs in another pile, attempting to line them up chronologically. Most of the photographs had the year stamped on their backs in faded ink, which helped immensely. Several were undated, but he could make educated guesses based on how old he looked in the picture.

When he'd finished collating them--there were more than two hundred--he flipped through them one at a time. An impromptu slide show of his life. He paused at one picture, dated 1978 and yellowed with age. He'd been wearing a blue t-shirt and red shorts. A plaster cast encased his arm from knuckles to elbow, a memento of his dirt-bike assault on Murphy's Hill. As he had come down a rut in the hill, the bike shimmied underneath Charlie and bucked him like an angry bronco. As he plunged to earth, he stuck an arm out to break his fall, which it did. It also broke his arm in six places, leaving him with the equivalent of a bag of broken glass. The cast was covered in signatures. Charlie tried to make out the signatures in the picture, but they were too blurry.

Another picture, this one from July 1980. At the beach, Charlie's arm slung around the shoulder of his best friend, Jimmy Shuman. Jimmy moved to Iowa City before that school year started when his father took a job with a medical supply company. He remembered the day that the Shumans' moving truck had pulled away from 238 Wrigley Avenue, Jimmy yelling from the cab of the truck that he'd come back and visit. Charlie had never seen Jimmy again.

More pictures. Junior prom, to which he'd taken Erica Heely. She looked beautiful, even with the big hair and electric blue dress with even bigger shoulder pads. The last Charlie heard, Erica was a pediatrician in Seattle. They were in the traditional prom pose, Charlie standing behind her, his arm draped across her waist.

As Charlie continued thumbing through the photos, something began to gnaw at him, like a rat nibbling on some old cheese. He went through the stack half a dozen times. Graduation. Christmas morning. Random pictures of buddies and girlfriends that had drifted in and out of his life like a morning fog. As he ticked through one picture after another, something began to bother him, like an itch between his shoulder blades, one he couldn't reach. Something was missing.

Then it hit him. He hadn't seen a single baby picture in the stack. In fact, the earliest dated photo was from September 1973, when he was three years old. There were a few undated photos from around the same time. He was about the same height in those earliest pictures, and either way, he was nowhere close to infancy.

The fact that the first record of his presence in the Dallas home was dated less than four months after the First National Bank robbery wasn't lost on him either. He tried to push that out of his mind as a coincidence, but it was growing increasingly difficult. He didn't have all the pieces, and he didn't know what the puzzle would look like if he ever completed it, but he was certain he wasn't going to like what he saw.

He scoured the boxes again for more pictures and came across a few stragglers, these from the day he left for college. Those were the last pictures taken of the Dallas family, as Emma Dallas was in the ground less than eight weeks later. He stood up, stretching and wincing. His back ached from the hours he'd spent hunched over the boxes.

He stepped out onto the back porch and lit a cigarette--*Careful*, he told himself, *you'll be hooked on these things again before you blink*--and took a long drag. As he smoked and listened to the ocean deliver its eternal beating to the coastline, he tried to make sense of his latest revelation. First, was it even a revelation? Maybe his parents hadn't bought a camera until he was three. He thought back to his childhood, but remembering specific events from anything before the age of seven or eight was like trying to bail out the Titanic with a spoon. All he had were ghostly images from different years that swirled together in a thick soup. His earliest concrete memory was from his first day of kindergarten in 1975. It stuck in his mind like a road sign that read *Life Starts Here*.

He crushed out the cigarette and dropped the filter into an empty beer bottle that he'd left on the railing, then went back to the storage room. He was determined to find some record of his life with his parents before September 1973. A birth certificate. Immunization records. A picture of him in his mother's arms in Sacred Heart, the hospital where he'd been born. Didn't every mother in the hospital get a free picture of her newborn? Even his bronze booties would do at this point. Smoky's words echoed in his head louder than ever, like the Doppler effect of an approaching jetplane.

You sure about that social security number?

No, Smoky, Charlie thought, twirling his wedding band around his finger. *No, I'm not too sure at all*. He dropped to his knees and started digging through the boxes with the panic of a man digging out a child buried in an avalanche. There had to be something here. Had to be. A stack of bank documents caught his eye, and he flipped through those for a few seconds before he paused. A receipt dated June 20, 1973, from the Madison Bank in Richmond. Stapled to the receipt was a small envelope, about the size of a baseball card. He broke the seal and removed the contents. A wad of tissue paper.

"Dammit!" he yelled, his voice muffled in the cluttered room. He grabbed the tissue and flung it in disgust, expecting it to flutter to the ground. Instead, it shot across the room like a pebble and thudded against the wall. Charlie cocked his head, then crawled on his hands and knees to where the tissue had landed. He unfolded it and found a small key. A number was stamped across the rounded edge.

It was a key to a safe deposit box.

JOHN WAS tired of his sessions with Dr. Elsa King. He was tired of the investigation into Agent Michael Vitelli's murder. He was just tired. Yet here he was, for his sixth session with the good doctor. Soon, he'd be done. He wanted to go back to work without the albatross of these sessions hanging around his neck. He wanted to find Charlie Dallas and this other shooter, whoever he was, and get back to hunting down the bad guys.

He scratched his chin with a thick thumbnail; it made a soft hissing noise, which appeared to nudge Elsa from her daydream. She peered at him over her reading glasses, which she'd been wearing the whole time. Usually, she just held them in her hand.

"I'm sorry," she said. "Did you have an answer to my question?"

Had she asked a question? Maybe he was the one in the daydream.

"What was it again?" he asked, slightly startled. He prided himself on being in control of every situation in which he found himself. But now, he felt as vulnerable as the day that he'd found Richard Zetlan's body.

"Have you given any more thought to our discussion from last time?"

"I suppose," he said, not having any idea what she was referring to.

"You're not being truthful," she said, a touch of disgust hanging in her voice.

"Isn't that a little aggressive, doc?" John asked, leaning back against the couch. "Aren't you supposed to be all touchy-feely?"

"Not when you're quitting on me."

"I'm not quitting!" he erupted, jumping to his feet and towering over his therapist. The power in his voice frightened him, and he looked over at Dr. King, afraid that he'd scared her into a stroke. She was smiling at him. *Jesus*, he thought. The woman had a brass set on her.

"OK," she said. "That's more like it."

"What do you want from me?" he asked, his voice suddenly small and distant. He sat back down on the couch.

Now she did take off her glasses, wrapping them with her short, stubby fingers.

"I want to know what happened," she said. "I want to know about that scar."

"It's in my file," he snapped at her, reflexively touching the dead, twisted flesh on his shoulder. "I'm sure you've read it."

She crossed the room and picked up Hood's personnel file from her desk. "This? I still haven't read it. See for yourself." She tossed the thick envelope over to him. He turned it over and saw that the sticker that verified the envelope had not been opened was still intact. He caressed the raised FBI seal embossed on the sticker.

"You don't know who I am?" he asked.

"No," she said softly. "I want you to tell me."

He stood up and stretched, then went to the window. Stretching out before him was a clear summer day, the sky blue and infinite. In the distance, sunlight glinted from a distant airliner, a tiny diamond shimmering against a field of blue. He thought about the passengers on that flight, cool and comfortable, maybe a little buzzed from an in-flight cocktail. The weather was clear, high pressure dominating the eastern seaboard. They probably couldn't even tell they were six miles up.

"Flight 605," he said suddenly. He turned away from the window, blocking the sun and plunging the room into shade. The temperature seemed to drop ten degrees in an instant.

"What's Flight 605?" she asked.

"Do you believe in God, Elsa?"

"I do," Elsa said.

"You won't," John said.

Elsa was silent.

"How come you never read the file?" he asked, nodding toward her desk.

"Didn't I tell you?"

"That not forming bias bullshit?" he snorted. "I didn't buy it."

"My, my, my," she said, her southern twang thicker than ever, as if she'd turned up the gas underneath her vocal cords. "Aren't we the clever one?"

He shrugged.

"That file," she began, "is none of my business. If I

can't get you to open up about the important things in it without me reading it, then I'm not worth much as a therapist. I feel like I'd be cheating you."

"Don't you worry about your patients lying?"

"No," she said. "I know they're lying. The trick is to get them to want to tell me the truth. If they don't want to be honest with me, then I'm no good to them. To you."

"Oh."

"Now then," she said. "Tell me about the scar."

John Hood coughed softly into one hand. He leaned forward and clasped his hands, tenting his fingers, elbows on his knees.

"I got burned. A long time ago," he said. He knew he was pulling back on her. They were here, at the threshold, but he was too afraid to go beyond it, into the wastelands of his mind.

"Go on," she said. She wasn't going to let him quit.

"It doesn't matter," he said. "It was a long time ago."

"Sure it matters," she said, her voice softening, taking an almost hypnotic quality. "You're the sum of all your experiences. Good and bad. You need to understand how the bad fits in, how it prevents you from growing emotionally."

John was silent now, his eyes glassy and wet. Then he spoke.

"Flight 605 was an Atlantic Airlines 737, non-stop from Newark to Orlando," he said, closing his eyes. "On December 20, 1981, the flight took off on time, carrying two hundred and eighteen passengers. Eight-twenty-nine in the morning. Temperature at takeoff was twenty-nine degrees. There had been some freezing rain that morning, and it was overcast."

In his mind's eye, John could still see the terminal shimmering as the airliner cleared the tower on takeoff. He stretched as far as he could to peer out the window, then settled back into his seat to read. That was when the pilot's voice, which had sounded so strong as they waited to take off (*We're number 3 for takeoff, ladies and gentlemen, we'll be up and out of here in no time...*) had become small and scared (*Folks, uh, we're gonna have to, uh, put her back down. Uh. Pull--*)

"Two minutes into the flight, the pilots lost control of the plane. The plane was at 12,000 feet. They tried to return to Newark for an emergency landing. Forty seconds later," John continued, "the plane crashed in a fireball just short of the runway."

Elsa sat perfectly still. She remembered this plane crash. It had made headlines not only across the country but around the world. Something about the crash. *Had his family been on the plane?*

John was back in seat 26E as Flight 605 entered its final approach. The screams of abject terror. The stench of human waste as the horrific scene unfolded and loosened more than a few bowels on board. He still woke up a few times a week in the dead of night, sheets drenched, the death howl of the doomed passengers echoing in his head so loudly he was afraid that if he opened his eyes, he'd see their ghosts hovering over his bed, wondering why he hadn't joined them. He saw his parents, draping their bodies over his own in what should have been a futile attempt to save their only son. He heard the pilot's last desperate call to the tower. Evidently, the pilots had accidentally activated the intercom during their battle to save the aircraft. Amid the terrified din of the passenger cabin, John had been able to hear the *whoop! whoop!* of the 727's emergency equipment in the background. The hollow dead in the pilot's voice, as if the Grim Reaper himself had taken over the controls.

"Tower. We're not gonna make it."

The last thing he remembered before impact was a pretty young woman in the seat across the aisle, maybe twenty-five years old, hunched over in the crash position, crossing herself. Then blackness.

"My God," she said, more to herself than to John. "You were on the plane."

He nodded.

"It took a dozen fire engines to put out the flames," he explained. "Everyone aboard was presumed dead. A few minutes after the crash, a firefighter spotted someone stumbling in the wreckage. He was babbling about the crash, covered in cuts and scratches. His clothes were charred black. They thought he was a runway employee who'd gotten caught in the debris field. He couldn't remember his name, and no one recognized him."

Now Elsa did remember the crash. The man had gone on and on and on about having been on the plane, but everyone discounted his story. No one could have survived the crash--it had been too fiery, too devastating. Finally, they checked his name against the passenger manifest. Indeed, he had been on the doomed jetliner. She looked up at John, who was staring at her with dead eyes.

"Unbelievable," she said, hoping that she hadn't compromised that clinical detachment that was often critical in a course of treatment.

22

U lysses arrived back at the hotel shortly before five. He went straight to the front desk, where the hotel clerk was blankly studying a sheaf of papers on a clipboard. His eyelids seemed to be drooping with fatigue.

"I'm expecting a fax," Ulysses said, giving the false name under which he'd checked in.

The clerk placed his palm on the counter and bent over toward the bin under the counter. He shuffled through some papers, then shrugged his shoulders.

"No faxes for you, sir."

"Shit," he said.

The clock on the wall behind the counter read 4:57 p.m. There might still be time. He whipped out his cell phone and re-dialed the number for the State Corporation Commission. *Civil servants*, he thought, as he went through the process of requesting another copy of Cowboy Limited's annual report. The SCC employee who took his call was an anomaly, seeming almost happy to help; still, Ulysses didn't dare comment about their failure to send it the first time, lest he still be waiting for his fax when the sun went red giant and swallowed Earth. After relaying the hotel's fax number, he ended the call. Rather than going back to his room, he decided to wait for the fax in the lobby. Pacing like an expectant father in the delivery room, Ulysses's heart soared when he heard the familiar whine of an incoming fax less than three minutes later. The clerk handed the fax to Ulysses, who thanked him and returned quickly to his room.

After lighting a cigar, Ulysses eased onto the bed and began to read. He made it through only a few sweet puffs of tobacco before kicking down the footstool and planning his next road trip. He knew where to find Charles Dallas. Whistling a little jingle, Ulysses packed up his belongings and carried them downstairs, his bags slung over his shoulders like wounded soldiers. This was it. One more job, and it would be time to retire. No more jobs. No more worrying. When Dallas was dead, Ulysses would hightail it to Mexico. He climbed into the car and picked his way through the city to I-95, which would carry him south to I-40 and follow a trail quite similar to one Charlie had taken only a few days before.

CHARLIE LOOKED AT HIS WATCH. It was nearly dinnertime. Dammit. Far too late to get to the bank today. Besides, he didn't know how he was going to get to the box. He wasn't the registered owner, and there was the little matter of his status as a fugitive. He was the next of kin--*OK, that had become debatable*, he thought grimly--maybe that would be enough. Maybe he could talk his way into it. Tricky. Very tricky.

As Charlie wracked his brain, trying to devise a plan to get his hands on the box, another thought bloomed in his head. It had been there since Sanibel, buried under a thin layer of his subconscious like a seedling, just waiting for the right fertilizer. Just before he and Susanna had left for dinner, he'd checked his messages on his cell phone.

The phone was long gone, but maybe his account was still active. He should still be able to access his voice mail. Using the prepaid cell phone that Devo had given him, he punched in his voice-mail number and followed the prompts to access his account.

"You have one saved message," said a pleasant female-sounding electronic voice.

Click.

"Hey, it's Mick. I got a lead on that bank robbery. Call me back."

The caller left a number, which Charlie scratched down on his legal pad before hanging up.

The caller was a private investigator named Mickey Duncan, a former cop who'd lost his badge after a pattern of overly aggressive interrogations of suspects. On his fortieth birthday, Mickey, perhaps feeling a little down about the latest turn of calendar pages, beat to death a juvenile suspect who took a swing at him. In a quiet agreement, the family agreed not to sue the city as long as it dumped Duncan from the force. The police chief, who hated Duncan for many reasons, namely for sleeping with his wife, was ecstatic. Michelle Henderson, the city's Commonwealth's Attorney, decided not to prosecute Duncan for two reasons. First, no one was willing to cross the thin blue line and testify against him. Second, and more importantly, the city's top prosecutor was in the middle of a dogfight campaign against her hardnosed former chief deputy, who had run on a platform that Henderson was far too soft on juvenile offenders, who often grew up to be adult offenders. Henderson hung onto her job by the slimmest of margins, but her opponent's attack TV ads, juxtaposing mug shots of juveniles (of course, with their faces blurred) with the mugshots of their adult selves, charged with more serious crimes, had hit home with the voters. She wasn't about to arrest a decorated police officer for defending himself, even if he had continued delivering his size-thirteen boot to the boy's head for nearly a minute after he'd dropped him to the floor.

With the threat of a criminal prosecution, as well as his badge, behind him, Duncan applied for and received his private ticket after convincing the state board of professions that he possessed the requisite moral character to operate in a quasi-law enforcement capacity. Along the way, he and Charlie had connected. In a quid pro quo arrangement, Mickey tracked down people who didn't always want to be tracked down and photographed them in situations in which they rarely wanted to be photographed. In return, Charlie helped Mickey get access to various events via press pass, a practice the paper officially condemned but secretly encouraged as long as it meant it would sell more papers. If the publisher could sell more papers by dropping bags of puppies into the James River, Charlie was certain they would do it.

Charlie dialed the number that Mickey had left.

"Go," a voice answered on the second ring.

"It's Dallas."

"Hoo, boy," the voice bellowed, starting to laugh. Duncan was originally from Texas, and he hadn't lost one hint of his accent. It seemed to have gotten thicker over the years. "I was wondering if I was gonna hear from you."

"Yeah, I'm in a bit of a pickle."

"Don't tell me! I've had two cops come by asking me about you. Real feds!"

That sent a chill rippling through Charlie's body. It was too late to ask Mickey for help. The cops had already flagged him.

"And?" he asked, afraid of the answer.

"And what? I ain't tell them shit. You know you got nothing to worry about."

"I hear there's a reward."

"The hell with the reward. I wouldn't wipe my ass with their money!"

"You have a lead on that bank robbery?" Charlie asked. He appreciated the loyalty, but it was time to steer the conversation back on topic.

"You're calling me about a story?" Mick bellowed. "Don't you have more important shit to worry about? I mean, come on--"

"The robbery fits into this somehow," Charlie said, raising his voice, desperate to cut him off.

"Into what?"

"Into my current situation."

"You must be shitting me."

"I'm serious," Charlie said, anxious to get to the point.

He liked Mick a lot, but the man had a hard time focusing. "Please. I'll fill you in later. What's the lead?"

"Remember a few months back, you asked me to get a copy of the account holders at the time of the robbery?"

Charlie did remember. While investigating the historical record of the robbery, he'd come to suspect that the thieves had some connection to the bank, whether as employees or customers. The robbers had been familiar with bank procedures and security protocols. Namely, they had been familiar with the fact that on the morning of May 15, 1973, the bank had two million dollars in cash on hand. It had been a hunch, granted, but one Charlie thought was worth playing. And now it looked like Charlie had been right on. He wondered if this had been what tipped off the thieves and set off the current course of events.

"What'd you find?"

"I paid off a teller to get me a list of the activity on each account in the weeks after the robbery," he said, rustling through some papers.

Charlie felt a wave of heat sweep through him, making him feel very uncomfortable. He wanted to get this conversation over with as quickly as possible. He had the feeling someone was watching him. Maybe the cops had bugged Mick's phone. His friendship with Charlie had not been lost on the police.

"How'd you do that?" Charlie asked, curious. It wasn't like they had computers sitting on each desk back in 1973.

Mick made a clicking noise with his tongue. "And therein lies the problem. I've got a file half an inch thick, and I haven't had time to go through it. Honestly, I kind of forgot about it when I heard you were in trouble."

"You still have your contact at the bank?" Charlie asked hopefully. Such a conduit of information could certainly come in handy.

"Naw, she got fired," he said. "She told me they sent a letter to each of the account holders, or their heirs, considering many of them are dead now, explaining the security breach."

"When was this?" Charlie asked, sparking a suspicion in his mind.

"Let me think for a second," Mickey said. "It was just getting warm out because the teller made some comment about it. Maybe two months ago."

"When did she get fired? When did the letters to the account holders go out?"

"A week ago. I called you right when I found out. They fired her as soon as they found out."

Charlie's heart sank. That couldn't have been what had drawn the robbers out of hiding. It was too close to the wedding.

"Hey, Mick?"

"Yeah?"

"How come the police didn't follow this lead back in '73?"

"Beats me. You're the one with the police report."

That was true.

"I need that file you've got."

"I figured as much. Where are you?" Mick asked.

Charlie chewed on his lower lip while he decided how to frame his response.

"I'm on a pay phone," Mick said.

"Captain Pete's," Charlie said. "Holden Beach."

"Holden Beach?" he replied. "That's five hours from here."

"I need your help, buddy."

"Five o'clock. Tomorrow afternoon," he said after a long silence. "I could use some time in the sand."

"I owe you," Charlie said, tears welling up in his eyes. For the first time, he felt like he was moving forward in his impromptu investigation rather than treading water.

"No shit."

Charlie killed the line, tossed the phone aside, and took a deep breath. He wondered if it was possible. Whether the identity of Susanna's kidnappers was tucked away in Mick's dusty old file. A new sensation began to wash over Charlie. Part guilt. Part redemption. It was his fault that Susanna had been kidnapped. His quest to unmask the First National Bank robbers had quite possibly cost him the life of his wife. And yet, he ached to piece the puzzle together. His own life story was interwoven with the story of the First National Bank robbery.

Time to get back to work.

He dug through the mess in the living room and plucked the 1973 police report from the files. Why hadn't the police followed up on the customers' account activity in the weeks after the robbery? Unusual activity would have certainly created red flags for anyone doing even a half-ass job of investigating. He dug through his notes, looking for his interview with the lead detective on the case. Howard Collinsworth. He'd been on the force for five years and had earned his shield at twenty-nine. He was a few days shy of his sixtieth birthday when Charlie interviewed him eight months ago.

Charlie had met with him only once, for about an

hour, and he didn't remember much of their meeting. Luckily, his notes were relatively clear; quickly transcribing his sources' words was one of his gifts as a reporter. It was a handy skill to have in the journalism business. No fewer than three threatened libel suits had disappeared when Charlie's notes had been shown to the allegedly libeled party.

Charlie read through his notes several times, focusing particularly on Collinsworth's recollection of the investigation into the robbery. In several places, mostly in the margins, Charlie had written *Nervous ???* near Collinsworth's comments.

"So," John said, wiping his eyes with the backs of his hands. "What does your psycho-babble bullshit have to say about that? I was on that plane. My old man had scrimped and saved for two years to get us plane tickets to Disney World."

"Why did you ask me about God earlier?" she asked, ignoring his barb.

"Because if you'd been on that plane as it went down, you wouldn't believe in God either."

They sat in silence for a moment, a pair of spent fighters catching their breath.

"May I ask you a question?" she asked in a way that said she was going to ask no matter what.

She had the steely determination of a pilot who was struggling to save his plane, John noticed.

"Whatever."

"What was the cause of the plane crash?" Elsa asked.

John laughed, a harsh guffaw filling the room.

"That was the thing," he said. "The ground crew forgot to de-ice the wings. Such a simple thing. And two hundred and seventeen people died because of it. Can you believe it?"

"It's a terrible thing," Elsa said. "But. . ."

"But what?"

"Why are you here?"

"They made me come here," he snapped. Then, seeing her look: "Anger."

"What did you decide was the root cause of the anger?"

He shrugged.

"Come on, John. We're so close."

"I see things in black and white."

"Why?"

"I don't know!"

"Yes, you do. You just told me."

"Because of the crash?"

She said nothing, not wanting to lose him at this critical moment. She decided to backtrack a bit, take him slowly to where he needed to go.

"What happened after the crash?"

"They took me to the hospital," he said. "An eight-inch piece of the fuselage stuck to my arm. That's where I got this." Methodically, he folded up his sleeve, voluntarily exposing his scar for the first time in his life. The scar ran from his neck, over his shoulder blade, down to the crook of his elbow. The dead, twisted flesh virtually screamed at the now-silent room.

"How long were you in the hospital?"

"Overnight. We didn't have any living relatives, so

they had to figure out what to do with me. I met with Child Protective Services for most of the night after they sewed me up."

"Where did you go after that?"

"Foster care," John said. "I bounced around a few homes until I graduated from high school two years later. Then I managed to get into college, and off I went. I've been on my own since then."

"What was foster care like?"

He shrugged. "It's not that the foster parents didn't care. They just needed the stipends to make ends meet. I lived in three different homes. They really left me alone. I graduated from high school and that was that."

"What about the victims' relatives? Did you ever reach out to them?"

"I went to a memorial a year after the crash," John said. "But it didn't go well. I got the impression they resented me for surviving. I could see it in their eyes. Why me? Why not their sister or husband or daughter? I never spoke to any of them again."

"Do you remember anger being a problem back then?"

"No. Like I said, they left me alone."

"What about in school? Any problems there?"

"My senior year, it got out that I was on the plane. Apparently, some kid in the class had a fascination with plane crashes, and he put two and two together. The other kids didn't know how to deal with that. So they started leaving me alone too. No one knew what to say to me."

"Have you ever been in a fight?"

"Sure," he said.

"I'm not talking about struggling with a suspect," she said. "When you're off duty. At a bar, at a football game, like that."

"No."

"Never?"

He shook his head.

She uncrossed her legs, then recrossed them, which told John she was about to change gears again. His heart hammered against his rib cage, and despite the chill of the office; warmth spread across his midsection.

"When they issued the final report on the crash, how did that make you feel?"

John thought back to the day that Atlantic Airlines and the National Transportation Safety Board issued its final report on the crash. A seven-hundred-page tome, complete with charts, graphs, and illustrations, all basically saying one thing. Someone forgot to de-ice the wings. An NTSB official had delivered the report to John's foster home and had shaken his hand demurely, as if John were a ghost. John stayed up all night reading the report. It astonished him. Such a simple thing. No mysterious mechanical failure. No pilot error. No freak meteorological incident. Just a dumb runway employee who'd been thinking about something else--a fight with his wife, what he was going to have for lunch--and 217 innocent people had died.

"All I could think was how a little simple oversight..." His voice trailed off. "If he'd just checked the wings. That's it. If he'd just checked the wings."

John paused and took a deep breath.

"Everything we say is confidential, right?"

"Yes, pretty much. As long as you don't pull me into

that gray area and tell me you're going to shoot up a McDonald's after our session today."

"Fair enough," he said, satisfied with her answer. "A few years ago, I pulled some strings and got the name of the guy working the flight that morning. Hector Elizondo. The one who hadn't checked the wings for ice. He lived in Rockaway Beach at the time. I drove up there and sat outside his house, waiting for him. I watched him pull in, grab some groceries, and head up to his front door. He was a fat guy, balding, wore old clothes that were too tight. I almost got out of the car, but I decided not to."

"Why didn't you?"

"Didn't know what I would do. Didn't really trust myself."

"What do you mean, you didn't trust yourself?"

He cocked an eyebrow at her.

"Probably a good idea," she said without the slightest hint of sarcasm.

"I waited until he got inside, then I drove home. I never saw him again. I knew if I did, I'd probably kill him."

"What would you have liked to have said to him?"

"How he could've been so stupid, for starters," John said, his voice rising, as if the runway crewman was in the room with them. "Check the wings, boom, the plane makes it to Orlando, and I'm not a footnote in aviation history. I don't go to bed wondering what horrors are waiting for me in my dreams."

"Look, I can't imagine your frustration," she said softly, trying to reassert her control over the session. "But--"

"You're about to get clinical on me, aren't you?"

"Yes, so pay close attention, I'm only going to say this once."

"Excuse me," he said. He was tired and in no mood to put up a fight. He was going to let her say her piece, and then he'd be done with it. He did some quick math in his head. This was his last session. He was off the hook. Thank God.

"As simple as the crash seemed," she began slowly, "it really wasn't."

He looked at her as if she'd slapped him across the side of the head.

"The runway guy, sure, he screwed up," she said. "But the pilot, didn't he have a responsibility to double-check the work? And the air traffic controller? Shouldn't he have had his eye on the air temp? Shouldn't he have said, 'Hey, 605, it's a little nippy out there, check your wings?' Back to the runway guy. Who knows what was going on in his head? Maybe something distracted him. Maybe his wife or his kids were sick, and he was worried about them. Maybe he checked the wings and decided they didn't need de-icing."

"He said he forgot," John snapped, his head reeling from Elsa's machine-gun evaluation of that fateful morning. "I read the transcript of his NTSB interview."

"Fine, whatever," Elsa said. "The key thing is that there could have been many factors at play here. Tragically, these factors combined, and you know the rest."

John leaned forward, elbow on his knee, and he rubbed his eyes. Cloudbursts of color filled the blackness behind his eyelids. This was more than he'd bargained for. Barriers he'd built for years began to crack. It had been so easy to direct his anger at Hector Elizondo alone.

"But more importantly, your focus on this one man has caused you to see things two-dimensionally."

"You ever heard of Occam's razor?" he asked, cutting her off. Right or not, he wasn't ready to cash in his entire belief system without a fight. His sessions with Elsa had helped him realize that yes, he'd lived his whole life based on one driving principle.

"Sure," she answered.

"What is it?" The fact that she knew what it was didn't bode well for his winning this argument.

"The philosophical belief that the simplest explanation is usually the correct one."

"Exactly."

"Usually," she repeated, with emphasis. "John, I agree with you that things aren't always as complicated as they seem or as people make them out to be. If a woman suspects her husband is cheating on her, he probably is. But when you try to force this guiding principle into every situation you encounter, inevitably, there's going to be conflict. Conflict within yourself that ultimately needs an outlet. Sometimes things do get complicated. We live in a complicated world with a lot of interdependency."

John was silent. He had no answer for this.

"I want you to do something for me."

"What?" he mumbled. He felt like an overmatched boxer, his opponent gaining the upper hand and circling for the knockout blow.

"Think back to your worst episodes," she said. "When you just absolutely lost it."

A montage of rage flashed through his mind.

"What set them off?"

"I don't know."

"Come on," she said. "Concentrate on them. Live through them again. Even if it's painful or embarrassing."

"A couple of tough cases," he said, his eyes closed, his chin nearly touching his chest. "A relationship gone bad. That kind of thing."

"Do you see?"

He was starting to see. The vagaries of the Dallas case began to trickle into his consciousness.

"What can I do?" he asked.

"Try to realize that not everything fits into a neat little box," she said. "Sometimes it does. Hell, most of the time, it does. But open your mind to the possibility that there may be another answer, one hiding beneath the surface. One clouded by a seemingly correct one."

He nodded. "I'll try."

She exhaled and leaned back in her chair, obviously spent mentally.

"Good."

23

John's first instinct was to drive to Phillips' Pub, spending the rest of the day and night drinking pints of Guinness and eating his weight in chicken wings. He managed to fight off the urge, but only barely. The thing that kept him going was the trinket he'd found at the Sleep Rite Motel. He'd made an appointment with a jeweler named Lucas, a nutjob who specialized in strange jewelry, the kinds of gems and stones that the chain stores didn't advertise around Christmas. The FBI had used him on several occasions, and despite his general weirdness, John found him to be fairly helpful. On one occasion, Lucas had deduced the significance of a charm dropped at a murder scene, which led the FBI and local cops directly to the murderer. It wasn't entirely altruistic on Lucas's part; his cooperation made sure John didn't leak his name to the local police narcotics unit, or even worse, the DEA. That would have seriously crimped Lucas's low-level marijuana business that helped supplement his income.

A steady rain was falling by the time John made his way to the corner of Sixth and Grace, where Lucas's little shop made its home. The air was still thick with humidity, giving the afternoon a greasy, soupy feel to it. Lucas' shop, Metal Works, made its home in the basement of a restored three-story Victorian, and Lucas rented the space from the VCU music professor who owned the place.

John descended the stone steps carefully, as they were slick with rain, and jangled the bell as he stepped inside. He was met with the burnt cinnamon smell of incense and recently smoked marijuana. The joint was like a dungeon, illuminated by blacklight and dull red bulbs. John wasn't sure how anyone spent any length of time here without going mind-blowingly insane. Then again, considering the proprietor, John wasn't convinced anyone did.

The shop consisted of a single room lined with display cases that were stuffed with every manner of rings, bracelets, necklaces, and earrings, along with studs and rods that appeared suited to pierce any part of the human anatomy. One case displayed necklaces made from what appeared to be human bone. Charms depicting dragons, snakes, snarling hyenas, and other creatures of the night filled a box on one counter while another overflowed with various polished and unpolished rocks. Richly colored tapestries hung from the wall.

A curtain at one end of the room fluttered, and Lucas stepped out in response to the bell's jingle. His thick, round face sank when he saw who had come calling. He was about John's height but weighed about twice as much. His thin red hair was pulled back in a ponytail, which did nothing but call attention to his severe acne problem. He wore baggy jeans that looked dirty even in the dim light and a baja-type pullover. John had never been able to get a good read on the guy's age, narrowing his estimate to somewhere between twenty and fifty.

"Lucas, what's happening, my man?" John asked.

"I thought you said you wouldn't tell the cops about me," he said softly. If there was one thing Lucas didn't like, it was confrontation.

"Sorry, Luc, I can't stop them from doing actual police work."

"They've been hassling me," he offered. "It's hurting my business."

"And if you go under, I'll definitely miss our little chats."

Lucas squealed in anger, the high-pitched whine of a small boy who hasn't gotten what he wanted.

"I need you to look at something," John said.

"Why should I help you?"

John reached across the case and yanked Lucas by his ponytail. The man's head whipped around like a top.

"Because if you don't, I'll put your head through this display case. And then I will call the DEA and bust up this little ring you've got going here."

John let go of the ponytail as quickly as he'd grabbed it, Elsa's words sneaking up on him. John shook his head. "You know, one of these days, I'm just going to arrest you myself."

Lucas scrunched up his nose in disgust and said: "Let me see it."

John dug in his pocket and extracted the item, slapping it down on the glass counter. Underneath, a small

replica of a human skull stared back at him. The eye
sockets were void and black, and the entire skull glowed
in the strange light of the room. *Jesus*, Hood thought. *As if
I don't get enough of this at work.*

With a small magnifying glass and a flashlight, Lucas
began studying the butterfly-shaped trinket. John wished
he could come up with a better word for it, but "trinket"
was all he had.

"I didn't make this," Lucas said. "But I wish I did."

"I'm glad you like it," John said. "Maybe you'll find
one in your stocking next Christmas. Any idea who did
make it? Or even better, who bought it?"

"Do you even know what it is?" Lucas asked with the
air of someone who very rarely had the intellectual upper
hand and thoroughly enjoyed it when he did.

"No, and I don't care."

"You should."

"Why?"

"Because this is a one-of-a-kind item, made for one
specific person."

With the charm in the palm of his hand, Lucas illuminated it with his flashlight.

"These are Army dog tags, twisted and molded
together to make the shape of the star. But you can see
the original names still on the tags. Look."

Now he handed John the magnifying glass and shone
the light on it himself. Sure enough, they looked like real
dog tags.

"They seem too thin to be the real thing," John said.

"That's the beauty of it," Lucas said. "The designer
thinned them out to make them more malleable but
preserved the original metal stamping. It's brilliant."

"Can you separate out the tags?" John asked, a plan forming in his head. "While keeping the names on the tags intact?"

"I think so," Lucas said. "It's going to take an hour or so."

"Give me each one as you finish."

LUCAS LAID out the five dog tags on the counter like a Texas hold'em dealer and handed Hood a magnifying glass. With pen in hand, he scratched out the names that appeared on each tag. Anderson Hensley. Philip Barker. Edward Bourne. Joseph Pinero. Anthony Burnette. Five men. Hood returned the tags to the evidence baggie and folded up the slip of paper bearing the men's names.

"A little somethin' for the trouble?" Lucas asked hopefully.

"Get out of my face," John said, spinning on his heel and marching out the door.

He drove back to the field office, which sat in the northeastern corner of Richmond amid a collection of warehouses and tractor-trailer drop lots. The building occupied about half a city block and housed twenty-four agents and sixteen support staff, along with the countless files and computer hardware necessary to combat crime in the twenty-first century. The office was physically divided by unit, so each agent assigned to a specific group worked with his fellow unit members. Each unit was headed up by a unit chief, all of whom reported to Hood, who in turn reported to Thomas Bagwell.

He went straight to the Intelligence division, which

had access to a number of databases, including certain ones maintained by the Department of Defense. In this database, John hoped to track down the five men identified in the dog tags, which he hoped would lead to Vitelli's killer. To do that, he went straight to the office of Dan Case, an agent in Intelligence with a knack for synthesizing a large amount of raw information into a more useful format.

As always, Dan's door was open, giving a passerby a window into the chaos that was his office. Stacks of printouts littered the floor like snowdrifts, along with case files, computer disks, reference books, and his passion, model sports cars. He must have had about two dozen of them in here. Corvettes, Porsches, Alfa Romeos. A sixteen-year veteran, Dan was several years older than Hood, married to a pediatrician and father of five boys.

Dan was on the phone when Hood poked his head in, and he waved John in. When John met his stare, Dan rolled his eyes and pointed at the receiver. He covered the mouthpiece and said, "I don't know where they get these idiots to run VICAP." VICAP was an acronym for Violent Criminal Apprehension Program, a database that helped law enforcement compare and connect crimes they were investigating to unsolved crimes that already had been cataloged.

"Sit down, sit down," Dan whispered, pointing to the two chairs. John shook his head, preferring to stand, even if both chairs had not been occupied by file boxes. A few minutes later, Case finally ended the call.

"Gosh," he said, shaking his head as he replaced the receiver. A devout Christian, Case's expletives rarely strayed further than 'gosh.' "They weren't much help. What's up?"

John explained the history behind the dog tags and the men's names. As he finished, Case was already tapping away at the keyboard of one of his three desktop computers that manned his office like silent sentinels.

"You can get this stuff on that computer?"

"John, don't you read the tech updates I send out?"

John scratched his head and looked away. He had about six months' worth of them sitting in his office. The idea of going back to street-level duty seemed more appealing than ever.

"Forget it," Case said. "Yes, we can get it. Bagwell's part of a committee that's trying to link us with as many government databases as we can. The Pentagon was not happy with the idea, so we let them set it up. We don't get a lot of information from it right now. They call it a beta version, say they'll upgrade the information in the coming months. I think they're just blowing smoke up our . . . well, you get the idea.

"OK, Anderson Hensley," Case said aloud, typing the name in simultaneously. "Born in Detroit, June 1947, served in Vietnam in the Fourth Infantry Division, Second Armored Cavalry." He repeated the process with each of the names from the dog tags.

"Interesting," he said as his fingers flew across the keyboard. His typing accelerated, as if he was anxious to confirm some newly developed suspicion.

"What?"

"These guys all died in Vietnam," Case said.

"Lots of guys died in Vietnam," John said.

"Yes, thanks for the history lesson, Professor," Case

quipped. "These guys all died on the same day. October 29, 1972."

"Really?"

"Yes," Case said, pointing to the screen. John stepped around the desk and peered at the screen over Case's shoulder.

"Do me a favor," John said. "I need to get back to my office. Can you cross-reference these names, see what the link is between them? Is there enough information for you to do that?"

"I think so."

"Call me whenever you find something."

IT WAS NEARLY eight o'clock when Case finally called. John had just finished a set of pushups, a hundred of them, and his arms burned with fatigue. He pushed the speakerphone button on his handset as he dropped into his chair, and Case's voice filled the room.

"You found something?" John asked hopefully, wiping his sweaty brow with the back of his arm.

"These men were all Army," Case said. John could hear him shuffling with papers in the background.

"What happened to them?"

"I couldn't get a lot of details, but here's what I could find. On the morning of October 29, 1972, their squad— twelve of them—were on patrol in a little town called Buon Ma Thuot, about 200 miles northeast of Saigon. They got ambushed by a squad of North Vietnamese soldiers posing as villagers, and eleven were killed."

"Eleven?"

"Yeah, there was one survivor, a second lieutenant named Ervin Coleman. Born in Richmond, Virginia. He put up a fight, picked off half the Vietnamese soldiers by himself until they just gave up and left him alone. He was up for a Medal of Honor, but he never got it. Not sure why. That part was classified. There's nothing in his record after that. I couldn't find out if he was wounded, if he was discharged, if he was sent home. Nothing."

"What about a current address? I don't suppose we'd be that lucky."

"Well, my clean-shaven friend, today is your lucky day. His number's unlisted, but I tracked down an address, and the identifying information seems to match up to his service record."

"Beautiful," John said, getting up from his desk. "Thanks. Can you send me the file on Coleman?"

"Sure."

Hood pressed the speakerphone button again, killing the line. Silence engulfed the room as John tried to process this new information. He tried to picture Coleman on that morning, watching his comrades die, one by one, coming to that terrible realization that he was all alone. John knew the feeling. He wondered about the gaps in Coleman's service record after the Buong Ma Thuot incident. What had happened to him? Had that been the first step in a chain of events that ended with him killing Mike Vitelli? These questions and others rattled around his head as he put together a fourteen-man team to raid Ervin Coleman's home.

∾

THIRTY-ONE MINUTES LATER, a pair of black Chevy
Suburbans glided to a halt in front of the small cottage
where Ulysses, born Ervin Coleman, made his home.
The men were dressed in black pants and navy blue
SWAT windbreakers, large enough to slip over the
Kevlar body armor protecting their vital organs. They
moved swiftly and in harmony, parts of a single whole.
Each man carried an H&K MP5 submachine pistol and
was strapped with a nine-millimeter Baretta pistol.
Eight agents, paired off in two-man teams, took posi-
tions at each corner of the old building. Two more
agents scurried down the narrow alley on the west side
of the house and covered the back door. Two crept up
the stairs to Apartment No. 5. Two more agents trailed
behind, carrying the miniature battering ram that
would serve as the key in case no one answered the
door.

Officer Tim Norton secured his weapon in his right
hand and pounded on the door three times with his left.
The knock echoed down the stairwell and into the street,
where a small crowd of onlookers had gathered. This
wasn't your everyday sort of thing in this neighborhood.
No answer.

"Ervin Coleman!" Norton called out, fully expecting
to find an empty apartment. No way he'd come back here.

No answer. Norton turned and nodded at the pair of
agents behind him. Officer Catherine Burke radioed the
two agents at the back of the house, who prepared their
own inward jailbreak. Norton's colleagues stepped
forward with the ram, which looked very similar to a steel
log with handles, reared back, and delivered a single
blow to the door, right at the deadbolt. The door tore

away from the frame like an overdone turkey leg from its socket and toppled over into Ulysses's living room.

The four agents rushed into the room, pistols raised, shouting, "Everyone down!"

A few seconds later, all fourteen agents were inside, scouring the apartment like rats looking for food. When they were satisfied the apartment was empty, they turned their attention to securing evidence. Outside, two city police cruisers had sealed off the block, and an FBI evidence van had arrived on the scene.

Norton was picking through some papers on a desk when Burke called out his name. She was scanning a document she had found in the tray of the fax machine.

"This is time-stamped late this afternoon," Burke said, handing the document to him.

The document was a printout from the State Corporation Commission. Cowboy Limited. 231 Ocean Blvd. Holden Beach, North Carolina.

"This is where he's headed," Norton said.

As HE EXITED off I-95 and looped onto I-40, Ulysses touched his fingers to his necklace, as he often did whenever he needed some luck. Like before a big mission. Problem was, the necklace wasn't there. Panic squeezed his heart, and he began pawing around the seats and center console as he merged into traffic from the on-ramp. An eighteen-wheeler roared by him as he drifted into its lane, but he scarcely noticed the twenty-ton behemoth that nearly flattened him. He checked his mirrors quickly, then swerved into the breakdown lane at sixty miles an hour, kicking up a cloud of dust and gravel as he did so. He clawed through the detritus in his vehicle, flipping up dirty mats and unrolling wads of used napkins. Nothing. "Dammit!" he bellowed to no one.

When he'd searched every square inch of the passenger cabin, he stepped outside and repeated the process in the trunk, knowing full well he wouldn't find it in there. He climbed back into the driver's seat, pounded the wheel with his fist, and lit a stale cigarette he'd found in the glove compartment.

"Shit!" he yelled. He pounded the steering wheel again to the cadence of his profanity. "Shit!"

It was gone.

The clasp had been a little shaky the last couple of weeks, but he'd been putting off getting it fixed. And now he was paying for his indiscretion. Unbelievable. No use worrying about it now. He gave the dashboard one final thud, then pressed the accelerator to the floor. The Bronco fishtailed to the right before the treads caught, and he zoomed back into traffic.

What a shitty day this was turning out to be. First, the fax from the SCC had never shown up at the hotel. He'd had to call them back and have them send a second copy. And now this.

24

By the next afternoon, Charlie was a mess. He had slept poorly, no more than twenty minutes at a stretch, and never deeply. He had spent more time pacing the house than asleep, and his nerves were shot with twin blasts of caffeine and nicotine. He wondered if he'd be able to quit smoking again. If he ever got out of this alive. He shook his head. If he got the chance to worry about whether to go with the nicotine patch or the gum, he'd consider himself lucky.

Time was running out on him, on Susanna, on his entire existence. Eventually, someone was going to track him down here, whether it was the kidnappers, the police, or God forbid, the FBI agent's killer, here to finish the job. He just didn't know where else he could go. He could only hope that the information that Mick was supposed to deliver would open more doors for him, doors that would eventually lead him to Susanna's kidnappers and hopefully to Susanna herself.

Mick hadn't called him today. Charlie hadn't expected

him to, but deep down, he wouldn't have minded a quick phone call, a "Hey, Charlie, I'm on my way, no one's following me, and we're gonna nail these bastards." It would have helped a lot. At four, he ate two peanut butter sandwiches and drank sixteen ounces of water. He wanted to drink more, but that was all he could drink and be confident that his bladder wouldn't rupture inside of an hour.

He packed his few belongings, as well as his notes on the bank robbery, the safe-deposit box key, and the attached receipt. Looking at his gear laid out on the coffee table, he realized he'd been reduced to the life of a nomad. Although he'd found some refuge here, he didn't know where he'd be spending that night. Maybe here. Maybe in a hotel. Maybe in jail. Amazing how easily one took for granted his day-to-day routine. Human nature was something else. Your average American bitched and moaned about the rut of his life and lived for his two weeks of vacation each year. But when that vacation came, and the last day or two rolled around, he was ready to get back to the routine he knew. The commute, the stop for coffee, the arguments with the wife, the job-induced stress headaches. Charlie himself would have given anything to know he'd be sleeping in his own bed, back in Richmond, Susanna curled up against his shoulder, leafing through a Cosmo.

A glance at his watch told him it was time to move. The seafood market was about two miles away, which Charlie estimated would take at least twenty minutes on foot, considering his extra load. He stepped out onto the porch, locked the house, and made his way down the steps. It was a brutally hot day, the kind where waves of heat shimmered off the blacktop and the humidity was so thick that it killed any hope of a cooling breeze.

At the end of his street, he turned west on Ocean Boulevard. The sidewalks were thick with beachgoers headed back to their houses after a long, carcinogenic bath. A blue Ford Bronco slowed and turned onto his street. Charlie didn't notice it.

ULYSSES WATCHED Charlie down the road, confident that he'd found his target. He looked different than his picture, but who else would be hoofing it down this street, on his way out of town, a heavy pack strapped to his back?

Easing up on the gas pedal, Ulysses coasted down Sailfish, away from Ocean Boulevard. He couldn't risk a U-turn right now; Dallas might get spooked and create a scene. Ulysses would have to hang back and trail from a safe distance. Luckily, he'd brought binoculars, and besides, Dallas was on foot; he wouldn't be going anywhere fast. Still, Ulysses couldn't afford to lose him. He might not be able to track him down so easily the next time.

Ulysses pulled into the driveway of an unoccupied house and stepped out of his truck. Stretched his legs, made like a tourist reaching his destination after a long drive. With his binoculars, he kept Dallas in his sights. He was about half a mile away now, jogging slowly. A few minutes later, Ulysses got back in his car and began the slowest car chase of his life. He stayed well back, venturing no closer than a quarter-mile of Dallas.

Ulysses wondered where the man was going. Off the island? Without a car? It was a long walk back to Richmond. He didn't seem like he was planning to hitch right now either. Maybe when he was back on the mainland. As he followed, Ulysses mentally inventoried his weapons and tried to decide which one would be best for the job. Hell, maybe he could use the Bronco to take care of him.

Nah.

Too risky. No guarantee of success. Maybe he rolls over the hood, up the windshield, and onto a soft strawberry patch, gets up, and memorizes Ulysses's license plate. He'd have to give up the truck, and he loved this truck. Plus, all it would take was one mildly observant witness to take down a license plate. Even a partial was all the police would need.

Best to just follow him. For now.

JUST A FEW MILES to the east, John Hood approached the little hamlet of Holden Beach with half a dozen agents from the Wilmington field office. The agents rode in three unmarked cars, escorted by two more police cruisers, courtesy of the Brunswick County Sheriff's office. John was silent, anxious to capture Dallas and Coleman, but careful not to unnerve the Wilmington agents, who had not warmed to him since he showed up early that morning. They still weren't sure that Dallas would be down here, but Hood felt a strong sense this was where Dallas had fled. Somewhere familiar, somewhere he'd feel safe and comfortable. And had it not been for the ingenuity of a man who was probably out to kill Dallas, they might not have found him this quickly.

Despite his best efforts, he had not secured a flight to Wilmington the night before. Bagwell made the call, deciding that the operation could best be handled by the local field office. Hood had told him he was going to Wilmington, whether it was by plane, car, train, or on the back of a giant Texas jackrabbit. He would be there for the collar.

"Just get out of here," Bagwell had finally said, defeated. He sounded like a man tired of dealing with a huge pain in his ass. John knew that a reversion to street duty might be more than just a career option. It might be forced upon him. Maybe in the Omaha field office, or somewhere equally sexy.

Up ahead, the causeway rose like a steel and concrete dragon. The cavalry zoomed over it, the police cruisers' lights flashing, breaking the serenity of the beach community, the equivalent of shattering a beer bottle to announce the start of a bar brawl.

MICK DUNCAN SAT in his Ford pickup just outside Captain Pete's market. A cigarette dangled from his lips, and his Yankees baseball cap was pushed low over his brow, shielding his face from the blinding sunwash. He was in a Ford F-150, big and roomy.

Every few minutes he poked his head up like a gopher and scanned the scene around him. The building, which also housed a fancy-looking seafood restaurant, was perched right on the dock of the sound and was surrounded by a dusty, gravel-coated parking lot. The building was held together by nothing more than wooden planks and goodwill, considering the beating it took every summer from thunderstorms and other tropical systems that ravaged the eastern seaboard. A trawler was currently docked at the pier, unloading its catch for the day. From the looks of it, they'd brought in a good catch. Several of the shrimpers leaped across the void between the dock and boat for a quick smoke in the shadows.

The dashboard clock read 5:02. He hated it when people were late. Even two minutes late. He stepped out of the cab into the blazing heat and paced around it. He pitched a half-smoked cigarette to the lot and smoked another one. He checked the clock again. 5:08. *Where the hell was he?*

CHARLIE'S LOAD was heavier than he expected. By the time the causeway came into view, his arms burned, and his legs ached. His level of fitness was not ideal. He hadn't worked out much since meeting Susanna. He crossed the intersection feeding onto the bridge and took a left at the next block.

A wave of relief rippled through him. Mick was there. The guy had come through. Charlie had imagined Mick stumbling around Richmond all day with a hangover, certain that he was supposed to be somewhere. But that didn't matter now. The guy was here.

"Mick!" he called out, dropping his bags to the dusty ground.

"Damn," Mick said softly. "You look like hell."

They shook hands.

"Thanks for noticing."

"My pleasure."

"You've got the files with you?"

He nodded and leaned in the driver's side door while Charlie scanned the area around them. He felt so exposed here, hoping they could wrap this up and--

And what? Charlie didn't know what he was supposed to do next. Should he hitch a ride back to Richmond with Mick? Would Mick even take him?

PERFECT.

Ulysses had parked about two hundred yards away from Duncan's pickup truck, just behind one of the causeway's thick concrete pylons. Behind him was an abandoned tennis court, its net missing, its surface cracked and overgrown with weeds. He set to work assembling the Barrett M82A2 rifle. Without taking his eyes off Charlie and the other man, Ulysses expertly put together the large pieces of the rifle. A scope. Within sixty seconds, he had chambered a round and was mechanically ready to fire. Now he just had to prepare himself mentally. In this line of work, you only got one chance.

He peered through the scope, thankful for the good weather. Clear, no wind. He altered the trajectory ever so slightly to account for the soupy humidity that could affect the bullet's flight path. Then he willed himself into an almost meditative state, slowing his heart rate, slowing his respiration, so that his shot would not be at the mercy of his body's physiological responses.

He was ready. Ten. Nine. Eight. Seven. Six. Five.

"DAMMIT!" barked Mick.

"What's wrong?" Charlie asked nervously.

"Oh, nothing. The file just fell between the seats."

"Jesus, you scared the shit out of me."

"Sorry."

Mick leaned further into the cab and reached across the passenger side. He felt around for a bit, then clamped down on the file with three fingers.

"WHAT's on the back side of the house?" Hood asked. Shielding his eyes from the sun, he watched the blacktop disappear underneath the car. If his calculations were correct, they were less than a quarter-mile from the turnoff.

"A small yard, backing up to a canal," said one of the Wilmington agents. He had a plat of the neighborhood spread out across his lap.

"No back way out then."

"No."

The caravan turned north onto Sailfish and rolled toward the cottage.

A LINE of thunderstorms had rolled through earlier that afternoon, soaking the town with an inch of rain in less than an hour. The storms had been fierce but short and had left residual clouds slipping across the sky like lost tourists. One such cloud had slid in front of the sun like a blanket; for the past few minutes, it had provided welcome relief to the hundreds of sunbathers dotting the coastline a few hundred yards away. At this moment, however, the cloud decided to move on to points east and released the sun's bright rays from captivity.

The day brightened instantly, and a ray of light glinted across Ulysses's line of sight at the precise moment he had applied sufficient pressure to the trigger. He blinked the blindness away, and the movement of his eyelid shifted the rifle ever so slightly. *Four. Three. Two. One.* The boom of the rifle echoed under the causeway.

CHARLIE TOOK the file and immediately opened it, unable to resist the urge. He was greeted by an index of names, dates, and transactions. He closed the file and told himself that now was not the time.

"Thanks," Charlie said, extending his hand and stepping toward Mick, who was back in the driver's seat.

"Sure." They shook. "What are you going to do-"

BOOM!

Charlie dropped to the ground and rolled, scraping every exposed inch of flesh against the rough, gritty parking lot gravel. As he tumbled to the ground, he heard the distinct sound of metal piercing metal. He continued rolling, not sure what had happened.

The sound that Charlie heard was the armor-piercing round from Ulysses's rifle, slicing through the pickup's chassis and into the fuel tank. Mick never had a chance. The hot bullet ignited the vapors in the half-empty tank, like a match to tinder-dry brushland, and the truck exploded, consuming fuel, plastic, metal, and human flesh in the resulting holocaust.

The fireball mushroomed like an atomic cloud, shooting burning debris for a hundred-yard radius. The blast wave blew Charlie about fifty feet across the parking lot; it was as if a giant, invisible hand had picked him up and thrown him aside. His face smacked the gravel full bore, and the tiny rocks tore his flesh like the teeth of a wild animal.

JOHN'S HEAD swung east as the sonic boom reached him, and he watched the ball of flame erupt in the distance.

"Holy Christ!" the driver barked. "What the hell was that?"

"I don't know," said Hood. "Let's check it out."

"Negative," the driver said. "Our orders are to raid the house. Let the locals handle that. We don't even have jurisdiction."

"Forget our orders," Hood said, jabbing his thumb in the direction of the fireball. "That's what we're looking for."

"No," the driver said. "We raid the house first. The locals can check that out."

"Now!" barked Hood.

The agent, whose name was Winston, seemed to hesitate. He slowly moved his foot to the brake, giving John his chance. The car slowed to a crawl, and John flung the door wide open. He jumped from the car and bolted around to the driver's side.

"What the hell are you doing?" Winston yelled. His eyes were as wide as saucers.

John ripped open the driver's side door and grabbed Winston by the collar, then dragged him onto the baking asphalt. He drew Winston toward him, their faces inches apart. John could feel Winston's hot, ragged breath on his face. "I told you, that's where we needed to go."

"You're a psychopath!"

John shoved him out of the way and jumped back into the car. He pressed the accelerator to the floor, and the air filled with the smell of burnt rubber as he spun a U-turn and headed back out toward the main road. One by one, the other cars in the caravan slowed to a halt, and their occupants stepped out to observe the scene unfolding before them. One agent from the closest car sprinted to Winston's defense, but John was already gone.

"Should we follow him?" Winston asked, rubbing his forehead where he'd scraped it.

"Naw," he said. "Let's raid the cottage first. Then we'll go get that bastard."

Ulysses was paralyzed. He'd missed. Badly. Thirty precious seconds ticked away before he remembered the necessity of vacating the premises. He didn't bother with breaking down the rifle; he just tossed it into the back of the Bronco like a loaf of bread. He got in, revved the engine, and hit the gas. As he spun the wheel and bounced across the rough hardtop, he took one more peek at the target area. The husk of the Bronco was still burning, sending a thick plume of black smoke into the afternoon sky. About fifty feet away, Charlie's soot-stained and battered body stirred slowly.

In a panic, Ulysses cut across a small access road instead of following the same one he used to drive in. He didn't see a jagged piece of Mick's pickup lying nearby, shot here in the force of the explosion. His right front tire caught the edge of the metal shard and blew out; the Bronco yawed and pitched to the right. A tremor of fear rippled through his body as the truck began to shimmy, and he pulled the wheel hard to the left. All of the Bronco's kinetic energy seemed to gravitate to the fatally wounded tire.

Oh, shit, he thought, as he felt the top-heavy vehicle begin to tip.

He yanked the wheel hard to the left; the force of Ulysses's attempt to regain control of the vehicle finally overtook the truck's ability to remain upright. The Bronco tipped onto its side with a loud crash and lay still like an injured animal on the African prairie. Not wearing his seatbelt, Ulysses tumbled to the truck's new floor--the passenger door. His head smacked against the door frame with a loud thud, and warm liquid oozed across his scalp. White light filled his field of vision before he was able to regain his bearings.

"Goddammit!" he bellowed. Of all the luck. Bad enough that he hadn't finished the job. Now he'd lost his ride out of Dodge. *OK, relax,* he told himself. Everyone's going to be focused on the explosion. He was just an innocent bystander. Just concentrate on getting out of here. He wedged his body around the front seats and snaked his way into the rear cargo hatch. His footlocker had popped open in the crash, and gun parts were strewn about the cabin like a child's toys. A Glock had gotten wedged in the tire well, and Ulysses grabbed it as he made his way to the rear hatch.

His head ached. He pressed his palm to the back of his skull and brought his hand to his face. It was slick with blood. He wished he could stop for a few minutes and rest, but he figured that would be a bad idea. The cops would focus on the explosion for a while, true, but then they'd start looking for what caused it. He had to get out of here.

A few painful bursts later, he reached the rear hatch. And then it hit him. No handle back here. Shit! He'd have to shoot out the window. He pushed back a few feet, covered his face and ears with his free arm, and fired a single round into the window.

THE REPORT OF ULYSSES' second gunshot of the afternoon pricked John's ears as he approached the scene of the explosion. He took his foot off the gas and scanned the area underneath the causeway. To his right, about fifty yards away, he could see the ruined remains of Duncan's pickup smoldering in the afternoon sun. A man-shaped husk, resembling a burned scarecrow, lay on the ground near the truck. Hood wondered if he'd finally found Charlie Dallas.

His peripheral vision caught sight of something

moving to his left. He swung his head and saw a second figure, on his hands and knees, crawling away from the wreckage. Hood braked hard, and the wheels locked; the car fishtailed before coming to a halt. He tapped his hip for his weapon before bursting from the car.

ULYSSES PULLED himself through the sea of glass, shimmering and brilliant in the sunshine. His headache had evolved into a dull throb. He checked the P229 pistol--three rounds left in the clip. That would be enough to keep him safe. When he looked up, he saw a man crawling towards him. He looked at him carefully, then realized that this was the man he'd come here to kill. *Unbelievable.* Sometimes luck was better than Darwinism. He pulled the slide back and chambered a round.

CHARLIE'S HEAD WAS SPINNING. The blast wave had left him a little loopy, and he was having a hard time regaining his bearings. One thing was certain though. The game was up. He was too weak to get much farther under his own power. He made certain the file was still tucked under his arm, then rolled over to a sitting position, his legs crossed underneath him. In the distance, but closing rapidly, he could hear the growing wail of emergency sirens. He'd show them the files, tell them everything that had happened, starting in Sanibel, and hope for the best. That would have to do. These law enforcement types, they were reasonable people. He hoped.

"I'm sorry, Susanna," he whispered. "I did all I could."

He took a deep breath; his lungs filled with hot, acrid smoke, and he felt lightheaded. From the corner of his eye, he spotted someone moving toward him. The man was armed, his weapon by his side. They made eye contact, and Charlie slowly raised his hands over his head. His left arm burned where the flames had licked his skin. *Don't startle him*, Charlie thought. *Make it nice and easy*. He was twenty yards away, then ten.

When the man raised his sidearm to a firing position, Charlie's heart began pattering a little more quickly.

SHIT, John thought, breaking into a run. The armed man was almost on top of the second one. He drew his weapon, grunting as he sprinted across the dusty parking lot.

"Put the gun down!" he barked, leveling his weapon and assuming a three-point firing stance. Thirty yards or so. A shot from this distance was an easy one for John, but he was hoping to take everyone alive if he could. If not, well, John thought back to his training--cops were trained to fire into a target's torso, which, as luck would have it, was usually a lethal shot. Ulysses's head, which had been focused on Charlie, perked up suddenly and turned toward the new threat.

Ulysses's weapon followed its owner, like a tank turret revolving toward a new target.

"Down, now!"

Ulysses slowly removed one hand from the barrel of his gun and held it up, palm out. John exhaled, relieved. He was going to surrender. Then, just as quickly, Ulysses took one step forward, like a quarterback stepping up in the pocket to pass, and balanced the butt of the pistol in his free hand. Before John could react, he heard the report of the gun. He felt the hot burn of a round whizzing past his face.

Desperate, John squeezed his trigger three times in less than three seconds. The pistol roared but stayed level; the shots stayed pure. The bullets hit him square in the chest, forming the points of a bloody triangle. The force of the bullets' impact slammed him to the ground like he'd been run over by a truck.

John stumbled forward and dropped to one knee. He wasn't sure if he'd been hit; he was afraid that once the adrenaline wore off, he'd see the red stain already blossoming on his shirt.

A few seconds passed, and he became satisfied that he hadn't been hit. He refocused his attention on Ulysses, who was perfectly still. His weapon had been jarred loose and was lying about three feet away from his body.

It was over.

25

"Please tell me you're a cop," Charlie said. The front of his shirt was caked with dust and grime, and he was in the back seat of John's car, handcuffed.

"I am," John said, reaching into his pocket and removing his credentials. He held the badge near Charlie's face, and Charlie read each line carefully.

"FBI," Charlie said.

"That's right." John folded the creds and slipped them back into his pocket. "Tell me you didn't kill that FBI agent back in Richmond."

"What?"

"I need to hear you say it."

"I didn't kill him," Charlie said softly.

John felt like he was having an out-of-body experience, as if he was watching the scene between Charlie Dallas, fugitive, and John Hood, FBI agent. Every fiber of his being told him that Dallas hadn't killed anyone, but the whole scene just made him want to laugh. He was gambling his whole career on a hunch. A hunch!

"Alright, I believe you. I just needed to hear it from you. But that being said, I'm probably not the best guy to have as your main supporter."

"What do you mean?"

John watched a seagull swoop in from the causeway and land softly on a nearby trash bin. The cavalry would be here soon, and he was going to have two big problems. One was assaulting Agent Winston. Two was the suspect he'd just shot and killed. He'd be placed on administrative leave immediately for the shooting. Standard operating procedure. With a suspension thrown in for good measure. He'd then be thrown so far off this case, he'd have to read the newspaper to learn anything about it.

Another thought occurred to him. Mashing the pedal to the floor and getting out of here with Charlie Dallas in tow. He couldn't. It was the equivalent of pushing his career to its knees and blowing its brains out. And besides, what evidence did he have that Dallas was innocent? Maybe he and the dead guy had been in on Vitelli's murder together, and the dead guy had turned on Charlie. It happened all the time. But if he just waited for the bureaucratic machinery to process the scene, the truth might be lost forever.

"What were you doing with Vitelli?" John asked suddenly, turning his head toward his prisoner. Charlie's head was low, his chin resting on his chest. Charlie looked up with a firmly set jaw.

"I'm looking for my wife," Charlie said, his voice thick with heartbreak. "She was kidnapped."

The wail of emergency sirens drew ever closer, and John could see the oscillating red lights of approaching police cruisers. He was running out of time. Three cars bounced into the parking lot and zoomed toward the scene; officers erupted from the cars like they'd been riding in ejector seats. One cruiser pulled up alongside John, and John immediately showed him his badge.

"What the hell's going on here?"

"Looks like a car bomb. Got a witness here," John said, nodding toward Charlie. "He was near the blast, he's covered in glass. I'm going to run him up to the local emergency clinic, get him patched up, ask him some questions."

The officer, an older man with skin leathered from years of beach patrol, nodded, clearly confused by the catastrophe that had struck his peaceful community.

"OK, roger that."

"I'll bring him back to the precinct after a doctor checks him out."

John propped his elbow on the doorframe and gave the local his biggest smile. He eased on the gas and headed out as a fire engine, two ambulances and two more police cruisers arrived on the scene. Behind them was a news van from Wilmington's NBC affiliate, Channel Five, which had the good fortune of being on the island to cover a sea turtle hatching that evening. Instead, the reporter's story would be picked up by CNN that night, and the reporter would be on national television.

~

"ALRIGHT, DALLAS, TELL ME EVERYTHING," John demanded. They were headed north on Route 17, which would lead them back to I-40 and ultimately, Richmond. Charlie was in the back seat, his hands cuffed behind his back. He was covered in minor cuts and scratches, and he smelled like he'd been barbecued, but otherwise, he was in decent shape. "When was your wife kidnapped?"

"A week ago," Charlie said.

"Why didn't you call the police?"

"They told me they'd kill her."

"So they contacted you?"

"Twice," Charlie said. "Once in writing, in our hotel room, to tell me they'd taken her, and once by phone when I got back to Richmond from Florida."

"You were on your honeymoon."

"Yes."

"How did Vitelli fit into all this?"

"I don't know. They ordered me to go to Belle Isle, and Vitelli was waiting for me. Like he'd been expecting me."

"Assuming you're telling the truth, it sounds like you were set up."

"That was all I could think of."

"Who'd want to set you up?"

Charlie told him about the First National Bank job, and his suspicions that the robbery and Susanna's disappearance were somehow connected. He left out his personal connection to the case. He needed to establish this guy's trust first before he dropped that craziness on him.

"Any idea who the robbers are?"

"No," Charlie said, defeated. "But I must've gotten close. Otherwise, why go to all the trouble?"

A good point, John thought. Like hungry rats, Elsa's words gnawed their way out of the basement of his mind into the forefront of his conscience. Not everything was as simple as it seemed.

"Why are you helping me?" Charlie asked.

"What makes you think I'm helping you?"

"You lied to that cop back there. You haven't called me in yet. I'm the biggest fish in the FBI pond right now, and you haven't told a soul."

What are you doing? John wondered to himself. Sitting here, peeling away the layers of his soul to a man who was a wanted fugitive, who in all probability was the bad guy. Elsa King or no Elsa King. *Good thinking*, John. *Brilliant career move.* Still, there was the ballistics report. Dallas hadn't been the shooter. The man he'd just killed probably had been the shooter, and he looked like he was here to finish Dallas off himself. The missing wife. The fact that Charlie Dallas didn't have any more reason to kill Vitelli than the Easter Bunny did. On the way down to Wilmington, he'd read the latest progress report on the investigation into Dallas's life. Perfectly ordinary. No bad debts. No criminal record, save a few speeding tickets and a DUI when he was twenty-two. No secret bank accounts or credit cards, no P.O. boxes where he received kiddie porn. His life hadn't triggered a single red flag suggesting that there might be more to him than what appeared on the surface. Any theory pinning Vitelli's murder on Dallas was just not going to hold water. He decided to answer Dallas's question. The truth wasn't going to hurt anyone.

"Because I was about to get kicked off the case," Hood said. "And I don't trust anyone else to finish the job right."

Charlie nodded his head and considered the agent's words, still stunned beyond belief. He'd just been hoping that no one shot him when they found him, and that was probably being optimistic. Cops did not tolerate violence against one of their own. Now it seemed he had an ally of sorts. Granted, allies always had their own agenda. He wondered what this guy's was.

"What's your name?" Charlie asked.

"Hood. John Hood."

"Look, Agent Hood, I just want to find my wife. That's all I care about. I want to find her." He added: "One way or the other."

"We've got about two days to put this thing together," John said. "After that, both of our mugshots will be on the news. Hell, maybe we'll be cellmates. I'm putting my ass out on the line for you, and to be honest, I really don't understand why."

Charlie looked at John Hood's eyes. He saw pain and rage in them, and it scared him a bit.

"A man trying to help me died in that explosion," Charlie said. "His name was Mickey Duncan."

"I'm sorry," John said.

"Me too. But he gave me information that may help me figure this thing out. I could use your help."

"If it will help find Mike's killers, then I'm right behind you."

Charlie nibbled on his lower lip, then decided to come clean with the rest of the story. Hood had a right to know. They had built an uneasy trust between each other, like the still-wet silk of a spider's web. Too much stress on it, and it would collapse. But leaving out crucial details would stress the link just as much.

"There's something else I haven't told you," Charlie said.

Here we go, John thought. *Here's the confession that proves I was right all along, and that Elsa King doesn't know shit.* "What?"

"My life is somehow connected to the bank robbery."

"What the hell are you talking about?"

Charlie told him the story about the tattoo on his foot, and how his parents told him it had come to be there.

Maybe not, John thought. "But what does that have to do with anything?"

"It's all a lie. There was no storm on the night I was born. And the tattoo on my foot matches the charm on the necklace that the woman in the picture was wearing. You're the first person I've told about it."

"I don't understand."

"I don't either," Charlie said. "But I might have a way to find out. I found a key to a safe-deposit box in my parents' house down here for a bank back in Richmond. Can you help me get in it?"

"I think so. I'm pretty tight with some of the magistrates up there. We'll go get a warrant when we get back to Richmond and go to the bank tomorrow. You know which bank it's in?"

"Madison Bank. Downtown."

"Yeah, I know it. What else do you have?"

Charlie held up the file Mickey had died delivering to him. "This is a record of the account activity at the First National Bank in the two months immediately before and after the robbery. Accounts opened and closed, large deposits and withdrawals, that kind of thing. I've been working on the theory that the bank was an inside job. I think that we can narrow the list of suspects by looking at this list."

"How'd you get your hands on that?"

"You probably don't want to know."

"You're probably right."

John returned his attention to the road, and Charlie began digging through the inch-thick stack of bank records. Charlie started with accounts closed in the month before the robbery and came up with one hundred and eleven names, which he scribbled onto a legal pad, a tricky task in a moving car. This seemed like the best approach. Someone who closed his account before the robbery might have been anticipating a run on the bank's funds immediately after the robbery. And that someone would only know about the bank's potential cash flow problem if he or she was planning on creating a cash flow problem. It was like looking for a specific grain of sand on the beach.

He ticked off each account holder's name as he plowed through the list. By the time the sun went down, he'd made it through four letters of the alphabet. Callahan. Collins. Collinsworth. Cowan. Daniels. *Whoa*, he thought. Charlie went back up the list. *Collinsworth*. All accounts closed on May 14, 1973. Howard and Amanda Collinsworth. *Jesus*. Collinsworth had been the lead robbery detective on the case. Now he knew why the police hadn't investigated this angle. Collinsworth ran the investigation, so it would have been easy to look the other way.

"Son of a bitch," he muttered.

"What is it?" John asked.

"I think I've got the names of two of the bank robbers."

26

"Why hasn't he called?" Patrick Jessup said, holding the prepaid cellular phone in his hand like it was a bomb and wondering if he'd be able to defuse it in time. Lindsey was sitting in the corner, chewing a slice of cold pepperoni pizza, wondering the same thing. She checked her watch. It was thirty-five minutes past eight. Ulysses was supposed to call no later than eight. If he didn't call by then, the assumption was that he had failed his mission, either by getting caught or getting killed. Still, Lindsey had made it more of a soft deadline than anything, thinking it was unlikely anything would go wrong. Ulysses had found Charlie, and finally she had started to relax.

She'd started getting nervous around eight-fifteen, and twenty more minutes had ticked by since then. She wasn't even that hungry, but food might take her mind off things, and that surely the phone would ring before the tasteless frozen pizza had heated up.

"Why hasn't he called?" Patrick said again.

"How the hell should I know?" She jumped out of her chair, grabbed the plates, and tossed them in the trash. "Jesus!"

"Hey, I wasn't done eating," Patrick protested.

"You are now. We've got work to do."

"What kind of work?" he asked, his voice weak and small.

"Just shut up for a minute."

Deep down, Lindsey had suspected that it would come to this. That ultimately, she would have to take care of Charlie herself. Ulysses had been a good man--*wow*, she realized she was already referring to him in the past tense--but stable was not a word she would have used to describe him. If he had been able to get rid of Charlie, great, but her hopes hadn't been high. His share of the money was gone anyway. He'd blown through it like a firestorm on a hot, dry summer day.

All the cash he'd ever need to start over, exorcise the demons of Vietnam and who knew what else, and he'd blown his chance, frittering it away on booze, women, drugs. She hoped he was dead. That way, they'd be rid of him for good. Even if he'd gotten caught, however, she wasn't too worried about that either. If there was one thing he did bring to the table--and there wasn't much he did bring--it was loyalty. He would never rat them out. And besides, they were ready to disappear. The little hacienda in the little coastal town in Brazil was paid for and titled in one of her several aliases. She'd taught herself Spanish, eventually becoming fluent over the years. Patrick never had much interest in it, thinking they'd never need it. But she was always prepared for the worst-case scenario, no matter how remote.

"It's time to go," she said to him with her most serious voice.

"To Brazil," he said dejectedly.

She nodded.

Part of it was that he didn't want to become an expatriate. He liked drinking beer and watching football, hanging out with other retired cops with whom he had a lot in common except the size of his retirement fund. She'd promised him a satellite TV connection that would deliver every NFL game every Sunday. Hell, he could have baseball, hockey, and basketball. It kept him quiet, happy, and out of her hair. But it would never be the same as sitting in his old recliner, chugging Olympia beer.

"So what do we do next?" Patrick asked. He lit his pipe again, and he seemed to have calmed down. Maybe made his peace with their ultimate destiny.

"We draw him out."

"How?"

Lindsey's heart was pounding. It was time to play their last, best card. Really, it was their only card.

"With our biggest poker chip."

27

When Charlie's eyes were fried from plowing through the bank records, they stopped for dinner at a truck stop, and Charlie ate a low-grade piece of steak and three scrambled eggs, his first hot meal in days. John picked up the tab, and they were back on the road. It was just after ten p.m. when Charlie and John caught the first glimpse of the downtown Richmond skyline. The trip had taken almost five hours.

Ahead of them, downtown office towers loomed large in the shadows, standing sentry over the Friday nightlife in the various clubs and bars below. Northbound traffic was light, and they had made great time coming up I-95. About two miles shy of downtown, John took an exit off the interstate and looped onto the Chippenham Parkway, which fed into the city's southern suburbs. He then exited onto Midlothian Turnpike and headed west, picking his way through an urban jungle of car dealerships and fast-food restaurants. While they paused at a stoplight, John whipped out his cell phone and speed-dialed a preset number.

"Nicola, it's John Hood," he said. "Not much, not much. Listen, I need your help. Yeah, for a safe-deposit box. We'll be there in five minutes."

As promised, five minutes later, John pulled into an apartment complex and killed the ignition. He started to alight from the car, then hesitated. "You better come with me," he said to Charlie. "This neighborhood's not safe, and the cuffs would make it tough for you to defend yourself."

"Thanks."

The thirty-second walk to Nicola's apartment reminded Charlie of his near-fatal trip to Carrolton Oaks a few days before. No Trespassing signs were plastered everywhere, but Charlie got the distinct impression that the signs were not complied with. And as if to underscore the fact that fear knew no skin color, Charlie saw three young white men loitering on the second-floor landing, passing a joint among them. The largest one, wearing baggy shorts and no shirt, seemed unconcerned with the large handgun planted in his waistband, displayed for public view.

John knocked on the apartment door three times, and Nicola immediately opened the door, as if she'd been waiting on the other side. She was a tiny woman with deep brown skin stretched tight over a compact, athletic frame. Her black hair was pulled back in a ponytail. Charlie pegged her as a Filipino native, about twenty-five years old. She stepped forward and gave John a quick peck on his cheek. Charlie followed Hood inside her apartment, which exuded a sense of calm and peacefulness. Very little furniture cluttered the small space. A recent bestselling novel was face down on a large, comfy-looking chair in the corner. Jazz bubbled softly from unseen speakers. Something top shelf, like Davis or Coltrane.

"Where you been all my life?" she asked in accented English.

"Trying to get you out of my head," John said.

"Listen to the guy," she said, turning to look at Charlie. "Such a heartbreaker. Come in, please sit down."

Charlie smiled awkwardly, as if he'd just poked his head behind the curtain that John kept draped across his personal life. John coughed into his hand, and the three of them sat in silence for a few moments.

"The warrant?" John said, way too late to avoid that sense of awkwardness.

"Oh, yes," Nicola said, a big smile nearly swallowing her small face. "Always with the business, this one. Convince me to give you this warrant."

Charlie was somewhat familiar with the warrant procedure. To get a search warrant, John had to convince Nicola that he had probable cause to believe that the safe-deposit box contained evidence connected to Vitelli's murder.

"This man was a witness to the agent's murder. The FBI has reason to believe that—"

"Whoa, whoa, whoa!" she said. "What reason to believe? Whose safe-deposit box is it?"

John sat back against the couch, crossed his right leg across his knee, and fiddled with his shoelace.

"It's his parents' box."

"What do his parents—" She stopped when John

leaned forward and took one of her small hands in his thick, meaty paws.

"I need this warrant," he said, giving her a look that Charlie knew she'd be powerless to resist and that told her the usual rules of probable cause just weren't going to apply tonight. Some closed chapter in both of their lives, and John was cashing in the goodwill he still had built up back there.

"I could lose my job," she said, her eyes wet and glassy with tears.

"This is Charlie Dallas," he said, putting his hand on Charlie's shoulder. "His wife's been kidnapped. We're trying to find her."

She got up and went over to an end table, where she retrieved a wrinkled pack of cigarettes from a drawer. She lit one, took a drag, unspooled her ponytail. She smoked in silence for a while, then asked: "Do you have anything remotely resembling PC?"

"Show her," John said to Charlie, pointing to his foot.

As he unlaced his shoes, Charlie thought about how best to convince this woman that issuing this warrant would not be career suicide. He removed his shoe and showed her the tattoo.

"I'm a newspaper reporter. I'm investigating a bank robbery that occurred thirty years ago."

"So?"

He extracted the folded-up newspaper photograph of Denise Vaughan from his pocket and handed it to Nicola. She studied it for a moment and then shook her head absently.

"What am I supposed to be looking at?" she asked.

"Look at the necklace."

Drawing the picture close to her face, she squinted and studied the photograph.

"OK, so they look alike," she said.

"My parents told me I was tattooed on the night I was born," Charlie said.

"Why would they--"

Charlie held up a hand, cutting her off. "It doesn't matter. It was a lie. My parents lied to me about the origin of this tattoo, and I don't know why. But I think that safe-deposit box may answer the question."

"What does that have to do with the agent's murder?" she asked.

"I believe that his murder is connected to the bank robbery."

She shook her head, then muttered softly, "Jesus."

John turned to Charlie and said, "Why don't you step outside for a minute?"

Charlie nodded. "Mind if I have one of those cigarettes?"

She handed him the pack, and Charlie stepped outside, where he fired up a smoke and leaned against the railing. He debated pressing his ear to the door, but that seemed a bit juvenile. Either she'd give them the warrant or she wouldn't. His ear pressed to the door wouldn't make a whole hell of a lot of difference. He pictured the vault at the Madison Bank, black and empty right now. His parents' box, shut tight for how many years now? What the hell was in it?

Nicola's door cracked open, startling Charlie. He dropped the cigarette, and it arced end over end to the ground, spraying orange embers like an Independence Day firecracker. John's thick figure was silhouetted in the doorway. Charlie followed him back inside the apartment.

"I'm sorry," Nicola was saying. "I can't take this kind of risk. This is my job. I can't afford to lose it."

"I understand," John said. "I wouldn't want you to do anything you don't feel--"

"Please!" Charlie cut in. "You have to help us!"

"No, I don't have to do shit!" she howled.

"Listen to me!" Charlie was yelling now, his eyes tearing, his voice was thick with phlegm. "I'm begging you. My wife is out there somewhere. I don't even know if she's alive. But this box is my last hope to find her. And I can't get it without your help."

"I'd like you to leave now," she said, pointing to the door.

"Let's go," John said, clamping his hand down on Charlie's shoulder and steering him to the door. No other words were exchanged before the men stepped back outside. The door slammed shut behind them, muffling her sobs like a blanket.

"You said there are other magistrates we can go to, right?"

John took a deep breath and exhaled it slowly.

"Right?" Charlie said again, hysteria returning to his voice.

"No."

"What do you mean?"

"I mean I don't trust any of the other magistrates. She was our best shot."

"It's worth a shot though, isn't it?"

"Look, she was the only one I could even trust not to turn you in. Hell, not to turn us both in."

Charlie's heart went cold.

"Fine," Charlie said with a steeliness he'd rarely heard in his own voice. "I'm going to have to get it myself."

John drove them back to his house and set Charlie up on the sleeper couch in the living room. They had spoken little on the drive back, agreeing to devise a plan after getting some sleep. Trying to get some sleep at least. Charlie pressed the backlight button of his watch, which glowed with the bad news. Three-eighteen a.m. What did someone need to get into a safe-deposit box anyway? Social security number? Date of birth? Maybe a password? A photo ID? *You'll find out tomorrow*, he thought, as he finally drifted off to sleep.

THEY RODE DOWNTOWN IN SILENCE, each sipping large cups of steaming coffee. Charlie had burned his tongue a dozen times like a dopey laboratory rat that couldn't figure out that the piece of cheese was tied to an electrified plate. His mind was on the box. He'd finally given up on sleep around six and taken a long shower, hoping that would pump some life back into him. His eyes were thick with fatigue, and he felt like he was trying to think at the bottom of a gravy boat.

Traffic wasn't helping either; it was thick, and the expressway flowed about as freely as motor oil. After what seemed like an eternity, John took the 7th Street/9th Street exit downtown, then turned north onto Seventh. The Madison Bank occupied a large concrete building at the northwest corner of 7th and Olivet, where the bank had made its home since 1947. The gray building cast a cold shadow along the adjacent sidewalk. Rumors that the building was haunted were rampant and part of the city's lore.

"I'll wait here," John said, pulling up alongside the building. He activated his hazard lights and shifted the car out of gear. "Make it quick."

His heart nearly in his throat, Charlie jumped out of the car and hurried inside the heavy glass doors. The bank lobby was huge, and every sound seemed magnified by a factor of ten. Even his sneakers echoed in the cavernous room. The bank had been open only a few minutes, so there were less than a dozen employees and customers inside.

"May I help you, sir?"

Charlie turned at the voice and saw a heavyset woman at a desk in an enclosed cubicle, smiling at him with unnaturally white teeth. Her makeup was thicker than the caked-on grease of a burger joint, and her perfume was overpowering, almost a presence in and of itself. Charlie rubbed his beard and approached her. He felt like everyone in the bank could hear his heart pounding, but he knew that his disguise was solid. *Relax*, he told himself. *Just relax.*

"I'd like to get into a safe-deposit box."

"Your name, please?" she asked, so sweetly that Charlie wanted to strangle her.

He hesitated for a moment, a moment that stretched between them for a second, then longer, then Charlie was certain she knew he was stalling. She eyed him pleasantly while Charlie looked at her desk. A nameplate bearing the name Linda Butler was at the edge of the desk.

"Charles Dallas."

It was out of his mouth before he even realized it. The way you turn your head in a crowded shopping mall when you hear someone call your name, even when you know the voice doesn't belong to anyone you know. He wasn't even sure whose name the box was in. His parents'? His own? He had no plan here. What did he think, they would just open the box up for him? She tapped a few keys, a wide smile plastered on her face. And then the smile disappeared. Her eyes left the screen and rolled east to west, from one side of her eye sockets to the other, as if to see who else was around, who else was looking.

"Shit," he muttered, just loud enough to draw her attention from the computer screen.

That was all Linda Butler needed. She pushed her chair away from the desk and stood. "If you'll just wait here, sir." The sweetness was gone.

Charlie turned to flee the bank when he felt a hand drop on his shoulder. They had him. A bank security guard. An off-duty cop. He turned slowly and was shocked to see John Hood standing behind him, his FBI credentials dangling from his fingers.

"Hood, FBI," he said with authority.

"Yes, sir," Linda Butler said.

"This man trying to get into a safe-deposit box?" he asked.

Linda Butler's eyes widened, and she clapped a hand to her chest. "Yes. Yes, he is!"

"I'm taking him into custody," he said. "I'm going to

do it very quietly, so as not to disrupt the business of the bank. Do you understand?"

She nodded fiercely, as if she'd narrowly averted death on this summer morning.

"Check your fax machine," Hood said. "The warrant is coming over as we speak. And then I'll need the contents of the box. You have the key, don't you, Mr. Dallas?"

Charlie nodded once, stunned beyond belief.

"Good," Hood said. "Ms. Butler, who's the manager of this bank?"

"I am."

"Very well," he said. "Can you bring the box in here?"

"Yes."

"Now go get the warrant, and bring the box in here. Mr. Dallas, give her the key."

He did, and Linda Butler went to retrieve the warrant and box, leaving Charlie and John alone. Charlie cut his eyes to the lobby, where business went on, although the tellers appeared to be whispering to each other and glancing their way whenever they got a free moment.

"What the hell is going on?"

"She had a change of heart," John said coolly.

"Thank God," he said. "I was about to get nailed. Why'd you let me go through with it?"

"I don't know," John said. "Half hoping you could do it, half hoping that Niki would change her mind after a sleepless night. She's a good girl, wants to do the right thing, the moral thing."

"Hell of a gamble, wasn't it?"

"You have any better ideas?"

"No, I guess not."

John poked his head around the corner of the cubicle and scanned the lobby. More eyes had turned their way as the bank started to fill with customers. More customers meant longer lines, longer waiting, more interest in what the tellers were whispering about.

"I'm going to cuff you now," John said, leaning back inside the protective shell of the cubicle. He nodded toward the center of the bank. "We've got an audience."

Charlie nodded again.

Linda stepped back around her desk just as John finished locking the cuffs into place around Charlie's wrists. She set the long, narrow box on the table, which clanged heavily against the wood desktop.

"I hope you don't mind the handcuffs," John said in a calm voice.

"As long as they're not on me, I suppose," Linda said, giggling nervously. John joined her for a chuckle. Linda Butler opened the box with Charlie's key and stuffed the contents into a large envelope; Charlie watched her like a cobra watched a snake charmer. She handed the envelope to John.

"Who rented this box?" John asked.

Butler checked her computer screen. "Eric Vaughan rented it on May 19, 1973. He paid five hundred dollars for a lifetime rental."

Four days after the First National robbery. And the name--Eric Vaughan--created a faint spark of recognition, which he tried to fan like a charcoal grill on a damp, windy afternoon.

"Has anyone else accessed the box since that day?" he asked.

She checked her screen. "No. Never."

"Thanks for your help," John said, tucking the envelope into his back pocket.

With his hand on Charlie's elbow, John led his prisoner out of the bank with no fanfare. Customers and employees gawked, but the men stared straight ahead and stepped back out into the warm, humid morning.

"Thanks," Charlie said when they were back in the car. John reached behind Charlie's back and unlocked the cuffs.

"Sure," John said as he eased back into traffic and deactivated the revolving light on the roof of his car. "It's only my career." He tossed the bulky envelope onto Charlie's lap.

"Well," John said. "Why don't we take a look at what's inside?"

Charlie carefully tore open the flap and slid out the contents, a couple of documents and a few old photographs, yellowed with age. The photographs were of an infant and a woman that appeared to be Denise Vaughan. The baby was a pudgy boy, maybe a year old, dressed in blue coveralls and bite-sized sneakers in each of the three pictures. He flipped to the second picture, also of the baby and his mother. The third one was like a kick to the stomach, drawing a loud gasp from his throat. In it, the baby and its father were cheek to cheek, both smiling widely.

"What?" John asked. "What is it?"

"This remind you of anyone?" Charlie asked, holding the picture up for John to look at.

Even occupied with his driving duties, the point Charlie was trying to make was not lost on John.

"That guy looks just like you," he said.

Charlie nodded. There was no doubt. From the chin to the eyes to the curve of the nose, there was no doubt that Charlie was related to the man in the picture. The baby's features were a bit more amorphous, but he didn't have any trouble guessing that he was the baby in the picture.

Charlie tucked the pictures away and turned his attention to the first document, an official-looking paper with stamps and seals and notarized signatures. The words *Certificate of Live Birth* were striped across the top.

"What is that?" John asked, his eyes focused on the heavy traffic around them.

"Birth certificate," he said as he scanned the information on it. *Jesus*, he thought, as his eyes bounced from one data field to the next. Name. Casey William Vaughan. His eyes locked on the box reflecting the baby's date of birth. July 18, 1970.

"Whose birth certificate is it?"

"I think it's mine."

28

Thomas Bagwell's bite of filet mignon was suspended in mid-air when his cell phone began chirping. He set his fork back down on his plate and glanced up at his date for the evening. She smiled at him and sipped her chardonnay. *Dammit*, he thought. His first night out in months, and it was about to be destroyed. He could just tell. He'd finally found a woman he was actually interested in, and he'd been looking forward to this evening, a dinner at Morton's, for a week. He told his staff that he wanted to enjoy a work-free night.

"I'm sorry," he said to Erica Cooper, a well-respected architect in Washington D.C. She smiled demurely and returned her attention to her lobster tail. Recognizing the phone number flashing on the caller ID, he got up from the heavy oak table and hustled from the dimly lit dining room. He stepped outside and ducked around the side of the building, where he could get some privacy.

"Is this about Hood?" he asked, dispensing with pointless pleasantries. He was not in a pleasant mood.

"Yeah," said Jerome Hudson.

"What happened?"

As best he could, Hudson explained to his boss the details of the incident at the seafood market.

"Jesus Christ."

"One other thing," Hudson said. "A phone call came in over the main switchboard at 1931."

Bagwell checked his watch. About twenty minutes ago, he calculated. Hudson went on. "Caller claimed to have kidnapped Susanna Dallas, and he wants to talk to John Hood to arrange for her release."

"You mean the caller asked for Hood specifically?"

"Yes."

"Goddammit." At this rate, he'd never be able to fire the jerkoff. "Proof of life?"

"Digital photograph was emailed immediately after the phone call with today's *Washington Post*," Hudson said. "Emailed from a disposable email account, opened with a fake name. We're working on the IP address of the computer that sent the email. The lab confirmed that the photo is genuine."

"Have we even confirmed that she's been kidnapped?" Bagwell asked.

"No one has reported seeing her since the day before Vitelli died."

Bagwell scratched his head. "OK, our priority is saving the victim, assuming she is a victim. Get in touch with Hood, and get him in contact with these alleged kidnappers. I want traces and recorders on everything."

"Yes, sir."

"Hey," began Bagwell.

"Sir?"

"You think I can finish my dinner before I come back to work?"

"I think so, sir."

Thomas Bagwell stopped at the restroom and readjusted his tie. Hudson was a hell of a good agent. If Bagwell could get rid of that lunatic Hood, maybe he could elevate Hudson to ASAC. Now then. He had a nice piece of meat waiting for him back at the table. And a decent filet mignon, too. He smiled at that. That had been a good one.

CHARLIE SPENT the day at Hood's house, going through the documents over and over again. There hadn't been much to go through, but Charlie was riveted by everything in the envelope. Especially the birth certificate. When you were a kid, you knew your birthday above all else. It was your day. No chores. Presents. You pick dinner. Cake and ice cream. You were finally the age you were telling people you were anyway. Who was Casey William Vaughan?

Charlie wasn't quite sure how to put his suspicions in words, so he told Hood he wasn't sure what the information meant. With that, Charlie had relegated them to the always popular strategy of hurry-up-and-wait. It drove Hood crazy. He spent the day on the phone, talking in hushed tones. They spoke little.

Fear buzzed through him as he came up with one explanation after another about the information in the safe-deposit box. One theory kept coming back like a bad cold sore. He hated to admit it, but it was the one that, as crazy as it sounded, made the most sense.

Charlie had been born Casey William Vaughan, but, at some point, he'd become Charles Xavier Dallas. The obvious questions were when, how, and most importantly, why? Somehow, his past was tied into the First National Bank robbery. He opened his files again and flipped to the earliest news clippings on the robbery.

There! The bank teller, the one that had been taken hostage and murdered--her name had been Denise Vaughan. *Vaughan was a common name, sure, but an awfully big coincidence in this case*, Charlie thought. *What if she hadn't been an innocent bystander? What if she was somehow wrapped up in the robbery plot?* He flipped through the police report. Detective Collinsworth had commented in his notes that the robbers had "extensive knowledge" of the bank's layout and its security procedures.

And closer to home, a far more important question. Was Denise Vaughan his mother? More of his childhood flowed through his subconscious like an underground river. He remembered on several occasions, people had commented that he really didn't favor either of his parents. Naturally, he'd never thought anything of it. His mom had said that he took after a long-dead grandparent. And that was the end of it. Again, why would he suspect anything was amiss?

He dozed during the afternoon and evening, and he dreamed about Susanna. Nothing specific, no sitting on a beach or skiing down a mountain. She'd just been there, and he felt warm. It was one of those dreams where you start making that transition across the spectral threshold, and you do everything you can to stop the dissolution of the dreamworld.

When he woke up, John was tapping the edge of the sofa.

"Time to move."

He rubbed the sleep from his eyes and sat up. Blood rushed to his head, making the room spin around him.

"It looks like I've been given a stay of execution," John said, sitting down on the couch next to Charlie. "I just talked to my field office. Someone claiming to be holding Susanna--"

This launched Charlie to his feet. "Is she OK?"

"I don't know. Please let me finish."

"Sorry," Charlie said softly. He sat back down and took a deep breath.

"Someone claiming to be holding Susanna called the FBI's main switchboard and asked to talk to the lead investigator on the Vitelli case. Actually, they asked for me specifically."

"Have you talked to them?" Charlie asked.

"No. They're going to call here. Tonight."

"Were they able to trace the call?"

"No."

"So we just wait?"

"Pretty much," John said. "But it's a good sign. It strongly suggests that your wife is still alive."

Tears welled up in Charlie's eyes. It was the first time since he went on the run that he felt like there might be a light at the end of the tunnel. A real light, he hoped--not a light on a locomotive headed right for him.

"They can trace the call when it comes in, right?" he asked hopefully.

"The perpetrator said they have call-trace detection software," John said. "They said if we try to trace, they'll kill her. The bitch of it is that such software actually exists, and we can't be sure if they're just yanking our chain. I am going to record the call, and we're going to patch in the guys at my office."

While they waited, John fixed two bowls of canned spaghetti, and they ate it in front of the television, hunched over wooden TV trays. They watched Sports-Center and said little. Charlie picked at his noodles, but he wasn't that hungry. He forced down most of it, conscious of his need for strength.

"Will other agents be coming here?" Charlie asked when they were finished eating. The thought made him extremely nervous, as he was aware of what cops did to people they suspected had killed another cop.

"No, they're going to let me handle it," John said, clearing the bowls and running them under the spigot in the kitchen sink. "The prevailing theory is that you killed Vitelli, so I convinced them that the wise move would be to keep this operation close to the vest. Only a few other agents know I'm with you. I've got to keep my boss apprised of what's going on. Otherwise, he's given me a lot of rope. I think he's hoping I hang myself with it, but that's a risk I'm willing to take."

"Why are you doing this?" Charlie asked. "Isn't this a big risk for you?"

"Because I've got this terrible feeling that something's going to get missed otherwise," John said. "Someone's gone to a lot of trouble to make it look like you were behind the murder. I've got no choice but to do it this way."

They went back to the living room and waited. While Hood cycled through the channels, Charlie tried to get a sense of the man based on his living quarters. The television was ancient, a strip of distorted bleed-through across the top of the screen. A built-in book-case in the far wall was stuffed with various publica-tions on law enforcement techniques, philosophies, and procedures. The couch was threadbare, the stuffing exposed in many spots, but it was soft and comfortable.

At eight-thirty, John Hood's phone began to jangle. He picked it up on the first ring and pressed the speaker-phone button so Charlie could listen in. Meanwhile, he speed-dialed his office on his cell phone and placed it next to the landline speaker so that Bagwell could listen in.

"John Hood," he answered.

"Listen very carefully," the caller said in the same mechanical voice that drenched Charlie's insides with ice. "Tomorrow. Noon. Be at the payphone at the north-west corner of Georgia and Copperas Streets in Naples, Florida, tomorrow at noon. You'll receive further instruc-tions there. Just you and Dallas. We'll have the area under surveillance. If we so much as think anyone else is around, she dies."

"Got it," John said.

"Let me talk to her!" Charlie snapped.

John glared at him while the line went silent.

"I just want proof she's alive," Charlie said, muting his tone considerably.

"Very well." The sound of shuffling, then more silence. Then:

"Charlie?" a soft but firm voice said. Tears immediately began streaming down Charlie's face. It was her. No doubt, it was her.

"Susanna! Are you OK?"

More confused sounds followed.

"That enough proof for you?" the mechanical voice asked.

Charlie's chin dropped. It was going to have to do. At least she was alive.

"One other thing," the voice said. "Bring all your files, notes, audio or video interviews, story drafts, outlines, notebooks, anything and everything you've ever written down on the First National Bank job. I want originals. If I ever see another story on the robbery from your paper, I will kill both of you."

The line went dead.

"You get that, Thomas?" John asked, speaking into the cell phone. "We're going to take a charter."

"You're going to fly?"

John paused. "Yes."

Now another silence filled the room, leaving Charlie to wonder what he'd missed.

"I don't like this at all," Bagwell said. "This is extremely unorthodox. What if you all get killed?"

"Disavow me," said John. "If it all goes bad, then blame me. Say I went rogue."

John could almost see Bagwell pinching the bridge of his nose, his face wrenched into a rictus of pain.

"Alright, Hood," Bagwell said after an interminable silence. "We do it your way."

"Thanks."

He ended the call and slipped the phone into his pocket.

Charlie was still staring at the speaker. He looked catatonic. His brain was trying to lock onto two revelations at once, either of which would have been stunning alone. Immediately, his brain began trying to analyze the tone of Susanna's voice, as if he could tell from her single spoken word how she was doing, whether she was hurt, emotionally stable, and so on. Another part of his brain, spinning just underneath the Susanna portion, was fixated on the caller's identity. He'd been right. The most important thing now--no, the only thing now--was saving Susanna.

29

By the time the sun rose over the East Coast the next morning, Charlie and John were aboard a Piper 150 turboprop, heading south toward Florida. John tried to doze in his seat but found himself focused on the sound of the engine. *Who was he kidding?* Your first time back on a plane after a crash, you didn't just take a Tylenol PM, tuck a pillow behind your head, and nod off.

But they had to be in Naples by noon. That was the deal. Susanna Dallas's safety was more important than any trauma-induced phobia or post-traumatic stress disorder that he carried with him like a day pack. And so he'd made his stand to Thomas Bagwell, whom John knew would fold on the issue when he said he'd fly down himself. The truth was, it was better this way. He hadn't had time to think about it, dwell on it, relive Flight 605. Before he knew it, they were on board, shooting down the runway and leaping into the predawn sky. The fact that they were on a little puddle jumper hadn't bothered him

either. He'd never been on one before, so he had no basis
for comparison. In fact, it was probably easier than
getting on a sleek 737 with pretty flight attendants and
personal TV monitors mounted in the headrests. Flight
605 had been a 737, and that flight hadn't really gone all
that well. The flight attendant had been a thirteen-year-
old boy's wet dream (*he remembered she was beautiful: she
was still beautiful today, even though he met her in the last
fifteen minutes of her life and the lives of everyone around him.
Live every day like it's your last, they say, but was everyone
on 605 living that day like it was their last? Tower, 605 is a
dead stick*). A wan smile drifted across his face. *That's right,
John, make jokes. I'm sure that's healthy.*

Across the aisle, Charlie sat hunched over in his chair,
peering out his window into the early-morning mist as
they cruised. There was some high cloud cover, muting
the power of the rising sun, but the view was still stunning. It reminded him of the night Susanna had disappeared, the couple standing on the balcony watching the
sun set. The air swirled around the small plane like it was
a living presence. Charlie was probably as close to God as
he was ever going to get, so he thought it would be a good
idea to start praying for the end of this hellacious
journey.

They had spent the night combing the white pages
for a private charter, calling more than a dozen places
before they found someone willing and able to take them
on such short notice. An outfit called Cavalier Aviation
had finally answered the call, and pilot Dave Connelly
was their de facto driver this morning. He was a nice
enough fellow, especially so when John had paid him six
hundred dollars in cash.

It had been a smooth flight, only a few bumps, most of it at about 20,000 feet. At that altitude, Charlie had been able to watch the southeastern part of the country twinkle to life as lights flickered on and systems powered up, signaling the start of a new day. At about eight-thirty, Connelly began his descent into southwest Florida, breaking through the clouds and into the stagnant atmosphere that blanketed this part of the country. It was a sunny morning, visibility obscured only by the shimmer of heat convection.

"Fellas, we're about ten minutes out," Connelly said, holding his hand over the microphone attached to his headset.

This broke John's trance, and he turned his attention to the confusing chatter between their pilot and the air traffic controller at the Naples Field Regional Airport.

"Got some light crosswinds," a faraway voice said. "Nothing to worry about."

"Roger," Connelly said.

"You're at the outer marker."

Pull up! Pull up!

Whoop! Whoop! Whoop!

"Looking good, you are cleared to land, see you on the ground."

Through the cockpit window, the world rushed at them with surprising velocity. John's stomach lurched the way it did when he came up on a stopped car too fast, realizing he'd have to mash the brake pedal to avoid a fender bender.

As promised, ten minutes later, the tires squealed, and the aircraft shook as they touched down on the runway. Much rougher landing than on a commercial jet,

Charlie noticed. He peeked over at John Hood, whose face was the color of chalk. He didn't look too hot.

"You OK, man?" Charlie asked.

John's head swung around to each of the windows, as if to verify they were actually on the ground. Then he nodded.

"You look like you're about to crap out on me."

"I'm fine," he said, mopping his drenched brow. His short-sleeved polo shirt stuck to his thick torso, darkening in the perspiration. John looked around, not sure what to make of the first successful aircraft landing of which he'd been a part.

Charlie watched him for a moment, not sure what to make of his companion. Was he having second thoughts about the mission? Couldn't be. If there was one thing this guy seemed to lack, it was second thoughts. He was like a heat-seeking missile. He'd locked on his target and would fly headlong toward it until he got it or got killed. Charlie couldn't decide if that was a good or bad attribute to have in a partner, if partner was even the right word to describe his association with the rogue FBI agent.

Or maybe he just didn't like to fly.

THE SMALL PLANE rolled to a soft stop near the small terminal, and the pilot went to work on his post-flight checklist.

"You guys can pop the hatch," Connelly said, pointing toward the left side of the plane. "The terminal's right over there."

John swung the door open, and the pair jumped the

four feet down to the concrete runway, bags slung over their shoulders. The airport was already hopping. Mechanics and pilots were calling back and forth to each other in a nearby hangar. It was hot as hell, much stickier and more oppressive than Richmond. Deodorant alone wouldn't cut it down here. This was antiperspirant country. Charlie checked his watch. It was nearly nine o'clock in the morning. Three hours to go.

John called a cab from a payphone near the terminal while Charlie chain-smoked from the pack he'd stuffed in his bag. After hanging up the phone, John took a seat on the curb.

"Those things'll kill you," he said.

"You want to live forever?" Charlie asked.

They waited almost an hour, but the cabbie never showed. By ten, Charlie had finished the pack and paced a groove in the concrete. He was driving John crazy, but even he had started checking his watch.

"Call'em back," Charlie said.

John did, and when he was done, he slammed the receiver against the cradle.

"What?" Charlie asked.

"The dispatch never went through."

"Shit!" Charlie shouted. "We're running out of time."

"I know."

John checked their surroundings. They were in the parking lot, sizzling and blindingly bright. The small airport was located on the outskirts of Naples in an area that was still relatively undeveloped, partially because it was close to a landfill, but mainly because the developers that owned it had been indicted for tax evasion and bribery.

John saw a car turn onto the airport's access road, approaching them from the north, and an idea came to him. He stepped into the roadway and waved his arms like an island castaway signaling a passing plane. The car, a cherry red Mazda convertible, slowed to a crawl, and John flashed his FBI credentials. Charlie watched but stayed well behind John. The driver was an older guy, bald except for two white strips of hair running along the flanks of his scalp. His skin was golden brown, and his elbow was propped on the open window. He matched Charlie's picture of a retiree in Florida. John stepped forward and leaned toward the window.

"Sir, my name is John Hood, and I am a special agent with the Federal Bureau of Investigation."

"What's this about?" the man said, reaching up and taking John's credentials. He studied them, having lived in Florida too long to simply accept someone's word that they were with the FBI. There were more handguns than people in this state, and the Everglades were stuffed to the gills with missing persons.

"We need to commandeer this vehicle," John said, his credentials dangling from his hand. "You'll be reimbursed for the wear and tear and any damage that comes to your car."

"Oh, no," the man said. "You can't have this car. My grandson is a U.S. Attorney. I know how these things work. You need a warrant."

John didn't have time for semantics. He reached for his hip and pointed his Sig Sauer in the man's face.

"Now, sir." He kept his voice level, worried that he'd scare the old man into a coronary.

The man, a retired certified public accountant from

East Lansing, Michigan named Edgar Rourke, was not scared. He'd been carjacked twice and robbed once, so this was nothing new. It did, however, reinforce his decision to pack up his wife and his condo at Del Boca Vista Phase III and move the hell back to Michigan. John handed Edgar one of his cards as he stepped out of the little roadster.

"Oh," Rourke said, his voice sauteed with sarcasm, peeking down at the card, "you'll be hearing from my attorney, John Hood, Assistant Special Agent in Charge."

As LUCK WOULD HAVE IT, Mr. Edgar Rourke had a new map of the Naples metropolitan area in his glove compartment, including an index of street names and an easy-to-use grid superimposed over the map.

"OK, we're only a few miles away," Charlie said, the map spread out across his lap.

They were headed northeast now, away from the blue-green waters of the Gulf. Charlie gazed out across the flatlands that stretched out before them, broken up only by the occasional cluster of palm trees. Charlie was keenly aware that Sanibel was only a few short miles off the nearby coast. Sanibel. Where this whole nightmare had started. He wondered if they had kept Susanna down here since they took her.

A traffic signal ahead reminded Charlie of his navigational duties. He checked the street name against the map. Then: "Turn left here. This is Copperas. Georgia should be the next big intersection."

Their destination came into view less than a minute

later. A gas station stood at the northwest corner, and John could see the payphone on the perimeter of the lot. A tall marquee stretched into the clear sky, its message simple: GAS. Except for a pickup parked by the small outbuilding, the filling station was deserted. It was old school--no mini-mart, no credit card reader at the pumps. As their car crawled toward the phone, Charlie could see the pumps didn't even have digital readouts, just old-fashioned counters. An old man wearing jean shorts and no shirt fiddled under the hood of the pickup. He glanced back at the sound of Charlie and John's arrival but paid them no mind.

Charlie checked his watch again. Eleven-forty-five.

"Why'd they send us all the way out here?" Charlie asked, stepping out of the car.

John got out of the car as well and took a long look around. He could see why the kidnappers had picked this location to make their next contact. There was nothing around for miles, just black asphalt cutting through the tropical flatlands.

"To make sure we're alone," John said.

"How would they--"

John held a finger to his lips. "Because they're watching us right now."

Charlie froze.

"Only way to be sure we don't have backup lurking somewhere," John said. "They said just you and me, and they meant it. It means they're showing a modicum of intelligence."

"I'm glad you approve," Charlie said.

"I just like to know what we're dealing with," John

said. "Besides, the smarter they are, the less likely they'll do something stupid, like kill your wife."

This revelation stunned Charlie silent.

"I wish I had some binoculars with me," John said. Shielding his eyes from the sun, a bright bronze dot burning mercilessly overhead, he scanned the horizon for telltale signs of surveillance. The glint of distant binoculars. An out-of-place vehicle. Nothing.

"See anything?" Charlie whispered, staring off into the emptiness, not sure what he was looking for. Mosquitoes the size of helicopters dive-bombed at them, leaving painful red welts on their exposed arms.

"Nothing."

~

THE PHONE RANG AT NOON. John grabbed it on the second ring and tilted the receiver away from his ear so Charlie could listen in.

"This is Hood."

"It's nice to see you can follow instructions," the caller said, the voice hidden behind the alteration equipment. "Do you have the material?"

"Yes."

"Good. See, this won't be hard at all."

John tried to leach clues from the call. Male? Female? Panicked? Confident?

"Tonight," continued the caller. "Eight o'clock. Shark Valley entrance to the Everglades. Drop Dallas off at the guard station and wait there. Tell Dallas to start walking toward the main compound. We'll find him. Once we confirm we have everything, he and that pretty little wife of his walk back out. Understand?"

"Wait a second--" John said.

"Understand?"

"Yes."

"If you deviate from our instructions, she dies."

"They'll catch you, you know," John said, his temper starting to rise. "You know what they do to people who kidnap and kill someone? They strap you to a little gurney, and a doctor swabs your arm with alcohol, and they stick you with a needle, and two minutes later you're dead."

John's suddenly belligerent attitude was making Charlie nervous. He didn't think the pissing-off-the-kidnappers approach was such a hot way to go.

"You still don't know who we are, do you?"

"We will soon enough."

A dismissive laugh echoed through the earpiece. "By then, we'll be gone. You'll never see us again."

"You killed a federal agent! You think we're just going to forget about that?"

"Earth's a big place, Agent Hood."

The line clicked dead.

John slammed the phone against the receiver. Then he picked it up again and banged it a dozen more times, matching an obscenity with each echoing bang of the phone.

"Take it easy!" Charlie said, grabbing him by the shoulders. "We've got work to do."

John snapped his head toward Charlie's voice, his eyes manic and bloodshot.

"We've got work to do," Charlie repeated. "And I need your help."

John struggled to rein in his fury like a wild thoroughbred.

"Please," Charlie begged. "I just want to get my wife back."

John stared into Charlie's wild, desperate eyes. This guy needed him. Maybe there was more to his job than just catching the bad guys. For every bad guy, there had been a victim. He'd forgotten that. Or maybe he'd never really gotten it. He thought back to the families of murder victims, parents of children snatched from a shopping mall, businesses cleaned out by con men. Survivors in their own way. They'd had their own Flight 605, plummeting into a world of chaos where nothing would ever be the same again. And now, this reporter, struggling to keep his life in the air.

"Let's go get your wife," John said.

30

L indsey Jessup went over the plan once more in her mind. And again. And again. Flawless execution. That was the key. She--*OK, they*, she told herself, *they* might hold all the cards, but she reminded herself that she was inviting two pretty determined players to the table. She couldn't afford to underestimate them or their drive. After all, Charlie Dallas had nothing to lose. That was important. Even if he didn't know the whole story. And the FBI agent was a professional. Again, not someone to mess around with. Still, she needed to remain confident. After all, hadn't she been the one that had kept them safe and secure all these years? Just the right balance of respect and confidence. She'd be ready.

"Excuse me, ma'am?" a voice startled her from her daydream.

Lindsey looked up from the rack of postcards and saw a squat woman wearing a park ranger uniform. "Yes?"

"The bookstore's closing in a few minutes," the ranger said. "This side of the park closes at six."

Lindsey looked over at Patrick, whose nose was in a picture book of the Everglades. *Idiot*, she thought. Other than the three of them, the Shark Valley Visitor Center was empty. The last tram of the day had pulled in a few minutes earlier, and tourists fresh from a two-hour tour of the park were streaming through the parking lot to their cars, baking in the late-afternoon sun.

"Is it that late already?" she asked, peeking down at her watch.

"I'm afraid so," the ranger said, obviously pleased that someone else had lost themselves in the park's majesty.

"How about I close up for you, Maggie?" Lindsey said, peering down at the woman's name tag.

Maggie cocked her head and looked strangely at Lindsey. Lindsey wasn't too worried about excessive eye contact. She was wearing a floppy, wide-brimmed hat and large sunglasses that all but swallowed her face.

"Beg your pardon?"

Lindsey reached inside her tote bag and pulled out a bundle of cash; the plastic clasp binding the money together was stamped $10,000 U.S.

"I'll close up."

"What the hell's going on?"

"Just take the money and leave," Lindsey said. "I won't take anything, and I won't do any damage to the park. Come back tomorrow morning, and I'll be long gone. You'll never see me again, and no one will ever come looking for that money. I promise."

Maggie, who made $21,000 a year, had two kids, and was in the middle of a nasty divorce, looked at the brick of cash like she was in a trance. She shouldn't. She couldn't. Yet somehow, her hand was reaching for the money all the same.

Patrick drifted over to the door and flipped the Open sign to Closed.

"I still need to close out the register," Maggie said. "I make a deposit every night."

Lindsey nodded.

"Make it quick."

"OK." Her hands quivering, Maggie took the money and shoved it deep into one of the extra pockets of her cargo pants, as though she wanted it as far away from her as possible. She spent the next ten minutes balancing the register tape against the cash in the drawer. As she folded the money into the bank bag, she started laughing.

"What's so funny?" Lindsey asked.

"There's three hundred and sixty dollars in this bag, I've got ten grand in my pocket, and it's just really damn funny to me," Maggie said. "Here're the keys to the store. Leave them under the mat when you're done here. Don't ever let me see you again."

"Don't worry," Lindsey said.

Maggie tapped her pockets once more to make sure the money was safe, then ran for her car in the corner of the parking lot as if all the demons of hell were after her. Lindsey watched Maggie's car disappear in a cloud of dust as it squealed out of the parking lot and back out to U.S. 41.

"Are you sure about this?" Patrick asked. "This can be a dangerous place."

"I grew up down here, remember?"

"I know, but it's been such a long--"

"Drop it," she said.

He quieted down, tucked his lips into his mouth.

"How much longer?" he asked once he felt he'd served appropriate penance.

"An hour," she said, pleased that he was back on task.

She went outside and listened to the quiet symphony of life around her. The Shark Valley entrance was on the north end of the Everglades National Park, and unique because it provided access to the Shark River Slough, which was their ticket out of here tonight. She'd scoped the area out yesterday, where she'd found a canoe tucked in some sawgrass bordering the river. The slough fed through the Glades and twisted east to a small lake, where they would ditch the canoe and hike back to the Tamiami Trail. Miami International Airport was fifty miles to the east, and from there, the rest of the world was a few short hours away. She leaned over the railing and peered down into the water. The surface was quiet except for a river otter cutting a channel toward the far side of the marsh. The sawgrasses swayed in a soft, warm breeze.

"I don't like the idea of taking the canoe," Patrick said, stepping in beside her. He lit his pipe and took a long drag from the stem.

"Put that damn thing out," she said. "The smoke's bad for the ecosystem."

"Sorry," he said, then: "Jesus."

"What the hell's the matter with you?" she asked. "We're getting ready to put our lives on the line, and you're acting like a goddamn six-year-old."

"Why can't we take care of them both back out at the main entrance? Go out that way? It'd be a hell of a lot safer."

She smacked the railing. "Are you really this stupid?"

"What do you mean?"

Her head had started to throb, and her jaws clenched together. Patrick was quickly becoming a liability. The last thing she needed tonight was an X factor, but that was what this was turning into. She ran through a mental checklist of their various accounts--she had sole authority over all of them. It had been easier to dish out money to Patrick via an allowance. But if this attitude kept up, he could get them both killed.

"If Dallas is dead, who's going to take the fall for Hood?" she asked with the impatience of a frustrated schoolmarm.

"Oh."

"Remember, the ranger saw us. Money or no money, she still might talk."

"Right," he said, but she could see in his eyes that he still wasn't convinced.

And that was how she made her decision. She'd begun thinking about it a few days ago, but she'd held off, hoping that he would redeem himself, get with the program, provide her with the support she needed. It wasn't going to happen. She could see that now. She guessed that she'd known it all along, but she'd lied to herself. Time to remedy that.

"Come here," she said, pulling him close to her and wrapping her arms around him. She held him tight and long while her right hand slipped inside her bag, where she'd packed more than the money she used to bribe the ranger.

With her right hand, she unsnapped the sheath covering the blade, then withdrew the hunting knife. He hugged her tight; she felt his hot, salty tears dripping onto her neck.

"I'm sorry," he said. "I'm just scared."

"You don't have to be scared anymore," she said, plunging the eight-inch blade under his ribcage. It slid into him like peanut butter. His body bucked once as his brain, slow as it was, realized something was terribly wrong. He stepped back from her, groping for the mortal wound in his abdomen. Slick blood coated his hands and arms.

"Why?" he asked, growing pale.

She stepped forward and shoved him over the railing. He was bigger than her, but he was in no position to resist. He tumbled backward and landed on his back in the shallow river, staining the murky water with blood. He flailed briefly, boiling the waters around him, then was still. Lindsey watched with sadness, wishing it hadn't had to end this way.

About twenty yards away, a triangle-shaped shadow on the surface of the water made its move, gliding toward Patrick's figure. Lindsey turned and walked away as the twelve-foot alligator opened its jaws.

31

John and Charlie raced east on U.S. 41 or, as it was known down here, the Tamiami Trail. The two-lane highway connected Tampa and Miami, hence the name, and helped facilitate the boom that had started here fifty years ago and showed no signs of letting up. One of man's only visible inroads into the ten million acres that constituted this strange, slow, wide river of grass, the Trail cut through the heart of the Everglades. Mangroves, which looked like trees that had been uprooted from the ground, floated magically in the water. Sawgrass plains stretched to the horizon. They passed a few roadside diners and trinket shops, mostly operated by the Miccosukee Indian tribe, but little else.

At about seven-thirty, John saw a sign indicating the entrance to Shark Valley was a quarter-mile away. He slowed down and eased off the main road onto a scenic turnoff. The sun, low in the sky, streaked the grassy ocean in gold highlights. They got out of the car and looked out to the horizon.

"You ever heard of the green flash?" Charlie asked.

John shook his head.

"They told us about it when we were down here for our honeymoon," Charlie said, pointing toward the fiery orb in the sky. "If the sun catches the clouds right as it sets, you see a green flash of light."

"Oh."

"Yeah," Charlie said. "I was hoping we'd see it while we were down here. I remember looking for it right before we left for dinner. I didn't see it."

John was silent for a few minutes. Then he said, "they're going to try to kill you, you know."

Charlie spotted an alligator at the edge of the marsh. It slid into the water and disappeared with the stealth of a nuclear submarine.

"Yeah, I figured as much," he said. "But they haven't really left us with much choice, have they?"

"No, I guess not," Hood said.

Wishing he'd never brought it up, he changed the subject. "I've got a GPS tracking device that I brought with me," he said. "I can keep an eye on you with it."

"What if they search me?"

"Relax. Wait until you see it."

John rifled through his bag and removed a small transmitter attached to a black fastening strap.

"This will fit under your sock," he said. "I have the tracking device in my bag. Coverage is a ten-mile radius, and I'll always know where you are. If they see it, tell them it's a brace for a weak ankle. The circuitry is buried inside the band."

Charlie rolled up the leg of his jeans and wrapped the transmitter around his ankle. When his sock was pulled up, the transmitter was virtually invisible. It made him feel a hell of a lot better. John fiddled with the transmitter for a few moments. "It's working."

"Thanks," Charlie said.

"We should go," John said. "It's ten of eight."

JOHN TURNED south off the Tamiami Trail and bounced over the poorly maintained gravel path leading to the Visitor Center. The gate was down at the guard station, but the booth was empty. Ahead of them, they could discern the outline of the few buildings that made up the Visitor Center. The edge of twilight had arrived; it was difficult to see anything beyond a hundred yards or so.

"I think we should wait here," John said.

Charlie nodded. He found a pack of cigarettes in the center console, and he pressed one between his lips. A shaky hand punched in the car's lighter; when it popped out, Charlie jumped. He couldn't steady his hand long enough to light the smoke.

"Here, let me," John said, reaching over for the glowing cylinder.

Charlie took a long drag and blew the smoke out in a long, thin stream. His hands occupied, he began to settle down.

"Someone's coming," John said a few minutes later. Charlie had forgotten to take a second puff from the cigarette. When he looked up, the inch-long cylinder of ash broke free and dusted Charlie's bare leg. He extinguished the cigarette in the ashtray.

His heart began pounding so hard he could feel it in

his ears. Narrowing his eyes, he could make out a car approaching them, headlights off. It kicked up a small cloud of dust behind it, partially obscuring their view. It looked like one of the four horsemen of the apocalypse riding in.

"Stay calm," John said. "I'll have my eye on you."

Charlie grabbed his bag and stepped out of the car, holding his arms high in surrender. *This is it*, he thought, *this is it*. He began walking toward the car, suspecting this was how condemned men felt as they walked toward the death chamber.

John drew his Baretta, chambered a round, and laid it on his lap. Just in case things went bad. He hadn't worked many kidnapping cases. There were basic procedures to follow--ensuring proof of life, making sure the victim wasn't actually part of the plot--but that was about the extent of his training. If the kidnappers established contact, they usually demanded a ransom. The victim's family would deliver a bag of money with an extra little bonus--exploding dye packs. If it got that far. More often than not, the victim was killed. This was especially true of business executives kidnapped outside the U.S. Typically, the masterminds hired mercenaries, who had as much respect for human life as they did human waste, to snatch the victim. Often, they tired of babysitting the victim and just killed him, hoping they could fake it long enough to get the ransom and disappear without delivering it to their employers.

This, however, was off the charts. John could only hope that Charlie was smart enough to pull it off. Now that they had solved Vitelli's murder (the bullet taken from Vitelli's body matched the gun that had been in

Coleman's hand when he died), the kidnapping had become secondary. Oh, sure, they'd throw a few resources at it, but the truth was, it was no longer a prime directive. The FBI had plenty to keep it busy in this post-September II world.

HIS HANDS STILL UP, arms burning, Charlie approached the car.

"Stop," a mechanical voice called out. Well, at least it was a familiar voice.

As difficult as it was to believe, the thought actually soothed Charlie's shredded nerves. The voice continued: "Tell your partner to go back out to the main road and drive west for two miles at sixty miles per hour. You have thirty seconds."

Charlie jogged back to the car.

"They want you to get out of here," he said to John. "Two miles west."

"You get a look?"

"No. Go on, get out of here. Is the GPS working?"

"The hell with that," John said. "We need to make sure she's not in the car."

"They wouldn't have been dumb enough to do that," he said. Then, hopefully: "Would they?"

"I doubt it. But you never know."

They opened their doors simultaneously, making it look like the little roadster had sprouted wings. John drew his Baretta and pointed it at the other vehicle.

"Get back in the car, Agent Hood," the voice bellowed. "This doesn't concern you."

"I'm going to give you three seconds to give up," he called out, slinking forward one step at a time.

"If I don't check in with the correct password in fifteen minutes, she dies."

"You're bluffing," John said. "Kidnapping's one thing, but murder's something else. You sure you've got it in you?"

"Why don't you ask your colleague from the boat ramp?"

The words were a punch to the stomach. John grunted loudly and increased the pressure on the trigger. *Just a little more*, he thought, *just a little more*. Charlie sidestepped toward John and placed his hand on the FBI agent's shoulder. His breathing was shallow and ragged, and his jaw buckled with tension.

"Relax," Charlie said. "I'll take it from here."

"No," John said. "I can't let--"

"Listen to me," Charlie said. "I'll do anything it takes to save Susanna. Just do what they say."

"Fine," he said, holstering his weapon. He got back in the car.

"GPS is working, right?" Charlie asked, hoping to get Hood settled down.

John checked the receiver.

"Yeah."

Charlie took two steps away from the car, and John backed straight out to the main road. He paused to check for oncoming traffic, then roared west on 41.

Charlie was alone.

32

C harlie stood on the side of the path, listening to the soft hum of the Everglades. Within seconds, it had enveloped the drone of the Mazda's engine as John sped away. The other car, a Ford Taurus, probably a rental, sat idling on the path, its headlights burning. It looked like some nocturnal beast, waiting to strike. The driver thumped it into gear and coasted up to Charlie.

"Get in the driver's seat," a woman's voice said, startling him. For a second, he thought it was Susanna. But it was different. Rougher. Older. Fatigued. "Keep both hands on the wheel."

"Where's Susanna?"

"Not until I see the files," she said.

"No," Charlie said, holding the bag tighter against his body. "You let her go, and I give you the bag. Look, I've got no reason not to give you the bag once I know she's safe. If I try to screw you, you can just kill us."

"Turn around here," she said.

Charlie spun the wheel and hit the gas. The access road opened up on the parking lot, which was rimmed by an outbuilding and three covered shelters. A row of vending machines glowed brightly under the shelters and seemed out of place, like spaceships stranded on a strange planet. As he expected, the place was deserted.

"Where are we going?" he asked, a sense of isolation setting in like a deep freeze.

"To see your wife," Lindsey said. "Just like you asked. Follow the access road."

Charlie did, guiding the car around a fleet of trams and onto the main trail through the park. A fifteen-mile loop that started and ended here, the road had been built in 1946 by Humbel Oil, Exxon's predecessor, for oil drilling, before it became fashionable to save this unique land. Now it was a tourist attraction, running trams every half-hour for eight bucks a head.

The sun was very low in the sky now, casting a weak blanket of light across the marshy plains. The rains this season had been heavy, and the park was lush with green. A pair of white-tailed deer grazed by the side of the road, looking up briefly as Charlie and Lindsey passed by, then returning their attention to dinner.

"Who are you?" Charlie asked as they bounced down the trail.

"Don't you know?" Lindsey asked

"I know your name is Lindsey Jessup," he said. "You robbed the bank. You and four others."

"And living happily until you started your stupid anniversary piece on the robbery."

"Sorry to inconvenience you."

"What was the point?" she asked. "Why dredge up ancient history?"

"It was an important story," he said. "It wasn't like you guys knocked off a convenience store. People died."

"And you think I'm happy about that?"

"Like that makes a difference."

"Sure it does," she said. "It makes a big difference. All those people had to do was listen to us. If that woman hadn't lost her shit--"

"All you had to do was not rob the bank."

"You'd think differently if you knew the truth."

"Whatever," he said.

Charlie drove on in silence, keeping his speed under twenty, slow enough for him to learn a little about the surrounding terrain. Baby alligators, still cute with their black and yellow striping, scampered across the road ahead of him and disappeared into the culverts along the shoulder. In the distance, a sixty-five-foot concrete tower speared the evening sky, breaking the endless wilderness and shimmering in the growing humidity. A check of the odometer told Charlie they had penetrated about five miles into the park.

"See that little turnoff?" she asked a few minutes later. "Stop there."

Charlie braked gently, careful to follow the woman's instructions. He was so close to the end that he could taste it. He allowed himself one fantasy. Holding Susanna tight to his body and inhaling her smell. The closer he got to finding her, the less he cared about the robbery, the tattoo on his foot, the contents of the safe-deposit box. What was the point in getting himself killed over things that were deep in the past when he had so much to live for? He thought about John's warning--that the kidnapper would try to kill him, but he didn't think she would. She just wanted to go back to her robbery-fueled lifestyle, and that was fine with him. Maybe it was time for him to think about a new career path as well. But now her comment--*You'd think differently if you knew the truth*-- had stoked the fires again. Did this woman know who he was, where he'd come from?

"Who was Denise Vaughan?" he asked, turning toward Lindsey.

Lindsey snickered, her face tightening in a hideous wrinkle. "Curiosity got the best of you, huh?"

"She was my mother, wasn't she?"

"It's time to get moving," Lindsey said.

"Please," he asked. "I just need to know."

"Yes, she was your mother," Lindsey said.

"And Eric Vaughan was my father, right?" he added. "What else do you know?"

"I know a lot," Lindsey said. "There was only one thing I didn't know until recently."

"Which was?"

"What happened to you after the robbery."

"What did happen?"

"Do you want to see Susanna or not?"

He took a deep breath and exhaled. "Yes. Let's go."

They got out of the car and followed a narrow path to the base of the observation tower, where a spiral ramp twisted its way to the tower's apex. A huge alligator napped in the thick, wet grass abutting the path, ignoring Charlie and Lindsey.

Charlie tapped his bag gently, comforted by the feel of the gun tucked inside. He didn't think he'd get this far with it, and he didn't know what awaited them at the top of the tower, but he was glad to have it. He was surprised that she didn't search him. Probably because she knew he wouldn't do anything to risk Susanna's life.

"You're wondering if you'll have enough time to go for your gun, aren't you?" she asked, startling him. "Did you think I was that stupid? Remember what I told you. If this doesn't go exactly as I explained to you, you both die. Don't be a hero."

A low rumble of thunder echoed across the park. The air had thickened considerably since they'd parked, and fat raindrops began spattering the concrete around them.

"You ever been in a south Florida thunderstorm?" Lindsey asked.

Charlie didn't answer, focusing instead on the thick bolt of lightning that pierced down from the heavens. A sharp clap of thunder followed, making his ears feel like cotton was stuffed inside. *Dammit*, he thought. As if he wasn't out of his element enough in this hellhole.

"Almost there," Lindsey said.

True to her word, they made it to the top of the ramp just as the skies opened up above them. Rain flooded the tower like a dam had burst. They were on a circular deck, about fifty feet in the air, and had the weather been clear, they would've been able to see for miles. Bolted to the middle of the deck was a small ladder ascending to a manhole-sized opening in the canopy of the tower.

"Where is she?" Charlie yelled over the rain.

"Up," Lindsey said, pointing toward the ladder. "You first. And I'll take that gun now."

Charlie made a move inside the bag, his hands groping and fumbling for the cold steel.

"I wouldn't," Lindsey said.

He looked back and saw Lindsey, training her own gun on him.

"Throw it to the middle!"

Charlie held the gun by the barrel and slid it across the metal deck.

"Let's go!" she shouted.

The rain was coming down in sheets now, blowing in sideways and soaking both of them. The metal ladder was slick with rain, and in his haste to get up the rungs, he slammed his hand into the jagged edge, gashing it open. Warm blood trickled down his arm, mixing with the salty rainwater. He grunted in pain, but he was careful not to show weakness.

With his good hand, he pulled himself up onto the exposed top deck and collapsed in a heap, holding his hand close to his body. Using the lightning as a backdrop, he examined his wounded hand. The flesh between the thumb and forefinger had split open. He would need stitches, but that was going to have to wait.

Another flash of lightning illuminated the deck like a camera, and he saw her. Huddled by the concrete railing, ankles and wrists bound, duct tape across her mouth. At first, he thought she was dead. Another bolt of lightning, and they made eye contact. When she saw him, she began bucking and thrashing. His hand forgotten, he pulled himself to his feet and sprinted across the rain-slicked concrete and threw his arms around his wife.

33

Charlie held Susanna tightly. Then, steadying her head with one hand, he ripped off the duct tape in one fell swoop. She grunted with pain, her eyes tearing and reddening.

"Are you OK?" he asked.

She looked at him with her wide, green eyes.

"Yes."

"You're not hurt?"

She shook her head. He helped her to her feet, and she balanced herself by throwing an arm around her husband's shoulder. Lindsey had just pulled herself up through the opening and had her gun aimed at both of them. Charlie reached for the strap around his neck and threw the bag across the deck.

"It's all in there!" he shouted.

The storm had worsened and seemed to have settled directly overhead. Angry bolts of lightning split the sky, close enough to make the hairs on Charlie's body stand up. They had to get out of here soon. Even if Lindsey

Jessup didn't kill them, the lightning easily could, and they would be just as dead.

Moving the gun from one hand to the other, Lindsey bent down and picked up the bag; she draped the strap over her head and across her shoulders, then put both hands back on the weapon.

"Now you let us go," Charlie said. "We had a deal."

"Sorry, Charlie," Lindsey said. "There's been a change in plans."

"No!"

"I can't take the chance that you'll try to nail me for this again."

"I won't, I promise," he said. "I don't care about the story."

"You're lying."

She was right. He didn't think he could ever forget about the story. It would haunt him for the rest of his life. But Lindsey Jessup didn't need to know that. He needed to stall her. She drew closer to them, the gun steady and level. The maw of the muzzle looked like a tiny black hole, capable of sucking the life out of anything that crossed its path.

"Then tell me the truth," he said, injecting a tone of defeat into his voice. "I want to know what happened."

The rain had tapered off as the storm cells continued moving east. Above them, the stars had begun to shine through, as if some unseen deity had thrown a handful of diamonds across a black cloth.

"Alright," she said. "If it's that important to you."

She glanced at Susanna then back at Charlie.

"The bank job was your parents' idea," she said.

"What?"

"Your mom worked in the bank as a teller, and your dad was an auto mechanic," she said. "You were about two, maybe a little younger. I was working as a seamstress, and my husband was a detective on the Richmond police force."

"Collinsworth," Charlie said, a big piece of the puzzle clicking into place. "That was how you knew I was working on the story. I met your husband at a diner for the interview."

"Right," she said. "We flew into Richmond for the meeting. Imagine our surprise when we saw you were the reporter."

"How did you know who I was?" he asked, knowing what her answer would be. His face had given him away.

"Because you're the spitting image of your father," Lindsey said, laughing. "I thought Patrick was going to have a stroke right there."

Charlie shook his head in disbelief. "And that was when you came up with this scheme to frame me."

"Correct."

"Why not just kill me?"

"We couldn't take the chance that someone would follow your work," Lindsey said. "Killing a reporter these days. It's too risky. We were worried you'd become a martyr."

Devo had been right. This whole thing had been nothing but a setup.

"So you were going to pin the FBI agent's murder on me, then get rid of Susanna, weren't you?" He pressed his hand to her back, reveling in her touch, even if it wasn't going to last long.

Lindsey cocked her eyebrows in agreement.

"Why an FBI agent?"

"We wanted you to get caught quickly. We figured the FBI would track you down in no time. I have to say, I'm impressed you lasted as long as you did."

"Why even bother kidnapping Susanna?" he asked. "There was no reason for her to get involved. You put her at risk for nothing. For nothing!"

"We had to make sure you would be there."

"And you just killed that FBI agent."

"We had to do what we had to do."

"So why'd you rob the bank in the first place?"

"Your parents wanted a better life for you," she said. "They didn't have any education, they didn't have any money, and they didn't have much hope for the future."

"And so you all decided to rob the bank?"

"Hey, times were tough," she said. "The bank was going to foreclose on our house. We were in debt up to our eyeballs."

"Who else?"

"Why is that important?"

"Because someone tried to warn me," Charlie asked. "He was supposed to show me proof of what happened. He said he was there that day. He knew about the tattoo on my foot. But I guess you killed him. The evidence was destroyed."

Lindsey shook her head.

"It was never supposed to turn out like this."

"Who was he?"

"One of the others. There were six of us in all. Really, it was never supposed--"

"Yeah, I'm sure you're devastated," Charlie said, cutting her off.

"Shut up," she barked. "You have no idea what it was like. How tough it was for all of us."

"So what happened then?"

"A week after the robbery, Eric and Diane told us they were going to turn themselves in."

"Why?"

"I guess they couldn't live with themselves."

Things were falling into place for Charlie now.

"So you killed them."

"You think we wanted to? They gave us no choice. When you told Patrick your name, we thought it was a strange coincidence," Lindsey said, running a hand through her wet hair. "Then when we saw you, we realized what became of you. We knew the Dallases too, but your parents were closer to them."

"Who was Charlie Dallas?"

"Their little boy," Lindsey said. "He died about six months before you were born. Leukemia."

"Why did they change my name?"

"That I don't know," Lindsey said. "When your parents decided to turn themselves in, they'd already given you to the Dallases. We didn't know what had happened to you. Maybe they were worried that you'd end up in foster care. So the Dallases just raised you as their own without going through the regular channels."

"Or maybe you were going to kill me as well," Charlie said.

"Look," she said, her voice rising. "We all made a deal when we robbed that bank. If we'd let your parents go to the police, we all would have gone down. Jesus, if they'd just kept their mouths shut! They had no idea who we were. And the best part was--"

"Your husband knew how to steer the investigation in the wrong direction."

"Exactly."

"So what happened to my father?" Charlie asked. "I've seen the news clippings on my mom."

She didn't reply.

"Just another missing person, right?" Charlie said.

"Just a girl trying to get by," Lindsey said. "Hey, don't stand there and be all judgmental. This was your parents' idea. The blood of the people that died in the bank is on their hands, too."

"And the tattoo on my foot?"

"Your momma wanted you to carry part of her with you."

A cool breeze rustled across the observation deck, chilling Charlie's rain-soaked body. The truth was that he was chilled to his very core, and that didn't have anything to do with the rustling breeze. Charlie couldn't dispute Lindsey's words, no matter how much he wanted to. Despite their motive, making his life better, his parents had been killers and thieves. He briefly debated asking Lindsey who had actually killed the hostages, but he wasn't sure he wanted to hear the answer. Even if his parents hadn't been the shooters, it didn't change the fact that innocent people had died because of them.

He glanced over at Susanna, who looked back at him with shell-shocked eyes. His own past had nearly been her doom. And his own. It was as if his parents had reached for him from beyond the grave and destroyed his life. Because of them, he'd been living a lie for nearly thirty years. Because of them, he'd nearly lost his fragile new family before the foundation had even had a chance to set. Because of them, he'd been denied a chance to know his own real family. Because of them, he was going to die here. Another thought occurred to him. The terrible burden that the Dallases had been forced to bear. He wondered if they even knew the truth about the robbery.

He wanted to hate his biological parents, but he didn't know how to. He wanted to hate Lindsey Jessup, but who was to say his own parents wouldn't have done the same thing had the roles been reversed? Oh, sure, it was all fine and good that they'd decided to turn themselves in. But that was a little like putting the condom on after the girl was pregnant. He doubted it made much difference in the lives of the families of the two victims.

"So that's it?" Charlie asked, hoping that there was nothing else to learn.

Lindsey eyed him with a look of near-amusement, a smirk on her face. As he returned her gaze, he realized that there was something else. Something she hadn't told him. Something he knew that he didn't want to hear, but that he would have to know if he was ever going to have a normal life. No one would give him that shit-eating smirk unless she had one more hand grenade to stuff down his pants.

"Well," she started, her eyes bouncing from Charlie to Susanna and back again.

"Please tell him," Susanna begged.

A loud bang drew their attention to the base of the tower. It sounded like a gunshot, but he couldn't be sure. The Everglades after dark was often full of miscreants running drugs, burying bodies, or hiding cash.

"Don't move!" Lindsey said, scurrying to the edge of

the deck and peering down. Charlie thought about rushing her and pushing her over the edge. Even if she got a shot off, the chances were good that she'd miss. No. Too much of a risk. There had to be another way.

"Let's go," she barked, pointing the gun at Susanna. "You, little missy, hands behind your head. And you, Chuckie, you lead the way. You try anything, and she dies."

John stared at the little roadster in disbelief, as if it was in cahoots with the kidnappers. He'd never been in a car that had backfired before. *Of all the luck*, he thought. Rage began to swell inside him. *Fight it, John, fight it down. Charlie needs you. What's done is done.* He told himself that the echo of the backfire would have made it impossible to pinpoint its origin. *You can still get the drop on them. Just be smart. Be smart.*

He checked the receiver; Charlie was closing in on him, but he couldn't tell if they were coming down from the tower or from behind it. He gave the car one last disgusted look, then drew his weapon and removed the safety. The ramp was about fifty yards away; he primed his ears and thought he could make out the faint sound of footfalls on the concrete. Looking around for cover, he ducked onto a second trail that branched off of the main path. His eyes slowly adjusted to the darkness.

A few seconds later, he saw three figures descending the final stretch of ramp. They looped around the back side of the tower toward the Shark River Slough, a channel of deeper water that flowed south out of the park like a storm drain. John checked the receiver and kept a bead on Charlie's location. He stayed close to the treeline and moved softly down the trail toward the tower, where he heard muffled voices. He held his breath, but he couldn't quite make out what they were saying. He checked the receiver again, but the marker had gone dead.

Dammit.

When he was convinced that they were out of his line of sight, he sprinted the last thirty yards and ducked behind the low concrete railing guarding the ramp. He pressed his back against the wall and slid around the perimeter, bringing him to a flat glade bordering the slough. He could see his targets by the shore, wading in ankle-deep water. That would explain the demise of the transmitter. The device was a lot of things, but waterproof wasn't one of them.

John got the distinct impression he was being watched. It wasn't Charlie or his companions. They were working to push a canoe into the water. Shit. Once they pushed off into the water, he would lose them. It was too dark to follow along the shoreline through the thick mangroves and sawgrass. Again, he got the impression something was looking at him. He moved his head from side to side; then he saw it. A pair of almond-shaped eyes peeking at him from a few yards away. The head tilted slightly, sizing John up the way a construction worker eyed an all-you-can-eat buffet at the end of a long day. John took a deep breath and let it out slowly, careful not to startle the alligator.

The woman with the gun motioned her captives into the canoe. She checked her rear flank, then climbed into the canoe with them. Charlie shoved off with one of the oars. The canoe bobbed into the still water and then eased away from the shore. A spotlight popped to life, giving Lindsey a welcome eye on the road ahead. Seeing the light arc toward him, John dropped to the ground, pressing his body to the soft terrain, ever mindful of the nearby gator. His heart was pounding; he knew what he had to do. He just couldn't believe that he was about to do it.

"KEEP ROWING!" Lindsey said. With one hand, she kept her gun trained on her hostages; with the other, she swept her spotlight across the slough for obstacles.

Charlie pulled the oars through the water, his arms burning with each successive stroke. He kept one eye on the water, keenly aware of the thousands of ancient killing machines that made their home in these dark and marshy waters. What would they do if a gator decided to take a chomp out of their little boat?

"Where are you taking us?" he asked through gritted teeth. His arms felt like pieces of heavy steel, and his back had joined in on the fun as well.

"Never mind that now," Lindsey said. "Never mind."

He threw a glance toward Susanna, wondering if they could somehow formulate a plan with fleeting glances and narrowing of the eyes. She returned his gaze, but he just saw fear and confusion in her eyes.

"Was it worth it?" he asked. The main thrust of his question was to stretch out their little cruise as long as possible, but he was curious. After all, his parents had been friends with this woman.

"You mean the robbery? You're goddamn right it was worth it. For the last thirty years, I've lived my life the way I want. I didn't answer to anybody. I didn't spend a meaningless existence stuck in an office, two weeks of vacation a year, working for a miserable little retirement. I've been all over the world. I've ridden a camel in front of the pyramids. I skied the Alps. I ran with the bulls in Pamplona.

"I'm sorry those people died. But I would do it all again in a second. Everyone wishes they could do what we did. We just had the sack to do it."

ALL THINGS BEING EQUAL, John Hood would have rather been anywhere else in the world than where he currently found himself. Shortly after the canoe had pushed off, he had sprinted headlong into the slough like a triathlete and grabbed the stern of the canoe. A tiny ridge of wood provided a small handhold, and Charlie's relentless rowing pulled John through the river like a water skier.

He was unarmed, having left his weapon on the shore. A gun working properly after getting wet was a coin flip. It would have been nice to have, but he did have the element of surprise on his side. But he was going to have to act now. He wasn't sure how much longer he could hold on. And there was always the matter of gators. You just couldn't escape it down here.

"THAT'S ENOUGH," Lindsey said in a small voice. "You can stop rowing."

Charlie released the oars and dropped his arms into his lap like lead weights. The forward motion of the canoe pushed them forward a few more yards before it slowed to a halt. It rocked gently in the dark water. Time was up, Charlie realized. He was out of answers. His arms were too fatigued to make a lunge for the gun.

"Please," Susanna said. "You've got what you want. Let us go."

"I like her," Lindsey said to Charlie, nodding toward Susanna. "She's got spunk. I can see why you married her."

"Then let her go at least," Charlie said. "This is between you and me."

"Really, I would love to," Lindsey said. "But I've got this problem. I can't leave any witnesses. Damn prosecutors."

Lindsey set the spotlight down, which cast a strange-looking golden path across the slough, as if they'd somehow stumbled into Oz. Then she pointed her gun squarely at Charlie's chest.

"No!"

The water around the canoe exploded as John launched himself into the canoe, like some mystical bass that had finally surrendered to its fate after being pursued for years in a local river.

"Thahell?" Lindsey muttered, squeezing the trigger of her pistol. Two shots flew wildly into a nearby cluster of mangroves. Charlie exploded from his seated position and hurled his body across the canoe into Lindsey's side.

Flustered, she lost her grip on the gun, and it clattered to the slick bottom of the canoe.

Getting his bearings, John saw the gun lying under one of the canoe's built-in benches. Above him, Charlie struggled to subdue Lindsey, who was a lot stronger than he'd expected. Charlie grabbed her arms and tried to pin them behind her back, but she delivered a swift kick to his left knee. It buckled, and he lost his grip. She turned and delivered a cold hard punch to his nose, breaking it. *Guess she's been working out for the last thirty years*, he thought, as his head swam with stars and white light. Lindsey shoved him square in the chest, and he tumbled backward against the unforgiving wood of the canoe. He felt a rib crack, filling his chest with white-hot pain.

John steadied himself on one knee as the canoe rocked and rolled, and then made a move for the gun. At that moment, Lindsey turned and delivered a soaked sneaker to his face. It was a glancing blow, but enough to upset his balance. Lindsey dropped to her knees and began fumbling for the gun. Desperate hands skittered across the damp wood, while the canoe took on more water as it continued to sway. Charlie groaned at the side of the canoe.

"Charlie!" Susanna cried, climbing over the wrestling bodies underneath her. "Are you alright?"

He grunted. "Help him," he begged, motioning toward John.

Susanna stood and eyed the struggle before her, unsure of where to pitch in. Lindsey had draped her legs across John's arms while she reached for the gun. She put her hands around the barrel and struggled to turn it to a firing position. John drove his head into Lindsey's stomach, eliciting an audible gasp, and he wrenched his arms free. He reached blindly upward, where he found purchase on Lindsey's slick arms. Wrapping his rough hands around her wrists, he kept the gun pointing skyward as he pushed himself to his knees.

"Put it down!" John shouted. "It's over!"

"Go to hell!" Lindsey howled. "I'll kill you all!"

Her strength was considerable, but she was significantly weaker than the FBI agent. He slowly brought her arms down and prepared to clamp her narrow forearms with a single hand. As he released one hand from her, the canoe bucked, tipping sideways and gulping water like a fish. *What the hell?* John thought, losing his grip on the crazed woman.

She gripped the butt with both hands and took dead aim at John Hood. As she squeezed the trigger, the boat was hammered again, altering her shot ever so slightly. One round caught John in the shoulder, which he regretted but preferred to its original destination--his heart. A lucky break, he realized. One he'd better not let get away.

His shoulder on fire, John staggered across the unsteady canoe and reached for the muzzle of the gun with his good arm before Lindsey could fire again. He could feel her fingers fumbling for the trigger, but she was struggling with the same problems he was--the water had slicked everything like a buttered casserole dish.

"Let. It. Go," he barked. "It's over."

Nothing but grunts in return. *Dammit*, John thought. She wasn't going to give this up easily.

Their bodies were pressed together now, as if they were preparing to tango. Through his river-soaked shirt, he could feel the cold steel pressed against his body. *Is that a gun in your pocket, or are you just happy to see me? Jesus, John, get the goddamn gun.* His shoulder felt like it had been dipped into molten steel. Lindsey drove her fist into the spongy wound with her free hand. John screamed.

EACH BREATH CHARLIE took felt like a knife through his chest, but John's howl burned into him even harder.

"I've got to help him," he said, pushing himself to his feet. "Stay here."

Susanna crouched by the edge of the canoe while Charlie stumbled into the fray. Rearing back, he delivered a single punch to Lindsey's ribs. He couldn't help feeling a certain sense of satisfaction as he felt her body slacken against John's. Still, she held the gun fast, like it had been superglued to her hand.

"Now, John, now!"

John pushed into her as hard as he could, knocking her off balance and easing the pressure from his gunshot wound. In the same move, he spun the gun toward Lindsey's body and pulled the trigger. The boom echoed through the silent majesty of the Everglades, then faded away like a fireworks show.

Lindsey groaned and stumbled backwards, a small red stain blooming on her lower abdomen like a rose. She tripped over the bench and then crashed over the side of the canoe into the water with a mournful howl. John went for the rail, where he finally saw what had been ramming the boat. A giant alligator had clamped its jaws around Lindsey's side and was pulling her under the water.

John glanced back at Charlie and Susanna. His arms were wrapped around her, and he was whispering into her ear. John sank in the corner of the canoe and wiped his face.

34

After a quick trip to the hospital, Charlie and Susanna spent the next day in the FBI's Miami field office being debriefed on what had happened out in the Everglades. Physically, Susanna was OK. Mentally, on the other hand, it would be a while. Charlie was going to have one hell of a headache for a while, and breathing wasn't going to be any picnic either. Besides the eight stitches in his hand, Lindsey had broken his nose, leaving him with a raccoon-mask bruise around the perimeter of his eyes, and he'd cracked two ribs against the edge of the canoe. Whenever he did manage to get a decent breath past the shattered ramparts of his nose, it got drawn against his ribcage like a saw.

Through a window of his small interrogation room, Charlie watched palm trees sway in the breeze under bell-clear blue skies. Susanna was in another interrogation room, as the FBI wanted to make sure they hadn't engineered this whole thing together. He shifted in his seat, wincing at the fiery burn of his cracked rib.

After realizing that there would be no rescuing Lindsey Jessup from the alligator, John and Charlie turned their attention to guiding the battered canoe back to shore. The slough was a dangerous place, even from the relative sanctuary of the canoe. Eventually, they had made it back to shore and staggered out of the canoe like three old friends stumbling out of a bar at closing time. John walked ahead of the couple to give them some privacy, which Charlie appreciated. He held Susanna tightly, and she sobbed into his shoulder as the events of the past week sluiced from her mind.

On the way to the Miami field office, John had called Thomas Bagwell and told him the good news. Bagwell arranged for the SAC of the Miami field office, Dan Williams, to meet them. Charlie and Susanna spent the night in separate lounges under armed guard while Williams debriefed John. Bagwell had taken a 6:00 a.m. flight to Miami and joined the festivities while Charlie and Susanna enjoyed a breakfast of bagels and coffee. Alone. Charlie wanted to know when he could see Susanna again, having been whisked away from her the moment they arrived in the office. *No matter*, he thought. *It would be over soon enough.*

A phalanx of agents and Miami-Dade County cops descended on the park after John called in the rescue, undoubtedly scaring the pants off Ranger Maggie. Early the next morning, a pair of agents followed a cloud of flies and vultures to the badly mangled body of retired detective Howard Collinsworth. Apparently, he hadn't been the good eating for which the gator had hoped.

Although the FBI didn't believe that Collinsworth had voluntarily gone for a swim in the canal, cause of death would be difficult if not impossible to imagine.

Charlie returned to the present and sipped a Sprite, cold and clean. He couldn't remember the last time he'd enjoyed a drink so much, and he didn't think he ever would again. He was ready to finish up these interviews, pack up his wife, and head over to the Miami airport-- maybe he'd cuff her to his wrist this time. From there, they could set off for a real honeymoon. This time, they would go to Hawaii, cost be damned. He was fairly certain they had earned it.

His mind drifted back over the past ten days like fog creeping down from the hills. He thought about his parents and the Jessups. The Dallases. Their lost little boy. Devo. Mick. He thought about his real name. Casey Vaughan. Not a bad name. But it didn't feel right. The Dallases had raised him as their own after suffering their own unimaginable tragedy. They were the only parents he had ever known.

He was sorry that his birth parents had died. He was sorry he had never gotten to know them. But they had chosen their path and paid the ultimate price. He never asked for an inheritance. Wouldn't being good parents have been enough? Maybe nothing would have satisfied them.

A knock on the door snapped him back to the present. John Hood poked his head in.

"Mind if I come in?"

Charlie shook his head, and John took a seat in the empty chair on the other side of the table.

"How you holding up?" he asked.

"Pretty fair," Charlie said. "How's Susanna?"

"They're still talking to her, getting some minor details ironed out," John said. "Since all the suspects are dead, they're going to try and wrap this up as quickly as possible."

Charlie picked at a piece of dry skin on his chin. "Thanks," he said quietly.

"For what?"

"For not giving up on me," Charlie said. "I know it must have been tough to go against the grain to get behind all this. Especially when I looked so guilty."

"The truth was, the forensics established you couldn't have been the shooter early on," John said. "I just assumed that you and the shooter were in on it together. Seemed like the easiest answer."

Charlie nodded.

"Let me ask you something," John said. "You ever figure out the story behind that tattoo?"

"No," he said. "All I can think is that my parents had me inked up right before they handed me over to the Dallases. Maybe they knew their lives were in danger. Who knows."

"I guess."

"So what's next for you?" Charlie asked.

"Oh, I've been suspended," John said.

"What? After all you did?"

"Well, let's see. Here's what I did. I disobeyed orders, assaulted a fellow agent, killed one suspect, left the scene without good cause, and then fed another suspect to an alligator. That means a shitload of paperwork. Especially now that there's no one left to prosecute. These guys need something to make their lives worthwhile."

"You don't seem all that concerned."

"Screw'em," he said. "I need some time off. And maybe a new career."

"A new career?"

John shrugged.

"I wouldn't," Charlie said. He took a sip of his soda. "I'll sleep better knowing you're on the job."

John chuckled as he pushed himself to his feet. "If only you knew." He extended his hand, and Charlie shook it. "Good luck to you. To both of you."

He turned and disappeared through the door.

SUMMER BURNED ITSELF OUT, and the world eased into fall. Charlie returned to the paper, but Susanna decided to take the semester off from teaching. Considering what she'd been through, the school was happy to give her the sabbatical. Susanna spoke little about her ordeal. Charlie was curious about what happened on the night Susanna disappeared, but he didn't want to push her. The FBI recommended that she meet with a counselor, but she demurred.

She spent her days reading, plowing through four or five novels a week. She went to bed early and slept soundly. Charlie would come to bed and watch her sleep, waiting for the nightmares that people experienced after a traumatic incident. They never came. More often than not, Charlie was the one staring at the dark ceiling, one hand under the pillow, until the green numbers on the clock glowed with the bad news.

One Saturday morning in early October, they sat at

the breakfast table, sipping coffee. Susanna's nose was buried in a John Grisham hardcover. Outside, the first true hint of fall had crisped the air under a canopy of blue sky. The windows were open, and a slight breeze made the kitchen fresh and airy. Someone nearby was burning leaves.

"I'm worried about you," he said, setting his mug on the scarred table with a thud.

"I'm fine," she said, never looking up from the page.

"But I'm not," he said.

She sighed, marked her page with the cover flap, and put the book aside.

"What's wrong?"

"I'm sorry," he said.

The guilt had been nibbling at him like a hungry rat since he'd made the connection between the kidnapping and his work on the robbery. It was his fault that this had happened to her. Yes, before all this happened, he'd been secretly hoping to crack the thirty-year-old mystery. Pulitzers had been won with lesser stories. Maybe turn it into a book, become a best-selling author. Thoughts of lunches in fancy restaurants with important New York agents and movie rights sizzled in his mind. He'd already come up with a title.

"For what?" she asked.

"It's my fault," he said, his voice cracking. He breathed deeply, forcing back the tears he could feel welling up in his eyes.

She reached across the table and took his hand in her own. "No. You were just doing your job. I know that." A smile crossed her face. "I'm sorry, too."

Now it was his turn. "For what?"

"For going to the bathroom."

A laugh escaped from his throat. Then another, and another, until his body was shaking with laughter. The tears did come, but not from sadness. Charlie's face reddened. Susanna, her mouth covered with her hand, joined in.

"Want to tell me what happened?" he asked when they'd settled down.

She twirled a lock of hair around her index finger and gnawed on her lower lip.

"OK," she said after a moment's hesitation.

"Did you make it to the bathroom?"

"Yes," she said. "Remember, it was around the corner from our table. That woman came in the bathroom, said she was the manager. She told me you'd collapsed at the table. They were taking you to the hospital on the mainland. She said she would give me a ride to the hospital, so we rushed out of the restaurant. I was freaking out, Charlie. I thought you were dead."

"So you never went back to check to see if I was still at the table?"

She shook her head. "Why would someone make something like that up? All I could think of was getting to the hospital."

"Then what?"

"There was a car waiting outside, motor running," she said. "I remember thinking at the time that was a little odd, but I let it go."

"Did you go back to our room?"

"No," she said. "Why?"

"They left me a note in the room," he said. "On the nightstand."

Susanna was quiet.

"I wonder how they got in the room," he said. "I remember locking the room when we left. It was locked when I went back to look for you."

"The man took my purse," she said. "The room key was in it. That was when I knew something was wrong."

"Then what happened?"

"I remember driving to a small airport. That was the last thing I remember," she continued. "I think they drugged me. I was pretty out of it for the first couple of days."

She squeezed his hand. "At least I was out of it. I can't imagine what it was like for you. Not knowing what happened."

He pushed back from the table and took their breakfast plates to the sink. Nothing was said for a moment while he ran the spigot over the crumbs.

"What do you think they were planning to do with me?" she asked when he shut the water off. "If their plan had worked?"

"I don't know," Charlie said, looking away.

"They were going to kill me, right?"

"Probably," he said. "Get me for both your murder and the FBI agent's. I'm surprised they didn't plant drugs all over the house. Really put the nail in my coffin."

He held back a string of obscenities. What was the point? Lindsey Jessup was dead. Her husband was dead. All six of the bank robbers were now dead. It had taken thirty years, but they were all now square with the house, their debts paid off.

∼

In December, Charlie's five-part series on the bank robbery and Susanna's kidnapping ran in the Richmond Gazette. The story went viral immediately. Two days before Christmas, Charlie went on the Today Show, chatted with Matt Lauer, stayed at the Waldorf. He went alone, not wanting to put Susanna through the wringer. He was nominated for a Pulitzer, but he didn't win. A high-profile literary agent called while he was in New York taping the morning news shows and asked him if he'd thought about writing a book about his experiences. "It'll be huge!" she'd said. "Fucking huge!" She'd be happy to represent him, work out the details, make him a ton of money. Maybe kickstart a brand-new career.

Charlie said he would think about it and hung up the phone. It was Christmas Eve. A light snow was falling, but it was expected to change over to rain before midnight. A white Christmas was unlikely. Charlie and Susanna had reservations for dinner at Morton's, a fancy steakhouse downtown they'd been wanting to try. No time like the present. It wasn't like either of them had any family to go home to.

He climbed onto the bed, propped a few pillows behind his back, and flipped through a recent copy of Sports Illustrated. Charlie read a story about the NBA, then another about the NFL playoffs. As he turned to Rick Reilly's column on the last page, he heard the hiss of the shower cut off and the floor creak as Susanna stepped out of the shower.

"Got any breath mints, babe?" he called out after a few minutes. Susanna was still in the bathroom. She was taking an awfully long time, especially for her.

"Try my purse," she said, her voice cracking slightly.

"You OK?"

"Yeah. Fine."

Charlie shook his head. Her purse was on the bureau across the room, and he got up to retrieve it. Inside the main pocket, he found lip gloss, her keys, and a mangled stick of gum. As he reached for the gum, he changed his mind, deciding that he really wanted a breath mint. He unzipped a side pocket and dug his fingers inside. There wasn't anything resembling a box of breath mints, but his fingers brushed against something else. He pulled it out and held it up to the light spilling from the small lamp on the edge of the bureau.

He turned it over in his hand, looking at it the way a 49er might have after finding gold in his pan. His brain recognized it on sight, but his soul refused to accept it. It couldn't be. There had to be a valid explanation. There had to be a good reason why Susanna still had the key card to their hotel room on Sanibel. The one Susanna said the kidnappers had stolen from her.

THE DOOR to the bathroom creaked open, and Susanna emerged, looking fresh and radiant. Her hair was swooped up in a towel, and she looked warm and cozy in her thick bathrobe. She was holding something in her hand as well. It was about six inches long, about the size of a magic marker. Charlie looked up at her, blinking heavily, as if he'd just looked right into the sun.

"Guess whaa-aatt?" she asked playfully before seeing what Charlie was looking at.

"What the hell is this?" he asked.

"Don't you want to hear the good news?" she asked, waving the home pregnancy test stick like a party favor. "I'm pregnant."

"I thought you said they took this from you," Charlie said coldly, ignoring her announcement. This had to be dealt with now before it slipped into the past, behind baby showers and folic acid and doctor's visits. It demanded an explanation. He was damn sure he deserved one. His mind was rolling through uncharted territory now, making new connections, delivering bad news with clinical coldness and detachment. His mom would have said he was getting married too fast. After all, he'd only known Susanna for seven months. Seven months.

His mind backtracked, the way it does when you finally realize you've taken a wrong turn. He'd met Collinsworth about eight months ago. It had been the first real spring day, when warm air hugs you like an old friend. Winter had been stubborn, hanging on into the first week of April, just as baseball season was getting underway. And then magically, mystically, Susanna had walked into his life. At the group meeting. Asking him for a drink.

She'd played him for a fool.

He pinched the bridge of his nose, thinking back to the observation tower in Shark Valley. Right before John had shown up. Lindsey Jessup's response when he asked her if there was anything else he didn't know. *Well...* The smirk, he'd wanted to smack it right off her face. And now he knew.

"So who was she?"

Susanna crossed the room and handed him the test stick. He threw it aside like a used tissue.

"Please look at it. I'm having a baby!"

"Who was she?" Charlie asked again, his voice rising.

"She was my mother," she said, crossing her arms defiantly.

"So all this," Charlie said, spreading his arms out. "It was all a lie."

Susanna sat on the edge of the bed facing him. Her chin drooped to her chest.

"What were you waiting for?" he asked. "To slit my throat in the middle of the night?"

"No," she whispered, shaking her head violently. "It wasn't like that at all."

"But that was why you married me."

She nodded almost imperceptibly. Charlie's legs gave out, and he crumpled to the floor in a heap.

"Why? Why? Why?"

"They were my parents," she said. "I'd have done anything for them."

"You mean for the money," Charlie said, his voice cutting through the air like a power saw.

"No," she said. "I didn't want them to go to jail. I didn't think anyone would get hurt."

"Our parents were murderers and thieves!"

"I know that now."

Charlie screamed, a deep, primal howl from the depths of his burning soul. The neighbors heard it, and a few got up from their turkey dinners and looked apprehensively through their blinds at the rapidly darkening neighborhood. For a few of them, Charlie's scream haunted their

Christmases for years to come. Charlie lunged to his feet, grabbed Susanna's purse, and hurled it at the decorative mirror over the bureau. The glass splintered into a million tiny shards, each reflecting a ruined image of the room like the wreckage of the two lives standing there.

"The hell did you stick around for?" Charlie asked. "After it was over?"

"I fell in love with you," she said. "I didn't want to go through with it."

"Jesus Christ."

"Really," she said, sobbing, throwing her arms around Charlie. "I couldn't believe how hard you worked to save me. I wanted to have a normal life. I wasn't going to let her hurt you out there. You have to believe me." She held him tight and brushed her lips across his mouth. Charlie pulled free of her, and she tumbled to the ground in a tangle of robe and towel.

"Get the hell off me."

Susanna sobbed.

EPILOGUE

Charlie parked the Honda Civic by the curb and hurried inside as the rain intensified. It was late spring in Richmond, meaning a perfectly beautiful day could turn into a soaker in a matter of seconds. He shook off the umbrella, then folded it up before stepping inside the WonderKid Center, where Emma spent three days a week making a mess of fingerpaint, cookies, construction paper and lately, little boys.

She was in the corner, sitting in a small blue chair, an oversized children's book spread out across her lap. Something tickled her fancy, and she began giggling, throwing her head back with pure glee. Her blond curls bounced like pogo sticks, and her face lit up like a fireworks show. He watched her play, and it reminded him of how innocent she was. Her sleep was easy and deep. Uncluttered by the worry and heartache that enveloped him. For now, at least.

"Emma!" he called out. "Time to go."

"Daddy!" She threw the book to the floor and stum-

bled across the room in that half-drunken state that all
two-year-olds seemed to perpetually be in. She was
getting better, though, steadier, and she didn't fall nearly
as often as she used to. He scooped her up and held her
tight while she smacked his face with kisses. He smelled
the sweet mixture of juice and cookies on her breath, felt
the remnant crumbs against his cheek.

"Walk, Daddy, walk." Meaning she wanted to do the
walking.

He set her down, and she hustled to the door. Charlie
nodded to Vanessa, Emma's daycare teacher. He felt
guilty about her spending so much time in daycare, but
she seemed to enjoy it. Socializing her and whatnot.
Getting her used to the tangled web that everyone spun
in their own lives.

"Good night, Mr. Dallas."

"'Night."

They stepped outside, where the sun had peeked out
again for a quick show before setting. The rainstorm had
ended as quickly as it had begun.

"Oooh, sunshine," Emma cooed.

He strapped her into her car seat, gave her a sippy cup
of juice, and climbed into the driver's seat. He looked at
his daughter in the rearview mirror while she drank her
juice. There was no mistaking it. She was the spitting
image of Susanna. It was becoming clearer with each
passing day. Emma sang unintelligible lyrics to an unintelligible song, blissfully oblivious to the circumstances
that had led to her very existence.

He thought back to the night he'd discovered the
truth. Susanna agreed to turn herself in, and the two of
them had met John at the field office. John had listened to

her tell her tale with stunned disbelief, and then he had arrested her. There had been no emotional breakdown, no crying, no resisting. She simply looked back at Charlie as John led her out the door and said goodbye.

In exchange for dropping the remaining charges, Susanna agreed to plead guilty to voluntary manslaughter in the death of Mick Duncan, and she was sentenced to five years in Evergreen Correctional Center for Women, out in the southwest part of the state. Six months later, she gave birth to a healthy seven-pound, four-ounce girl in a local hospital. Charlie named her after the woman who had raised him, and Judge Mitchell, the juvenile and domestic relations judge in the City of Richmond, had granted him full custody of their daughter.

Charlie had called the literary agent back and agreed to write a book. He finished the manuscript four months after Emma was born. After a few dozen revisions, the agent sold the book at auction, netting a low six-figure deal for Charlie. Publication was only a couple weeks away. The book advance was nice, but it wasn't quit-your-job money. Besides, he would always be a reporter at heart.

Charlie had not been back to the prison since Emma's birth. Susanna wrote letters every day, begging Charlie to let her see her daughter. He ignored most of the letters, but when he did respond, he wrote that he didn't think it would be good for Emma. That was bullshit, and he knew it. She was too young to know the difference. The truth was that it wouldn't be good for him. And part of him wanted to punish Susanna. For the ruin that she'd brought on his life. Her own life. Her baby's life. A baby that, for all intents and purposes, should never have been born.

But Emma had been born, and Charlie loved her more than the air he breathed. And she had a mother that was a convicted felon. Always a nice thing to have on your resume. Part of Charlie didn't think Susanna deserved to have her in her life. But things were about to change. Susanna had been a model inmate and was earning one day of credit against her sentence for each day she served, effectively cutting her sentence in half. She was scheduled to be released in less than a month. And she was planning to petition the court for visitation rights, whether Charlie agreed or not.

Could he deny his daughter her mother? Could he do to Emma what the Collinsworths had done to him? It wasn't exactly the same thing, but would it matter to Emma? She was going to want to know who her mother was. Maybe not today, maybe not in a year. But eventually. And the time would come when Emma would want to make her own decisions.

But not right now. From the backseat, Emma cooed, "Home, Daddy!"

Home. Keeping one hand on the wheel, Charlie reached back and squeezed Emma's ankle.

"That's right, baby. We're going home."

∾

∾

∾

THANK you for reading GOOD AS GONE. To stay up to date on new releases, discounts, and other book-related news, please join my mailing list at www. davidkazzie.com. You'll also receive two pieces of exclusive bonus content available *only* to newsletter subscribers.

ABOUT THE AUTHOR

David is the author of nine novels, several of which have appeared on Amazon's Kindle Top 100 bestseller lists. He is also the creator of a series of short animated films that have nearly three million views on YouTube and were featured in *The Wall Street Journal*, *The Washington Post*, *Huffington Post*, and on CNN.

He lives in central Virginia with his family.